DUNGEON LIFE

BOOK 2

DUNGEON LIFE

BOOK 2

Khenal

Podium

Cover design by Istvan Straban

ISBN: 978-1-0394-5396-8

Published in 2024 by Podium Publishing
www.podiumaudio.com
Podium

To Aranya, who was more confident in the story than I was, and who encouraged me to start posting it in the first place.

DUNGEON LIFE

BOOK 2

Chapter 1

Up in the clouds and a little *sideways* is a place the Angel of Prodigals likes to think of as her office. The nature of infinite reality makes that a little moot, as she can get from anywhere to anywhere, but she's always enjoyed the idea of Heaven being literally in the clouds. It also makes her job easier to give the newly passed humans a bit of what they expect.

Those ready to continue on get a different sort of orientation. Those who have lived and are ready are those she doesn't really deal with. She deals with the ones who have been cut short. Humans say He works in mysterious ways, and the angel thinks trucks are a very good example of that.

They're not the only way for someone to get to try again, but being hit by one is a lot more common than she would have suspected. Perhaps her kin should be wary of treading on the street as much as they avoid the threshing floor.

However they come to her, she is to help the prodigal sons and daughters prepare for their next journey, and be prepared to welcome them home when they return.

One such son decided to take the path untread. An option she was starting to think was only put there to guide the humans to go over the entire list. It's a strange option, to be sure, to become a genius loci, a dungeon.

In all her time with this Purpose, nobody had even given that option a second glance, yet that one seemed drawn to it. She had almost thought the option was not actually an option, as she wasn't allowed to give much extra information about the small piece of creation the prodigal would be locked to.

When she watched the son start to transition, she feared he might rage at what his decision wrought, feared he might fall astray. But after a few moments of confusion came determination and curiosity. She watched him grow and adapt to his new existence.

She watched as he did what humans always do: their best, with no idea what the consequences could be. He found his core, the crystallization of his life, and he protected it. He hid it, and he welcomed the outsiders. He could have killed them, and even been rewarded for it, but he forged his own path, and has been reaping the benefits greatly.

New friends, new allies, battle fought and hard-won, challenges met and overcome in unexpected ways, fulfilling the requirements of his new life without even realizing it. She can see the ripples through the local kingdoms, even from several realities away. She can't fully see what the changes will bring, but she has faith that the prodigal son will be a great benefit to that world.

It's impressive how much impact someone can have, even when technically immobile. The prodigal is his domain, his awareness spread over all his territory. He has his defenses in the form of his spawners and his scions, to protect his core and challenge the delvers who would come to explore his territory. He has his resource nodes, tempting flames for the moths around him, though he takes care to ensure they don't immolate themselves.

He has forged friendships with the outsiders, from children to jaded adults. He has claimed two as his residents: one as a natural extension of friendship; the other as a desperate act of protection. An evil dungeon has been defeated, reclaimed, and its resources repurposed. A fledgling dungeon has been taken under wing, guided, and helped.

Eyes are starting to be drawn to the prodigal son, and she can tell he will be drawing those same eyes to a threat very few are aware of. She will need to keep a special eye on the prodigal son who has chosen to call himself Thedeim.

Chapter 2

The new day brings a new delver, and thankfully, not of the scythemaw variety. It feels weird to have the old ratkin delving, but it sure looks like that's what Old Staiven is planning to do. Looks like he's warming up by checking the herbs in the backyard first.

"What's your secret . . ." he grumbles to himself as he gathers quite a bit of ochredill, and I mentally smile at that with equal parts humor and relief. Looks like the master alchemist wasn't able to recreate the Bottled Lightning, despite knowing what it's made of. I wonder if it's a magic thing, a dungeon thing, a me thing, or a Queen thing? Either way, I might be able to start giving small vials of it away as rewards occasionally. I don't think he tried to drink it, but it seems like the kind of thing to be a rare reward at most. Even if he can't recreate it.

The aged ratkin looks over at the maze for a few long seconds before shaking his head and turning back to the house. I wonder if he doesn't like his chances against Tiny, or if he wants to do something different from the gnome. Either way, he pauses on my porch to look at the notice board and the various hanging signs for quests.

"Such a strange dungeon," he says to himself as he takes his time to read the notices and consider the quests.

Hey, Teemo, mind asking him what's up?

My Voice has no problem with that, and soon, the rat pops out of a shortcut near Old Staiven.

"Rhonda's teacher, right?"

The ratkin looks confused for a moment before smiling and looking at Teemo. "I had forgotten the dungeon had a Voice. I was a bit more interested in the leftover traps from Neverrest than in socializing last time."

Teemo smiles at that. "Thing really appreciated the help with those, too. He's gotten a lot better with the runework, as well."

"I should think so. He seemed a rather focused hand. Has he had any breakthroughs with Lifedrinking?"

My Voice deflates a little and shakes his head. "Not really. He's learned a lot about taking enchantments apart from studying it, but no real progress on easily nullifying it."

"I hope he's not too hard on himself. Countless mages, clerics, artificers, and more have tried to find a counter to that foul enchantment, but none have succeeded."

"Heh, but none of them have the Boss giving them weird ideas to try for it."

Staiven laughs at that. "Those weird ideas are partially why I'm here, actually. I'm out of that lightning essence tincture and was hoping to get more. And maybe get a look at whatever other alchemical oddities I might be able to get my hands on."

I dunno if I'm willing to give him access to the Liquid Steel or the Healing Essence, and I'm definitely not ready to let him into the secret alchemy lab, but if Queen wants to talk shop with him, that'd be fine.

"Thedeim isn't sure how much to give you access to just yet, but Queen can compare notes with you. It'll be a bit before she's ready, though. She's working on a thing right now. Maybe in an hour or two?"

"That should be fine. I was going to see how dull my edge has gotten by doing a bit of delving anyway. I still need to get some spell spores, too," says the ratkin with a nod. He reaches up and takes the quest to kill a widow, nodding to himself. "This should be a good way to stretch my legs. My venom stocks are a bit low . . ."

Teemo looks a bit uncertain about the elderly ratkin fighting something like one of my widows, but I get the feeling it won't be out of his ability to handle. "Do you want a tour, or to just explore on your own?"

Old Staiven smiles at the rat. "Thanks for the offer, but I think I'll explore on my own. If I'm going to take the time of a scion, I'd rather it be of the Alchemist, no offense. And I should do a bit of delving to help pay for that time."

With that, he heads inside, and Teemo returns to working with Thing. Their progress on the bag of holding is going slow but steady. They both have a lot of other things they're busy with anyway, and the affinity expansion is definitely more of a long-term project.

I go ahead and keep an eye on Staiven as he explores the manor and deals with the denizens therein. They're all used to delvers enough that they start slow and ramp up from there, though the Alchemist is more than a match for the spawns in the house. I could have them all converge on him at once, but that's hardly fair. And I'm pretty sure he'd deal with them all at once with an actual alchemical thing instead of just bonking them with his staff.

I bet he has some Kinetic affinity on it, too. Even Freddie would be jealous of some of the distance he gets on my various rats, snakes, and whatnot.

He drinks a bottle of Lightning Resist before heading up to deal with the attic boss, and I let him have fun with an electric spider swarm. He seems to actually have fun with it, too. He runs around, swinging his staff and avoiding the worst of the attacks as he sprinkles some dust around, which seems to be some kind of contact poison. It must only work on spiders or something, because he doesn't seem concerned at all about getting it on himself. Maybe he's already taken an antidote?

Either way, he's soon dispatched the boss and looted the chest, and continues up onto the roof. Poe peers at him from his nest near the chimney as he approaches. The ratkin holds his hands up as he gets closer.

"I'm in no rush to make the same mistake that one party did. I just want to see if I can get a few cast-off feathers," he explains as he slowly moves forward. I can feel Poe asking what to do, but I leave him without an answer for now. He awkwardly watches as Staiven pulls a few feathers from the nest and gives my Marshal a respectful nod before turning toward the belfry.

Oh, don't be like that, Poe. It was only awkward because you made it awkward. Heh, watch how Jello interacts with people if you want to get better at it.

Staiven looks around the various planters, taking samples here and there but not taking any seeds. A few of the bats watch him as he works, so he speaks to them. "I never could get the hang of actually growing herbs. Always was easier to go gather from the wild or pay adventurers to do it for me. I should come back again sometime. So few adventurers know how to properly handle so many herbs."

He looks out over the yard as he finishes gathering, watching the delvers fighting and gathering, and soon, he eyes the cave in the yard. His gaze flicks up to the bats, and he speaks again. "What do you think? Should I take that cave or try the basement?" The fruitbat just yawns and wraps itself in its wings in reply.

"I imagine you'd take the cave rather than go through the house, hmm? I'll try that, I think." He nods to himself as the bat nods off, and he heads back through the house and out to the yard, then down to the cave. He meets a group of miners getting ready to head in and chats a bit with them.

"Where would I most easily find a widow?" he asks the leader after some small talk. The elf shrugs.

"You could just come with us for a bit. There's an access tunnel that goes down to the caverns, which is where we want to mine. There's a branch that leads off to the spider lair from there, so you should be able to spot one without too much difficulty."

"I think I'll do just that, thank you." He joins their party, and they head deeper, fighting my various spawns in the tunnels. They go fairly slowly, but Old Staiven doesn't seem to mind. I bet he gets a lot of his metals from these guys . . . or if not these guys, whoever these guys sell the ore to.

They part ways as the tunnel splits, with the miners going deeper and Staiven looking down the winding tunnel that leads to my spider lair. He takes a few minutes to prepare himself, even tying a few bits of leather to his staff. I can see they're some kind of rune or something, but I don't know what they actually do. I could ask Thing, but I don't want to interrupt him . . . And I kinda want to be surprised.

Staiven takes his time creeping down the tunnel, hoping to have some element of surprise on his side, or at least not to get the attention of more than one spider. Luckily for him, there's only one in the tunnel right now. They spot each other at the same time, and each freezes for a moment before they both spring into action.

The widow scurries up a wall and along the ceiling, hoping to use height to her advantage, but the ratkin tracks her without fail. He points his staff and shouts to send a beam of yellow magic at her. "Fumble!"

The widow immediately loses her footing, but manages to stick the landing and keep coming at him along the floor for a few moments before tossing a line of silk at him. He dodges out of the way, and it hits the wall, but the spider pulls on it and uses the force to propel herself forward.

"Whoa!" he exclaims, getting his staff in the way of her fangs. "Repulse!" he shouts, sending her backward before she can overpower him. He follows the motion with a whirl of his staff, one of the tied-on runes flashing. "Blizzard!"

Wind and snow buffet the spider, forcing her to hunker down and giving the delver time to breathe and pull out a flask. He lets the blizzard end as he throws the flask and swings his staff in an arc as a familiar attack shoots from it. "Windblade!"

The widow dodges the blade, but that puts her in the perfect position for the flask. It gets split by the blade and spills oil over the large spider. She doesn't have any issues with her footing as she warily circles Old Staiven, looking for an opening. He pulls out a pouch and tosses it against the top of the tunnel, sending little pink particles around.

The spider flinches back from the movement, but after a few moments, she resumes her circling. It doesn't take long for it to become clear something is weird about the particles, as her motions become sluggish and her stance uncertain. That's all Staiven needs to finish the fight with the old classic.

"Fireball!" The impact sends the spider onto her back, and the oil ensures he quickly gets his experience. "Snuff!" he shouts, then leans on his staff as the fire poofs out, leaving a crispy outside to the widow, but I don't think much heat actually transferred too deeply inside. It better not have, if he wants the venom he said he was after.

"Huff . . . Whew! Never seen them jump like that before," he says to himself as he catches his breath then walks to the dead widow. "And, if I did it right . . ."

He leans his staff against the wall and grabs her fangs, then carefully pulls. He grins as they slide out easily, along with a bit of the mandible and the venom sack. "Perfect! Cook them just right, and the venom sacks will slide right out." He smiles before chuckling at himself and gathering his staff. I guess he's gotten pretty used to Rhonda being around to learn stuff.

It'll be a nice change of pace for him, I imagine, to be able to talk with someone who can teach him a thing or two. Queen is done preparing the solution that should grow the quartz pickups, so the two can talk shop in the public lab soon.

Chapter 3

Teemo goes and gets Staiven so he and Queen can talk some shop. I'll leave them to it, too. Queen knows what she should and shouldn't relay, as does Teemo. She's tried to talk some with me about alchemy, but it's a bit outside my wheelhouse. I understand the concepts of mixing things and most of the technical terms, but I'm a mechanical engineer, not a chemical one.

It kinda makes me understand how Teemo's been getting better at just relaying information without having to understand it. I guess this'll be good practice for him, as well as good PR with Staiven. I'm pretty sure most magical stuff around here is either from me or him, and I prefer my competition to be more friendly than anything else.

Speaking of friendly competition, the trio have been coming back to tackle the hard gauntlet, and they've been behaving themselves. They do a few encounters on the way, but they don't go trying to start crap with my scions or my residents.

They've been making quick progress through the gauntlet, too. They'd be going a lot faster if there wasn't an actual line to try it. From the chatter, a few of the more distant guilds want to be the first to finish it, but the local guild isn't going to let them have it without a fight.

With the trio having *joined* the local guild, they have quite the advantage, seeing as they managed to work through it to escape me. I've been sure to mix things up some, though, so they don't have a free ride. My favorite reaction from them had to be when they saw someone doing the salmon ladder properly the first time, instead of their little tower maneuver.

I've also added an element of time management in the final section, too. Even with me being easily able to change the specific answers, people were just endlessly theorycrafting what the solution could be. So now, they get washed out after a couple minutes, though it resets with each section of the puzzle they manage.

I've also been wanting to talk with the halfling and see if she knows anything about scythemaws. From Leo's opinion, she doesn't seem the most "one with nature's balance and harmony" of druids, but she's still a druid of *some* flavor. Maybe she's an expert in scythemaws and we don't know because we haven't asked?

I mean, I doubt it, but it's possible.

Queen

Oh, the Emperor should try to keep this one. She can feel a thirst for knowledge from this one, and not like Honey's thirst. The Bee Scion treats information like honey: something to be stored and appreciated for its own sake. She understands its sweetness, but doesn't feel the need to partake, to *apply* it.

But to ants like Queen? Sweetness is to be gathered and used; shared with the colony and utilized. Sweetness that sits there is just going to make a mess. Of course, honey doesn't go bad, but the Ant Scion still likes her metaphor.

And this Staiven may look like the ratkin the Emperor uplifted, but he is an ant at heart. He hungers for knowledge and is willing to share his own to get it. It also doesn't hurt that he recognizes her talent.

"It takes that much of the Bottled Lightning to grant the essence to a denizen? You must have quite the lab hidden somewhere, then," says the old ratkin, and Queen gives off a pleased scent at that. She's so happy the Emperor's Voice can understand her native language of pheromones. It makes things so much simpler.

Teemo smiles at him. "She thanks you for the compliment. Her lab really is something, but not for visitors, heh."

"Can you show me anything here, then? I could give a few pointers or even a recipe for something in return?" says Staiven as he looks over the public lab. It's not the best of labs, but it's leagues ahead of her first. She still cringes when she thinks of how primitive the first one was: dirt floors, go-juice being produced atop small leaves and other things to try to minimize the contaminants. She still remembers how elated she was when the Emperor gave her her first bit of glassware!

She shakes off her nostalgia to focus on the now, and on the Alchemist's request. *Is there anything specific he'd like to see?*

"Anything in particular you want her to make?"

"Could she make the Bottled Lightning? I have the ingredients, at least as far as I'm aware, but I haven't been able to make it myself," Old Staiven explains as he pulls out some ochredill and spell spore.

Queen is surprised he hasn't been able to produce it. It's easily the simplest thing she can make, with her supply more limited by the growth of the ingredients than the difficulty in making it. She can't even fathom how the process is eluding the elderly Alchemist, either.

She takes a few moments to consider the process, checking and rechecking for anything the Emperor wouldn't like to share, but it really is simplicity itself!

Well, the original version, at least. In her lab proper, she can distill out exactly what she needs from the reagents and get a lot more product. There shouldn't be any harm in showing the most basic recipe for it.

Her mandibles quiver in excitement at the idea of him somehow still failing it. It'd make no sense! Or rather . . . it would mean there's more for her to *learn* about alchemy. Some fundamental she's missed! While she doesn't like the idea of missing something so foundational, she very much *does* like the idea of *discovering* something foundational.

She quickly relays the basic formula to the Emperor's Voice, who gives her a strange look.

"That's really it?"

Yes.

He shrugs. "Alright. Well, Staiven, she says all you have to do is grind them together in equal parts, with a little water to help everything mix."

Staiven sighs at that, but nods as he produces a knife to start chopping the ingredients for easier grinding. "I was afraid it'd be something like that. I tried every method I could to get them to recombine after separating the sample I got the last time I was here, but nothing worked."

Queen perks up at that, so Teemo questions, "Really? Is that a known thing?"

The Alchemist nods as he sets aside a small portion of the chopped ingredients and motions for Queen to do her thing. She sees no harm in it, so sends her ants to process the go-juice in the old way.

"My old mentor used to say that, way back in antiquity, it was thought alchemy could only be performed in dungeons. The unique mana flows in them can influence the process in unknown ways. But as the ancients worked and experimented, they eventually started to figure out how to produce various things even outside dungeons," he explains as he works, his hands deftly grinding the herbs into a fine paste.

"The first true Alchemist was said to have gained a unique affinity with his class, or so the legends say. Personally, I think he was the first to gain the Meta affinity that most crafting classes get. Whatever the truth, he was supposed to be able to make anything a dungeon could.

"Nowadays, though, Alchemists make all sorts of things that dungeons don't. Maybe the processes are too complex for them? Who knows. But look," he says as he shows the results of his work.

The texture is perfect, the mix fully homogeneous, and yet, it just looks like an unpalatable tea. He motions at Queen's work, where she already has a few shining droplets of the go-juice.

"There's still something about dungeon alchemy that we just don't know. I can tell I've done it just as she has, if only on a larger scale, and yet, something eludes me," he laments, though not too deeply. Queen very much likes this Staiven and his ant heart. Setbacks happen but can be overcome.

Teemo gives her an odd look at her request, but still relays it. "She wants you to put the mortar down so she can try something."

"Of course," Staiven replies, and sets it next to her busy ants. Quickly, she has them swarm the contents, specifically using her alchemical storage ants for it. This sort of thing is their job, after all.

Her pleased scent returns as the mixture is quickly finished in her ants, and they start adding it to her sample in the little dish she was working in.

Staiven chuckles at what he's seeing. "See? Something about dungeon alchemy is different. Or maybe I didn't use enough ant spit in mine."

Teemo laughs at that, and Queen can't help but enjoy the joke. She does think he has a point, though. Not about the ant spit, but about the scale. She knows it takes mana to infuse the ingredients, but she and Staiven are working on a different scale at the conceptual level. If watching the Zombie Scion gain affinities has taught her anything, it's that the conceptual level is vital when it comes to magic of any kind.

Chapter 4

Leo's been working with the tundra wolves to get them into shape to actually go and help the Southwood, and I've been slowly absorbing the information Tarl gave me on it, as well as everything else. It takes time to properly process all that, and I've been busy trying not to freak out over the scythemaws.

At least the stupid swordgators seem content to be on my back burner for now—thank goodness for small blessings—even if they feel like a sword of Damocles hanging over my head.

I'm pretty sure in the myth it was hanging over the guy's throne, for some reason. I don't remember if it ever actually fell on him. I'd brush up on my Greek mythology, but it's a little out of my reach, heh.

Anyway: Southwood. It's a long way off. No wonder Tarl is gone for like a month when he goes to visit. It's at least a hundred miles of rough country to get there, and the winter will only make it rougher. I've talked with Poe about sending some ravens with the wolves to act as messengers, and he says they should be able to handle it, especially if they can ride the wolves and hunker down for warmth.

My Warden and Marshal have been working on coordinating, and it's been going pretty well, what with the practice of having Honey's bees along for a lot of expeditions. None of them will be going to the Southwood, though. It'll be *way* too cold for them to do much of anything.

They're sending a few scouting parties where the map says they should need to go, and are practicing a bit of a pony express system for relaying reports and results of the expeditions. It's working pretty well so far; we've got two outposts set up already. They're not Outposts with a capital *O* yet, or whatever the official designation might be. I dunno if there's not an official term for it yet, or if I've missed some requirement for them. Either way, they're just a little spot in a thicket and a small alcove in a hill that the wolves and ravens can rest and recover in. They don't exactly have running water, and I'm not planning on moving in anytime soon.

Still, I think the system will work, and Leo and Poe are both looking forward to organizing further afield, so I give them the go-ahead. I get the feeling Leo wants to go with the first actual force I send to try to help, but that's for later. I probably won't stop him, though. Leonidas is a name that wants to stand in the face of the impossible tide, after all. I just hope it goes better for mine than the one in history.

I'm also working on upgrading my Earth elemental spawner, and it spat out something that sounds a lot scarier than it actually is: a living rockslide. It *sounds* like something that would just obliterate everything in its path. It *looks* like a pebble swarm.

To be fair, it *is* more dangerous than it looks. For smaller invaders, it might as well be an actual rockslide, and for larger, it's quite the tripping hazard. They're cool. I'm letting them wander around more or less as they like, and they mostly like the tunnels and caverns.

I'm considering asking Poe to send some on expedition into the underswamps and/or aquifer when I feel the familiar feet of Tarl on my grass. He doesn't get the typical birb greeting, though, as he's over in the graveyard section, rather than the manor. He doesn't make any declarations, either . . . Is he here on personal business, then?

He spots Grim and simply nods at him as he walks slowly through the gravestones. He clearly has a destination in mind, so my scion leaves him be. He's seen the look of someone needing to pay respects enough times to recognize it.

I should probably give him some privacy . . . but I can't help but follow him, trying to be quiet and respectful. As if anyone could notice my presence, anyway. The elf's hands idly brush over a few of the tombstones, a small smile teasing at the corners of his lips. Yeah, Grim's done amazing work in here. I'm proud of him.

Eventually, Tarl comes to a stop in front of a grave and simply stands there a few minutes, lost in thought or memories.

Inspector Listor Greybrows
Honored Mentor
Loving Husband and Father

"Your focus isn't quite as subtle as you think it is, Thedeim," he says evenly. I'm just glad I lack the ability to crap my pants now. He gives a bittersweet chuckle as I try to take my focus elsewhere. "You don't have to go. It'd be rude of me to demand that. Besides . . . I could use someone to just listen." He pauses and looks at the tombstone, trying to gather his thoughts. "Where do I even start?

"Well, I guess I should say he's not my dad. Listor was an orc from the Wanderlands. He always had this innate understanding of dungeons. I couldn't have asked for a better mentor. He was understanding, both of people and of dungeons. I think I'm decent with one, at least."

He sighs and looks out over the wall of the cemetery.

"He died not far from here. We could only put up a memorial stone and embed his badge in it. Hullbreak Harbor killed him. Yeah . . . the other dungeon." He shakes his head before continuing. "It wasn't always belligerent. In fact, it was a pretty standard toybox. Good fishing, good pearling . . . It even eventually got dwellers who were happy to trade.

"And then . . . disaster struck. You can read what details we managed to get from the survivors, but an accident killed a few of the merfolk, and Hullbreak went mad. Listor was delving at the time." His hand gently rests atop the tombstone, where the fallen inspector's icon of authority sits. "This is all we got back."

He sighs once more and straightens slightly. "That's the risk of the job, and why people were so nervous around you at the start, you know? Nobody wanted a repeat of Hullbreak. Everyone else is content to just ignore the water dungeon, and it's happy to ignore everyone else, too." His hand slips into a pocket and pulls out a letter, which he spreads out on the tombstone for me to inspect. "But ignoring a problem doesn't make it go away."

Please, dungeoneers, help us. Hullbreak is starving. His spawners are fading; his nodes atrophying. He just wants to protect us, but he's killing himself to try to do it! Save my people and my home!
Yendo

"A seagull left that for me, at the guildhouse. As far as I can tell, it's from one of the dwellers. I don't know how they managed to get this message out, but I can't ignore it. Hullbreak killed my mentor . . . but I don't think I can blame it for that. I know *he* wouldn't blame it for that.

"But I don't know how to help it. How to help *them*. Hullbreak only avoids being labeled murderous because it doesn't send out hostile expeditions. How can I help it if it will just kill anyone who tries?" He closes his eyes in frustration, and soon feels a hand on his shoulder.

Opening his eyes, he sees a yellow daffodil offered in the other bony hand of my Skeleton Scion. My Voice speaks from the shoulder of my Grounds Reaper. "We'll figure something out, Tarl. Thedeim will put things right," he promises for me, and the elf takes the flower with shaking hands and sets it atop the tombstone.

Ah, such a terrible day for rain.

Chapter 5

Tarl eventually calms down and heads home to recover. A good cry—er . . . *rain shower* can take a lot out of someone, but it's good to let it all out sometimes. I can't blame him for having complicated feelings about Hullbreak. Honestly, when he started his story, I was making vague plans to kick in Hullbreak's door and give it the Neverrest treatment.

But in the end, it's a bit more clear what the situation is. Neverrest was rabid and had to be put down. Hullbreak is a wounded and starving beast. I might have to put it down, too, but that's the last resort. There's still hope to get it fed and healed. But how?

Focusing on the reports and stuff he gave me, the details don't really give me anything to go on. Almost every delver inside when the accident happened was killed by the sharks and other denizens of the dungeon. Any who managed to get out were able to survive, but it's pretty clear that Hullbreak doesn't want anyone from the outside coming in.

I'm also starting to suspect I might be part of the reason why it's starving now. The seagulls that I've been dealing with for a long time are probably from Hullbreak, or at least some of them are. The wasps were mostly from Neverrest, after all. I still have some wasps that attack, but not nearly as many. I think Hullbreak was basically sustaining itself on Neverrest's wasps and what raids on me it could get away with.

But now, with Neverrest gone and my defenses much improved, there's not a lot of profit in raiding around here. So . . . how can I fix it? Raid it right back?

Maybe? I have the excess mana to spend on failed raids, but what would I actually raid *with*? It'll probably figure out that something is weird if I try to send spiders or snakes or other things that clearly don't belong in the ocean. I'm sure it'd still take the mana, but it'd also keep its guard up, which I need to avoid if I'm going to help it.

I need information, too. Everything the ODA has looks to be at least a decade out of date. I don't want to try something like this with old information. I'll probably only get one chance, and then have to resort to the Old Yeller treatment if that fails.

Although . . . I wonder. If we have old info on it, how up to date is its info on what's been going on around here? I could pretend to be Neverrest, at least as far as raiding goes. I don't have the wasps, but I *do* have undead. Skeletons would probably be the best to try to raid Hullbreak with, if I want to do that kind of act.

I'll need to be careful about it, though. Too many, and it'll put its guard up even more surely than if I sent random stuff against it. But if I send a slow stream of skeletons, it should assume Neverrest has graduated from wasp harassment into undead harassment. And with it focusing on bigger invaders, I might be able to slip in a few who are sneakier.

I think I have two options with that, but I'll need to do a bit of testing. I might as well get the skeletons in on the testing, too. Just because a movie says skeletons can walk around underwater without much issue, it doesn't mean they actually can. I mean, that same movie thinks two guys can walk a rowboat upside down underwater without a bajillion pounds to help weigh it down. Buoyancy does not like having big air bubbles under the water.

Anyhow: testing. I don't want to use the underswamps or the aquifer for this. I don't need to go stirring up the scythemaws before their mating season or migration season or whatever it is they actually are going to do. So that really just leaves the hard gauntlet for testing. That's not too bad, though. It's pretty deep, and if nothing else, my denizens can be lifeguards while they're practicing in there.

I ping a couple rockslides, a handful of skeletons, and several of my more transparent slimes to head there so testing can get underway. The rockslides make quite a splash when they dive in, but they are thankfully unhindered by the water. Well, not *fully* unhindered. Water has a lot more resistance than air, but they don't need to breathe, seems like. So rockslides pass the first test with flying colors.

The skeletons are in next, and they have a bit more issues. They're quite a bit lighter than the rockslides, so they have to be more careful with their movements. If they move too fast, they basically propel themselves backward, which isn't ideal. I'm also going to need to leave my various plant-skeleton combos out of this mission. Saltwater does not like plants that are not used to it.

I'll just need to give my skeletons some kind of weighted shoes or something.

Heh, if I had access to limestone, I might be able to give them actual cement shoes. As it is, I'll probably end up tying rocks to them to keep them grounded. It'll give them a good base to be stable from, at least.

The slimes are the last to show up, which isn't a surprise. Even with shortcuts, they're pretty slow. Jello even comes to see what everyone is up to. The various slimes slip into the water, and Jello follows. While most of them aren't quite as clear as I'd like, Jello is basically invisible. If she wasn't my scion, I'd send her to get intel on Hullbreak. Thankfully, one of the oozes is also more or less invisible in the water, so I'll be sending some of them.

From the bond, I get the feeling Jello would like to go, but I gently tell her no. She still needs to find a good gopher or a good gremlin to convert. And, if Hullbreak actually manages to spot her, it'll definitely lose its crap. Scions in another dungeon are one of the biggest dangers we seem to face. Hard to make a friend if you show up to their house carrying a bomb. It doesn't matter how many times you assure them you won't use it, you're still a new person in their house, and pose a clear danger.

So now that I know who I'm sending, I need to figure out *how*. Even with me being on people's good sides, I don't think they'd appreciate skeletons, rockslides, and slimes just strolling down main street. So how do I get them to the dungeon in the bay?

They'll use the stairs I built over the wall in the graveyard. I have just been using them for the wolf expeditions on the surface, but I don't see any reason my other denizens can't use them too. First, though, I want to get the route scouted as much as possible. As far as I can tell, they should be able to just hop the wall and head roughly northwest to the ocean, then more or less north under the water to get to Hullbreak Harbor.

But I want to be sure, so I have Poe and Leo send a few expeditions along the planned route. I don't want to send my other stuff only to discover they'll be stomping through someone's big garden, or trip over *another* baby dungeon, or somehow unseal some unspeakable evil or something.

But if it all goes to plan, Operation: *Mend the Break* can actually start. I hope I'll be able to get it to open up to me and delvers, but I'm not exactly holding my breath on that one. It's been isolated for too long. Had to fight and scrape for existence for too long. There's very little chance of this happening without someone having to be smacked a few times to listen. I don't think I'll have to eat Hullbreak, though. While Violet is calm and small enough for me to just mentor, I think my most likely action with Hullbreak will be to subjugate it and make it my vassal. That's hardly the best option, but like with a lot of wounded and scared animals, sometimes dominance has to be asserted.

It'll be a delicate process, though. I have to show it there's no point in fighting me, but also that I don't want to hurt it. If it thinks it can fight me, it'll hurt itself and its dwellers to try to keep doing what it thinks is best. And if it thinks I want to consume it, it'll fight tooth and nail because it won't want to die.

It'll be a tough tightrope to walk, but if I can strike that balance, Hullbreak might be able to be released back into the wild and thrive on its own. If I *can't*... Well, the zoo is a better option than behind the shed.

Chapter 6

With the route to Hullbreak being scouted, you'd think the home front would be nice and quiet. Or at least, *I'd* hope it'd be nice and quiet, but there are two things looking to ramp up. First: we're starting to see more scythemaw activity. None are wandering out of the water yet, but we're definitely seeing more of them closer to shore.

So not quite DEFCON 1 . . . or is it DEFCON 5? I always forget if it counts up or down. I'll just say we're at DEFCON 3: a moderate pucker but still nowhere near a panic. The bypass isn't done yet, and I seriously doubt it will be done by the time this thing kicks off, but I'm not ordering Coda off the project. I've given him the suggestion, but he wants to keep working. I'm proud of that bat.

The second thing that's ramping up is the Spiderkin Enclave. It looks like they've figured out what the bottleneck was. It was their leadership. Folarn may have been stepping up into the role, but she very clearly doesn't actually want the role of leader. So, between the various preparations for dealing with scythemaws and making their enclave the best it can be, two other major figures have arisen, each from the other two main spider types.

From the widows and orb weavers comes the Master Seamstress Norloke. She seems to be more of a pumpkin spider than a widow, which is interesting to me. I would have thought one of the widows would have stepped up, but that's just not the case. I think partially because Norloke is just a really good fit for leadership.

She's a bit chunky and quite orange, as any healthy pumpkin spider should be, and has that air of a mom who knows everything that happens under her roof; the kind to wield a wooden spoon both to make dinner and to keep rowdy children in line, yet can be softer and more caring when needed, too. She's definitely more focused on keeping the enclave running smoothly and dealing with internal issues, though.

From the hunting/jumping spiders, we have the Huntsmistress Vernew, who seems to be based on a jumping wolf spider, or at least what we used to call them back home. Small and lithe, colored in various stripes of gray, she's one of the smaller jumpers, but probably the best hunter. It was actually her plan that led to them getting that one scythemaw not long ago.

She's pretty brash and boastful in the enclave, but is all business when out on a hunt, at least so far as I've been able to tell. Some of the expeditions spot her doing her thing—or more often, cleaning a kill after she's done her thing. She seems focused mostly on hunting, obviously, but also on other threats that the Deeps might send the enclave's way. She's also the most spiritual of the three and keeps a small orange gemstone on a string of her own silk on her at all times. I wonder if she might become a shaman or something instead of a ranger.

And of course, Folarn of the tarantulas is more or less the military leader and reluctant face to outsiders. She's very good at keeping her people safe, but a bit out of her depth when it comes to the other duties of leadership. Norloke is excellent at keeping them housed and clothed, but despite her expert wielding of the mom voice, she's not a fighter. And Vernew can keep the spiderkin fed and talk about the Weaver of the Threads (me, *bleh*), but has little desire or skill to do much else.

Which I think is why they were stalled for a bit. I think Folarn understands the problem, though, so she's asked the other two to meet with her to discuss things. Folarn's home is rather spartan, unsurprisingly, but she has done what she can to make her guests comfortable. She has a few different slings hanging from the ceiling for them to relax on and has prepared a couple cave lobsters for them to eat.

Vernew is the first to arrive, and greets the large tarantulakin with a smile. "Folarn! How're you doing? Those delvers aren't making you rub a bald spot on your butt, are they?" she jokes before hopping onto a sling to lounge. Folarn simply rumbles a soft chuckle and shakes her head as she moves to relax on her silken floor.

"No, they're no trouble. Aside from the inspector and the two green children, it's mostly miners who venture this deep. They've traded for a few things, but say they can't do much more until we become officially independent from Weaver Thedeim."

Vernew slightly bows her head at my name. "Yeah, I hear the ratkin had to deal with the same thing. But you said you think you know why our bars are stuck?"

"Yes, but I would like to wait for Norloke before explaining. If I'm right, it will require at least us three to resume the progress of our bars, and our Ascension to true dwellers and spiderkin."

"I like the sound of that. The delvers have all kinds of interesting things to trade for, and we might be able to do some hunting up there once we're recognized. Maybe we can get some bread from that bakery across the street, too. The Reader of the Web says the Weaver of the Threads likes baked stuff. I've never actually had any!"

Folarn chuckles once more. "Scion Tiny is likely right about that. I've heard some of the miners complaining about only being able to afford hard biscuits for a week because of a failed wager on something. The Weaver likes to see all enjoy the small comforts in life. Scion Honey says it is mostly wheat, and I've seen a picture of the plant. Perhaps we can obtain some and try to get it to grow down here."

Vernew winces a bit at that. "I don't think it'll work. At least not without someone with a good affinity for it. Stuff down here grows way differently than on the surface."

Folarn shrugs. "You'd know better than I. Still, I think we could figure out something." The two chat for a few more minutes until Norloke pokes her head in at the entrance.

"Folarn? Ah, you're both already here!" she says with a smile. Folarn gets up to embrace her while Vernew simply waves.

"Come take a sling and relax. Folarn says she has a plan to get our bars finished."

"I do, but first, let us enjoy a meal together. If my plan works, I feel we will be doing so regularly."

Norloke looks interested in the idea but is patient enough to climb into a sling and accept a cooked lobster from her host. The three eat quickly, and for me, it's like watching a train wreck. Their mouths have so many moving pieces . . .

You'd think they'd make a huge mess, but no. All those pieces grab and move and . . . *bleh*. This must be how some people come to be afraid of spiders and bugs. Thankfully, it doesn't take them long to eat, and once they're done, it seems Vernew can't hold her curiosity in check.

"So? What's the idea?!" she asks with excitement, earning a motherly smile from Norloke and an amused sigh from Folarn.

"I have, reluctantly, been taking the role of leader of the enclave for a while now," she starts. The two simply nod. "But there is much I can't do." She looks over to Vernew first. "I can't go out and hunt, or go out and gather. While I'm certain I could fell any beast out there, with the possible exception of a scythe-maw, I'm also certain I would ruin much of the meat."

"Yeah. Spears and javelins are great because they put smaller holes into important bits. A big axe would kill the thing dead but make a huge mess to try to dress," the small spiderkin says, nodding. Folarn nods and turns her attention to Norloke.

"And while I can keep the enclave safe from outside danger, I can't give them homes and jobs and guidance."

"Oh, don't sell yourself short. But I get what you mean. Trying to keep the fighters fit while also trying to organize and place everyone . . . That'd be too much for even tarantula strength to bear."

Folarn nods at that once more. "Then you two see the problem. I can't run this, but I think you two, together, can."

Vernew stands in her sling and points a dramatic and accusing finger at the larger spiderkin. "No way! You're not getting out of this that easily!"

Norloke smiles and nods at that. "You most certainly are not, no. The outsiders are too used to you now for you to try to step into some quiet, subservient role."

Folarn looks pretty unhappy at that, but she doesn't argue. "Fine. We three together can run this enclave. Vernew: the hunting and the spiritual needs of our people. Norloke: the internal needs of clothing, housing, and peace between ourselves. And I will handle our protection . . . and our diplomacy, if you two insist."

The two smile wide and nod, with Vernew speaking first. "Think of it as punishment for trying to get out of this."

"You're much better at it than you think you are, Folarn," adds Norloke. Folarn doesn't look too convinced, but she's not going to try to overturn the decision of her fellow councilwomen.

While I'm glad they figured out the hurdle, the timing makes me a bit nervous. I think they'll want to do a ceremony like the ratkin did to finalize the transition, and they sure seem to want to do it before the scythemaws do their thing.

On the one hand, it makes sense. They'll probably have to wait quite some time for the scythemaws to settle down, if they try to wait.

But on the other hand, they'll be fully independent, so they can't respawn if the worst happens.

Ugh, it's no wonder Hullbreak went nuts when some of his dwellers died. They're like my children, in a way, and I want to see them succeed and do what I can to protect them.

But I won't make Hullbreak's mistake. Maybe my perspective is weird from having died, but . . . danger is a part of life. People can be bottled up, and sure, they might survive. But people don't want to simply survive. They want to *live.*

Chapter 7

Your minds are all made up, then?" asks Teemo of the aranea triumvirate, and the three spider ladies all nod. Folarn speaks first.

"Not just ours, but all of us in this enclave. My fellow tarantulas are no strangers to difficult fights, and we understand the desire to protect. But we must have the room to grow to become better protectors."

Norloke speaks next. "The weavers are also in agreement. We all appreciate the intricate and robust web you've created, but we must have the space to create our own, to hone our own craft."

Vernew speaks last, looking the most nervous of the three. "The hunters *need* to be spiderkin. Your Weave is glorious, but there is even more to see and experience outside! We need to see it, and hopefully, help you integrate it, Weaver."

Teemo sighs at the three, mimicking my own reaction. I don't doubt their conviction, and they're not wrong about needing room to grow, space to learn, and wonders to see. I just wish they'd delay until after the scythemaws. But they're all resolute in this, and not just the triumvirate. I can feel the anticipation in the other aranea. They know the scythemaws will be trouble, but they want to be able to stand on their own feet to face it.

"Thedeim respects your decision, even if he disagrees with it. It's still *yours* to make, not his. You'll be doing the ceremony soon, then?"

The three nod, and this time, Norloke speaks first.

"I believe Aranya will be by shortly after sunset to officiate."

Vernew speaks quickly after her, not quite able to hide her excitement. "Elder Larx said he'd be showing up, too!"

My Voice can't help but chuckle a bit at that. "I think Tiny wants to come and watch, also. The Boss says he's going to have Rocky and Fluffles watching the entrances so all of you can be present."

Folarn smiles and bows slightly at that. "We thank the Weaver for that. My warriors would never shirk their duties . . . but nobody wants to be left out of this."

The final confirmation made and prep done, Teemo takes his leave. It's not going to be too long until sunset, so there's not a whole lot I can do before the ceremony. I wonder if that was part of the point of them wanting to do it quickly. Not so much that they worry I might try to stop them, but more to try to minimize *my* worry. Kinda ripping the bandage off.

I go ahead and focus in on Rocky and Fluffles as they spar, and can't help but admire the progress the two have made. My Boxer is a force to be reckoned with. He hasn't been working on expanding his affinities since gaining Kinetic, instead focusing on honing his control with them. I think he saw Fluffles's progress and identified a hole in his own training.

Part of that hole are his magical defenses. The few spars that Fluffles has won against Rocky have been when my wingnoodle would just grab him with telekinesis, and Rocky would have to tap out. Getting his own Kinetic affinity has helped him to be able to parry Fluffles's invisible grabbers. I think Rocky is starting to apply some Fire concepts to his Kinetic defense, too, because I can see something a lot like ash, but made of mana, when he parries. I'm not sure how else to describe it.

It's a really good way to spend the Kinetic energy that's trying to get him, too. All the potential goes into the "ash," which just fades into nothingness without letting the energy actually impact Rocky. It makes me think of the ablative tiling on a space shuttle. He's got a long way to go before he hits *that* kind of efficiency, but he's got the concept now.

And for his offense, he's working hard on Antipode. I'm surprised he has that idea, but I guess it must have slipped through the bond at some point. I probably *shouldn't* be surprised he's picked that up. Lucca and Nadia's Antipode spells are too cool for me *not* to think about them when I see him practicing. He hasn't been able to make it click yet, but I know he'll figure it out eventually.

As for Fluffles, my coatl has been progressing incredibly well with his Kinetic control. I can feel him examining the mana ash in the moments during their sparring that he can spare, trying to figure out how it works. He hasn't managed to wrap his head around Fire or Ice yet. In fact, I think he's going to be getting Wind before those two.

I can feel him brushing up against the concept to let him expand his telekinesis into Wind affinity. He can feel the air with his wings, knows he can push against it to fly. He just hasn't put together that he can *grab* the air with his telekinesis. I mean, it might not be how to expand into Wind affinity, but something about the idea just feels right.

I'm not sure which of them I should put facing the underswamps. There still haven't been any scythemaws wandering on the shore, but the expeditions are starting to see heads breaching the surface. I don't know which of the two fighting scions would be better suited to stopping a potential incursion. Fluffles still has the raw power advantage, but Rocky is simply the better fighter.

Actually . . . I shouldn't think about who would be the best fighter for it but who can get there quicker if they're *not* stationed facing the swamps. In that light, the choice is easy: Rocky will be facing the potential path of the scythemaws during the ceremony. If anything happens, Fluffles should be able to cross through the enclave much faster than Rocky could.

And if Tiny will be down to watch the ceremony, too, that should be security handled, hopefully. I can't imagine anything overwhelming those three quicker than the enclave could evacuate. Well, I *can* imagine a few things, but none that would actually fit down there.

I have Teemo give out the posts before letting him do his thing, which he'll be doing *with* Thing, looks like. The two are both interested in the bag of holding. I think Teemo is finally starting to understand how it works, so he and Thing are working hard to replicate the enchantment.

I idly watch them to pass the time, and soon, Aranya awakens and does her morning (dusk?) routine. She even invites Yvonne to come, but she politely declines, to nobody's surprise. My kobold meets up with Larx, and soon, everyone is gathered in the enclave.

Much like with the ratlings-turned-ratkin, Aranya starts everything off once everyone is ready.

"Aranea! You have had a difficult journey to this point, but you have persevered to reach the culmination! Lord Thedeim has given you the opportunity to be more than just denizens, and you have worked hard to achieve that! Lord Thedeim smiles at your efforts and offers you the protections he can while you prepare to truly become dwellers.

"It is a dangerous path to walk, but a fruitful one. Lord Thedeim provides as he can, but there is an entire world out there to explore and discover, friends and enemies alike to meet. He's not made a secret of this, but you still continue, braving the strange and the new. There will be difficulties, but there will be opportunities as well. I know you can and will face them as they come, and will be able to find the benefits hidden in the hardships, and will weave a strong tapestry that Lord Thedeim will be proud of."

She steps aside, letting the triumvirate of Folarn, Vernew, and Norloke take the attention of all gathered. Vernew speaks first, though she gives Tiny a bow before she starts. "The Weaver of the Threads was so strange for us at the start. Even with time and the progress of the bars blurring our memories, we all remember the strange designs he had for us all. Hunt the invaders, guide and challenge the delvers. Grow ourselves."

Norloke stands and gives Tiny a bow. "We wove traps for the invaders. We wove secrets for the Weaver of the Threads. We made signs. We helped guide the flow of delvers, putting our clumsy strings where we thought they could help, and watched how they were integrated with graceful ease."

Folarn stands and gives Tiny a bow. "We have protected the core from the very start. The Reader of the Web and Guardian is a testament to how seriously we take that responsibility. Now, we will protect not only that but ourselves, and those outside. We all know of the looming threat of the scythemaws. Instead of cowering, we will face them without the benefit of the cycle of the Weaver.

"If our threads are to be sheared, so be it. But we face that danger with the full knowledge of it. We may watch it pass beneath us from our webs. We may descend and pluck our prey from the hordes. But whatever we do, it shall be by our will. We will always hear the advice of the Weaver of the Threads, but it is not forced upon us. We will strive and struggle, and though our web may be tattered by wind and foes, we will rebuild. We are spiderkin! Beautiful as our webs may be, our *people* are what supports us, not silk. We are far stronger."

With that, the bars wink out. After a pregnant pause, the spiderkin all roar with applause and begin the celebration. Aranya and Larx stay and mingle, and Tiny continues to watch as well. I can feel him tapping into his Fate affinity, and a few concepts pass through the bond to me. This was something important, and not just for my new spiderkin. It's like it's a new spoke in a web. A new anchor point to be built on.

Chapter 8

Maybe a day after the dweller ceremony for the spiderkin, the scythemaws start leaving the water. It looks like the ones in the underswamps are a bit ahead of schedule of the ones in the aquifer, or the aquifer ones are a bit slow. Either way: Happening level is raised to *It's*.

The spiderkin are as prepared as they can be, mostly watching the scythemaws from high up on the walls and from the ceilings. They're only in danger if they slip, and I don't think I've ever seen one fall. I'm still nervous about the whole thing, but they're being diligent and watchful, which is all I can really ask.

The only thing they have on the floors are the lobster ponds, and even those they managed to cover with a few big slabs of stone. I'm pretty sure the tunnel horrors could easily get through, and I even spot a few scratching at the lids, but none put in the effort to actually get in. They can probably smell the lobsters and don't really care too much about them. They have cave lobster at home; no need to get at these ones.

Besides, food seems to be on the bottom of the list of their priorities right now. Looks like it *is* mating season, with a bit of migration thrown in. I can't say for certain, but it looks like the male and females both have their own competitions. I can't say definitively which is which, because they all look like big, armored lizards with mandibles to me, but I do see two basic sets of behavior going on right now.

One set is settling in and spreading out. The bigger and meaner ones are more or less settling in the middle of the spiderkin village. I think they want to be closish to water, but not too close, and the biggest ones are stomping around to settle their nesting area, seems like. I don't know if the spiderkin will need to run them off or not. I don't think the scythemaws will be able to cause any trouble, but I also don't know if they'll like the village going on overhead. It's still early, though, so we'll just have to wait and see how they behave, and if the enclave decides they want the beasties further away.

The other group seems to be the males, and they're trudging through the various tunnels, fighting and marking the walls. The one in the front seems to be the strongest. First one to the other side gets first pick of the lovely ladies, I suppose. Considering how much fighting is going on, they'll probably be fighting their prospective mates to find a good match, too.

Their fighting is loud and looks pretty brutal, but I'm not seeing a lot of lasting injuries. I did see what looks like a younger buck manage to snap a scythe off of one of the horrors in front of him in the rough line, but that seems to be about it. The other ones ahead of him have been giving him wary looks, but I think he's happy in his new place, at least for the moment. We'll see if he lets success go to his head.

Heh, listen to me. I'm a nature documentary. I'd probably lose my funding for how much I'm interfering in their natural stuff, though. They're still delvers to me, so I'm going to send at least some encounters to mess with them.

Unsurprisingly, they don't care about my various nodes at all. They also don't pay much attention to the living rockslides. I think they just don't process the little pebble swarms as things they should bite at, and their nature makes it difficult for the denizens to mess with them much. The slimes and oozes are similar, and most of the maws either go around or ignore them.

Stalactsprites have been surprisingly effective, though. They haven't killed any of them, but the things dropping on them from the roof tend to make the maws vacate the area, which is worth a nice bit of mana. The one thing the maws *do* pay attention to are the widows and other larger spiders I have to throw at them.

I don't know if there's some rivalry or if the maws prey on something spidery in the water or what, but they attack the spiders on sight, if at all possible. I even sent a large group of spiders at them to see what would happen, and they actually banded together to fight them off. I think the pecking order changed a bit from that fight, too.

My testing of the scythemaws aside, the surface is aware of the new danger in the Deeps. I've been sure to keep the ODA well informed of what's going on, so delvers know the deeper tunnels and caverns, while not off-limits, are a *lot* more dangerous than usual.

That doesn't stop all of them, though. There're more than a few quests to bring back some part or another from a scythemaw, so the more adventurous delvers are weighing their options. Even Yvonne and her party are getting in on the action. They've been trying to get Aranya to join them, too, as a more dedicated support role so Aelara can lean more into her offense. So far, everyone is just spying on the big lizards, trying to suss out any weaknesses or find one injured or sick or something. I've been keeping the few healing slimes I have on standby, just in case something happens.

Oddly, Grim has been taking an interest in the whole thing. He still tends to the cemetery and the flower garden there, but he also has been showing up around the delvers who want to take a look at the scythemaws. It feels less like he's waiting to reap and more like he's a butterfly flapping its wings.

I've seen him wave an encounter off from one duo of delvers, and they were able to get into a little hiding spot to observe some scythemaws just before the beasties arrived. He's swept up some sand in one area, spread some in others, and even set a rock at a precarious balance, which tumbled and drew the attention of a maw so a solo delver could slip away before being spotted.

I was confused at first, but I think he's using his Fate affinity to help delvers. He's got Death affinity, too, so he can probably tell if things would go poorly for the surface delvers. It's like watching a *Final Destination* movie, but the coincidences are keeping people from dying rather than killing them in convoluted ways.

He gets a thumbs-up from me for it, and I think he can feel my appreciation through the bond, too. He's stoic and hard to read from the outside, but the sense of accomplishment I get back lets me know he gets the idea.

Violet is taking the whole thing really well, too. She's saved up quite a bit of mana and could expand at any time, but I've been encouraging her to wait to see how this plays out before she tries that just yet. She has her two scions now, too. They're both still pretty weak, but she has them. For now, they're mostly staying in her Sanctum with her core. I've pointed out she could start working on making one strong like Tiny, but she doesn't seem to be too worried about that.

Her Mushroom Scion is pretty interesting, though. It looks to have Knowledge affinity, and has been slowly spreading beyond Violet's borders. Right now, it's more focused on keeping an eye on the aquifer maws than anything else, which is fair. Aranya, Yvonne, Aelara, and Ragnar have been using the little dungeon as a bit of a forward observation base, coordinating with Teemo to help them get in and out.

He hasn't made any shortcuts from me to Violet yet because I want to make sure she has room to grow. There are a few in the unclaimed tunnels, but only big enough for Teemo to use, nothing bigger. They're a lot easier to hide in my territory, and I don't want to go accidentally making problems for Violet when she expands and suddenly finds all kinds of security breaches in her new area. Still, Teemo is a Scout, so this kind of thing is right up his alley.

Aranya is actually having fun with the delvers, too, quietly and carefully observing the maws as more and more slowly fill the tunnels.

"I cannae believe ye' outran one a those, Aranya," says Ragnar as they all relax behind the doors. My kobold smiles at that.

"It wasn't for very long. By the time I stumbled into Thedeim's Sanctuary, I was on the brink of exhaustion," she points out.

"It must have been incredibly hungry to chase you all the way to his territory," says Yvonne as she goes over the observations they've made so far. "It looks like they mostly prefer to hunt in the water."

I give Teemo my own theory on the matter, and he relays it. "Maybe it was wanting to fatten up for the migration? They don't seem too interested in eating right now, so maybe they need to eat a lot beforehand?"

Yvonne hums at that and adds it to the notes. "It's possible, and it would explain some of their behavior. We need more information to know for sure."

The elven woman speaks up. "Luckily, there are people willing to pay for that kind of information. So little is known of the horrors, we could claim they sprout little wings and disintegrate into butterflies, and there'd be little evidence to contradict it," she says with a smile, and they all laugh at the idea.

"I'm most curious to see if they lay eggs or give live birth. If they lay, we might be able to try to domesticate them. Can you imagine having one as a mount?" asks Yvonne. Only Ragnar seems to like the idea.

"Och, that'd be a sight, aye. Th' best mounts in Homehold're jus' dire moles. They're nae very intimidatin', though."

Aelara giggles at that and nods. "I've seen them before. Those star noses are somehow hideous and adorable at the same time, and their little beady eyes always look more lost and innocent than what should be on a mount bred for war."

"Aye, but they're still th' best option. But if we c'n get *scythemaws* fer Homehold, we'd be bloody rich!"

"Don't go counting your tunnel horrors before they hatch," points out Aranya with a smile. "They seem pretty troublesome. They might not take to domestication."

Ragnar shrugs, and Yvonne speaks once more. "We'll just have to see. I think a lot of parties are getting close to trying to kill one, and then we'll have a better idea of how they work."

"Are we close, too?" asks Aelara. Everyone looks at Yvonne and her notes. My birb resident considers the question before answering.

"Maybe. If we can get Violet to help, it might be even easier. We could try to lure one in here, separate it from the rest, and then only have to deal with one, instead of however many might take notice out in the open."

"It'd also get her quite a bit of mana if it dies in here, too," points out my little kobold, and the others look like they like the idea.

"Violet?" asks Teemo, to get her attention. "Would you be willing to let them lure a scythemaw in here and kill it? You should get a lot of mana once it's dead."

Violet seems more nervous about that idea, but she doesn't reject it right away.

"She's not saying no, but I think she'd like us to have a more concrete plan before trying."

"Aye, so would I," agrees Ragnar. "Jus' 'cuz I'm th' shield, dinnae mean I want more dents 'n I have t' take."

They all agree on that and get down to brass tacks with planning.

Chapter 9

Aranya, Yvonne, Ragnar, Aelara, and even Teemo are all for luring a scythemaw into Violet—who is also onboard, tentatively—but as they all sit down to plan, they realize something: how will they actually lure the scythemaw in?

"They dinnae seem ta be hungry," points out Ragnar as the group carefully peers out of Violet's doors. A couple of wild critters scurry by occasionally, but the maws don't seem to care about chasing them down to eat.

"We could try having the Boss send a spider? They seemed to like to go after those," suggests Teemo, but Yvonne shakes her head.

"They're a little *too* interested in the spiders. If they notice it on the ceiling, we could draw in more than one. And Thedeim seems reluctant to make shortcuts to allow them to get here unseen," she points out.

"What if we try throwing rocks or something at one?" suggests Aranya, and the others weigh that option, with Aelara voicing her opinion first.

"It'd be risky, but would be easiest to pick exactly which one we want."

Yvonne nods at that. "If they behave like other territorial nesters I've seen, the weaker ones will be more aggressive in guarding their territory than a stronger one, which should make it easier to draw it off. If we bide our time, we can even try to instigate something, too. Wait for a stronger one to eye its territory, draw it toward us, and if the stronger one moves in, the weaker will have little other option than to try to come get us. We even have a clear territory here in Violet that it might want to claim."

Violet doesn't seem happy with that, but Teemo does his best to ease her concerns. "We won't let it *actually* claim you for its nest, Violet. We're just planning around how it thinks. All the maw would see is an unclaimed area, and then we spring the trap."

Are you guys going to be able to handle even a shrimpy scythemaw, though? The one Tiny fought was pretty gnarly, and I've spotted a few that look even meaner.

Teemo relays my concerns, and they all nod.

"We're certainly not strong enough to just go charging out there to fight all comers," says Aelara. "But that's what the plan is for. We'll lure in a smaller, weaker one and deal with it once the doors are closed. If something goes wrong, we'll take an emergency shortcut back to Thedeim's territory. You can do that, right, Teemo?"

My Voice reluctantly nods. "It'll be a drain, but I think so. It'll be even more of a drain to properly collapse it afterward . . . But yeah, I think I can."

"Sounds like we have a plan!" says Ragnar with a wide grin. "We'll draw the beastie here, I'll keep its focus, and you lot put it down b'fore it turns me intae dwarf jelly."

They all nod at the simple plan, and Teemo relays it to Violet. She still seems a bit nervous about it, but she gives her permission. She even points out to Teemo a patch of puffballs to try to draw the scythemaw through. She's not sure if it'll actually do much, but she'd like to contribute more than just the doors.

The plan set, the group returns to their careful scouting and observing of the scythemaws, looking for a good opportunity to try their plan. I nervously watch for a few minutes, but it's quickly obvious it'll take a while. Yvonne's party is experienced enough to be patient and wait for the proper time, and Aranya is smart enough to follow their lead. I should probably stop worrying about them, but it's not that simple.

Bah, leave the pros to do their job.

Obsessing will just wind me up, so I'll go do something else . . . like checking in on the not-so-terrible trio in the gauntlet. With the scythemaws in town, a lot of the adventurers are checking out the new show instead of competing to be the first to beat the hard gauntlet. It also helps that the trio have been significantly ahead in their progress, too.

They're back to the final room, and they're very close to victory. They're also very close to washing out again, though. They've traced the pipe they need to connect, and now, it's a matter of putting the handles on the correct valves to send the water where it needs to go.

"Mine should be set!" shouts the halfling, Mlynda, looking nervous and excited at the same time. She looks more in her element than I think I've seen her before, too, even without an animal companion.

"Done here!" exclaims Hark, the tanned elf, as he points a finger at his own set of pipes, taking a moment to double-check everything is how it should be. "Yeah, looks good! Vnarl?"

The troll leader of the group growls at his challenge. "My pipe goes into a box or something! It's not the only one, too! I'm not sure which is the right valve to close for it!"

"What does it look like?" asks the elf, knowing that the solution for one room is often hidden in a different one. I made this gauntlet to make sure people cooperate better, after all.

"We're low on time!" warns Mlynda, and she's not wrong. I don't have an hourglass or anything set up, but after getting washed out so many times, they're getting a feel for the rhythm of how long they have.

"*Grrah*, I'll just have to guess!" grumbles Vnarl to himself, setting the valves before running over to the main one for his room. "Ready? One!"

"Two!" follows Mlynda, hoping they have it right, and that even this brief delay won't wash them out. They still have about ten seconds, which isn't a whole lot, but plenty for this, at least.

"Three!" finishes Hark, and all three open the flow valves. It's a tense couple seconds as the water rushes through the pipes. They've had to endure this wait many times, and only once have they tasted victory after it's over.

Make that twice, now. They flinch as the doors open before they all laugh and rush through to the reward room. Their old stuff is long gone, but I think they'll appreciate their first true stash from me. And, atop the coins and stuff, lies a simple wooden board with words carved by my aranea.

First to complete the Challenge Gauntlet.

Vnarl grins wide and holds the sign high while the other two cheer.

"We did it!"

"What rank do you think we'll be?" asks Hark. Vnarl shrugs while Mlynda considers that, the guys checking through the loot to see if there's anything of special interest.

"Well, we're some of the top in the guild as far as raw power goes. That's probably one of the reasons he recruited us."

"Yeah, but a lot of the others are gaining fast. Thedeim is a great place to train," grunts Vnarl, looking forward to turning in this particular quest so the three can get back to some more typical delving. The gauntlet was an interesting challenge and test, but the troll knows where his particular talents lie.

"It really is. Did you know there haven't been any deaths in here yet?" asks Hark, and the other two look at him like he's lost his mind.

"Of course there have been deaths, Hark. You saw what that Raven Scion did to us!" points out the halfling as she joins the guys in sorting and gathering the loot.

"Yeah, I did. But we also survived, right? I'm telling you; I've been checking. There's been some good scares and some close calls, but nobody has died in here," he insists.

Vnarl still doesn't look convinced.

"Even if that's true, which I doubt, it'll only be a matter of time. Even the most peaceful toyboxes have had people die on accident."

"What if it's a Death- or Life-affinity dungeon?" insists Hark.

It's Mlynda's turn to give him a look.

"What makes you even think that?"

"Well, Yvonne is alive . . . or not. You know what I mean. He saved her. What if he's saved others? What if the close calls were closer than people think?"

"I think you're crazy, Hark. Death- and Life-affinity dungeons are pretty obvious in their affinities. Besides, other people would have that same condition if it was doing the same to them as it did to her. I think it's Earth affinity."

"Why's that?" asks Vnarl as he examines a pair of boots.

"It hasn't been content to just expand into natural caves and tunnels. It manipulates the stone to make what it wants."

"I think it's Water. The only reason it hasn't gone to the sea yet is it doesn't quite know it's there." The two look to Hark to see if he's changed his mind on what aspect I am.

"You're sure it's not Death?" he asks, and Mlynda nods. ". . . Then I think it's Life. That's why Yvonne is a weird kind of undead, and why nobody has died in here."

The other two shrug, then Vnarl speaks up. "Whatever affinity it has, we should finish looting and get back to the guild. We're still on the bottom rung until we turn this quest back in to Karn."

Chapter 10

I let the trio enjoy their loot and look back at Aranya and the others. They're still waiting, with Yvonne giving a bit of a play-by-play of the shifting hierarchy among the scythemaws.

Most seem to be more or less settled into their spots, but there's one who seems a prime candidate for them to draw out. It's a bit skinnier than the others around, but a whole lot meaner. I'd probably try for one of the others, but from how Yvonne talks about that one's position, it's going to be their best bet.

A larger one has been wandering around, and Yvonne thinks it's waiting for someone to make better progress on a nest before simply muscling them out. It'll probably get a few cuts from the fight, but there's little doubt it'd be able to oust the smaller one, and it seems to be the best one for it to go after, too. The others are big enough they might be able to break something, so the skinnier one would be the clear choice.

It's taking a while, though. Long enough for my attention to wander back to my spiderkin and their new enclave. I'm kinda surprised the scythemaws are mostly treating the cave like the enclave isn't even there, considering how much they seem to hate spiders.

In fact, the first couple days they were in there, they were always stomping around, growling, and generally trying to get the spiderkin to come down and fight. The spiderkin, of course, have no intention of going down there . . . at least as long as they finish up relatively quickly. The cave lobster ponds are safe, but they don't know how long the things will live without any help from the village.

The wranglers are fully confident that two weeks will be no problem, and are pretty sure they should be fine for a month or so. After that, opinions start differing, but they're happy to leave the concern mostly for the future. The male maws have started showing up and strutting their stuff for the ladies, but no business has been conducted just yet. If they're happy to lay fairly quickly and leave, the enclave can easily just wait. If they stick around to try to protect the eggs . . . we might have a problem.

It's a pretty outside chance, though, so they're content to wait. While it's possible the mother scythemaws will starve themselves protecting their eggs, Yvonne gives it pretty long odds.

And speaking of my favorite birb (sorry, Poe), she speaks up from Violet's doors, where she and Teemo are keeping a careful watch.

"The big one's back. I think it's time. With the males mingling now, she needs a nest if she wants a mate. Everyone remember their parts?" Everyone nods their heads. "Then get ready to open the doors all the way."

I watch through Teemo as the scythemaw swaggers through the area outside. She sniffs at a few nests, but the ones there growl and convince her it'll be too much hassle. She could probably take most of the scythemaws in the area, but they might get in some good licks. Yvonne calling that she'd bully the smaller one is right on the money, as she puffs herself up larger as she comes closer to the nest of the smaller one.

The outsider growls as she approaches, and the smaller one roars, leaving the larger one unimpressed. She roars again as the other steps a foot into her area, but doesn't yet attack. She knows this isn't a fight she can win, but she also doesn't want to give up her hard work.

A second leg intrudes on her domain, and it's time to put up or shut up. She dashes forward, mandibles wide open, and her foe meets her. They lock maws, and it becomes a lot like a sumo match: first pushed out loses. Of course, with the difference in size, the smaller one never stood a chance. If she had managed to avoid locking mandibles together, she might have been able to use her speed, but she didn't, and is pushed out without too much fuss.

She hisses and roars at the usurper, but the new tenant simply snaps her mandibles at the loser, showing she's more than willing to defend her new home.

Meanwhile, at the doors, Yvonne gets them open, and Aelara hurls a stone at it from across the cave. Everyone except Ragnar hides, and the grinning dwarf raps his hammer on his shield, taunting the angry tunnel horror. Whether it's the insulting look, irritating sound, or the seemingly empty room behind him, it doesn't matter: she charges.

Ragnar laughs and runs back inside, taking up position behind a patch of puffballs. As the angry creature rushes in, Yvonne and Aranya work to get the doors closed as quickly as possible. Aelara prepares an Earth spell as Ragnar stares down the charging monster. It doesn't seem to even notice the puffballs popping as it rushes through, though I can see a slowed effect pop up over the scythemaw.

"C'mon, ye wee beastie! I've pulled worse things than ye out'a me ale!" yells Ragnar as he plants his feet and blocks the scythes—one on his shield, the other with his hammer. Aelara releases her spell, rooting Ragnar to the spot and helping him deal with all that momentum while at the same time destabilizing the ground the maw stands on.

It roars in anger, and the dwarf responds with a laugh and a kick to the snout, causing it to rear back. "Och, ye'll be a grand tale to tell!" he shouts before getting his shield up just in time to block a swipe from its tail.

Aelara releases another spell, causing the floor under the maw to turn to sand for a moment, its feet sinking in. Then it hardens, leaving the monster restrained for a few moments. That gives Yvonne and Aranya the time to finish closing the doors and join in the fray.

"Thedeim's Temper!" shouts Aranya. A soft orange glow surrounds Ragnar's armor, shield, and hammer.

"Barrage!" yells Yvonne as she lets loose a handful of arrows at once. They don't do much damage, but they do draw the maw's attention for a moment, letting Ragnar step in and wallop it with his hammer.

"Hide's tough! Need to hit it in the eyes or mouth!" yells Yvonne, more to let the others know she needs to be at the front. Aranya doesn't have too much in the way of offense, even with the sword at her hip, but Aelara's Earth magic should be able to do a lot of damage if she actually decides to switch from hindering to damage.

The maw, though, isn't just going to take this lying down. With a roar, it frees its legs and swipes the debris at the ones in range. Ragnar whacks one of its mandibles from the opening, though, and I get the feeling he has the maw's full attention now.

"That's right, beastie! Keep yer eyes on Ragnar!"

The maw is starting to realize it's in trouble, so it attempts to deal with the small, bearded menace. It moves its head to swipe at him, getting Ragnar to raise his shield, before dipping low and cutting into the earth like it is butter. With a flick, Ragnar is sent cursing into the air before being snatched by the wicked mandibles.

"True Shot!" shouts Yvonne over the sound of strained metal, and the maw releases Ragnar with a roar as the arrow finds one of its eyes. He lands in a heap, but staggers to his feet with a manic grin. His chest piece has matching dents on the front and back now, and the orange glow has vanished. He coughs up a bit of blood, which only seems to make him grin wider.

"Weaver's Tangle!" shouts Aranya as she finishes another spell, this time doing something to the scythemaw. The others seem to take it as a signal and prepare attacks.

"Hol' th' line!" bellows Ragnar, red spittle flying as he stares down the enraged scythemaw.

"True Shot!" follows Yvonne, her arrow glowing slightly as she waits for the perfect moment to let it fly.

"Stalactite Call!" finishes Aelara, pulling a large spear of rock from the ceiling, directly overhead of the scythemaw.

The monster charges Ragnar, ready to meet and overcome his challenge or die trying, before a twist of Fate seals its doom. "Bold Gambit!" shout all four, their efforts combining. The orange glow nudges its leading foot just a little before winking out, causing it to fall into the gap left from when the maw sent Ragnar into the air. It stumbles with a surprised grunt, and Yvonne releases her arrow into its throat. The beast rears back in pain before the plummeting stalactite catches it right at the base of the skull and drives it to the floor with an echoing boom.

The party watches for a few moments to make sure the maw is dead, but the body doesn't even twitch. Nobody wants to be the first to declare victory, but Ragnar soon grunts and takes a rough seat on the floor. "Urg . . . 'm gonna feel this tomorra'," he groans, tracing the long dent on his chest armor.

That seems to pop the tension, and Aelara walks over to heal him with a smile and shake of her head. "I was worried when that thing grabbed you, Ragnar."

"Aye, how d'ye think *I* felt?" he jokes, looking over at Aranya. "What was that prayer y' cast? I could feel it fightin' tha' bite."

Aranya looks a bit embarrassed before she answers. "It's inspired by the ratkin, actually. They remember working in the forges when they were still denizens, smelting ore and making crude gear. They like to ask to be tempered to never shatter, only to bend under great force. A bent sword can be straightened or reforged much easier than a broken one."

"Weaver's Tangle is inspired by the spiderkin, then?" asks Aelara.

My High Priestess nods.

"They like to focus on his Fate aspect, saying he weaves small starts into glorious finales."

"I'd certainly call that a pretty glorious finale," says Yvonne as she examines the dead scythemaw, and the others all nod. Ragnar stands, seeming to be feeling much better after being healed, but his face falls as he looks at the dead beast.

"How're we gonna get it out'a here?"

Chapter 11

Everyone stands around the dead scythemaw, trying to figure out the answer to Ragnar's question: How *will* they get this thing out of here? It's too big and heavy for them to lift, and even if they manage to cut it into pieces, there's still the matter of all the other scythemaws between them and my territory.

"Maybe a shortcut?" suggests Aelara, but the others don't look too sure about that.

"Even if Teemo made one, we still wouldn't be able to lift the entire thing," points out Yvonne.

Teemo tilts his head slightly as I tell him I'll help, and he smiles once I explain. "The Boss says he's sending Fluffles to come get the scythemaw. He should be able to levitate the corpse without much issue, and probably us with it. Once back in Thedeim's territory proper, you guys should be able to get a cart and some laborers or something."

Ragnar grins at that idea. "An' we c'n parade this thing through town. I bet we're the first ta fell one." The others enjoy the idea of the fame that will bring, and then Yvonne speaks up.

"Oh, Aranya. Did you want to officially join the guild? Your prayers made that fight much smoother," she points out. The other two nod as the kobold considers that.

"What about my responsibilities to Thedeim?"

Teemo shrugs. "You know how his plans can change, but he's not planning any new enclaves for a while. I'm pretty sure the other spawners still have quite a few upgrades to go before any of them will be ready, too."

She thinks while the others idly chat and poke the dead maw, taking their time to examine their prize as they wait for Fluffles to get there. He has no trouble flying high and over the scythemaws, and they're content to ignore him. He earns the occasional growl when he flies over some nests, but that's it. Once he arrives and slips past the doors, Aranya seems to take that as her cue to announce her decision.

"I think I will join the adventurers' guild, if you'll have me in your party. You *are* allowed more than three, right? I've only ever seen trios or solo people. Sometimes a delver leading a noncombatant to the nodes."

Aelara nods. "There's no official limit to a party size, but three is the traditional number. It tends to give a good balance of roles while minimizing the need to divide loot and experience."

"You all are fine with me having a share of both?"

They all nod, and Ragnar speaks up. "Aye, lass. If na fer yer prayers, that maw could 'ave left me as half th' dwarf I am now."

Aranya smiles and looks to Teemo. "And Lord Thedeim is fine with this, too?"

"Yeah, he's fine with it. Just don't go leaving him *too* lonely," he says with a wink, and everyone shares a laugh. Fluffles hisses for everyone's attention, to see if they're all ready to go.

"I think we should climb aboard the scythemaw and pretty much just hang on?" suggests Teemo. The others agree to that plan.

Piling on, they all give Violet thanks again before Fluffles lifts the whole show with his telekinesis and flies out the doors.

The trip back is only slightly more interesting than the flight in. A floating scythemaw is a lot more attention-grabbing than just my wingnoodle on his own. Hisses, growls, and roars follow, but all the maws take more defensive than offensive positions as Fluffles goes past. They don't want a fight, but they want to try to establish themselves as something Fluffles doesn't want to fight, either.

I'm pretty sure he could take them, but he has more important things to do. He deposits everyone up on the lawn, just outside the cave entrance, drawing looks from everyone else on the surface. Aelara and Ragnar head outside to see about a wagon and a few "stout lads" to help load the thing, while Yvonne and Aranya stay with the body to make sure nobody messes with it.

The two get asked all sorts of questions, and Aranya lets Yvonne handle what information they get to hear. My birdkin is more familiar with the terms of the quest, after all. She gives out only the most basic of information; the maws are fast and strong, don't get grabbed, hit it hard to get past the scales, and so on.

Before too long, the other two return with a mule-drawn cart and a few . . . badgerkin, looks like? They fit the *stout lads* description, that's for sure. It doesn't take them too much time nor effort to get it loaded up, and the party heads off to turn in the quest and get Aranya officially signed up, while the other delvers return to their own delves.

The next couple days see more parties wanting to bag a maw of their own, but there's a lot fewer opportunities to snag one. The maws squatting in the

Spiderkin Enclave have settled in, with only a few of the larger ones deciding they don't like having my spiderkin overhead. So, with the nesting seeming to be settled, it's time for the guys to strut their stuff and try to impress a lady enough to do the nasty. As such, most maws are all gathered up together, and even the most reckless of parties would rather not try to fight a whole cavern full of horny tunnel horrors.

Still, dominance displays will always leave a couple on the outskirts, which is generally outside my borders in the hunting tunnels. I watch a familiar group as they prepare to head out: the same group who got the chest in my basement a while ago. The halfling is still done up in shiny armor with a sword and shield, though the shield is closer to a tower shield now. I'm pretty sure he had more of a kite shield back in the basement.

The spear elf still has his spear and chainmail, and the lady gnome still looks like a walking alchemy shop. They all look to be in pretty high spirits, though the jovial tone of their conversation quiets as they near my border and put their game faces on.

"Remember," says the gnome as everyone does one last check of their gear, "these things are dangerous. The Hardening Oil for Jurl's armor should protect him from the worst, but we'll all drink the Stoneskin potions once we have a horror picked out. The Keen Oil should help your spear get past the scales, Dirnos, but watch for the tail. I'm going to try a Frozen Fulmination when I get the chance. It might have more trouble breaking free of ice than from earth."

The other two nod, and the elf grins. "And if we're in over our heads, run back here and hope Thedeim can keep the angry maw from eating us, right, Quitly?"

The gnome sticks her tongue out at him before nodding.

"Right. The Fleet Ointment should help us stay unnoticed, and also help us run, if it comes to that."

With one more nod, the three head out, and I wish them luck. They seem to be the only ones risking a fight down there right now, with everyone else either doing more ordinary delving or giving the gauntlet or maze a try. The gauntlet has been less popular since the trio took the first true clear, but it's still an interesting challenge that keeps the delvers on their toes when the deeper sections are just too dangerous for more parties to play with. I watch a couple runs in there, and a few people in the maze, though I keep an eye out on my borders, just in case.

I start to get a bit worried for the group when I notice Grim making his way down to one of the tunnels, and I set a few healing slimes to follow him. There's only that one group that's hunting right now, so I hope things are going well for them.

* * *

Things don't seem to be going well for them, as I soon feel the elf sprinting into the tunnel with Grim, the gnome and halfling over his shoulders. The halfling is looking like a rabid can opener attacked him, and the gnome is looking pretty pale from blood loss. The culprit is probably that deep gash on her thigh. I can see something smeared over the wound, but I don't know what it actually is.

And not far behind comes a rampaging scythemaw, roaring and chasing as quickly as it can. Grim watches them all and motions at the elf before indicating the two red slimes behind him, then slowly walks forward. The elf rushes past him and gives the two slimes a weird look before the gnome manages a few pained words.

"Into . . . the slimes . . ." she groans, recognizing the healing properties even in her state.

Grim's scythe makes a rhythmic sound as he uses it as a walking stick, continuing his pace toward the tunnel horror, seeming to pay no mind to the scenes before or behind him.

The elf, apparently Dirnos, manages to get his companions into the jellies before he looks back. His eyes widen as he feels Grim tap into his true power. My Grounds Reaper's robes seem to softly billow in an unseen breeze as he comes to a stop, the scythemaw practically upon him. If I had eyes, they'd widen, too, once I took a peek at Grim's stats. He's got a few new titles.

Grim, the Grounds Reaper
Skeleton Scion
Bloom of Life
Touch of Death
The Bridge Between

Grim doesn't even move as the maw collapses like a puppet with its strings cut, a faint caw echoing through the tunnels. Momentum carries it to Grim's feet, where he reaches into his robe, pulling out a simple daisy, and lays it upon its snout. His task complete, he turns and walks back past the stunned elf and the recovering others. They're in no position to say anything, but he quietly swears once Grim passes out of his view, and he looks back toward the dead scythemaw.

"By the Raven . . ."

I don't think he's too far off.

Chapter 12

After they recover and get some people down to deal with the scythemaw body, it starts to feel like the scythemaw mania is about finished. Those three are considered pretty dang stronk and cautious, and if even *they* had to be bailed out of a hunt, it makes the other delver groups reconsider their options.

And speaking of delver groups: Aranya is officially part of the adventurers' guild! She's been getting to know everyone there better and hanging out with Ragnar and Aelara more, too. She's suggested to them asking to be residents, but neither is too interested, which is fine. My two residents have also been keeping an eye on various quests, which helps me adjust to demand.

In low demand now are scythemaw quests, for example. There's plenty of bits for the curious to play with, so the only quests left seem to be to observe them. It's still not exactly *safe*, but the maws are settling into homemaking to go with their baby making. There are very few solo maws left, so the various pairs mostly guard their territory and work on deepening their nests.

It's nice to have the delvers get back to more usual delving, at least. The crypt complex is busier than usual, thanks to the deeper caverns being taken up by the maws, but it's simple enough to aim the tougher spiders and other harder encounters over there, as well as the various plant/undead hybrids that are already calling that area home.

The scouting operations outside the borders are going well. Progress proceeds apace to get into contact with the Southwood. Leo has set a few packs to head there directly, now that we have a few little outposts established. I don't want him going himself just yet, though. I want to get him a bit more experience directing my denizens before I let him run off to an unknown fight.

The path to Hullbreak looks pretty clear, and I'm going to need to have Teemo drop in on Tarl and the Office of Dungeon Affairs soon, to let them know not to freak out if they see skeletons and stuff outside of town to the north.

Tying rocks to them is still my best option, seems like. I considered trying some metal transmutation, but there are a couple problems with that. The first is that saltwater does not play nicely with most metals. The second is that I just don't have enough of the stuff to transmute enough of the skeletons to make them sink nicely.

And the third: I don't want to tip off Hullbreak that I have alchemical stuff. It might think it's just a skeleton upgrade if I was able to transmute an entire skelly, but that is *way* too expensive to keep up for long.

So just rocks for now. Besides, it'll give my rockslides a good cover to get inside. With new rocks littering the seabed, other little piles won't stick out as much.

We'll be getting into the water from a steep, rocky beach. I'm pretty sure Hullbreak doesn't own that section, so we should be able to slip the slimes in without too much trouble. Poe is setting a flock of ravens at the beachhead just in case, to make sure Hullbreak can't get too close of a look at what's going on.

. . . I think that's basically all the planning I can do before actually doing this. I need to see how Hullbreak will react, and try to get information on his dwellers before I can do much more. First thing I'll probably have my spies try to do will be to get in contact with the one who wrote that letter.

Alright, Teemo. Go let Tarl know what we're up to.

Tarl

The inspector has been feeling . . . rather good lately, actually. He hadn't realized how much he was bottling up in regard to Hullbreak, and having Thedeim listen in was a great weight off his mind. And then the crazy dungeon promised to somehow make it right!

He chuckles at the idea as he helps organize the yearly paperwork. Telar does an excellent job keeping everything in order throughout the year, but even she needs help going through everything for the official records. And the tax collectors, of course.

"Has the Boss really made that much of a mess for you this last week?" comes a familiar voice from atop a cabinet, and Tarl smiles at the local Voice.

"Ah, hello, Teemo. And no, this isn't just from this week. We're getting started with the year-end paperwork. Tax collectors are more formidable than anything I've encountered in a dungeon," he replies with a smirk. He watches as the scion makes a couple jumps to land on his desk, and he decides he can take a quick break to chat. "Is something up?"

Teemo nods. "Yeah. Remember what I said in the graveyard? Well, the Boss is about ready to make his first move on that."

Tarl's face turns serious as he adopts his inspector mode, understanding this is an important business topic. "What are his plans with Hullbreak?"

"Well . . . *plan* is a bit strong, but he does have a few things he's going to be doing. He's going to send sacrificial raids of skeletons at Hullbreak to help keep it from starving, and he's going to infiltrate it to get more information."

"Sacrificial raids?" repeats Tarl, surprised Thedeim would go that far. "He's not just going to subsume it?"

"I mean, it's an option, but Hullbreak sounds like it's hurt and scared, rather than just outright evil and dangerous. He wants to try to talk to it."

"And if that doesn't work?" asks the elf, looking like he seriously doubts that will work.

"He'll try to Vassalize it."

Tarl's eyes widen at that. "He can do that already?!"

Teemo nods. "He technically could have done that with Violet, but he hasn't. She's still open to learning and doesn't just lash out in fear. Hullbreak . . . is probably going to take a heavier hand."

Tarl slowly nods at that. "He's aware Hullbreak won't just accept Vassalization?"

"Yeah, he knows it'll be a fight if it comes to that, and that it will probably come to that, too. But he wants to take it slow and careful; see if the carrot will work before he has to employ the stick."

The inspector sighs at that, not having much hope for the carrot approach but unwilling to call it a lost cause already. "Can I put his ability to Vassalize into the records?"

The Voice tilts his head slightly, listening to Thedeim, before nodding. "That's fine. Unless Hullbreak somehow comes to its senses without needing to be shown force, it'll be pretty obvious before too long anyway. Also obvious: people are going to see skeletons, slimes, and living rockslides to the north of town."

Tarl nods at that, then starts leafing through the more recent reports. "We'll start letting people know, if only so they don't flood us with reports. Speaking of pretty obvious . . . Where is it . . . Ah!" He pulls out the report he was looking for and holds it for Teemo to see. "Is this accurate?"

Teemo peers at it for a few seconds before nodding. "Looks like. That group went into the caverns to try to bag a scythemaw but got in over their head. Grim dealt with it."

"That simply?"

"That simply."

"How?"

Teemo shrugs. "I don't understand his magic, but I think his affinities tell a pretty clear story." He lets Tarl get a scrap of paper and a charcoal stick to take notes, then continues. "See, he started with Earth and Fate, because of Thedeim, yeah? Once he earned his Grounds Reaper title, he picked up Death."

Tarl nods at that. "Pretty standard so far. Scions tend to start with one affinity of their own, and one affinity granted by their dungeon. Titles often grant affinities, too."

Teemo nods and continues. "So, he's also been growing flowers and stuff, and listening to mourners at the graves. The Boss says he's managed to make the connection and expand his Death affinity into Life."

Tarl's eyes widen at that, and when Teemo doesn't continue, he fills the silence. "So Rocky isn't the only one he's been working on affinities with?"

Teemo chuckles. "He's been working with all of us, but he was surprised when he saw Grim had managed to get Life somehow. The Boss understands the link, but I sure don't."

Tarl doesn't understand any link either, but he's not exactly a mage. "And that somehow let Grim kill the tunnel horror without seeming to move?"

Teemo nods. "I'm not an expert, but I figure someone who has Life, Death, and Fate affinities could manage something like that without too much trouble."

Tarl stares for a few moments before sighing, crumpling the paper, and tossing it into the fire. "Not information to be shared with the guild at large. Any other terrifying revelations?"

Teemo chuckles and shakes his head.

Chapter 13

Hullbreak Harbor, First Mate

The great white prowls the waters, efficient movements seemingly lazy with how easy they are for her. She watches the invaders as they defile her home and her Captain with their mere presence, but she takes her time lining up to charge. The skeletons are slow and clumsy, but they can still do a lot of damage if they manage to grab on to her fins or tail. She spots her chance and charges forward, and the first skeleton in the group shatters under her assault. Simple bones are no match for the Voice of Hullbreak Harbor.

Sometimes, she wishes she could properly growl while under the water. Even at her most intimidating, trying to make any actual noise just sounds like a drowning landlubber. She internally shelves the frustration as she rips apart another skeleton. It's not like they'd even be intimidated anyway.

Neverrest doesn't seem to care too much about the undead it's sending, or maybe it hasn't figured out a better way to attack the Captain yet. She was vaguely aware the Captain had found another dungeon out in the town, but it seems their old foe Neverrest managed to subsume it. She can't think of any other way for the old cemetery to have gotten access to ravens.

Although . . . they *are* kind of fitting for it to have on its own. Whatever the reason, the Captain doesn't share everything with her, and he's not the most informed on what's been going on out there, anyway. She's just glad to see the Captain not starving anymore.

She's been a lot busier with the sudden stream of undead, but it's better than being bored and having plenty of time to watch her home and Captain slowly shrivel. The rush of mana from the first skeleton that morning was like fresh deepwater on her gills. The Captain quickly reinvigorated the shark spawner first, then started at least stabilizing the various nodes so the dwellers could be more comfortable.

The mana flow has lessened a little, now that the initial rush is over. Still, the skeletons are making quite a mess with their crude rock anchors. Stones litter much of the Captain's seabed, but a small mess is a fine price to pay to keep her Captain healthy.

He really doesn't like the new development of Neverrest raiding *him*, though, so he's trying to upgrade the seagull spawner back to a decent level so he can try to get a better look at the situation as a whole. He has his strength up now, but he also has his guard up. Neverrest has always been rather single-minded in trying to consume everything, but it's no fool. It'll realize eventually that its raids are only strengthening the Captain, and that it'll take more than just a thin line of skeletons to defeat him . . . even if the line seems never-ending.

She's sure the Captain will come up with something eventually, though. For now, they'll quietly build their strength and try to get the gulls to get information.

Thedeim

See, this is the kind of thing people mean about plans not surviving contact with the enemy. Most of the plan has been going great. The rockslides and slimes seem to be infiltrating without much issue, and Hullbreak seems to be a lot healthier already. Even the scattered initial reports are showing nodes and spawners healing and replenishing.

The sharks and fish returning in force I expected, too. I'm sending invaders, so of course Hullbreak will beef up his defenses. Unfortunately for me, I forgot about the seagull spawner. It's healing up, too, which will make keeping secrets more difficult. The slimes and rockslides might be practically invisible in the water, but they stick out a lot more on land. I don't think changing the number of undead I send will do much to stop it, either. If I try to send more, it might actually get strong enough to fight me more directly and *still* have gulls. If I slow the flow, it'll start starving again. So I'll just have to deal with the annoying little spyplanes.

I've asked Poe to keep a lot of ravens out to intercept as many gulls as possible, but it's only a matter of time before they start being able to spot things they shouldn't. So . . . how do I deal with this.

Problem: seagulls are going to eventually notice the line of rockslides and slimes among the skeletons. A lot of the path is covered by trees, but the beachhead and the stretch just past my walls are wide open. And I need to get a denizen back to get their actual report on what's going on.

Solution: Uh . . . ?

Well, I don't need too many more slimes and slides in there, so I can slow the rate of deployment. Maybe I'll just send them at night? I'm pretty sure seagulls don't do well at night. Hmm . . . I should probably also establish a bit of a beachhead actually in the water, too, come to think of it.

If Hullbreak has enough mana to work on the seagulls, it might get enough to try sending an expedition or two out to hit the skeletons before they even enter its waters. I really don't need it realizing I'm sending more than just skeletons under the waves.

I still need to get the information back here, though. My rats could do that . . . maybe. The gulls seemed to be more interested in my snakes than the rats when Hullbreak was able to raid me more consistently, but I'd bet they can handle a rodent at least as easily as they could handle a serpent.

Maybe dig a tunnel? It'd only need to be rat-sized . . . but that's a *long* way from the tree line to the shoreline. They'd also be in danger from the wall to the trees, but that'd be a lot easier to defend without giving away the position of the rocky beach.

Maybe I should send Coda out to supervise it? He should make it a lot easier for them to dig. He'd probably need to only go out at night, though he could also receive the reports from my little spies.

Huh . . . actually, that gives me a better idea. If I had thought about the tunnel before committing, it might have worked, but it's way too late in the game to try that now. If I had moles, it might be possible, but even with Jello hunting them more actively, she still hasn't found a viable candidate. Instead, I'll send Leo on expedition to manage my denizens. It'll be a good practice run for him before I try to send him off to help the Southwood. If things go pear-shaped, it'll be a lot easier to support him at the beach than way deep in the forest.

I nudge my wolf to expect Teemo, and nudge Teemo that Leo is expecting him. I explain as Teemo takes a shortcut, and Leo is sitting at attention once my Voice arrives.

"Hey, Leo. The Boss has a special mission for you, if you're ready."

The wolf barks, and Teemo smiles.

"He says he was spawned ready, heh. Okay, Leo, Thedeim knows you want to be the one to head the support to the Southwood. Well, consider this a practice run. He wants you to manage the operation to get info on Hullbreak. Getting the denizens all the way back here is too big a risk, so he wants you to set up a forward operating base in the woods near the beach and organize things from there.

"As far as Hullbreak should know, all you'll have access to are undead and ravens. You'll need to help get what slimes and slides are still needed into the water without it noticing, and Thedeim also wants a defensive perimeter under the water at the beach. Hullbreak is using gulls to try to get intel, and though we'll be slowing that as much as we can, it'll only be a matter of time before it sends sharks and such to try to hit the undead before they even get inside its borders."

Leo growls and yips as Teemo translates, and then gives my reply. "You can get access to the other denizens if you can keep Hullbreak from realizing they're Thedeim's."

Leo nods, and I can feel his mind churning with plans, my Warden preparing to protect my denizens and my plan, and hopefully, protect even Hullbreak from itself.

Chapter 14

Leo

Leo thinks as he prepares to go on his expedition. This is the most important thing the Alpha has asked him to do, and is possibly the most important thing he's asked *any* of his scions to do, so the wolf wants to do the best job he possibly can.

He first checks with Poe to see if there's any extra information he can get.

There is, but not much. It's mostly topography of the area, but that does at least give him a better idea of what he'll be working with. The rocky beach should not be too difficult to secure, even beneath the waves. There are a lot of large rocks and other things that would spell doom for a boat and also disrupt the waves. At low tide, it gives him several choke points that the skeletons can secure. At high tide, he's more uncertain of how to deal with them. Sharks and other dangerous denizens may be able to swim over, but they'd also risk dashing themselves on the rocks. He'll have to get a better look himself before he can make much in the way of plans there.

The biggest challenge will be the stretch of land between the beach itself and the woods he'll be hiding in. The Alpha is correct in transitioning to just skeletons to avoid the spying denizens getting spotted. He'd like to get even more inside Hullbreak itself, but he can't risk bringing in more for that. Perhaps he can get the delvers to help? A few quests to deliver boxes or barrels to the local docks, and slimes and slides could slip out and into the sea with minimal chance of being seen.

He nods to himself and files that idea away for later, in case it's needed. He still has the problem of actually *acquiring* the reports from the spies. He could use skeletons, but he'd prefer not to. Skeletons leaving the ocean would play against the idea of Neverrest just sending constant raids to try to gain mana or whittle Hullbreak down, so he needs to use something sneakier; something smaller.

His first thought is to try the rats, maybe at night. They're quick and should blend in well, but can he manage anything better?

He gets an idea and heads for the library. *He* can't manage anything sneakier than the rats, but he thinks Honey's bees would be an even better option.

He's actually quite fond of the bookish little bee. He had expected her to be annoying or useless with her idea to go get samples of things around the Alpha's territory, but had been willing to humor her if the Alpha was. But her bees have been proving themselves invaluable in getting details, and she has this infectious energy when she goes on about whatever weird thing has captured her interest at the time.

The bees only give him a passing glance as he enters the lab before continuing their own work. He soon finds Honey dissecting what appears to be a dragonfly of some variety, and he wiggles his rear in a pale imitation of a bee's dance of greeting. He's pretty sure he manages to say something crude each time, but it does a good job of gaining Honey's attention and making the mood light.

"Leo! How can I help you?" she asks, handing her tiny tools off to a few other workers while she focuses on her fellow scion.

"I was hoping I could borrow some of your bees, Honey. The Alpha has given me a task, and I think some bees would be perfect for one of the roles."

She buzzes in excitement. "The Hullbreak situation, right? I'd love to help, though I do have a condition."

"That is?"

"I'd like for my bees to be able to investigate the area when not actively doing whatever you're going to have them doing. What *are* you going to have them doing?" she asks, realizing she should probably know what she's agreeing to before she actually agrees to it.

"I will have them ferry the reports from the shore to my FOB, and ferry any orders I have back."

Honey buzzes in a little circle in approval. "Ah, messengers! They should be fine to do that, and they should have plenty of time to explore and find me new samples, too!"

"Once I get situated, I may be able to organize deliveries back here so you can examine things yourself, too. My priority will be on Hullbreak, however."

She floats side to side, waving off the concern. "That's fine. The Emperor's plans take priority, but there's still a lot of opportunity to *learn*!"

He nods. "Good. I'll return to get your initial contingent of bees before I leave for the expedition. Enjoy your work, Honey."

"You as well!" she buzzes happily before returning to her dissection.

Leo next visits the other insect scion, Queen, to see if the ant has managed to make any potions to breathe in the water. Her workspace is a bit more chaotic to his eyes, but he knows it's an illusion. Not a single ant is where Queen doesn't want it. They part for him as he makes his way to the main table, where Queen typically works on her experiments and notes.

"Ah, Leo. I hear the Emperor has given you a special task. You're here to ask my help?" she says without looking away from her ants carefully measuring powders.

"Yes. Have you made any progress on a potion to breathe underwater?"

It's difficult to read her expression thanks to both her size and her simple anatomy, but he gets the feeling she's smirking at him. "I have, but you don't want it."

He gives her a confused look. "Why wouldn't I want it?"

"Because breathing underwater is not actually especially useful. You need to be able to move freely underwater, too."

Leo still doesn't get it. "I can swim just fine, Queen."

She laughs and motions for her ants to pause so she can focus more on Leo. "Can you swim as well as a fish, Leo? How much more nimble is a fish than you in the water? Even if a fish could breathe on land, would you have any trouble fighting one if it flopped into the Emperor's territory? It will be the same with Hullbreak. Breathing will help, but *mobility* is the key to actually trying to win any fights with Hullbreak."

Leo frowns, not liking her tone but also not able to come up with any real retort. "Have you made any progress on *that*, then?"

Her confidence fades at that, and she eventually must shake her head. "No, unfortunately. The Emperor has given me some interesting ideas, but I haven't managed to make anything with the properties to try to use them yet. That rat-kin delver, Staiven, may be able to help with that. I believe he has formulae for what we want, but I also suspect it requires reagents I just don't have."

Leo sighs at that. "I was afraid of that."

"We still have some hope, though."

"Oh?" says the wolf, perking up.

"The Emperor has agents inside the harbor now, correct? I'd wager that any missing reagents can be found inside it. A few subtle snips, and we could have what we need to bring a fight to them, should the need arise."

Leo can't help but grin at that, glad he decided to come to her. "I'll keep that in mind! The Alpha hopes for a peaceful resolution . . ."

"But he *prepares* for the worst. The Emperor is wise and merciful, daring to hope without letting it blind him," said Queen.

Leo can only nod at that. "I'll keep you in the loop if it looks like the spies can sneak out anything from inside. The Alpha wants to get into contact with the dwellers, and they may have a much easier time of gathering than our invaders will."

"And I shall continue to work on the water problem with what we do have available. The Emperor has suggested I look into how oil repels water, to see if that could be useful. He thinks it will only be part of the solution, but a part is better than what we have now."

Leo nods once more and takes his leave, trying to think of what else he needs to do. He has the foreseeable problems planned for, and with the bees, he should at least have warning for anything *un*foreseeable. He needs to actually get out there and get the FOB started, then secure the beachhead before he can try to solve any other problems. Those two will certainly present issues, but if he keeps a level head, he's certain he can do the Alpha proud.

Chapter 15

I watch through Leo's eyes as he explores the woods, looking for a good spot to set up his forward operating base. It's a bit of a grandiose name for what's probably going to be a glorified hole in the ground. There are quite a few divots in the sides of hills, and hollows in some tree roots, but he hasn't managed to find anything quite to his liking just yet. That hasn't stopped him from sending a few orders, though.

The latest batch of skeletons are to stay near the beach to start securing it, and he's set up a line of rockslides along the beach so the bees won't have to try to dodge waves to be able to relay the reports. It looks like he's going to try to make some wooden spike walls to put atop the natural walls, to help keep any aquatic attackers from being able to actually get into the secured area.

He's letting the bees help him look for a good spot, too, so I'm sure they'll find something to his liking soon. If it comes to it, I should be able to sneak Coda and a few ratlings to expand whatever he decides to set up shop in.

I've also realized another problem with the plan, or at least the next step. I want to get into contact with the dwellers in Hullbreak . . . but how am I actually going to manage that? I might be able to skirt the rules with a few signs from my aranea, but they might be a bit too obvious. Driftwood is all well and good, but most of it floats rather than sticking to random rocks.

It's not a fatal flaw. At least not yet. Leo has gotten a few more reports already, and my spies are still settling in and getting a feel for what is normal in there. I don't believe they've spotted any dwellers yet. If their enclave is anything like the ones I've made, there's still plenty of room to hide it. I also wouldn't be surprised if the enclave is close to the Sanctum. That note made it sound like the dwellers are precious to Hullbreak, so it'd make sense to make their enclave as secure as possible.

It's looking like I only just managed to get out ahead of the seagulls, too. I've asked Poe to make it look like we're only barely able to handle keeping the gulls away from sensitive areas, even if I'm pretty sure Poe could easily go and scour the spawner from the little island or reef or wherever it's on all by himself. I need Hullbreak to feel comfortable before I spring on him how outclassed he is. Otherwise, Vassalizing him will take a lot more pain than is strictly required.

Hullbreak's defenses are swelling, and though my spies haven't found the spawners yet, I can get at least a rough idea of how strong he is by how quickly the skeletons are handled. I kinda want to overwhelm his defenses so my spies can get deeper quicker, but I need to take it nice and slow. I might have been able to get deeper with a more aggressive initial attack, but now is just too late to send another surge . . . Or too early, I guess. If I send another surge, I need to make it look like I've had to build up skeletons, and possibly send a new variety, too.

But either way, now is not the time to rush. Even though I really want to. It's times like this that make me miss having thumbs to twiddle, or an internet to wander for stupid stuff. It's a lot harder to distract myself when I really need to hurry up and wait. Watching my scions can help with that some, though.

Most of them are still doing what they do. Teemo has made just about all the shortcuts he can think to make, so he's taken to doing a bit of people watching and practicing his Fate affinity. I don't know where he got that dice from, but he rolls it sometimes to try to call what it will be. I'm not sure if he's trying to read what the destined roll is, or if he's trying to influence it himself, but he seems to be having a small bit of success with it, getting it right about twenty percent of the time. I may have spent a couple hours keeping track of it. Don't judge.

Queen and Thing have finished growing the crystal pickups for the axe, so now the former can focus more on trying to get a working aqua potion, or whatever she's going to call a thing that will let people both breathe and move properly underwater. A Water-affinity potion would probably be ideal, but I seriously doubt she'll be able to stumble over something like that anytime soon. A Mer potion might be more achievable, but that's not really saying much. The only thing we have that actually transforms something is the metal stuff, and I think turning something into a half fish would be even more complex than turning it to metal.

Thing has been running experiments with the pickups and working on the enchantments to take the electricity from the quartz and amplify it into the singing Tesla coils that I want in the hat. It seems like it's not too complicated for him, but it is delicate work, so he's going slow. They have a few spares, but he'd rather not break them by accident.

The actual axe head is making pretty good progress, surprisingly. The spiderkin have been able to walk along the ceiling and avoid the scythemaws, and they have been visiting my ratkin to help forge the blades. It's a pretty good working relationship they have going, too. The ratkin have been making various steels while the spiderkin forge them into weapons, and they all do the testing. Most of the blades either shatter or bend, but they're taking good notes and have discovered a lot of interesting ways to not make an axe.

As for the recipient of the axe, Slash has managed to pick up a lute or something from somewhere. Maybe Tiny captured a bard in the maze? Either way, he spends a lot of his time in the tunnels, just practicing. There's not a ton of digging to be done right now, so he has the free time. He's got a long way to go to live up to his namesake, but he has to start somewhere.

Jello is hunting moles and gremlins with more focus than I think I've ever seen from her. I don't feel any frustration coming from her, but I do get a sense she feels like she needs to try something different with her approach. I tickle the bond with the idea of asking Teemo to help, and she readily accepts the suggestion. I let him know she'll be on her way, so he puts the dice away and goes to head her off at the pass. And by pass, I mean the lawn, where she's been hunting.

Jello

Jello hums as she works on the latest mole she's captured. She'll be able to calm it; she's not worried about that. She's just wondering what she's doing wrong to not find one that would want to join. She can already tell this one will just want to go. Leo would probably suggest she just eat it, but that feels kinda mean, to start calming it down only to eat it when it's not going to do what she wants.

Then the Voice in her head suggests asking Teemo, and she brightens at that. He's almost a mole, right? Maybe he'll have a better idea of what to offer them! She burbles happily as she makes her way toward the nearest shortcut, only for the Voice's Voice to appear from it.

"Ah, heya, Jello. The Boss says you could use some help with the moles?"

She jiggles in affirmation. "Yes! He wants to get a mole so he can have a new spawner, but none of them want to join! They all just want to leave. Should I . . . just eat them?" she asks, clearly uncomfortable, but Teemo smiles and shakes his head.

"Nah, you can keep catching and releasing them. It's their choice to stay or go. Have you been trying to use your affinity to find one who would want to stay?"

"Jello's been trying but hasn't had any takers. Should she try offering them something more than just soft dirt to dig and a warm spawner? She can't think of anything else to offer a mole."

Teemo thinks on that for a few moments before shrugging. "I think that's about all we can offer. Well, that and friends."

"Oh, friends! Right! How could Jello forget that? That should make it a lot easier!" She wiggles in happiness before Teemo speaks up.

“I think the Boss wants me to help you try to use your affinity to find a good one, too. Have the moles been feeling any different?”

“Yeah, some. Jello can tell which ones she can actually calm down, and which ones are just kinda . . . *off.* But Jello still hasn’t found one that would stay. She’s even tried with gremlins, but no luck there, either,” she says, slumping a little in defeat.

Teemo gives her a reassuring smile. “That’s what I’m here for. The Boss says I’m starting to get the hang of luck with this dice I found. The numbers don’t sound too impressive to me, but he says it’s still ‘statistically relevant.’”

“What’s that mean?”

The Voice smiles and climbs atop the big cube of slime. “It means that, even if you’ve gotten zero, I might help you get *one.* It’s not a huge number, but it’s still more.”

Chapter 16

Slash

Simple notes drift through the tunnels as the Earth elemental gets familiar with the lute Tiny gifted him. It sounds completely different from the snippets of music he sometimes hears through the bond with the Composer. He's known from shortly after his creation that the Composer had a special role to give him.

The Composer was uncertain if Slash would be up to the task, and if he's honest, Slash wasn't sure either. He was allowed to simply explore Composer Thedeim's territory, to see if anything else might catch his attention or inspire. He supposes something did, too.

His fingers wander the strings as he thinks back. The Bat Scion had been directing some digging. As an Earth elemental, Slash could make it go much quicker, so decided to join in. And that's when the Composer sang.

He's tried asking the Voice about the song, but even he can't give much more information. It's a song both melancholic and somehow triumphant, of someone in a bad situation. Yet, instead of succumbing to despair, they work hard at their impossible task. They're not quite accepting the poor bargain, yet not outright rejecting it, either. The Voice knows the words, but they don't give much extra detail, except that it's about mining.

It's also a much different song than what Slash hears when the Composer usually thinks about him. Those songs are full of energy and life, beautifully complex melodies played on harsh instruments. Songs of danger. Songs of life. Songs of battle. The axe the Composer is creating is supposed to be able to create those kinds of sounds.

His fingers pick notes faster as he imagines bringing those songs to reality, and he winces as he notices.

No, this lute is not for those songs. And yet, there *are* songs he hears sometimes that could fit. Some are simple little tunes that often serve as jokes or drinking songs, or even nursery rhymes. But there are also haunting ballads, beautiful and sorrowful. His fingers stumble along the strings as he tries to play them, his inexperience not letting him even manage a pale imitation.

He shakes his head to clear it, choosing to focus on what he *can* manage, instead of what is still so far out of his reach. He goes back to remembering the digging again, the rhythm guiding his movements, and even guiding the movements of the ratlings. The bat would even sing at the rock at times, and Slash could feel it trying to sing back to him. While the bat used it to help guide the digging, Slash was inspired to give it a different use.

He knows that, to be the Bard he wants to be, he needs Thunder affinity. Or Sonic, as the Composer calls it. Whatever its name, he needs it. He also knows affinities can be expanded. The Zombie Scion is the most successful at it so far, and has given Slash the only advice he can: to pay attention. The affinities are not so rigidly separate as they first seem. Slash would like to argue that, but he's felt the proof in the very earth around him. With the right circumstances, the stones will sing. If simple stones can sing, *he* can sing.

He reaches deep into his Earth affinity as he plays one of the simplest songs he's heard from the Composer, about the stars in the sky. It doesn't have the kind of deep wonder of so many of the other songs, but the simple notes loop easily, letting him almost meditate. He can feel the movement of the earth around him. The beat may be slower than most would notice, but it's still there. He works to slowly bring the beat up a bit around himself, even as he slows the beat of the music he's playing.

Fittingly enough, he knows he needs to bring them into harmony if he's going to attain Sonic affinity.

The Adventurers' Guild

In the hours before dawn, the tabby catkin enjoys a bit of quiet with a pipe and a book. Berdol feels he has a pretty good gig, especially now that Fourdock has a proper dungeon for people to gather in, rather than having to make long trips out to the Southwood or try to nab a few scraps from Hullbreak before fleeing.

Thedeim has definitely made his job a lot easier, and a lot more profitable, too. It's strange that the dungeon decided to name itself instead of just staying as Fourdock Dungeon. Then again, Thedeim is a strange dungeon, so it probably shouldn't be too much of a surprise.

He sets his book aside as he starts preparing for the day's delving, hooking his various hiltless knives to his leather armor. He wonders if he should invest in something heavier, now that he doesn't need to hike for a week or more to get to a job, but he pushes the idea aside. He's used to the lighter weight, so he'd have to change too much to adjust to something like scale mail.

The solo adventurer snuffs his pipe, dumps the embers, and crushes them underfoot at the room's hearth before heading down to the guild board. He had tried to get into a more permanent party, but most adventurers around here have a lot more ambition than he does. He doesn't need to avenge some tragedy, or pay off some loan shark, or even try to support some lifestyle beyond his means. He just likes delving, and he's pretty good at it.

As usual, his focus is on the daily hiring of escorts for gatherers. They don't pay the most, but they're quick and easy. It even lets him make friends and professional acquaintances and get small discounts for various things. He scans to see if any of the smiths have quests, but has no luck today. While he might not want to get new armor, a couple of his knives are getting a bit dull. He's got a decent bit saved, but a few quests to get him a discount might let him get something truly special.

Today, he decides to start simple, taking a quest to escort an herbalist. Looks like they just want a trip around the yard and into the house; shouldn't take more than an hour, two at most. They don't want to visit the belfry garden, so this should be a great way to warm up for the day. Maybe he'll be able to get a quest from the dungeon itself, too. He's had a few clients stop to see if the aranea want anything in specific to be gathered, so it's a good chance to get his own quest. He doesn't even need to do it just around that one client. They're not tied to the quest, so he can take his time and kill a dozen rats over several clients, or whatever quest looks convenient.

He actually got a sock to match one he got a week ago. When he was younger, he never appreciated good socks. But now? The pair is some of his favorite loot he's gotten. Maybe he'll try a harder quest. He's seen a few people with the silk shirts around town, and they look very comfortable. He can imagine himself with his pipe and a book, relaxing with a silk shirt in front of a fire.

Yes, he'll keep an eye out for a harder quest.

At the dungeon's gates, he meets his client: a featherkin whose clothing looks to be more for pockets than for modesty. His modesty is well and truly covered, though, and Berdol thinks the featherkin could give most bags of holding a run for their money for storage space. He meets the bird's eyes and nods from across the way, offering his hand to shake once he gets closer.

"Pleased to meet ya. I'm Berdol. You left this quest at the guild?" he asks, holding up the notice. The featherkin nods and speaks, his voice a bit high and full of nervous energy.

"Yes! I've been hearing of this new dungeon, and I wanted to get as much as I could before winter sets in!"

"You from a bit more to the south?"

The bird shakes his head. "Almost due east, actually. My village is by Lake Gofnar. Oh, uh . . . I'm Hijyn."

The catkin nods and starts toward the gates. "I've been past that area a few times. The local dungeons don't have much for herbalism?"

"Oh, they do! It's just that there are ingredients here that we can't get back home," he reasons, his voice getting quieter as they get closer to the gates. "Is the dungeon dangerous? I mean, I got the basic information from the Dungeoneer's, but . . ."

The cat smiles and nods as he opens the gate. "But you're hardly an adventurer, so you don't know how dangerous it can still be, yeah?"

The client sheepishly nods, and the cat waves it off.

"Nothing to be ashamed of. We adventurers appreciate the work of alchemists as much, if not more, than the work of smiths and enchanters. It takes just as much dedication as adventuring does, just a different kind," he says, giving a short little speech he gives to a lot of his new clients. Not only does it make them feel better about hiring people like him—it's even true. Delving would be a lot more dangerous if not for the various crafters.

"As for the dungeon, it's pretty safe, but you're going to pick up at least a little bit of fighting experience. You have a dagger?" The featherkin nods and shows the simple weapon. "That should be fine for the yard and manor. I'll point out the things you should be able to handle, and I'll deal with the rest. The most dangerous thing we should encounter are a couple vipers, maybe a small spider swarm if the dungeon is feeling rambunctious."

The client looks nervous at that. "I'll have to do some fighting? Isn't that what you're for?"

Berdol laughs at that. "I can, but you'll get a lot more herbs if you contribute. That's how this dungeon works: the more effort you put in, the more reward you get. If we actually do end up fighting a spider swarm, there's a good chance something will just happen to fall out of the garden up in the belfry for you. But you'll have to contribute to the fighting for that."

Hijyn still looks uncertain, so Berdol decides to just guide him toward the patches in the backyard, not bothering with the quests on the porch for now. He'll let the new guy deal with an encounter or two just to ease him into what it's like before showing him more of the weirdness of Thedeim. And, thinking of encounters, he spots what's practically the traditional probing encounter of the dungeon: two rats and a viper.

"Here we are, looks like the dungeon is ready to see what we're made of. Thedeim's cooperative, so he's not going to kill us, but he's also no toybox that will just hand over the loot." Berdol draws two daggers and lets his Metal affinity draw two more for him, the floating blades taking a defensive position before his client. "To start, just don't get hit. I'll deal with the viper, and then show you how to handle a rat, okay?"

"Uh . . . okay?" comes the nervous reply.

Berdol smiles at the answer and prepares to get down to business. The new guy will be fine. He's had clients flee, and clients demand he just keep them safe, but Hijyn here is willing to pull his weight. Depending on how he does, they might even be able to go after the attic boss and get him into that garden after all. Going above and beyond the letter of a quest makes for a happy client, and happy clients are repeat clients.

Chapter 17

There's something in the air today, but I can't place what it is. The bakery across the street isn't making anything too special, as far as I can tell, though the delvers are of the opinion that *everything* there is special. I wonder if the spiderkin are still wanting to try their hands at baking, once the maws clear out?

But whatever the situation is on my dwellers learning to bake, I can feel *something* in the air. I'm pretty sure it's not Hullbreak about to do something nasty, at least. It feels more like the tension before getting to jump out at a surprise party, rather than the tension of a looming threat. I've even asked Tiny, and he's not telling much. All I've been able to get Teemo to wheedle out of him is that it's not a threat, but that's it. I could probably order him to spill the beans, but that'd be a dick move. Besides, if it's not an actual danger, there's no need to be so rash.

Even if my curiosity is driving me to distraction.

Freddie

The young orc hums an upbeat hymn as he walks down the street. He's in mostly ordinary clothes, though he has his round shield on his back. He wears it partially as a connection to the Crystal Shield, but also because it's the perfect size for Fiona to cling to and peek her head over his shoulder.

He and Rhonda have been pretty busy the last few weeks with their training and studying, but they've been able to keep in touch with their spiders. He had been surprised when Lucas slipped through the shutters in his small room at the church, and surprised again with the small letter he was carrying.

He smiles as he thinks of his short friend. Her hat may be a bit large for her head, but it might be a tad small for her brain. Having their spiders send notes not only lets them keep in touch when their situations keep them apart, but it also helps the two arachnids keep healthy and active. In fact, the last letter Rhonda sent him is why he's walking to the bakery just outside Thedeim before dropping in to surprise her. Her master says she's doing very well in her studies and is giving her a bit of a break today. His own work has been going very well, too, so he also has the day off. What better way to spend it than with a bag of sticky rolls and his friend?

The bell above the door to Cobble Bread dings as he enters, and the large troll woman smiles at him from over by the oven. Freddie sometimes wonders if she's bigger around than she is tall, not that he could blame her. If he had to spend every day around the wonderful things she bakes, he'd fare no better.

"Ah, Freddie! It's been a while! I was starting to wonder if those god-botherers had gotten you to swear off sweets! That, or your beastie decided to wrap you up as a snack, haw!" she says with a hearty laugh. Freddie can't help but chuckle with her. Many might take the term she used for his brothers and sisters in the Shield as an insult, but he's known her long enough to understand she tends to only insult those she cares about, and the more vile the better.

She does try to watch her tongue around him and Rhonda and the other children, at least.

"That'd be quite the test of my resolve, to swear off your baking, Freida! I've just been busy with my training, but I have a day off today. A dozen sticky rolls, please." He reaches for his coin bag. Delving with Rhonda and his stipend from the church have given him at least enough coin to be able to afford something like this.

"A dozen, eh? Looking to put on a second chin or two?" she says with a wide grin, knowing exactly how little room she has to speak, and starts moving the small pastries into a bag.

"Not just for me. I'm going to be visiting Rhonda today, too."

"Ah, good. She could use a bit more meat on her bones, too. Here, have a blueberry muffin for each of you, also. On the house." She gives him a motherly smile, dropping the two extra treats into the bag.

"Thank you, ma'am," he replies with an earnest smile, paying for his order. She waves as he leaves, and he has to resist the temptation and stay out of the bag of treats until he reaches Old Staiven's Emporium. He's still not certain what differentiates an emporium from a shop, but the place certainly has a different feel than the other places adventurers might look to if they want to gear up in Fourdock.

The bell dings as he enters, and he smiles as he hears his friend's voice.

"Welcome to Old Stai—Freddie!" Her polite customer service tone vanishes into familiar warmth as she recognizes her friend, and she dashes around the counter to jump at him. He kneels slightly and catches her as the two embrace . . . and then winces as she cuffs his ear.

"Why didn't you tell me you were coming? I could have put on some fresh tea!" she scolds him while he offers a quick prayer of mourning for his lost *quiet* friend, followed by a more earnest prayer of thanks for how much life seems to have improved for her. Gone is the quiet and nervous little goblin from the orphanage, grown now into a fledgling mage with an intense thirst for knowledge.

"You too, Fiona!" she gives the spider a glare, and the arachnid manages to avoid meeting her with any of her eyes. Soon, though, Rhonda giggles and gives Freddie another squeeze before hopping down and letting him finally defend himself.

"How am I supposed to surprise you with sticky rolls if I let you know I'm coming?" he asks.

Her eyes sparkle at the mention of one of her favorite treats.

"Watch the counter for me while I get some tea and some plates for the rolls, okay?"

He nods and makes for the counter as she dashes up the stairs to the living area. Fiona takes this as her chance to slip away and find Lucas, leaving Freddie with his thoughts and a smile on his face.

A couple fistfuls of mushrooms from a dusty basement have certainly resulted in quite the change for both of their lives. They both have places they truly belong, and a fulfilling direction to take in their lives. In fact, that's partially why he wanted to visit her: to be able to tell her face-to-face, rather than just in a note.

He's drawn from his thoughts as Rhonda comes down the stairs and joins him behind the counter to sit on her tall stool. She hands him a plate and sets her own down before setting the tea kettle on a small stand. She pulls out her wand made of simple black wood with a rough quartz set on the end, and aims it at the kettle.

"Heat!" she exclaims. A lick of flame settles around the base of the tea kettle. "There! That should only take a couple minutes."

Freddie chuckles. "Looks like your studies really *are* coming along well."

"Yeah! Master Staiven says I should have no problem solidifying an Ice Mage class. I mean, I got that fire spell without even looking at my notes!" she says with pride, and her friend can't help but burst her bubble at least a little.

"I mean, if a zombie fist fighter can manage it, so can you, right?" He grins.

She punches his side.

"Rocky doesn't count, and you know it! Thedeim's scions are weird, like how Grim ignored that Turn Undead," she fires back. Freddie can only laugh.

"You should have seen the look on the acolyte's face! He thought it was going to be the last mistake he ever made." The two laugh at that and enjoy a bit more small talk while they wait for the water to boil, enjoying a sticky roll each, as well.

Once the kettle whistles, Freddie decides it's a good time to talk about the other reason he's here. "So, you said Staiven thinks you're close to your class?" She nods, so he continues. "Head Priest Torlon says I'm close to finalizing becoming a paladin, too."

Rhonda gasps in excitement for her friend. "That's great!"

He nods. "It is. So I was thinking we should both head to Thedeim and try to get our classes later."

Rhonda thinks that over as she pours tea for the two of them. She waits to set the kettle aside before replying. "I can't think of any reason not to try. Master Staiven has been pretty quiet on how to actually *get* my class, and I guess the church isn't giving you much, either?"

Freddie nods. "Yea, they aren't giving me much else to go on. I've sworn the appropriate oaths to the Shield, but there's still something missing. I think figuring it out ourselves is part of the point?"

Rhonda nods to that and takes a sip of her tea, sighing at the pleasing hot liquid. "That sounds like Master Staiven, yeah. They can prepare us for what we want to do, but it's up to us to actually do it."

Freddie smiles around his own cup of tea and pulls out the two blueberry muffins, handing one to his goblin friend. "Just like with the spell spores."

"Yeah. If we want it, we need to go get it. It won't just be handed to us."

"Shall we go after Staiven gets back?"

"He's taking a nap right now, actually. Once he wakes up, though . . . yeah." Rhonda picks up her muffin and holds it high.

Freddie holds his muffin up as well and taps it to hers. "To getting our classes!"

"To our classes!"

They each take a big bite of their muffins, and after a few moments, cough a little before swallowing. Freddie manages to speak up first.

"A . . . bit dry . . ."

Rhonda nods and takes a drink of her tea, then after a moment's thought, dips her muffin in it and tries that. "It's good with the tea, though."

Freddie follows suit and nods. "It is, yeah. Heh, I think I know why Freida gave me the muffins for free." They laugh and enjoy some more small talk and good company as they wait for Staiven to finish his nap. Gaining their classes will be a great accomplishment, but they're in no big hurry. After all, there's still most of a bag of sticky rolls, and they won't eat themselves.

Chapter 18

Is it Christmas morning? Because it feels like Christmas morning. I don't see any presents, but I can still feel that kind of tension in the air. I even make sure things are going smoothly for the two big potential problems, in case I'm reading this energy in the air wrong.

The scythemaws are . . . well, as behaved as I can hope for, really. There's definitely some magic involved in their reproduction, because I can see the ladies are full of eggs. The males will probably get even more territorial once they get ready to lay. They're looking a bit skinnier, so that raises my hopes that they'll finish with their stuff soon and go back to the water.

Leo and the FOB are also doing as well as can be hoped. The spies are still slowly spreading out, and fresh spies have stopped flowing in. Leo found what seems to be a big hollow under some kind of bramble, maybe wild berries of some kind? It's too late in the year for any to still be there, if there were any in the first place. Either way, though, he has a nice spot to hide and direct the efforts against Hullbreak. I'll probably send Coda and a few ratlings to help expand it soon.

But neither of those are the source of what I'm feeling. I'm starting to think it's just in my head, but then I feel some familiar feet enter the main gate that draws my attention like a magnet.

It's the kids! Man, they haven't been back in . . . like a month? Not since the scythemaws showed up or so.

They're both looking good, looking healthy. Their spiders are also looking healthy and alert, too, which is also a good sign. The slightly less good sign is how uncertain the kids look. They're trying to look determined, but I've seen them in here enough times to know when they're *actually* confident.

"Uh . . . Thedeim? Can we talk?" speaks up Freddie. I'd nod if I could, but I can't, so I settle for sending Teemo to see what the kids need. He's still helping Jello look for a mole and/or gremlin to join us, but they still haven't managed one. They both feel like they're on the right track, though, so that's good. Teemo bids my favorite big blob of jelly farewell, and it's only a minute or two for him to pop out of a shortcut near the kids.

"Ah, hey, you two! What's up?" he asks, happy to see them.

The kids look happy to see him, too, but their smiles don't stick around too long under the weight of whatever it is they want to talk about. They exchange glances a couple times, and I can practically see them hot potatoing whatever the subject is, neither really wanting to be the one to start the conversation. Freddie eventually accepts the duty and looks at my Voice.

". . . Can you help us get our classes?"

What?

"What?" echoes my Voice, just as confused at the question as I am. "Shouldn't you be asking Staiven and Torlon about that?"

The two exchange looks again, then Rhonda speaks up this time. "Well . . . we have, but they said that's not how it works."

"How *does* it work?"

The kids shrug. "I dunno," they both answer in unison before Freddie elaborates. "But we're both pretty sure we're ready. I've taken the oaths; Rhonda has been able to cast a lot of things . . . but there's still something missing. We think it's something we have to figure out on our own, and our best guess is to ask you."

Ask *me*? Why? Hmm . . . is it a dungeon thing, or a me thing? Either way, I'm pretty sure that weird feeling is from these two, and I like the kids, so of course I'll try to help. But . . . how do I help them get classes? Is it similar to how my scions get titles?

Seems as good a place to start as any. I need something magic for Rhonda, and something uh . . . paladin-y for Freddie. Three. Yeah, three for each feels right, too. Thing, Queen, and Rocky for Rhonda . . . but who for Freddie? I've been trying to stay as far away as possible from the kind of stuff that might help Freddie. I could just throw him at the crypt complex? I think that would work, but I also *know* I can do better.

Well, I do have three people who are experts in that kind of thing, though I'll need to have Teemo ask them. Vernew, the small spiderkin mistress of the hunt; Larx, the ratkin elder; and Aranya, my own personal High Priestess. I don't think any of them know the specifics of how the Shield does things, but I don't get the feeling they'd mess anything up between Freddie and his god.

Yeah, I think I can make this work. I'll just need to . . .

Rhonda

The young goblin can only wait as the Voice seems to be listening to Thedeim, trying desperately to not lean closer in excitement . . . or nervousness. Anxiety?

Oh, this sounded like a much better idea back at the shop. But now that they're all here, her thoughts and emotions feel so jumbled up! She feels her friend's hand on her shoulder, though, and feels her confidence returning. Freddie thinks it's a good idea, too. It's difficult to get too worked up over something with him around.

Teemo chuckles at the two. "Well, sounds like the Boss is willing to help, and he's sounding pretty inspired about it, too."

"Is that good?" she asks, her natural curiosity spilling out before she can contain it. The Voice just grins at her.

"It's not *bad*, but the Boss's weirdest stuff tends to happen when he's inspired. You two sure you want this? Last time you tried something like this, you *both* ended up with spiders," he points out.

Rhonda and Freddie meet eyes, then meet the eyes of their spiders, and they smile. "Yeah," replies Rhonda. "We want this. Lucas and Fiona have been wonderful. I think if Thedeim has more tricks like them up his sleeve, we'll be just fine."

Freddie nods, then gives a small smirk. "He's not planning on giving us more spiders, though, is he? I'm not sure either of us has room."

Teemo laughs and shakes his head. "No spiders to bring along, no, but your first challenge will involve one. Well, if she agrees, at least."

The pair look confused at that. "*First* challenge?" asks Rhonda, starting to wonder if their big mouths have gotten them in deeper than they had thought.

"Three challenges, yeah. I'll be back in a couple minutes. I need to go ask Vernew if she's up for this." Before they can raise any objections, the Voice vanishes down one of his countless shortcuts, leaving them on their own on the lawn.

Lucas peers over the edge of Rhonda's hat at her, and she smiles, holding her hands out for him to jump into. "Yes, I meant what I said about you."

Fiona chitters as she peers over Freddie's shoulder, and he smiles and gently pats her. "Of course I feel the same, Fiona. I didn't come in here expecting to make a new friend, but that's what happened."

Lucas chitters, and the young goblin laughs. "No, I don't think you'll be getting company on my hat. That'd be too heavy, for starters!"

"And neither of us are trained to become tamers or anything like that," points out Freddie. "Still . . . I wonder what Thedeim will have in store for us."

Rhonda nods, looking off into the distance as she tries to guess what the dungeon is thinking. "I dunno . . . boss fights?"

Her orc friend shrugs. "Maybe, but that sounds a bit too simple. Teemo sounded like Thedeim has ideas. From a different dungeon, I'd be concerned."

"I'm *still* concerned, but more because I don't have any idea what he might do!" half jokes Rhonda. The four decide to lounge on the grass as they wait for the Voice to return, and he eventually does.

"Alright, that should be ready."

The kids stand, and the spiders resume their perches as Teemo clears his throat. "Thedeim has decreed you shall face three challenges to obtain your classes. The first of which is this: capture or otherwise subdue Vernew, the spiderkin mistress of the hunt. You must do so *without* harming Queen, who will be aiding her. Do this, and your first challenge will be complete. So says the Voice of Thedeim."

Rhonda suppresses a shudder as she feels powerful magic settle over her. From Freddie's reaction, he can feel the same. She'd wager their spiders can feel it, too. "So . . . how do we do that?" she asks. Teemo just grins.

"That's for you to figure out! Don't be too worried, though. Vernew has her own rules she has to follow for this, one of which is that the deep tunnels are off-limits. Those scythemaws are *way* too dangerous for you to go in there."

The kids nod at that, and he continues. "And that's about all. Go track her down, but don't expect it to be simple. The rest of Thedeim is open to you, and the denizens will encounter you as usual. And good luck. Vernew won't take it easy on you, heh."

Chapter 19

The kids exchange glances after Teemo finishes talking. Freddie is the first to break the silence.

"I think we're going to need more than a bucket of mice to capture this one," he says with a sideways look to Rhonda, who can't help but giggle.

"Yeah, we're going to need to dig deep if we're going to have any hope of capturing a mistress of the hunt," she agrees, and tries to think of what to do. "I don't suppose you know anything about her?"

"A little, actually," admits the young orc. Rhonda looks surprised and motions for him to continue, which he quickly does. "She's visited Elder Larx a couple times while I was also visiting. She's an adherent of Thedeim's and calls him the Weaver of the Threads. It's weird how she and Larx focus on different aspects of him."

"Anything we can use to try to catch her?"

"Hmm . . . not that I can think of, besides knowing at least what she looks like. She stands about as tall as you do, Rhonda, but she's all spider below the waist. She likes to use spears and javelins, or at least I've never seen her without them. I'm pretty sure she won't use them on us? She's quick and agile, too. And if she's a mistress of the hunt, she's probably really good at the whole hunting thing."

"So keep an eye on the ceiling. Good thing we learned that lesson early!" says Rhonda with a grin, motioning for Freddie to follow her around the house. "I think the first thing we should do is get some alchemical assistance. If she has Queen along, Vernew will definitely have some of her own."

"Oh?" asks Freddie as he follows, and the two soon encounter a couple vipers. They easily assume their stances and continue to talk, even as they deal with the fight.

"Yeah. Master Staiven says she's the best alchemist he's met in a while, and that she's the Ant Scion! Flash Freeze!" she shouts as one of the vipers spits venom at her. Her spell quickly freezes the projectile solid, making it much easier to sidestep.

Freddie decapitates a viper with his axe before stepping in to keep the other one busy while Rhonda prepares to finish it off.

"Icicle!" she shouts before hurling a small spear of ice at the distracted viper, catching it in the side of the head and ending the encounter. "Whew. Anyway, I think I want to make some agility and perception potions for us, so we can spot her and be able to chase her, too."

Freddie nods to that, and the two soon get to the herb patch in the back. While they gather and plan a bit more, I turn my attention over to Vernew and Queen, who are currently in the tunnels. They are not to be confused with the caverns, which are currently overrun with scythemaws. The spiderkin is happily walking along the wall, idly twirling her spear.

"You don't get out of the lab too much, do you?" she asks Queen, and my Alchemist releases a subtly sour scent. I guess either Vernew has hunted enough things by tracking pheromones to have a rough idea of what they mean, or my spiderkin still use pheromones to communicate at least a little.

"Not calling you out for it, just saying, is all. The Weaver of the Threads has you doing important stuff, so it's not like you know the whole place back to front. *I* don't even know His territory that well, and I'm always moving around!" she says with a shrug. The two continue for a few more minutes before she speaks up again.

"What do you think of the two delvers He has us testing?" This time, a pleasant scent comes from Queen, and Vernew nods. "Yeah, they're probably something special for Him to take a special interest in them. I've seen the orc boy a couple times. Seems like a good kid. Larx treats him like his own grandson, so he can't be *too* bad," she jokes as they come to an intersection.

"What do you think? Should we head up and see how well they can chase us, or head down and make them come find us." She frowns at the neutral scent. "No opinion?" She grumbles and taps the butt of her spear against the wall she's still standing on as she thinks, before seeming to come to a decision.

"We're going up. Even if they're supposed to be the ones after us, I'm a hunter, not prey. Besides, I haven't been to the surface too often. Maybe I'll get a chance to try to talk with the Reader." She grins as she starts heading up. "Besides, if it's unfamiliar territory for me, it might give the kids half a chance, hah!"

I watch her for a few more minutes as she goes, seeing her do a few quick forward jumps occasionally. Yeah, the kids are going to need to work hard to catch her, but that's part of the point. If it was easy, I don't think they'd be motivated enough to push themselves to get the best classes they can.

Back with the kids, it seems like those potions Rhonda wanted are not too difficult to make, as she has several brewed already.

"Okay, so, the perception potions are a bit weaker, but should last an hour or so each. The agility potions are stronger but won't last as long. So we'll try to keep the perception effect active, and only drink the agility ones once we actually find her."

Freddie nods at that and drinks his first perception potion, taking a few seconds to get used to noticing more than usual. "I might know where to try to look for her, too."

"Yeah?" asks the young goblin as she gets the spares sorted and stored on her person.

"Yeah. She'd often talk about the Reader of the Web with Larx. I'm pretty sure she meant Tiny."

Rhonda looks uncertain at that. "I don't think we can hide from him for that long in the maze. And we'd have to run from him while also trying to catch Vernew and Queen," she points out. Freddie doesn't look too concerned, though.

"Then we don't go in. We go *on*. I'm pretty sure it's not sticky on top. If she goes on top, we can try to ambush her around Tiny's lair. The maze itself is pretty flat, but the trees in his arena should give us places to try to hide. And if she goes inside, she should have to run the maze like anyone else. If you can slow her down, Tiny can get her, and we'll just pick her up at the maze entrance."

"That all depends on her actually going there . . . but it's not like I have any better ideas," says Rhonda with a shrug. The two head to the maze and send their spiders up to test that the covering will be enough to support them. Tiny doesn't make subpar webbing, and they quickly decide it should be fine. Freddie helps Rhonda up first by having her run at him and jump up off his shield, with him giving a good push to help.

It's a little more difficult to get Freddie up, though, since the bushes aren't really made for climbing. After a few minutes of discussion, Rhonda pulls out a small stone and takes her time inscribing a rune onto it. Freddie backs up, and at her signal, charges toward the thorny wall. At the last moment, Rhonda drops the stone and activates it.

"Earth Thrust!" The ground under Freddie surges upward, and he jumps with all his might. He just manages to clear the hedge and lands gracelessly on his face beside Rhonda and the spiders. The group takes a few minutes to enjoy the webbing and the unique view from atop the maze before simply walking over the top, toward the lumpy bulges of the trees in and around Tiny's lair.

The big lug, of course, feels the unusual movement on top of his domain, and actually lets a runner get much further than normal as he tracks down the kids. They give him a sheepish look once he appears below them.

"Uh . . . hey, Tiny," starts Freddie. "We're not trying to cheat the maze. We're doing something else."

The huge spider doesn't look very convinced, so Rhonda tries to explain. "See, we're trying to get our classes and asked Thedeim for help. So he wants us to try to track down and capture Vernew, who is getting Queen's help! Freddie thinks our best bet is to try to hide up here and hope she comes by to visit you."

Tiny considers that for a few long moments before giving a series of shrugs that ripple along his eight legs, much to the kids' relief.

"Oh, and if she *does* come by, can you try to keep her distracted?" asks Rhonda.

Tiny again doesn't look inclined, until the group uses their secret weapon: puppy-dog eyes! Even Lucas and Fiona get in on it, and Tiny is forced to relent under the onslaught of twenty big watery pleading eyes. With a whoop of triumph, the kids head for the webbed trees, and Tiny returns to chasing those who would brave his maze.

Chapter 20

Is bemused the right word? Knowing you've been had, but not particularly minding it? Whatever it's called, I'd say that describes Tiny's feelings on having been defeated by the kids' puppy-dog eyes. They're pretty good at it, and shameless in using it, too, heh.

I split my attention between the kids and Vernew, with the former refining their plan for how to catch the latter, and the latter obviously getting more excited by the idea of killing some time with Tiny. It looks like Freddie won't be even trying to use an improvised club or anything in the upcoming fight, opting to focus on his shield and grabs/punches. His hatchet could hurt Vernew, and even a club could accidentally crush Queen. So can his hands and shield, but the kids are pretty sure it will be safer all around if he doesn't use an actual weapon.

Vernew and Queen, meanwhile, are just enjoying looking around as they wander the yard. Queen's ants were and are important to keeping the various herbalism nodes healthy and growing, but she herself hasn't had much chance to actually see the fruits and herbs of their labor. Vernew has been to the surface a few times before, but I think this is her first time up here in the day, not counting any time she may have spent on sign duty before becoming a spiderkin.

She earns a few curious looks from the various delvers, but nobody tries to stop or talk with her. People are busy with their own stuff, and a new spiderkin doesn't even register on their scale of oddities around here anymore, I guess. I wonder if I should do something classic and play it fully straight, just to keep them guessing. If you only ever do weird stuff, it stops being so weird, right?

My own musings aside, Vernew grins as she sees the hedge maze, her legs shuffling a little in excitement. I'm not sure if Queen is physically capable of rolling her eyes, but Vernew at least catches the scent and laughs as she starts to climb the hedge.

"Maybe you'll understand it better once the Weaver gets an ant enclave. Ant-kin? Whatever they are, they'll want to get some of your time or just watch you doing your thing. Heh, they'll probably see you as even more mysterious and wise than we do the Reader. He has a pretty public domain, and you don't."

I can practically hear the "Hmph!" through the bond, and I'm pretty sure the pheromone she releases means the same thing, as Vernew just laughs again. Over at Freddie and Rhonda, their eyes widen a little as they hear new laughter in the distance. They try to subtly look around the web-covered trees, looking for the source, and it actually takes Fiona tapping Freddie's shoulder and pointing for them to spot their target.

Vernew strides forward, confident as she twirls an empty spear haft. The kids aren't the only ones who needed to adjust their usual setup for this. I don't think she's noticed them yet, but it's hard to say. She might be able to feel through the web like Tiny can. Even if she can, though, I don't think she knows how the top web is supposed to feel without two kids and their spiders on it.

Her eyes almost sparkle as she sees Tiny through the dense covering over his central lair. I can tell he glances at where the kids are, but he doesn't directly rat them out as he stands and walks toward Vernew. Rhonda and Freddie drink their potions and start to carefully advance as Vernew gives my Spider Scion a respectful bow.

"Reader of the Web! I hope I'm not intruding on your duties?" she asks, fidgeting a little as she realizes she's kinda barged in on his workplace. He waves a foreleg lazily, dismissing her concern.

"Oh, good! I was, uh . . ." she tapers off as she realizes she didn't have much of a plan to talk with him. An amused scent wafts from Queen, and Vernew glares at her for a moment, which only makes Queen laugh harder in her own way.

"I was hoping for some wisdom? Or maybe just to see you work? The Weaver has given me a task, and—" She stops as Tiny moves a little, and I can feel a bit of Fate magic reaching out to Vernew. She looks a bit defensive as the magic fades. "I *am* doing it! I'm supposed to test the two green children by forcing them to catch me! It's not my fault they're not—!"

"Ensnaring Gale!" shouts Rhonda as Fiona hurls a large web at Vernew. The summoned wind accelerates and widens it as it flies at their foe, but the mistress of the hunt is not so easily captured. She leaps into the air without looking backward, though she turns midair and lands to face the two with a look of shock and budding respect on her face. She even spares an accusing glance down toward Tiny.

"You *helped* them!" Tiny doesn't look even the least bit chastised as he relaxes to watch the ensuing battle. Vernew's attention is forced back to the fight on her hands as Freddie charges, and she catches his shield with a cross block. "Right, first rule of any hunt: don't get distracted!" she says before grinning.

She kicks out at Freddie's feet to try to trip him up, but he keeps his balance. The moment of solidifying his stance gives her a chance to slip away, and the two sides enjoy a small standoff.

"And here I thought it'd be a boring hunt with you two! Er, four," she corrects as the spiders chitter at her. She holds her empty spear like it still has the head on it, and Freddie keeps his shield up to catch any attack from her. He also keeps himself between her and Rhonda. She could jump over him, but he's not so far away that even something like that would give her more than a few moments with Rhonda and Lucas.

After a few moments, she grins and turns to flee, hopping up onto one of the taller web-coated trees and forcing the kids to chase her. They're no fools, though, and stay close as they pursue her, not giving her the satisfaction of breaking their formation and giving her an opening.

"They're good. I see why the Weaver likes them. Alright, Queen, which one was the distraction?" she asks as she watches the kids approach. My Ant Scion taps at the back of her neck, and she nods, letting one of her secondary hands grab a small sealed jar from her belt.

She's not the only one who was preparing, though. Lucas maneuvers his legs as Rhonda channels a spell, helping her keep the magic correct as she focuses more on movement. As they get closer, she takes over the spell and points her wand. "Black Ice!" The webbing and tree around Vernew quickly are coated with incredibly slick ice, and even the mistress of the hunt loses her footing. Freddie jumps and quickly climbs, closing the distance between them and Vernew.

The dweller tries to entangle him with some of her own webbing, but he brings his shield up, and the ensnarement finds no purchase. She bites back a curse as she tosses the jar up into the air. "You waxed his shield?! Fine, deal with *this*!"

She jumps after the jar and shatters it with her staff. Within moments, the area is covered in thick smoke. It looks like it's not difficult to breathe in, but visibility is basically nil in there. I can see Vernew grin as she slowly stalks toward the kids while they put their backs together after a few words, their spiders running around on the webbing beneath them.

"Who is the hunted now, hmm?" she says as she slowly circles them, using their movements on the webbing to guide her. "I didn't think I'd need this one, either, so consider me impressed, kids." She stops as she prepares to leap at them. "But there was only one way this hunt could have gone." She leaps forward, only to find Freddie's shield directly in her way. "How?!"

"You're not the only one with some alchemical help. Now!" responds Freddie before the webbing beneath them all collapses. Shouts of struggle and complaints drift from the cloud of smoke until it clears a minute or two later and reveals the result.

The entire group is tangled up in webbing, mostly of Tiny's make, though Lucas and Fiona contributed to actually make the larger spider's web work to entrap their prey. And themselves. The entire group awkwardly turns as one whole, limbs and faces sticking out of a big mess of silk.

"No, really—How?!" repeats Vernew, struggling against the tough silk around them all.

"Perception and agility potions," answers Rhonda. "We could hear you talking through the smoke. We knew you'd be just as blind as us, so we set a trap. We, uh . . . we weren't supposed to get caught too, though." Lucas and Fiona chitter apologies.

Tiny smiles in his own way at the scene as he gets up, and Vernew looks a bit embarrassed to be in this kind of situation where he can see. He turns the mess so Rhonda and Freddie can see him, and the aspiring paladin speaks up.

"This counts as catching her, right?"

Tiny

Today will be interesting for the large Spider Scion. Something big is coming, and even Weaver Thedeim has noticed. Not that he's *bad* at sensing the threads of fate, but it's more like he works them without even realizing it, so it's always interesting when he *does* notice.

Tiny, of course, refused to give him much detail, lest he influence the Weaver's work. He did at least concede to tell him it's nothing bad, though Thedeim still checked the various potential troubles anyway. It's good for him to reinforce those particular threads periodically.

The next couple hours were spent simply tending to the maze, harrying and hurrying the delvers who would like to get at the various bounties hidden in his domain. Not long before noon, though, he felt something new in his webbing. Movement on top of the maze?

He follows the vibration to eventually find several familiar faces, though from a perspective he hasn't seen in quite some time. Looking up through the webbing, he sees the two green children; he can feel the work of the Weaver all around them, now that he's looking. But what are they doing?

"Uh . . . hey, Tiny. We're not trying to cheat the maze. We're doing something else."

The large spider squints as well as he can at the two, still not sure what they're actually doing. It wouldn't be like them to try to cheat, but he can't think of anything else they might be up to on top of his maze.

"See, we're trying to get our classes, and asked Thedeim for help. So he wants us to try to track down and capture Vernew, who is getting Queen's help! Freddie thinks our best bet is to try to hide up here and hope she comes by to visit you."

Tiny considers that for a few moments. If Vernew is going to be on the move and not simply hunting, there is a very good chance she'll come by. The spiderkin always puts up a brave face, but she's still coming to terms with her place in the world and the weave. She often will visit or simply watch as he works.

He shrugs and allows them to stay on top of his maze. He starts to turn to leave them to it when the goblin speaks up once more.

"Oh, and if she *does* come by, can you try to keep her distracted?"

He's inclined to politely decline, but the children and their spiders are perfectly willing to use every advantage they have at their disposal and give him innocent pleading looks. He knows it's a ruse, and he's pretty sure they know he knows, yet they try anyway. He can't help but respect the moxie that takes, so he nods, much to their elation.

They move to hide among the webbed branches over his lair, and he moves to capture a woodsman who is trying to get a bit more than usual. He almost gets away, too, but his heavy load slows him just enough for Tiny to capture him and relieve him of his wood, as well as what seems to be a nice chisel, before he leads him outside the maze, tied up.

Later, he feels new and familiar feet atop his maze, and so he heads to his lair to greet her. He can't help but enjoy her nervous core that peeks through her confident and calm mask as they exchange greetings. The specifics of his greeting to her are rather lost in translation, but he gets across his general point with her most of the time. It doesn't take her long to get to why she's there.

"I was hoping for some wisdom? Or maybe just to see you work? The Weaver has given me a task, and—"

Tiny taps into his Fate affinity, weaving a subtle little vision of her at work, along with a questioning feeling. If the Weaver has given her a task, why isn't she doing it?

"I *am* doing it! I'm supposed to test the two green children by forcing them to catch me! It's not my fault they're not—!"

Tiny grins as a spider does once the children attack, and he settles in to watch the show. He's gotten glimpses of something the Weaver calls popcorn before, and it seems like it would be the perfect snack for watching something like this.

There is surprisingly little Fate magic involved in the fight, too. Just a few subtle little nudges to help the children with their plan, the magic slowly settling around them and changing to something else: the basic framework of their classes.

Once the fight is over and everyone is tangled in the ball of his webbing, Tiny stands to help extract them, and add his own little nudges. Oh, nothing so crass as actually trying to direct their growth into their classes, no. He just snips a frayed bit here, smooths a corner there, just a couple small things to help the children be what they should be.

He's reminded of something else that has drifted through the bond, usually when Thedeim is designing some new challenge like the maze or the gauntlet. Thedeim wishes to help the delvers grow, and there is a strange bit of wisdom from . . . a short foxkin? Tiny isn't certain, and he's never bothered to try to ask Teemo for clarification on the origin.

The wisdom is clear: don't try to turn your students into you, but rather help them grow into themselves.

Chapter 21

I laugh to myself as I watch Tiny untangle the group from the web, and manage to ask Teemo to be there once they're free so he can tell them about the next challenge. It looks like he'll have plenty of time, too. They've made a proper hash of the webbing.

"I count it as you catching me, even if the Weaver doesn't," says Vernew, who has to suffer the indignity of admitting defeat.

"You would?" asks Freddie with a mix of hope and surprise. "I get the feeling it's not a usual hunt that ends with you tied to your prey."

The spiderkin shrugs as much as she can right now. "I mean, it's not a *flawless* hunt, but you still have backup nearby to clean up the mess and put everything right. Even if recruiting the Reader is cheating . . ." she grumbles, and the kids laugh.

"Thank you for the help too, Tiny. We'd be in . . . well, a *bind* without your help," admits Rhonda with a giggle, and Freddie chuckles as well before speaking up.

"So, you call Thedeim the Weaver and Tiny the Reader?" he asks with curiosity.

Vernew strains to try to get a better look at him.

"Why . . . Oh, right! You follow the Shield! Yeah, I follow Thedeim, the Weaver of the Threads. The Reader of the Web is . . . well, kinda complicated."

"I'm not going anywhere," replies Freddie with admirable stoicism, even if Rhonda giggles at the understatement.

Vernew chuckles. "Heh, fair enough, kid. Well, the Reader was one of the Weaver's first scions, and is probably the most in tune with the Fate affinity they all have. We dwellers still have the vague memories of when we were still aranea, and feel a connection with Reader Tiny."

Freddie looks thoughtful at that. "But the ratkin don't revere Teemo like that . . . right?"

Vernew shakes her head, making the whole mass of webbing and people and spiders wobble a little, earning herself a deep chitter from Tiny. "Oh, sorry. Uh, the ratkin. Well . . . Teemo isn't . . ." She looks around, trying to find the words without sounding insulting. After a few more false starts, she sighs and just plows forward.

"He's not exactly majestic or mysterious. No offense to him, but he's just not. But he also doesn't pretend to be. The Reader will try to guide you to a truth, or let you figure out yourself that you're doing something stupid. Teemo will just tell you if you're being dumb." She sighs again. "Like if you underestimate a couple kids and don't use everything a certain Alchemist prepared for you because you let your pride get in the way."

Freddie looks thoughtful as the web ball slowly turns, considering Vernew's words. I can't help but feel a little proud of her. It takes a big person to admit when they mess up, and I'm glad she's not too prideful nor fearful to admit it. Tiny pats her head in encouragement, and I can practically see her resolve solidify. "I'll do better next time, Weaver," she murmurs in a simple little prayer.

"What else did Queen prepare for you to use, anyway?" asks Rhonda with curiosity, changing the subject and helping to keep Vernew from dwelling on past failures.

"Uh . . . let me see . . . Oh! She had a strength potion and a modified version of the go-juice for me. I, uh . . . I didn't think I'd need them to handle a couple kids. She also had a really weird one. Some kind of exploding ice trap or something?" She wriggles a little, though a look from Tiny gets her to stop pretty quickly.

"Exploding ice trap? That sounds a bit dangerous," says Rhonda, wondering just what kind of bullet they managed to dodge.

"Nah, it was . . . Queen, help me out here? What did it do again?" Tiny moves to let Queen hop into Vernew's face, and she takes a spot on her forehead as she tries to explain via pheromones. "Slower, please. Slower! It's all muddling together!" she complains. That's when Teemo finally comes out of a shortcut to save her. Well, metaphorically. Mostly. A little?

"Not majestic or mysterious, hmm?" Vernew withers as much as she can under his glare before he cracks and laughs. "I gotta keep you all grounded somehow! Hard to do that and keep an air of mystique, heh. Anyway, Queen, what were you trying to explain?"

He listens to her scents for a few moments before looking to Tiny. "Can you get me to her belt, please? This thing sounds cool, and I think a demonstration might be in order."

Tiny nods and points at a small hole in the webbing near Vernew's hip. Teemo slips inside quickly, and also quickly slips out with a sealed flask in his mouth. He sets it on the floor in front of Rhonda and collects himself for a few moments.

"Okay, so this thing is something Queen's pretty proud of. I'm not going to go over the technical stuff in detail. Sorry, Queen. No, I refuse. Maybe if it was Staiven, but it's not." He looks back to Rhonda and shakes his head. "Anyway . . . it creates an ice slick and also a disorienting bang and flash of light. It's based on something Thedeim knows about, and a few tricks that we've all been toying with. Ready for a demonstration?"

Rhonda nods vigorously, shaking Freddie out of his thoughts.

"Hmm?" asks the young orc, trying to figure out what he's missed while deep in thought.

"Alchemical ice slick explosion bomb!" replies Rhonda, not quite as helpfully as she might think. Freddie doesn't have time to try to get any clarification before Tiny picks up the flask and tosses it out into his lair area.

The glass shatters, and a coating of ice quickly forms on the floor, as well as a swirling, strobing mass of energy floating above the center of the slick. After a few seconds, it explodes with a bright flash and a loud crack. Instead of shattering the ice, however, it remains unharmed, all the energy seeming to have gone into the light and sound.

All gathered jump—or the best they can manage while in a big ball of web—and Teemo even falls over on his back with a surprised squeak. After a moment of stunned silence from everyone, Teemo rights himself. "Well, I think you did it, Queen."

"Yeah, but *how*?!" exclaims Rhonda, her eyes wide as saucers at what they just witnessed.

"I already said how." Teemo smirks over at Vernew, where Tiny seems to be getting close to unraveling the webbing keeping everyone ensnared. "See? I can do mysterious sometimes."

With one last flick of his legs, Tiny gets the webbing loose enough for everyone to spill to the ground with a collective grunt. Rhonda leaps to her feet and immediately has her notebook out, scribbling furiously about what she just saw, at least until Teemo clears his throat.

"You have passed the first trial. The second trial will be easier to find, but perhaps more difficult to pass. In the laboratory in the crypt complex await Elder Larx and Thing. They will have your next challenge. So speaks the Voice of Thedeim."

The kids whoop in triumph, and the spiders chitter in their own celebration. They all do a little dance, though there's no victory music yet. Slash will need his guitar for that to be a reality. After their celebration, they all dust themselves off and gather whatever they dropped. Freddie even gets Rhonda's hat and dusts it off before giving it to her.

"So, the crypt complex. We'll need to be on our toes on the way to the lab over there," comments Freddie as they make their way out of the maze.

"Yeah, I hear the church does a lot of training in there because of the undead, right? Think we'll have to fight through them?"

Freddie nods. "Teemo said we'd get normal encounters in the first challenge, and I don't think that'll change for this one."

"I'm glad he counted our capture. I thought for sure we messed up by getting caught in the webbing, too," admits Rhonda as they chat.

"Yeah, I'm surprised, too. I'm also surprised Vernew took it so well."

"What do you mean?"

"Well . . . she failed a task given to her by 'The Weaver of the Threads, I don't know if I'd be that calm if I failed something the Shield asked me to do."

"Maybe she didn't fail?" suggests Rhonda.

Freddie shakes his head.

"No, she did. But Thedeim wasn't upset. He didn't even set her up to fail, I think. She had Queen's help, too. If she had used that weird ice flask, she could have gotten away from us, but she didn't think she needed to."

Rhonda gives him a sideways look, knowing when he's working toward something. "So, why don't you think he was upset with her? He seems pretty relaxed to me, and I don't picture him being mad over something like this."

"Yeah, I don't think he'd be mad at her, but . . . what she said stuck with me. She'll do better next time. I don't think it's about him being mad at her, but more that it's about her being mad with herself. It makes me think of Head Priest Torlon's battered shield on the wall."

"Yeah?" asks Rhonda, not really seeing a connection there.

"Yeah. I always thought the chips and such were just there to be reminders of the grace of the Shield. But now . . . I dunno. That shield is all battered and scarred . . . but it never shattered. The mistakes don't define it or weaken it. It's still a shield. It can still protect. The marks are reminders to do better . . . and reminders that you shouldn't let a mistake break you."

Chapter 22

Thing

Threads of mana, a place of death, a single hand, life without breath.

The first seconds of existence are confusing. His nature says to seek and choke, to grasp and grab, hide and hinder. To be seen is to be destroyed. The directions from the Master are completely contrary to that. He is not to lead the subtle hordes of hands, but to learn the secrets of magic.

He's not even supposed to be learning how to destroy with the magic, unless one counts destroying magic itself. The Master has subsumed another dungeon, and finds magical workings he doesn't wish, and so he wishes them destroyed.

It's a shame, really. Taking a look at the enchantments, they're works of deadly art. He no more understands their actual construction than he understands how one would paint a picture, but he knows he'll need to learn if he's to follow the Master's desires.

The Master is understanding, knowing how well-made the enchantments are, and so doesn't expect immediate results. Instead, he is allowed to research and learn, using a lab deep behind the enchantments to discover the secrets of the arcane. He can feel the Master observing, but doesn't feel any compulsions, his Master content to let Thing learn on his own.

He can feel vague concepts drift past the bond; echoed and distorted whispers of the true workings of reality. Perhaps he'll be able to understand those secrets someday, but for now, he needs to understand the basics.

Learning is a humbling and time-consuming experience. The books and research materials are dense and carry the weight of the power of the knowledge within. They give their secrets reluctantly, seeming to fight him for it.

And yet, he sees and meets with those who seem to grasp the ideas so easily. The aged ratkin is knowledgeable, and accepting his help stings of inadequacy, but he has plainly been working on this sort of thing for decades. Thing would be a fool to ignore his advice.

But the truly humbling teacher is Rocky. A zombie, intended to be a simple fighter, and yet, he progresses in magic as if he were born to it. At first, Thing worried the Master may have been favoring the zombie, whispering the secrets into that rotting ear, but no. Rocky is simply driven, and Thing suspects he's smarter than even the zombie understands.

Conversing has been . . . a learning experience for them both. Rocky seems to have an innate understanding of the style of Master's magic, but little idea how to convey it. Thing understands the formulae, the structure, but has to rely on his instruments to actually manipulate and observe the mana flows properly. Working together, however, improves them both.

Time passes, and he dismantles the magic traps left behind, then creates the enchanted mandible swords for the Master's residents. He also fails to undo Lifedrinking, yet the Master doesn't rebuke him for it. He knows it is a nigh-impossible task, so is prepared for it to take time. Even with Thing hitting a wall in his progress, the Master is patient and gives him a new project: an axe.

It's a strange thing for the new Earth Elemental Scion, employing Thunder and Lightning mana to create an instrument. The complexity is staggering, but the Master provides guidance. The process is . . . so strange, so different from what Thing is used to, and something about it sticks in his mind. Something about the similarities between how thunder and lightning function. He can't quite place his finger on it, but he knows there's something profound there.

He will have to put that aside for the moment, though, as he has hit a wall in the progress for the axe as well, and the Master has seen fit to give him an assistant in the form of the young goblin who frequents the Master's territory. She is seeking her class, though Thing doesn't know what he can do to help her with that. The Master seems to think she can help with the axe, and though Thing doubts it, he will not defy the Master.

Rocky is an unlikely source of arcane knowledge and expertise. This goblin could be the same.

Thedeim

Freddie and Rhonda elect to take the streets over to the cemetery and crypt complex rather than try to slip through the tunnels, and I can hardly blame them. The scythemaws are mostly settled in now, but why take the risk?

I look in on Thing and Larx to see what they're up to. I didn't have Teemo tell them too much, other than their challenge should be something that doesn't involve fighting and should be something to help the kids with their classes. Thing looks to be planning to get Rhonda's help with the axe, specifically with getting the pickups to translate properly into the singing Tesla coils. The hat isn't finished yet, as I wanted to make sure the magitech amplifier setup would actually work before committing to the design.

I'm not sure how electricity and sound will help Rhonda with her Ice class, but something about it feels right, so I don't try to convince Thing to do something else.

Larx, on the other hand, seems to just be writing in a little book, trying to glean "wisdom" from how I run things. I'm not so sure how well that'll work, but he's over halfway through this one, so what do I know? As far as I can tell, he's planning some kind of debate or something? A discussion? Hard to say without having Teemo ask him.

Soon enough, the kids enter through the cemetery gates, and they even wave at Grim before they head into the complex. It's interesting watching them fight the various verdant skeletons and fungal zombies, as well as the smattering of more ordinary undead that still wander out of the spawners sometimes.

Freddie doesn't try to turn any of the hybrids, instead seeming to draw on the Shield's power to strengthen himself rather than weaken his foes. Rhonda's cold magic works pretty dang well to immobilize and weaken them enough on its own, seems like, and I'm actually pretty impressed at how well they're handling themselves in there. It gives me some confidence in them for the final challenge against Rocky and Aranya.

Before too long, they enter the public enchanting lab in the crypt complex, and Larx gives them a warm, grandfatherly smile and greeting. "Ah, you've made it! I hope Vernew didn't take her loss too hard?" he asks, motioning for them to take a seat. There's no need to rush into things, after all.

The kids nod and sit on some stools, and their spiders hop off and explore a little. Freddie soon realizes they were asked a question and shakes his head. "She seemed to take it with grace. Well, with as much grace as one can have when wrapped in a big bundle of Tiny's web."

"With a goblin, an orc, and two spiders," adds Rhonda with a smile. Larx grins at that.

"Ah, not the most graceful of victories, but accepted with grace all the same? Very good, very good. I'd offer you cookies or a drink, but Thing has made it very clear to me that this lab is not a place for snacks," he says with a laugh while Thing just shrugs . . . somehow.

"Master Staiven says the same thing. There's stuff in a lab you don't want to accidentally eat or drink, and delicate stuff can be ruined by a spill," points out Rhonda, earning herself a thumbs-up from the wandering hand.

"Indeed! So, without much to distract us, what classes are you two hoping to get?" asks my dweller with a gleam in his eyes.

"I've been training hard to become a paladin of the Shield," answers Freddie, and Rhonda quickly follows up.

"I want to be an ice mage! I like ice, but I also want the versatility a mage has. I think I've been getting pretty good with other aspects, and Arcane would be just amazing to have!"

Larx nods at that. "Those both sound reasonable, and I think Thing and I will be able to help in our own ways. For you, Rhonda, he would like you to lend him a hand," he says with a grin. Thing manages to convey a flat look before Larx continues. "To help him with a tricky bit of enchanting. The details go well over my head, but it's something about Lightning mana transforming into Thunder in specific ways."

Rhonda looks intrigued by that but manages to keep her questions to herself as Larx continues.

"And for you, Freddie, I wish to plumb the depths of your wisdom."

Freddie looks a little confused at that. "Quoting scripture?" he asks. Larx chuckles and shakes his head.

"That would just be you repeating *their* words. I want to hear it in *yours*. I won't pretend to be an expert in the finer details of what the Shield demands, but I get the feeling there are more than a few points it and Lord Thedeim would agree on. Are you both ready?"

The two nod, equal parts nervous and determined.

"Then let's begin."

Thing

The Enchanter wonders how well this will work, but he doesn't attempt to deny the wishes of the Master. He hasn't been able to make much progress on the amplifier for a while now, so a fresh set of eyes could do a lot of good.

He takes a few minutes to try to explain the details to the goblin, but even with Lucas trying to help, he doesn't get very far. He deflates a little and resorts to using the chalkboard to walk her through the process, which works much better. She takes meticulous notes and asks pertinent questions, and he finds himself enjoying being able to talk a bit of shop with her. She's not an expert yet, but she knows enough to at least understand the problems.

"So these will actually turn the vibrations from the strings into lightning? Wow!" Thing can't help but preen a bit at her appreciation of his and Queen's hard work. He knows the Master appreciates the work, but having an outsider feel the same is different, somehow.

"And then they go over here and make tiny lightning bolts to make the thunder?" She looks at the board and her notes for a few seconds before continuing. "But you want it to sound a specific way, because it's some kind of musical instrument?" She looks at the whole setup, looking a bit lost as to where to even begin. Thing understands that feeling all too well.

"Well, I'm no bard . . ." she starts before letting the thought trail off as she plucks a string, then puts her finger on it to pluck again. If it was working, it would make a higher note, but there's no appreciable difference in the sound produced.

Thing motions for her attention and assistance, and the two get to work to try to make it sound better. The working assumption is that there is some kind of interference, but there are a lot of potential places for it to come in. Connections are checked and rechecked, different pickups tried to see if those are the problem, and even the coils are put through their paces to see if there is something wrong with them, but everything seems to be working properly.

Rhonda slumps in her stool as Thing taps a finger on his notes, both trying to think of what the problem could be.

"This is some advanced stuff you're up to, Thing," she compliments, and that does at least lessen the sting of failure, even if it reminds him of his failure with the Lifedrinking enchantment, too.

"You and Queen both, and don't even get me started on Rocky, heh. Have you seen Queen's new ice bomb thing?" Thing has not, and so he motions for her to continue.

"I have no idea how she did it, but she made something that spreads an ice slick while building up energy for a really loud explosion! I don't know how she managed to mix ice, fire, and *thunder* of all things together into a flask!"

Thing nods at that, letting his mind wander how it would work. Rhonda wouldn't know about how energy works like he and Queen do, and the other scions as well. The ice slick is created *by* the building explosion as it sucks the energy out of an area and is then deliberately released as light and sound with little direction.

Hmm . . . sonic waves and electrical waves. What if the release on the coils isn't as properly organized as he thought? If the sounds are released wrong, they might be interfering with each other and canceling each other out.

Thing locks up as that thought mingles with the lingering bitterness of failing to defeat Lifedrinking. He had been trying to pick it apart or otherwise destabilize it. Harmonic interference should be able to just make it vanish!

He scrambles to clear a space on the workbench, and the confused goblin does her best to help, even ordering Lucas to put things away as Thing dashes about like a hand possessed. Once he has some room to work, he quickly creates a Lifedrinking enchantment, and motions for Rhonda to look closer. She gasps as she realizes what it is.

"Lifedrinking?! What's that have to do with . . ." She once again quiets as Thing starts weaving his new attempt at a counterspell for it. "Thunder? No, it's close, but . . . What are you *doing* . . . ?" she asks as she takes notes. Thing hardly hears her as he carefully works his magic, and he walks himself through the entire theory to help focus.

A wave has peaks and valleys. Simple enough. If two waves meet, they will add together; peaks become bigger, valleys become deeper. But they can also lessen each other. A peak and a valley meeting will produce a smaller peak, a shallower valley. If you match them up perfectly *wrong,* they will cancel each other out! It's much more complex when the waves move off of a simple piece of paper, and more complex still with magic, but he can feel it in his bones that it will work this time!

"Oh!" quietly exclaims Rhonda, and Thing realizes he's done it. The enchantment that's been his bane has just vanished like a bubble of soap. He's actually done it! He does a little dance before holding himself up for a high five, but Rhonda is staring wide-eyed at where the enchantment used to be.

"You did . . . something with thunder or lightning, and countered *Lifedrinking*?! How does that even work?!" she demands of him. Her need to know is quieted a little once she realizes she's been leaving him hanging, and she slaps her palm against his. "But seriously, how?! That implies . . . that implies *so much*!"

Thing worries as he realizes he might have spilled the beans on one of the few things the Master has wished to keep secret from the delvers, but he can feel pride and happiness from the bond. Master Thedeim is proud of him for solving the long-standing problem!

As Thing looks over at Rhonda, he doesn't even need his Fate affinity to see she's making great strides toward her class as she theorizes wildly and chases possibilities. He's a little nervous about that, but the Master trusts her and her friend. These secrets could be devastating in the wrong hands . . . but they could be revolutionary in the right ones.

Chapter 23

While Thing and Rhonda get ready to work on the quartz pickups, I pay more attention to Larx and Freddie. I always find it interesting to listen to philosophy and how people think, but I'm also curious about how paladins actually work here.

In the games I've played and run, paladins are lawful good, meaning they have honor for agreements and are good. The problem is that a lot of people don't understand how that actually works and end up playing lawful stupid instead. There's no shortage of horror stories about people playing paladins, falling, and being the only ones at the table confused about it, and there are also horror stories of people playing paladins being deliberately set up to fall by their DMs setting up situations where law and good conflict, and then simply forcing the paladin to fall no matter what they do.

But here, I don't know the mechanics. Is falling even a thing? I dunno. But listening in, I might learn. And even if not, I'll at least get a good idea of what kind of philosophy I've accidentally been teaching my ratkin. I may not appreciate the situation I'm in with them, but I do want to make sure they're doing things right.

The ratkin elder simply sits on his stool, looking somewhere between lost in thought and remembering a joke. Freddie sits on his own stool and fidgets as the silence drags on.

"So, uh . . . how do we start?" asks the young orc, and Larx finally focusses on him with a smile.

"Ah, a grander question than I think you realize," he says with a chuckle, but mercifully continues quickly. "That's what I was thinking on, actually. There's a lot of things we could start with, and while beginning at the beginning is usually a good idea, I think it might drag on a bit, hmm?"

Freddie simply nods.

"We could compare writings and have a long-winded talk about people who are well known for how long their winds are, but there's a bit of wisdom Lord Thedeim has given, and I think your Shield understands it as well: words are noise; actions are change. I've heard the Voice say this in many ways, and I've seen the truth of it myself. So let me ask you this, young Freddie: Why did the consecration of the cemetery go as it did?"

Freddie looks confused. "What?"

Larx smiles with a twinkle in his eyes. "Why did the consecration of the cemetery go as it did? Talk and think your way through it, lad. There was much more happening than a couple acolytes and an old rat."

The orc doesn't look very confident, but Larx hasn't led him astray yet. "Why? Uh . . ." He takes a few more seconds to get his mind into gear, then starts. "At the beginning? Well . . . Head Priest Torlon said we should go consecrate it, and sent the Head Acolyte at the time to oversee it."

"Good. Why?" prods Larx, and Freddie frowns as he actually thinks about the why of the mission, instead of just doing as asked.

"Because the Shield wanted it consecrated? It doesn't like undead, so that makes sense, right? And it's pretty plain why it wouldn't like undead, right? I mean, Thedeim's undead aren't bad, and Miss Yvonne is a special case, but most undead are just mindless destroyers."

Larx nods, glad Freddie is thinking things through now, and motions for him to continue.

"Okay, uh . . . other whys . . . Why send me? I was one of the people who'd delved in here the most and part of the Church, so I could give advice and stuff. And the Head Acolyte . . . was the Head Acolyte, so he should have been able to do the consecration without any problem."

"And yet there was a problem," states Larx simply. Freddie nods at that.

"Yeah. He tried to consecrate it, but that didn't work, then he tried to attack Thedeim, I think? That didn't work. Then *you* consecrated it just fine, and he got mad. Then he tried to turn Grim . . ."

Larx chuckles at the memory and nods. "Do you know why the first try didn't work to consecrate it?" Freddie gives an awkward shrug.

"Not really? I know he did the wrong kind of consecration, but I don't really know much about doing that kind of thing yet . . ." Freddie admits, and Larx simply nods.

"I've actually talked with the Voice about that many times because it's an interesting example of that wisdom I mentioned at the start of this. The consecration the acolyte tried was in the name of the Shield, but that cemetery is part of Lord Thedeim. Trying to dedicate it to the Shield would be forming a pact with the Shield, and Lord Thedeim declined."

Freddie looks confused at that. "Why would he decline?"

Larx grins wide at that. "Why *would* he decline?" he fires back, wanting Freddie to think through his question.

Freddie looks lost for a few moments as he tries to gather his thoughts and reconcile the idea of me and the Shield being at odds. Thankfully, he's not stupid, just inexperienced at thinking things through, but he gets there before too long. ". . . He's not against the Shield, or he wouldn't be helping us train with his undead, and the Head Acolyte probably wouldn't have been allowed to leave the cemetery that day. So why wouldn't he pact with the Shield . . ."

Larx relaxes and gives Freddie the time to think it through. After a few minutes, the young orc brightens. "Oh! What kind of pact was it? If it's anything like the paladin oaths, not everyone would want to take those. You don't have to be against the Shield to not take those oaths. Rhonda is fine with the Shield, but I don't think she'd even take the initiate vows, let alone the paladin ones." Freddie looks pretty confident, and Larx is looking pretty proud of the thought process.

"Exactly, Freddie. A bond is not to be taken lightly. While Lord Thedeim holds no ill will toward the Shield, he's not going to bind himself to it. So why was the acolyte so upset?"

Freddie looks like he's suffering a bit of secondhand embarrassment. "Well . . . I don't think he really respected Thedeim. I don't think he's done much delving, so he really only knew Neverrest, which didn't give him a very bright view on dungeons, I guess. When Thedeim rejected the consecration because of the pact, he must have thought he had another threat on his hands and tried to attack with that exorcism."

"And even you, Freddie, seem to feel Lord Thedeim would have been fully within his rights to strike him down on the spot. So why didn't he?"

Freddie takes much less time to start talking it out. "Well . . . Thedeim doesn't really do stuff like that. He's not against punishment and stuff, like with that one group who attacked Poe, but he only knocked them out. So . . . he just doesn't like killing people?" Freddie doesn't look too confident in that, so Larx motions for him to keep going.

". . . Why doesn't he like killing people? Huh." Freddie pauses at that. "Miss Telar says that dungeons gain a lot of power from killing, but Thedeim doesn't do that. I mean . . . *I* know killing people is wrong. A dungeon can know that too?"

Larx laughs and nods. "I wouldn't just worship any old hole in the ground, would I?"

Freddie shakes his head. "Yeah, I guess not. So . . . he didn't attack the acolyte because killing is wrong, and I think he wasn't really a threat? If the pact and the exorcism didn't work, I think the acolyte was pretty much out of tricks, even if he *could* have gotten special incense or whatever. And that's even without the fact that Grim is immune to turning."

"So what can you learn from that?"

Freddie thinks for a few moments, chewing over the memories in a new light. "To not jump to conclusions about someone, or even if they *are* a someone? I never really thought about it, but . . . Thedeim really is aware, isn't he? I never thought dungeons were that smart."

Larx just grins at him, and it takes Freddie a moment to realize he said he thought I was stupid right in the middle of a challenge I've given him. If I could, I'd be grinning too, and laughing as he tries to stammer out an apology. Thankfully, Larx calms him down and waves off the nervous stumbling over words.

"I think he knows what you meant, lad. I don't think he takes it personally, either. Even the Dungeoneer's Guild seems to be caught by surprise by him and what he does, so he can hardly blame you for doing the same. But I have one more question for you, Freddie. What happened to the Head Acolyte?"

"Well . . . he's just a normal acolyte now?" Freddie pauses and mulls the question over, not even needing the prodding from Larx to examine the situation in more detail. The young orc's eyes widen once he makes a few connections.

"Wait . . . Head Priest Torlon asked him to consecrate the cemetery. It might not be a direct mission from the Shield, but it's at least something it would want done, right? But the acolyte failed. *You* consecrated it, not the acolyte. I mean, it still got consecrated, but the acolyte still failed to do what the Shield wanted . . ." Freddie trails off for a moment before glancing upward, and I can only assume he's trying to look toward the maze. ". . . Like Vernew failed to do what Thedeim asked."

Larx beams with pride but doesn't say anything, not wanting to distract Freddie from his train of thought. "They kinda both let their pride get in the way of doing their task. But the acolyte didn't get kicked out. He just lost some privileges. He still has some anger issues, I think, but he's also working to get past them. And . . . I think Vernew will also work to do better, too, like she promised."

"And what can you learn from that, and how does it relate to the wisdom I shared with you at the start?"

". . . Don't get a big head just because someone important asks you to do something? And don't give up on someone if they fail?" Larx nods and motions for him to continue. "Because . . . it's easy to just *say* you forgive someone for something, but that's just noise. Giving them more chances is the action to let them change."

I smile to myself at that. Freddie's a good kid, and I think he'll be a good paladin. I think, no matter what kind of system or situation, the honor of a paladin is about actually *doing* good, not just saying it.

Chapter 24

Okay, well . . . that went a lot better than I thought. Not only does Freddie seem to be on a path to understanding what a paladin actually does, but Rhonda helped Thing to get a breakthrough with the Lifedrinking problem! I'm a *little* nervous about her getting hints about the deeper ways things work, but I don't think she'll be making any disasters with it.

But now that she and Freddie have finished their second challenge, it's time for the third and final one. It's going to be a bit of a practical exam, if you will. I give Teemo the TL;DR, and he heads off to go tell the kids.

The kids, Larx, and Thing are all relaxing a bit now, everyone taking a bit of a break. Freddie and Rhonda both have a lot to think about now, and the ratkin and hand can take a moment to bask in a job well done. Everyone sits up a bit as Teemo exits a shortcut, and as he seems to have everyone's attention, he goes ahead and speaks up.

"You've completed Thedeim's second challenge. All that remains is the third, which you'll find in Rocky's arena. He and Aranya will give you your last task. Thedeim says you'll need to apply what you've learned to succeed. He also says making a few more potions might not be the worst idea, heh. So speaks the Voice of Thedeim."

"What's the last challenge?" asks Rhonda, the little goblin hoping to get some information so she can decide what potions to make.

I let Teemo give them a hint, and he takes a few moments to phrase it how he wants. "It's not quite a combat challenge . . . but it's also not *not* a combat challenge."

Freddie smiles as he speaks. "Did you take the whole 'not mysterious' thing personally?" he asks, earning a laugh from Rhonda and Teemo.

"Nah, not really. You two are just lucky in getting to see me trying it out some. I like to be direct, but sometimes, it's not the best option," says my Voice with a shrug. Larx looks intrigued but doesn't press right now. I bet he'll be chewing Teemo's ear about it later, though.

"Oh, and Thing? Great job with the Lifedrinking! The Boss had practically given up on there being a good solution, but you got one!" Thing frantically starts signing, and Teemo laughs it off. "He knows it's still rough, but you can actually work on refining it now. Well, not *right* now. He'd still like you to work on the pickups first." Thing gives a thumbs-up as the kids stand and gather their spiders.

"Is Rocky's arena fully finished?" asks Freddie with interest, and Teemo shakes his head.

"It's all dug out, and some stuff is done, but the Boss wants a fancy ring for it to be completely finished. It'll still have plenty of room for your challenge, though, so don't worry about that."

Larx makes his exit as Rhonda gets to work on a few potions. They still have a few left over from chasing Vernew, and Rhonda adds to their stockpile with what she explains are strength and durability potions. Thing lets her use some of his reagents for them, probably as thanks for her help with the Lifedrinking. Before too long, she has several potions to add to what they already have.

With that, the kids make their exit and head through the catacombs to find the arena. At the moment, it looks a lot like an underground gladiatorial arena . . . which it kinda is, really. It's a place for fights to happen and for people to be able to watch. Maybe I can do some exhibition matches in here even without the ring? I know Rocky would be up for it. I should ask my other scions to see if anyone would be interested.

On the way there, I can see the kids doing things a little differently, too. Rhonda's spellwork seems a little less stable, which I think means she's trying to do things differently, or maybe trying to get a better feel for her magic. Freddie is also being a bit more attentive in his actions. He's not just getting in the way and holding various undead at bay, but also trying to knock them off-balance and being a bit more on the offensive with his shield.

It takes them a little longer than I might have expected, but they *are* experimenting a bit with applying some of what they've learned today, so it's not too surprising. When they finally get there, Aranya is relaxing on one of the benches while Rocky shadowboxes. My kobold isn't the only one on a bench, though. Looks like most of the Ratkin and Spiderkin Enclaves are here to see the show. She raises her voice as the kids enter, so everyone can hear her.

"Ah, you've made it. Welcome to Lord Thedeim's final challenge. In concept, it's pretty simple. But like with a lot of what He does, it won't be so simple to do. It's a bit of a game of tag. Tag me, and you win."

The kids look a little nervous as they wait for the other shoe to drop, or about the people watching, and my High Priestess smiles at that. "The catch is that

Rocky will be trying to stop you. And, of course, I'm not going to just sit around the whole time, either. Poe's Uplifting Wings!" She hops from the stands, and translucent wings sprout from her back, letting her land gracefully on the floor of the arena before they fade away.

Rocky takes up his position in front of her, slamming his gloved hands together and causing a swirl of fire and ice to envelop them before fire settles on one hand, and ice on the other.

"Are you prepared for this challenge?" asks Aranya solemnly.

The kids exchange a long look before nodding.

"We're ready, Aranya," replies Freddie, and the two drink their potions. Looks like they're going all out with them, too, going with the strength and durability ones, as well as the perception and agility potions. To be fair, though, they'll need everything they can get. I've told both Rocky and Aranya that this needs to be a serious test of their ability and resolve, so punches probably won't be as pulled as they might usually be.

As the final potion is quaffed, Aranya speaks. "Then, let the challenge begin!"

"Grah!" shouts Rocky as he performs an uppercut and a hard cross, the movements sending two blades of energy at the kids! With the distance between them, though, they have plenty of time to react. Freddie steps forward and kneels as he brings his shield up, letting the horizontal ice blade pass overhead and catching the fire on the symbol of his faith. As soon as that's dealt with, the kids run forward, trying to circle around, but Rocky can easily keep his position between them and their ultimate target.

Rocky sends a few more attacks as they close, but the kids handle them in much the same way. Rhonda pulls a stone from her pocket as they get near and passes it to Lucas to hold on to. Fiona hops free from Freddie as well as the group prepares to square off against my Zombie Scion.

Rocky grunts at them and motions for them to come closer, practically daring them to try him, but they're in no hurry to get into true melee range with him just yet. "Icicle Spear!" shouts Rhonda, sending a long and sharp shaft of ice at the undead.

Instead of juking it, he meets it with a punch of his fire hand. While the flames lessen and the spear vanishes into his fist, the ice around his other hand grows thicker. In a smooth one-two punch, he not only destroys the spear like it never existed in the first place, but he also launches his own icy projectile at Freddie. The orc plants his feet and yells for Rhonda to back up as the flying fist of ice quickly approaches. It hits and shatters on his shield, sending Freddie skidding back several feet, but leaves the young orc none the worse for wear.

Rhonda pulls out what I first think is another notebook, but instead of scribbling in it, it seems to be full of runes for various spells. "Where is . . . Ah! Fiona!"

she calls for the spider's attention as she prepares a spell, and Freddie slowly moves closer and closer to Rocky. He's still well out of melee range, but should be able to close the distance quickly, should he choose.

"Now! Shield Charge!" yells Freddie, and Rhonda holds her runebook high. "Misdirection!"

The rock in Lucas's grip flashes brightly while Fiona throws a large web net at Rocky. The ground shakes as several pillars erupt around and behind my Zombie Scion, leaving him in quite a pickle. The pillars will hinder his movement, Freddie is barreling down on him, and a large web is coming to entangle him. Moving will either get him tangled in the web or let Freddie around him to chase Aranya. None of these are viable options for the Zombie Scion.

He grunts as he lets the thermal energy around his flaming glove go out. He needs to focus on a different affinity to deal with this. A swift hook sends a blade of kinetic energy at the web, neatly slicing it enough for it to miss him. Another hard hook with the ice-encrusted fist meets Freddie's shield with enough force to stop even an attack like that in its tracks.

Except, instead of stopping Freddie, it passes through him without effect. Rocky grunts in surprise as the illusion takes a few more moments to dissipate, and it takes him a few moments more to realize what the kids have done. Freddie rode one of the pillars to jump over Rocky, just like how he got on top of the hedge maze. The large web net was never aimed at Rocky at all, but at the pillars behind him, forming a wall that would take him time to get through. Worse: he'd have to turn his back on Rhonda to try to deal with it, too.

He focuses his attention on Rhonda and the spiders as Freddie charges my High Priestess, but she looks delighted more than worried. "Teemo's Disjunction!" Freddie trips as the world seems to shift sharply to the right, and his sense of balance really doesn't like suddenly being on a completely new heading. He rolls and comes up quickly, but Aranya is already running.

Rhonda

The aspiring goblin mage tries not to show her nervousness as Rocky turns his attention squarely on her. Freddie had been apprehensive of her wanting to deal with the undead scion mostly on her own, but she *needs* this. After seeing the hint from the Frostbang vial and working with Thing, she can almost feel what Rocky is doing. She knows he started with Fire and Fate affinities, and expanded to get Ice and looks like Kinetic.

She doesn't know how, but she can feel *something.* It's like a whisper on the wind, or movement out of the corner of her eye; things that vanish once she focuses on them. She needs more. Needs to observe more! She grits her teeth and passes the runebook to Lucas as she holds her wand tight. "Windblast, page thirty or so. Bookmark and help stabilize me," she orders as she walks forward, Fiona moving to her side to help.

Rocky watches for a moment before resuming his fire-and-ice style, willing to meet Rhonda on her terms. A straight sends a wall of ice toward her and empowers the fire fist. Another straight sends a multitude of small balls of fire to rain upon her and the spiders.

The ice wall cuts off some of her maneuvering, but it also gives her a way to avoid the firestorm. Lucas dutifully helps stabilize her magic as she wrenches control of part of the ice wall from Rocky, reshaping it upward to protect her from the fire and giving her a moment to think.

"It's just like the grenade . . . Somehow making ice and empowering a separate spell. But that makes no sense!" Fiona motions to move, and Rhonda runs without a second thought, escaping the arced ice sheet just before Rocky's fist shatters the fortification.

"Windblast!" she orders Lucas as she launches her own spell: "Black Ice!"

Rocky raises his fists in the classic boxing block as a sheet of ice forms under his feet and extends behind him. Lucas invokes the rune for Windblast, and though Rocky clearly isn't harmed by the attack, the combined efforts send him sliding along the ice. He doesn't see much way to stop himself until the end, and so launches a smaller fist of ice at the goblin.

Fiona, however, isn't just about throwing webs. She holds up a stronger web between her forelegs like a shield and catches the ice, and Rhonda sags slightly with relief for a moment before trying to get back on her mental track.

How can ice empower other spells? That's the biggest question, and she has no idea how to answer it. It's clear it *can* empower other magic, but the secret eludes her. She doesn't get much chance to think, though, as Rocky reaches the end of the ice patch. Instead of getting off it, however, he seems to get an idea. He kinetically punches behind himself, sending him shooting back down the ice toward her this time. What's more, he starts creating more ice on the floor, right toward Rhonda! All the while, the conflagration on his other fist grows further and further in intensity.

How can he create heat and cold so effortlessly?!

Rhonda's eyes widen as it suddenly clicks. In *magic*, they're two different affinities. In normal life . . . they're temperatures. A word, a *concept* seems to whisper in her ear: **thermodynamics**. Her magic doesn't add ice—it removes fire!

"Lucas, stabilize!" she shouts as she digs deeper into her magic than ever before. It's amazing what kind of motivation a charging elemental Boxer can provide.

There, his control! Just like with over the ice, she can feel him moving the fire around, draining it from the floor to make ice, and imbuing it into his fist. She needs to fight that.

At first, it seems impossible, like lifting a boulder the size of Freddie. But she can feel it . . . she's doing it! Lucas helps stabilize her gains, letting her accelerate her efforts to redirect Rocky's control.

She and Rocky are both surprised when his control suddenly shatters. The flame around his hand vanishes, as does the ice he's sliding on, and he doesn't even have the time to put his guard back up before he's forced forward by simple momentum to slam face-first into the floor.

Freddie

Freddie doesn't like the idea of leaving Rhonda to tackle Rocky on her own, but he knows why she has to. He can feel the same need to be the one to face Aranya. There's something fundamental he can learn. He knows it.

Just like he knew he needed to leave Fiona to help protect Rhonda. With her help, his friend will never lack for a shield. He trusts his friend to overcome the odds and defeat Rocky, somehow, just as she trusts him to tag Aranya and complete the challenge for them both.

He focuses his attention on the fleeing kobold, sending a silent prayer to grant him speed. Even with the potion helping him, Aranya is still *very* fast. He smiles as a gentle warmth seems to wash over his legs, and the distance starts to close.

"Jello's Grip!" she shouts, and reality seems to *thicken* somehow around Freddie, slowing his movements significantly. He struggles to get through it as he tries to apply some of the lessons of the day to capturing Aranya. Why capture her? To get his class, duh. Why can't he capture her? She has Thedeim.

That doesn't feel quite right, but he's out of the . . . whatever it was, and the chase resumes. He's gaining. With the Shield's blessing, he's faster now! Just a little . . .

"Thing's Grasp!" Ethereal orange hands suddenly grip Freddie and hold him fast, and he has to fight his anger and frustration. It's not just that she has Thedeim's help—it's like she has all of his scions, too! How can he fight that?!

He struggles against the hands, though he stops after a moment. He can almost hear Larx in his head. How *can* he fight that? He refuses to believe that any dungeon less than a year old, even one as special as Thedeim seems to be, can be mightier than the Crystal Shield. Thedeim has allies, then so does Aranya. That makes sense.

But so does he. He first wanted to join the Shield because of the simple fact he wouldn't be alone. But the Shield has allies, then so too should Freddie! The hands finally fail and fade, and Freddie stands unopposed for a moment. A word comes to Freddie, foreign and strange, but perfect for him. A concept of togetherness and support in more than just battle.

His shield glows a soft blue, and several more ethereal versions materialize.

"Phalanx Charge!"

The shields work as one, moving and hemming Aranya in as Freddie rushes forward and grabs her arm.

Chapter 25

Freddie smiles in triumph as he holds Aranya by the forearm, the challenge done. If I could, I'd be smiling with him. I don't know how I was expecting the kids to beat Aranya and Rocky, but I wasn't expecting them to split up and face the two individually! The young orc's look of victory soon turns to one of uncertainty, even as Rocky drags himself to his feet without any hint of wishing to continue the challenge.

"Did . . . Did we win?" asks the orc, and Aranya laughs.

"Of course! You've tagged me, haven't you?"

Rhonda approaches the pair and hears that, but she also looks a bit confused. "But there's no big fanfare? No flash of light, rush of power . . . You know, dramatic stuff!"

Aranya giggles at that and shakes her head. "Have you two been listening to the adventurers at the guild? Classes don't tend to be that dramatic when they unlock, though sometimes the situations are dramatic enough to make up for it. Like, say, chasing down a fleeing priestess while her guardian tries to stop you?" she says with a smirk.

Personally, I'm enjoying their look of anticlimax as they check their status, and their reactions are . . . a bit odd. They each whoop with joy as they see they have classes, but the joy quickly gives way to confusion. Aranya can see that, and so speaks up.

"Is something the matter?"

"I . . . don't know?" offers Freddie.

"Yeah, it's . . . kinda weird," confirms Rhonda.

Curious, I go ahead and spend a little mana to take a peek. While they make sense to me, it doesn't take long for me to realize why they're confused.

I poke Teemo to head down there as the kids try to explain.

"Yours is weird too, Rhonda?"

"Yeah, there's . . ." she starts, but Freddie finishes her sentence for her.

"A word you don't recognize?"

The goblin's eyes widen at that, and she nods. "You too?"

"Yeah."

Aranya butts in, her own curiosity burning. "Well, don't leave me in suspense! What did you get?"

The kids exchange looks once more before Freddie speaks up. "I'm a *Legionnaire* Paladin of the Crystal Shield."

Aranya looks confused as Rhonda speaks up. "And I'm an Ice *Sage*." At my High Priestess's continued confusion, Freddie can't help but smirk.

"Yeah, that's why we're confused. I can feel that the class is . . . *right*, but I don't know what a *legionnaire* is."

"Yeah, I know I'm a caster, but I've never heard of a *sage* before."

"That's because they're some of Thedeim's words," replies Teemo as he steps out of a shortcut, doing a darn good job of catching up on his air of mystery. Aranya looks intrigued at that, but the kids don't seem to think it's anything too unusual.

"What do they mean?" they both ask at once, and Teemo hops up on Aranya's shoulder before responding.

"Well . . . I'll start with *sage*, since it's a bit simpler. In essence, it's a person of great learning and great magic. The Boss gave me the rundown of what you kids did, and I think *sage* is a pretty good fit for you now, Rhonda. You've learned one of the fundamentals of how Thedeim's scions do what we do. He's been careful about giving out hints with this, too. Imagine what something like Neverrest would do with just what you know about ice and fire now."

Rhonda winces as she imagines that, and Teemo smiles before continuing. "Still, the Boss can't make you keep quiet, and part of truly being a *sage* is in teaching. Just be mindful of who your students are, heh."

Rhonda looks pretty relieved at that, and Teemo turns to look at Freddie. "Yours has a bit of history behind it. In ages past, there was a society of warriors . . . or perhaps *soldiers* is the more accurate word. They fought with large round shields and short spears, and were experts in tactics and positioning. They would fight side by side, presenting enemies with an impenetrable wall of shields, and would stab out of the small cracks with their spears.

"A later empire, or maybe one born from the original society? The Boss isn't the best with history, so the details are a little muddy, but the idea of soldiers with shields, working together, was improved on. Instead of large round shields, they became more rectangular and easier to hold together in formation. They still sometimes used spears, but generally preferred short swords. They were the *Legion*, which means many. A *legionnaire* is one *of* the legion."

Freddie looks a bit shocked at that, and Teemo chuckles for me. "Yeah, the Boss and I both are kinda surprised the Shield hasn't managed anything like that before. Otherwise, I'm pretty sure it'd use that word, instead of one of Thedeim's."

"Many . . . so that's why I had so many manifestations?" asks Freddie, still trying to wrap his head around getting a class that has probably not existed here before. Teemo can only shrug.

"Probably? I don't know much about classes, and the Boss mostly just has guesswork. It'd be hard to be a legion of one, though. How about you, Rhonda? Do you have any questions?"

She slowly shakes her head. "Not really. I mean, I have a *lot* of questions, but I don't know what to ask first! I think I need some time to think about it and maybe ask Master Staiven what he thinks."

Freddie nods at that. "I'd also like to talk with Head Priest Torlon about what this means, too. I can feel a closer connection to the Shield now, but . . . I think I'd like to get his advice on what to do." He shakes his head, trying to clear it, but his mood lightens a bit as he feels Fiona climb onto his back. He reaches up and pets her some before returning his focus to my Voice.

"It's never simple with you, is it, Thedeim? We first came in here for just some spell spores, and both got put on a path for our lives. We then came in just for a familiar for Rhonda, and we both left with a new friend. Now we came in here for our classes, and you've gone and given us something weird. Again."

Rhonda grins at that. "It's our own fault, though. We've known from the start you don't behave like other dungeons. We should have guessed you'd be weird with classes, too."

Aranya and Teemo smile at that before Freddie speaks up once more. "Still, we should probably head home. It's pretty late, and people will probably wonder what we've been up to. Not to mention that we need to talk about our classes."

"I'll lead you two down a shortcut to the gates," offers Teemo, hopping off Aranya's shoulders. She speaks up before he can vanish down a shortcut, though.

"I'll meet you in the Sanctum after?"

Yeah, she wants to talk about those words, and probably more. It'd probably be a good idea, too. I'm not deliberately trying to keep this stuff from her; there just hasn't been much point. Well, okay, I *am* going to try to keep my origin from her, partially because these new classes are probably going to cause enough of a wave as it is. I don't need to go talking about other dimensions and being from them, especially since it seems like not only were humans never a thing here, but they seem to be specifically not *allowed* to be a thing. I can't think of any other reason why even Teemo can't hear the word.

"That'll be fine, yeah. The Boss isn't sure how much more he can explain, but just hanging out isn't bad." Aranya smiles and seems to accept that answer, and Teemo and the kids soon make their exit.

I try to gather my thoughts, and before I know it, Aranya and Teemo are both in the Sanctum. She bows her head and gives a little prayer before relaxing on her little hammock/cot/bed thing. There's gotta be a word for that, but I don't know it.

The kobold takes her time to get comfortable and regards my core—the large orange sphere with swirling depths—seeming to try to gather her own thoughts on the matter. "New words?"

My Voice chuckles at how much just those two words imply. "Yeah, heh. There are a lot of concepts and stuff floating around in there. Personally, I think that's why his core looks more active than Neverrest's did, or Violet's does."

"Where did he hear about those soldiers with shields? I've never heard of that kind of legend."

I take a few moments to measure my words before passing them on to Teemo. "The world's a pretty big place, and Neverrest has gotten a lot of weird bits and pieces from the people he killed."

"It's a tale captured from Neverrest?"

"It's a tale from far away, and a long time ago."

She seems to think on that for a while, then gives a sly smile. "And you're sure it's not something He made up, another of His strange concepts that just needed a little nudge to make it real?"

I don't know what to say to that, and Teemo doesn't seem to have any answer, either. Aranya's smile slowly turns to a grin as she takes the silence as an answer, then nods. "They're still both good ideas, and I think will be good for the world. I won't tell anyone," she promises.

Chapter 26

With the challenge done and settled, and Aranya relaxing, I can take some time to go over what else has been happening. It's not like everything else stops just because I'm distracted with something else.

It's looking like the scythemaws are finally starting to pack it up and head home. Poe says the expeditions down there have been seeing them laying and burying the eggs. I'm pretty sure I saw a documentary once that alligators (crocodiles?) do basically the same thing. I think they tend to put the eggs closer to water, though? If I had to guess, I think gators are the better parents, but I probably shouldn't count the monsters before they hatch.

Once a nest is buried, the male seems to head back toward whichever body of water he came from, but the lady is sticking around for a bit more. Probably to make sure nobody decides to dig her eggs up. The fact that she goes and stomps a few other divots around to be fake nests also lends credence to that. I'm definitely going to try to dig some up later, but that can wait. The spots just need to be marked on the map, and we can get at them at our leisure. Well, I assume. They probably will hatch well after the maws have to head home.

While it's nice to have that distraction winding down, there's still the issue of the kids' classes, and of course, Hullbreak Harbor. I got a boatload of mana from them getting their classes, but I'm not sure what to spend it on. I'm thinking I'll just hang on to it for now, no matter how weird it feels to have a big pile of it just sitting there. But I want to have some to be able to spend on whatever surprises Hullbreak manages to spring.

Leo's FOB is looking a lot more secure, and with the sun down, I even send Coda and a few ratlings to give it the finishing touches that Leo needs. The wolf is doing a great job organizing things, too. He practically has the entire underwater dungeon mapped out now. As suspected, the enclave seems to be around his core. Leo isn't a hundred percent certain on that, but we haven't been able to find it yet, and the places it could hide are pretty few.

He's also found a shipwreck that seems to be of serious importance. It might be where the core is, but my gut says it's in the enclave. Still, the fact that the Shark Scion seems to constantly patrol around it tells me there's something important in there. The slimes are working on getting a better look inside, but even from outside, they've spotted a merman in there.

I wonder if he's an important resident like Aranya and Yvonne are for me? If he is, spying on him could be a great way to get information. Still, we have to take it slow so nobody notices the slimes slipping in.

It also looks like Hullbreak is building up his forces under the waves, so I'm going to be slowing the flow of undead now. I think I've been giving him too much, and I *really* don't want him to be able to build up his strength. Besides, if I let the stream start to slow, I can build up my standing army. The risk is that he'll attack the beachhead, though, if he senses weakness. I don't know how something like that would go, either. I don't think he'll be able to just crush the forces there, but it won't be trivial to hold it while also keeping up the charade. Hmm . . . that *does* give me an idea, though.

See, if he attacks the beachhead, he's going to expect to see at least one of my scions. I don't know exactly how much he knows about Neverrest's scions, but I should probably assume he knows about the skeleton and the lich. Even if he doesn't, mimicking them would still make it look like the kind of thing Neverrest would have.

But Grim will never pass for the Skeleton Scion, and none of my other skeletons or other scions will, either. Nobody has the kind of armor he'd have, and all my skeletons only have two arms. Tiny could pretend, but nobody is going to buy that.

But I *do* think I can have someone pretend to be the lich: Rocky. He'll need a completely different outfit, but his mastery of several affinities should make him a very believable lich. He doesn't even need to breathe, so he can easily enter the water to help fight off whatever might be needed.

It'll take a little bit to get him ready for that role, though. First, I should probably make sure he's willing to pretend and to put on some other stuff besides his boxing gear.

I take a few moments to track him down, and find he's not in the usual places I'd see him training. Instead, he's in the enchanting lab, looking like he's having a talk with Thing. Curious, I poke Teemo to go check it out, and my Voice is happy to go look.

When Teemo exits a shortcut in the lab, Rocky seems to stiffen slightly.

Teemo raises an eyebrow at that. "You okay, Rocky?"

He shifts slightly toward a defensive stance for a few moments before he lets his arms drop and his head hang a bit. He doesn't seem to have replied, though, and soon, Thing signs some.

Teemo nods as my enchanter finishes. "Ah, okay. Thing says Rocky is trying to figure out how to fix the hole in his fundamentals."

Uh . . . what? He's far and away the scion that's been doing the best at expanding his affinities.

"Yeah, but he says that's just fancy moves. Rhonda was able to, as he put it, 'break his stance' with the magic and completely throw him off-balance. So he's asking Thing to help him with that," explains Teemo. Rocky slowly stands up straight, maybe expecting to be told to stop bothering Thing, but I'm not going to shoot down his attempts to improve his style.

How goes the work on the pickups? I ask, and Teemo dutifully repeats, then dutifully translates. "He says he's had a breakthrough. The coils were a bit too uniform, and the sound waves really were canceling each other out. He's tuning them to be better, but he says they're actually working now!"

Awesome! Alright, Rocky, you can help Thing with his stuff in here and get some better work on your magic fundamentals. That actually plays into something else I'd like you to do, too.

Teemo relays the message, and Rocky looks confused. My Voice just chuckles at his reply.

"He says, 'Whatcha need, Coach?'"

I'm going to need you to be able to pretend to be a lich. You'll have to be ready to toss off the gloves and toss on a robe, in case Hullbreak actually attacks the beachhead.

Rocky looks at his gloves like he's forgotten he has hands in there, then looks to Teemo and gives a grunt.

Teemo smiles as he speaks. "He wants to know if he can keep the mouthguard."

Hah! That shouldn't be a problem. Oh, I'll need Thing to make him some fancy enchanted stuff, too, to help sell the trick. It'll probably help Rocky with solidifying his control, too, if he helps.

They both seem to like that idea, and Thing helps Rocky get his gloves off for the first time in . . . ever? It doesn't seem like his hands are any worse for having been in boxing gloves for so long, but it's difficult to tell with a zombie. He flexes his fingers for a few moments before he does a few practice jabs, and I wonder if this is like him taking his limiters off . . . or maybe removing the training wheels?

While he gets used to bare air on his rotten skin, Thing seems curious about the gloves themselves. He gives them a few testing pokes before he struggles to crawl into one! I watch as he manages to sit back on his wrist, fully encased in the thick glove. He hops a couple times before falling off the table. He hits the floor with a muffled *plap*, and I can only assume he can't see while in it. Probably not surprising, but . . . how *does* he see?

He quickly wriggles himself out of the glove and telekinetically tosses it against a wall, much to the amusement of Rocky, Teemo, and myself. Rocky might be willing to fake being a lich, but I don't think Thing will be signing up to pretend to be a boxer anytime soon.

Chapter 27

Staiven

The aged ratkin steals a few seconds as he and Rhonda work to simply observe his apprentice. While he couldn't be more proud of her for gaining her class, they still have a business to run. These healing potions won't brew themselves, after all. She came in last night, looking equal parts exhausted and elated, and barely managed to say she got her class before stumbling off to her bed.

He hasn't been able to get much else out of her about it yet, but working together can be a great opportunity to chat, at least once the mixture is set to simmer. "So . . . your class, Rhonda?"

The young goblin's eyes brighten as she's reminded she hasn't had much chance to explain just what happened. "Yes! Freddie and I both got our classes! We asked Thedeim to help, and he set three challenges for us!"

Staiven nods and starts preparing ingredients for the Lightning Resist potions, and Rhonda cleans the various dirty glassware as she continues to talk. "First, we had to capture Vernew, one of the ruling triumvirate of the Spiderkin Enclave! Even more, she had Queen's help!"

"Oh, the Alchemist scion? I'd wager it was a difficult challenge to beat, then."

Rhonda giggles. "It was, but we also got pretty lucky. Vernew didn't take us as seriously as she should have. We only barely won, though, by catching her in a web trap . . . and catching ourselves, too. Tiny helped us out of the web, and Teemo told us we won. Queen wanted to show off a weird alchemical thing she created to help Vernew, but she never got a chance before we won. So they demonstrated it!"

Staiven waits a few seconds for her to say what it was, but a glance shows she's trying to get him to ask instead of just telling it herself. He smirks and decides to give her the satisfaction. It's part of her story about gaining her class, so she deserves to tell it how she wants.

"Well, what was it?" he asks, honestly curious what Queen came up with. From what he's seen of her work, she's got a lot of interesting ideas, like that water-breathing potion she came up with.

"It was a two-part reaction! First, it would spread a slick of ice and build up energy above the center of it. Then it'd release all that energy in a loud and bright explosion! But not in like a fireball, more like a thunderclap—more disorienting than damaging! I've been calling it a Frostbang."

"Hmm . . ." says the ratkin as he considers what a flask like that would require. "That's an odd combination of affinities. How large was the flask to be able to contain all that mana?"

"That's the best part! It was a normal size!"

Staiven looks at her like he doesn't believe her, and she just smiles wider. "Right?! I kinda know part of how it was done, too! That's how I got my class, but I'm getting ahead of myself."

He considers telling her to explain, but holds himself back. She'll get there eventually. "So, what was the second challenge?"

"It was a lot less strenuous than the first, at least physically. I had to help Thing with an enchanting array that would turn Lightning into Thunder mana for a weird instrument Thedeim is working on. I think it's some kind of lute or something? It uses plucked strings, at least. But no matter what we tried, it didn't make different notes! I was pretty sure it was beyond me, and I said so, but something about what I said seemed to make Thing realize something incredible!"

"What'd you say?"

"I don't remember . . . Something about how he was working with advanced stuff, kinda like Queen's Frostbang. All I knew is one second, he was working on the problem, and the next, he was clearing the workbench as fast as he could! And then, he created a *Lifedrinking* array!"

Staiven pauses in his work to stare at her. "What?!"

"Yeah! I didn't know what was happening until he motioned me forward to examine it, and I realized what it was! And then he *countered* it! He didn't collapse it—he just negated it!"

The ratkin puts down his tools to stare, and Rhonda tries to explain, now that she has her mentor's full, undivided attention. "I don't know *how*, but he did something . . . I dunno? I could feel it was somehow related to thunder or lightning, but it made no sense, like using Earth mana in a Windblade rune. Whatever he did, though, the Lifedrinking just winked out of existence."

Staiven's gaze grows distant as he tries to work through what Rhonda could have seen, but his imagination fails him. Using an array meant for one mana type but channeling a different one? It should just be a waste of effort! But he doesn't doubt Rhonda's tale. She has a natural eye for a lot of this, even if she doesn't know the technical details just yet. He shakes his head and focuses on her once more.

"I take it that counted for clearing that challenge?" She nods. "So what was the third one?"

"To get past Rocky and tag Aranya!" she exclaims with excitement.

"You two whittled down the Zombie Scion before chasing her, then?"

"Nope! I faced Rocky while Freddie went to go tag Aranya!"

He looks incredulous, and Rhonda just giggles again.

"I mean, I had Lucas and Fiona to help, too. We tricked Rocky with a team-up attack that let Freddie get past him, and then I got to see some of his magic close-up . . . A bit closer than I'd have really wanted," she admits, and Staiven is just glad she doesn't seem to be hurt.

"How did you beat him?" he asks, unable to fathom how his little apprentice could best that beast of a Zombie Scion.

"I figured out how he does his magic, then broke his control over it! He was kinda in the middle of an attack with it, and face-planted pretty hard when his control broke. That's how I got my class!"

Staiven can't help but give his apprentice a small smirk. "So you're a boxer now?"

She giggles and shakes her head. "No, I'm an Ice Sage!"

He looks confused. "An ice what?"

"A sage! I was confused at first, too, but Teemo said it's one of Thedeim's words for someone with a lot of knowledge and magic, kinda like a teacher, student, and mage all rolled into one." She practically vibrates with excitement at being able to talk about her new class, but Staiven is practically reeling from what she's said.

"How . . . ?"

"How did I get my class? Because of how I realized what Rocky is doing! Here, look!" She holds her hands out, forming a small ball of ice and a small ball of fire, but Staiven can feel she's hardly expended any of her mana to do it. "Rocky isn't just making both ice and fire! They're *temperatures*! He takes the heat out of one spot to make ice, and puts it into a different spot to make fire! He's just moving the fire around!"

Staiven sits down heavily on his stool, and Rhonda's excitement turns to concern. She lets the two opposing elemental balls equalize as she rushes over. "Master? Are you alright?"

"I'm . . ." He takes a few moments to try to collect himself. Physically, he's as fine as ever, but Rhonda's story seems impossible in so many ways. And yet, he saw her manipulate ice and fire like they're the same affinity! But it makes no sense.

At least there's an easy way to tell if she's telling the truth, or if she's somehow wrong about all this.

"May I scry your class?" he asks, and she nods without hesitation. It's hardly any effort for him to create a scrying enchantment on a handy lens, and he almost drops it at what he sees. She's an Ice Sage, and she's picked up the Fire affinity now. She doesn't have the Arcane affinity he would have expected, but if she's right about what she's learned, it might be a bit of a moot point. While Arcane can mimic a lot of other affinities, it's not especially powerful. If she tried to do that fire-and-ice trick using Arcane mana, it would have cost a lot more.

But how did she get a class he's never heard of before? It's apparently because of Thedeim, which probably shouldn't be surprising, but it *is* concerning. A young dungeon like that has concepts powerful enough to create new classes?

He tries to keep his hand from shaking as he sets the lens down.

"Did Freddie get a new class, too?"

Rhonda still looks concerned but answers him. "Yeah. He's a Legionnaire Paladin of the Crystal Shield."

Another strange word, another new concept, another new class. He's going to need to talk to Torlon later, and possibly Inspector Tarl . . . and *certainly* Thedeim. Rhonda didn't say it was her own word, but one of Thedeim's. There is a lot more going on in that dungeon than it's been letting on.

Before his thoughts can spiral too much further, wondering what Fourdock has gotten into, the distinctive scent of a potion on the verge of being ruined reaches his nose. Existential crises later. Potions now!

"Kill the fire and pull the heat out of the batch, Rhonda! Put your class to use saving our work!"

Chapter 28

Freddie

On a quiet night, a basket is left on the doorstep of the orphanage. The larger orc considers if this is the right thing to do . . . and has to conclude it is. The wrecked and raided caravan he found the baby in can't care for it, and he has no experience with trying to raise a child. Delving is too dangerous a task for a serious parent. The little bundle in the basket looks at him with a smile, tempting him to try it anyway . . . But no, this is what will be best for the baby orc.

He knocks and vanishes into the night.

"Freddie!" snaps the teacher, and he jerks to attention at his desk. It's not that he's *bad* in school; it's just that some of the teachers are so *boring*!

"Uh . . . yes, ma'am?" he tries, having completely lost track of what she was trying to teach. She glares at him until a quiet voice speaks up from the next desk over.

"Um . . . t-they're principalities," manages the goblin sitting there. The teacher squints at her, clearly weighing if she should punish her for speaking out of turn, or reward her for the correct answer. She settles on giving Freddie one more glance, making it clear that the goblin girl just saved him, before standing and resuming the lecture.

As she returns to the chalkboard, he gives his rescuer a wide smile, and she returns it with a more timid one. He should hang out with her at lunch.

Freddie wanders around, catching bugs, while Rhonda reads a little magic pamphlet from the library. While an actual teacher would be better for her, it's not like she can afford it. So the two just spend some time in the alley, relaxing after their lessons in their own way.

"So, do you know what affinity you have yet?" he asks as he pokes a large beetle with a stick. It raises its rear at him, so he leaves it alone for a few seconds, letting it return to a normal posture before he pokes it again. His friend shakes her head.

"Not yet, I'm getting close, though . . . I think. I'm not Earth, Air, or Water. I tried Fire, and that felt really wrong, so I'm gonna try Ice next."

"Ice would be pretty cool. It'd make shoveling the walk in winter a lot easier," replies the young orc as he flips the beetle over and watches its legs wiggle in the air to try to right itself. Rhonda absently hums at that, her focus more on the spell than her friend.

Freddie wishes they had been able to find anything interesting in the alley today. They're behind Old Staiven's shop, and sometimes, he'll throw out something cool, but today was a bust.

He's pulled from his longing by the sound of crackling, happy laughter. He looks to see his friend has managed to freeze a small puddle of water!

"Ice affinity!" she shouts in happiness, and Freddie can only be happy for his friend.

The two, once again, relax behind Old Staiven's shop after lessons, though now Rhonda can make a little ball of ice for them to toss back and forth. Their enjoyable waste of time is interrupted by the angry voice of the proprietor, though it's not aimed at them.

"Spell spore! Always out of spell spore! Blasted Neverrest never had any to begin with, Hullbreak has gone mad, and the Southwood is a fortnight trip at the least!"

The two kids exchange a look as the aged ratkin rants to himself. He's been getting more upset recently with the reduced supply, and probably also the reduced demand.

". . . And the ones who *do* bring me spell spore ruin half the harvest from not knowing how to do it! Does nobody know how to properly handle herbs anymore?! I've got plenty of books they could look into! Why, if they had an inkling of magic, I'd even apprentice them, just to have someone who could get me enough spell spores to brew something more than once a week!"

Freddie sees that glimmer of hope in his friend's eye, and just as quickly, he sees it smolder out. Where would they even get some spell spore? It's not like there are any dungeons close by that they could try to delve.

Freddie looks at the Church of the Crystal Shield from down the street, trying to build up his courage. Rhonda is talking to Old Staiven on her own, so he can talk to them on his own, right? He wishes he had paid a bit more attention in school when it came to talking about the various gods to follow. With how out of the way Fourdock is, though, it's not like he has a whole lot of options to choose from.

He does his best to steel his resolve, then starts walking. They're not just the one he's interested in because he doesn't know what else to do. He could always try to join the rangers or the guard or something. No, he *wants* to be a paladin. He wants to help people and keep them safe. Guards and rangers protect people, too, but the idea of always having help just feels right. And paladins look cooler, too.

As he gets closer, he catches the eye of an older priest sweeping the steps, and the elder wolfkin smiles at him. "Hello, young one. What brings you here today, with such fire in your eyes?"

Freddie pauses at that before answering honestly. "I wanna be a paladin."

Instead of laughing the declaration off, the priest leans on his broom and looks the young orc over from head to toe. "Hmm . . . Maybe."

"Maybe?"

"It's not the easiest path, but if it's the one you want to walk, I'll not be the one to stand in your way. Come, let's talk to the Head Priest. He can explain it to you better than I." With that, he opens the door for the both of them.

Freddie does his best to keep his nerves in check as the wolfkin leads him through the church. It's made a bit easier by the curious and friendly looks of the various people going about their business. Some are praying, some cleaning. There even seems to be a small group quietly chatting and joking.

He's lead through a door, down a hall, through another door, up some stairs, down some stairs, through a kitchen (where the cook passes him a sweet roll with a wink), until the wolfkin stops before one last door and knocks.

"Head Priest? I have a potential paladin initiate."

After a few moments, a replay comes through the door. Freddie can't quite make it out, but his guide seems to have no trouble. He turns to the young orc and steps aside from the door.

"Just be honest with him, and you should do just fine," he says before leaving. Freddie takes a deep breath and heads inside, where he finds a gnome sitting at a desk, a battered crystalline shield hanging on the wall behind him.

The gnome smiles and motions at a seat. "Ah, you're the new aspirant? A bit younger than most."

"Uh . . . is that a problem?" asks Freddie, stopping before getting into the seat.

The gnome shakes his head and motions for him to continue his intention to sit down. "It's unusual, but not a problem. What's your name?"

"Freddie?"

He smiles. "Hello, Freddie, I'm Torlon. Why would you like to be a paladin?"

The young orc fidgets, uncertain if he should call the gnome just by his name or not. "Well . . . I'm an orphan, and my friend is getting apprenticed to Old Staiven, so I figured I should try to get some training, too."

Torlon nods at that. "An early start can make things much easier. But why a paladin? The guards always have need of new recruits, and the rangers are likewise always looking for new blood."

"Because I wanna help people, and that's what paladins do, right? Help people, beat up bad guys, and look cool doing it?"

The gnome laughs at that with a wide smile, glancing behind himself at the shield on the wall. "That *is* the rough list of duties in order, heh. So why the Crystal Shield?"

"Because what's better at protecting people than a shield?" he replies honestly.

Torlon smiles like a proud grandparent. "Ah, leave it to the youth to cut so cleanly to the heart of a solution. Have you done any training or studying?" he asks, needing to gauge how far along the young orc is already.

"Rhonda and I delved the new dungeon! We got some spell spores so she could get apprenticed!" he replies with excitement, and the gnome looks surprised at that.

"The *new* dungeon?"

"Yeah! It's in that old manor in the center of town! I . . . uh . . ." He calms quickly, uncertain if he should admit anything else, but he's already in pretty deep. ". . . I don't think it's cleared for general delving just yet, but we were careful! And it's not very strong yet!"

"That's fine, Freddie. Just be careful. Fourdock has had poor luck with dungeons."

"I know, but this one is really cool!"

Torlon chuckles and brings the topic back to the original target. "I don't see any reason why you can't train to be a paladin, Freddie. You've been honest with me, and I can feel your determination. I'll get you a copy of our scripture so you can get more familiar with the specifics of what the Crystal Shield asks of its followers. Once you've read it, you can decide if you want to swear the acolyte oath and truly start on your chosen path."

"Does that mean you're gonna adopt me?"

"In the technical, legal term? No. You'll become a ward of the church, rather than of the kingdom," he says with a serious face before it cracks into a more familial smile. "In almost every other sense of the word, however . . . yes. We are a family, Freddie. Your brothers and sisters in the Shield will be here to help you as they can, even if you decide you don't want to swear the oaths. Protecting and helping people very rarely actually involves deflecting physical blows, and the Shield asks us to protect as many as we can."

* * *

Freddie sits on his bed in his small room at the church, staring at the large spider he got from the dungeon. What's he supposed to do with a big spider?! *Rhonda* was the one who wanted a spider, not him! If he didn't know better, he'd say the dungeon was messing with him on purpose!

As he grumbles, the spider wanders the small room, and he can feel curiosity through their bond. At first, he tried to ignore the bond entirely, hoping he could somehow release the spider, but a visit to the rangers squashed that hope quickly. He'll only be rid of her once she dies, and he can't bring himself to consider that thought for more than a few moments.

No matter how creepy she looks, he can feel her trust for him through the bond, and the idea of betraying that kind of trust makes him want to scrub himself in the river. He watches her poke at the shutters to his small window for a few moments, the arachnid trying to figure out how it works, before he turns to his studies.

Unlike in school, he actually finds the scriptures and history of the Shield to be interesting.

"I will be the protection for those without it, a barrier to those who would do harm, and an inspiration so as to bring more to the aegis of the Shield," swears the young orc, his head down. It's only the most basic of the paladin oaths, but also the foundation on which the others build.

He can feel a soft warmth inside him as the Shield accepts his promise and gifts him a tiny fraction of Its power.

"Rise, Paladin Acolyte Freddie. The Shield has heard your oath and found it to be true." Head Priest Torlon smiles as the atmosphere lightens, the ceremony complete. "How do you feel?"

"I feel . . . I don't know," he admits, not knowing how to explain the feeling, and Torlon gives a knowing nod.

"Well, if you're feeling up to it, I have your first paladin duty," says the gnome, and Freddie jumps to his feet. "I'll take that as you being ready, heh. With Neverrest gone, the cemetery needs to be blessed. Ordinarily, this would be a task for a more experienced and fully-fledged paladin, but I think the new dungeon has proven itself to be trustworthy. I'd like you to escort the Head Acolyte and some other priests to the cemetery, and see that those laid to rest there *stay* at rest."

Chapter 29

Torlon

Last night was a strange experience for the Head Priest. He might not have as close of a connection to the Shield as the High Priest in the Citadel, but he is the closest of anyone in Fourdock. So it came as a surprise to him that he could feel someone with a strong connection even before they entered the church.

It was even more of a surprise to see it was Freddie! He knew the lad had the potential to be a great paladin, but he didn't expect the lad to vanish for the day and come back with his class!

Perhaps most surprising of all was the vision he received from the Shield as he slept. Dream visions were always difficult to interpret. Dreams can be so ephemeral, and visions in general are often so vague, so combining the two can be a metaphorical nightmare, no matter how pleasant they are.

He saw snippets of Freddie's past, then a singular, vaguer vision of Freddie leading and inspiring a whole new generation of paladins, and felt the need to help the young orc in sharing what he'd learned. Upon awakening, he can't recall much more detail than that, but he trusts the Shield has given him at least the gist of what it wants: to guide and help Freddie.

He can't help but smirk to himself as he gets out of bed, imagining himself lamenting in all the most extreme ways over the most difficult task of something he'd do without even needing to be asked. He genuinely likes Freddie, and so is glad to take up such a "burden," and more genuinely happy with the Shield for being given something he is confident in doing.

It doesn't take him long to do his morning routine and head to the kitchen, hoping to catch Freddie there and maybe share a meal together. He quickly finds the young lad at a table having some simple porridge with some dried fruits and nuts, and even spots the spider, Fiona, not far away, munching on a rat. He waves at Freddie, and the young orc smiles and waves back. Torlon gets himself a similar bowl for his own meal and sits across from the new paladin.

"I see you've gotten your class," he says with a smile, and Freddie nods with excitement.

"So did Rhonda!"

"Oh? What did you two get up to, then? Not a lot of people get their classes together," Torlon says simply before digging into his breakfast. Freddie takes the cue to tell the story, and is all too happy to do so.

"So, I went and visited Rhonda, and we decided to go to Thedeim and see if he could help us with our classes. We both knew we were missing something, and you and Old Staiven were being kinda deliberate in not telling us, so we thought he might be able to do something."

"And it looks like he did, lad. A big part of a class is in figuring it out yourself, and challenging Thedeim's denizens is a good way to do just that."

Freddie nods. "Yeah, but we didn't just go and fight stuff! We actually asked him to help, and he gave us three challenges to complete!"

Torlon looks a bit surprised at that. "Challenges? Like when Thedeim asked me to go loot Tiny's chest?"

"Kinda? He actually got some of his dwellers to help, and even Miss Aranya! And some of the scions, too!"

". . . That sounds like quite the challenge . . . *challenges*, rather. What did you do?"

"Well, first, we had to capture the huntsmistress of the spiderkin, Vernew, and she even had Queen's help!"

"That's . . . the bee?"

Freddie laughs and shakes his head. "Nah, that's Honey. Queen is the ant and Alchemist. So we had to capture Vernew without harming Queen. Rhonda made us some potions while I tried to think of a good place to try to catch her, and I remembered hearing her talking with Larx about Tiny. I figured she might try to hide in and around his maze, so we got on top and convinced Tiny to distract her if she showed up.

"And then she did! She was talking to him, and we attacked, trying to get her in one of Fiona's webs with Rhonda's help, but she dodged and threw a smoke bomb or something. We decided to try to entangle her in the webbing Tiny has on top of the maze, and when she leaped at us, we struck!"

Freddie looks a little embarrassed. "It, uh . . . it worked, but we got tangled up, too. Me, Rhonda, Lucas, Fiona, and Vernew: all stuck in a huge ball of Tiny's webbing, just kinda hanging there and slowly turning."

Torlon does his best not to make a mess while laughing, easily able to imagine all of them stuck together like that. After a few seconds to calm himself—at least enough that he won't interrupt himself with another laugh—he manages a reply. "I take it that counted, then, since you have your class?"

"Yeah, it counted. Heh, I even asked, and Vernew said she counted it. And . . . I think that was one of the first things I learned about, and was kind of a theme for at least my part of the challenges."

"Oh?" asks the gnome, wanting to hear what wisdom Freddie had gained yesterday.

"I only had a vague idea of what it was, until the second challenge. I had to talk with Larx."

Torlon quirks an eyebrow at that, confused. "That doesn't sound like a challenge. You often go and talk with him when you can spare some time between your training and delving."

Freddie inhales deeply. "It definitely was a challenge. He wanted me to explain why the consecration at the cemetery went like it did."

Torlon nods in understanding at that. "Ah, that makes more sense. It was a bit of a delicate situation."

"Yeah, but he also asked me about the former Head Acolyte, too, and how actions have more meaning than words. Vernew worships Thedeim, but she failed to keep from getting captured by us, even though he specifically asked her to do that. And the acolyte failed to consecrate the cemetery, even though the Shield wanted it. But they're not just cast out for failing. They get more chances. Even if punishments have to happen, they can do better if they keep trying. It's kinda like the shield you keep on your wall. It has chips and dings, but it's still going to protect. It didn't break at the first problem."

Torlon nods along as Freddie talks. The lad is jumping around a bit in his explanation, but it's all core to the entire point of the Crystal Shield and what it wants of its followers.

"And then, for the last challenge, we had to face Rocky and Aranya in the arena!"

Torlon's brow furrows at that. "Rocky is the Zombie Scion with far more magic than usual, right?" Freddie nods, and Torlon continues. "So you faced off against the zombie while Rhonda went after Aranya?"

Freddie sheepishly shakes his head. "No, actually. She faced Rocky, and I went after Aranya. Rhonda said she needed to face him herself, though I was at least able to have Fiona help her. I was still pretty nervous about her fighting him, but she was pretty sure it had to be done. And I had the same feeling with having to face Aranya."

"Really? Why?"

Freddie shrugs. "I dunno? Something about her connection with Thedeim . . . I felt like I could learn something from it. And I kinda did, too."

Freddie continues before Torlon can even prompt him, the gnome forgetting his porridge as he listens. "So, a lot of her magic has her calling on aspects of

Thedeim and his scions. She called on Poe's wings to let her jump into the arena without hurting herself . . . and maybe to give her some extra speed. But with the Shield's help, I was able to outpace her, just barely. But whenever I'd get too close, she'd call on one of those aspects to slow or stop me, and she'd get away!

"It was pretty frustrating, because it felt like I wasn't just facing her or Thedeim, but all of Thedeim's scions, too! It hardly seemed fair she could call on so much help, but then I remembered why I wanted to become a paladin in the first place: so I wouldn't have to face stuff alone. I mean, I'm not exactly lonely, but having the help of you and everyone has been amazing for the hard times, you know?"

Torlon smiles at that and nods, and Freddie soon continues.

"So I thought, if she can call on help, so can I. And I was able to call a bunch of Shields to help corner her and grab her to win. I called it Phalanx Charge, and I just somehow knew it was a formation of a lot of shields."

Torlon's eyes shoot open at that, but Freddie continues before he can ask any questions. "And I got my class, too. I'm a Legionnaire Paladin of the Crystal Shield, a paladin of many. It's one of Thedeim's words, I guess? I'm still getting used to it, but . . . Well, let me show you."

With that, Freddie closes his eyes for a moment to focus, and several ephemeral manifestations of the Shield appear around him. Even more interesting, Torlon sees even Fiona move into a place in the small formation with her own shield, before they fade away and Freddie breathes heavily from the effort.

As Freddie catches his breath, Torlon's mind races at what he just saw. Every paladin he's had the chance to meet could only imbue their personal shield. While it would often grow in size to be an impenetrable barrier, it was still only one shield. With something like this . . . He doesn't even know what the potential power for good it could hold! So many possibilities, especially if Freddie can teach his way of thinking to other prospective paladins.

As Freddie returns his focus to his breakfast, the effort seeming to have made him hungry, Torlon can only offer a quick prayer for forgiveness for thinking guiding Freddie properly would be a simple task. He is no less resolved to do it, though, both for the Shield and for Freddie himself. That kind of power requires a firm will and resolve to not misuse. Thankfully, Freddie isn't the type to let something like that go to his head.

Chapter 30

With the scythemaws pretty much done with their fun, and the surprise fun of helping Rhonda and Freddie getting their classes finished, I return my attention to the problem of Hullbreak Harbor. I'm still trying to get more info and set up a few safeguards, but I think I'm getting close to needing to make a move.

I think. Maybe? I was never terrible at strategy games, but I also would tend to just turtle up until I had enough troops to steamroll. But steamrolling Hullbreak is pretty much the last thing I want to do. I think he can be theoretically reasoned with if his dwellers are safe. If they get hurt, though . . . I think it'll get ugly all around.

I just need to make sure I strike the right balance between preparing and not giving Hullbreak the time to prepare too much on his side. From the reports from Leo, I think he's going to try to strike the beachhead soon. I just wish I knew how soon "soon" is. He's started sending out expeditions, so he's sure to find the beachhead eventually.

So now, I need to make sure I have some contingencies for if he attacks. I would say "when," but there's no guarantee. He could find the beachhead and try to negotiate. I mean . . . I wouldn't put money on it, but it could happen.

Anyway, contingencies. First, who can I actually try to bring in to fight? Pretty much all my denizens who could work underwater are already doing stuff: the skeletons are doing their thing, the slimes and rockslides are being sneaky. Despite Queen's best efforts, I don't think she's going to manage a Water-affinity potion before this fight pops off, so I need to plan with what I have.

While Rocky should be a good plan A for dealing with an attack, I need to have a solid plan B in case the attack is too much for him to overcome. In which case . . . I think the subtle route will have to be tossed out the window. At least that will let me bring in some of my other scions. Not the best silver lining, but if I have to take the kid gloves off, it'll be time to lay down the law.

Jello will probably be very good underwater. While she still won't be very fast, the little bit of water testing we did a while ago showed she's not much slower in the water, either, so she'll be at her full strength. Probably even stronger, actually, considering how she practically vanishes when submerged.

Grim has a lot of potential, but I get the feeling he won't want to go on the offensive. He'd be an absolute nightmare on a battlefield, but that's just not his temperament. I might be able to get him to defend the beachhead while the others attack, but I'm inclined to not even try to push him for this. Besides, after seeing him stop that scythemaw like flipping a switch, I worry it could send the wrong message if he starts just ending whatever Hullbreak sends at him. Gotta wield destructive potential carefully if you don't want to have to keep using it.

Slash would probably do well underwater, but his involvement will depend on if we can get the axe finished in time. With the hurdle of actually making the sound finally cleared, we're basically just down to actually producing it now. The ratkin and spiderkin have settled on a good alloy for the head, and while it's not going to be the shiny stainless steel that I think would be perfect, it's going to be a proper weapons-quality steel, so I can't really complain. I don't even know if stainless steel would be good for an axe. Pretty sure it's what scalpels are made of, but there's a big difference between that and an axe. Besides, I still haven't managed to make stainless steel anyway.

The enclaves are now able to work on the top hat, too, with the aranea more than happy to weave the hat itself, and the ratkin working with Thing to get the magical Tesla amplifiers installed. Slash has been by to look at the work, but he's been staying out of it for the most part. He knows how to create music, not how to make an electric guitar. He *does* actually know how to compose music, too. He finally got the title of Bard from playing on the lute that I still don't know how he got. He's plucked out a few bars from a couple songs he must have overheard through the bond with me, but he hasn't tried to string them into a true song yet. I think it's because they're not designed for a lute. But there are also other songs he's picked up from the delvers, and even some of the dwellers in the enclaves.

Let me see, what other scions might be able to fight . . . Well, Poe can *kind* of fight. Which is to say he can *definitely* fight, but not too much underwater. He could deal with the gull spawner, but I don't think it's going to actually make much difference for what's happening under the waves.

Fluffles might be able to, but unless he pulls a Water affinity out of his serpentine behind, he's going to have trouble moving well. Which really only means I could bring Jello and maybe Slash to the party. The biggest problem with them being my emergency plan is that neither of them is especially quick. It's about half a day's walk to the beachhead from home. It's not a big deal for the skeletons, since they can just walk and don't have to be there in any real hurry. But if I need an emergency response, I need to get there in minutes, preferably seconds, not hours.

I do have an idea for that, though. *Hey, Teemo, you busy?*

My Voice is currently lounging on Yvonne's lap in the Sanctum, my lovely birb taking a chance to relax after having spent much of the last few days on paperwork. Taxes and inspections and such for the guild, as she explained it. Aranya is just glad she doesn't actually have anything new to report, seeing as she's only just registered as an adventurer recently.

I can see Teemo's ears twitch when I talk to him, and I can practically see him weighing if he wants to respond. I'm pretty sure he can sense my amusement at him shirking his duty because he soon sighs and speaks up.

"Nah, I'm not busy, Boss. Kinda deliberately not busy, even," he says. Yvonne smiles at his snark.

"Thedeim needs something?"

Yeah, I'd like you to make a new shortcut, please. I'm sure you could hear me plotting and thinking, and I want to be able to respond quickly if Hullbreak attacks the beachhead.

Teemo wrinkles his nose. "I thought you didn't want a shortcut from the inside to outside?"

I don't, but I have an idea for where to put it. Inside the tree line, past the cemetery wall for one end, and inside the tree line near the shore for the other end. You should be able to hide the entrances with more mundane means, and even if Hullbreak somehow finds it, we'll already know everything about it. If he tries to use it to counterattack, ambushing his forces would be a cakewalk.

Teemo thinks on that for a few seconds as Yvonne rubs his head, and he soon nods.

"That should work, Boss. How big do you need it?"

I just need enough for Jello and Slash. If you can make it fit an army, that'd be nice, but I really only need it to be able to handle them. It'll be a bit of a last resort to use, since it'll give away that I'm not Neverrest, but I'd rather have it and not need it, than need it and not have it.

"Yeah, that shouldn't be a problem, then."

"What are you going to be doing?" asks Yvonne, sitting up a bit more so she can focus better.

"The Boss wants an emergency shortcut through the woods to the beachhead, in case Hullbreak attacks there."

Yvonne's eyes light up. "Ah, I had forgotten you were making moves against the water dungeon! Is there anything we can do to help?"

Teemo shrugs. "I mean, I wouldn't mind some company outside. Ragnar and Aelara can see what we're up to, right, Boss?"

Yeah, that should be fine.

"Boss says you all can take a look. He's clever, and he talks like he's vaguely familiar with stuff like this, but your party has more experience with fighting and such. An extra perspective would be nice to have on everything. Think they'll be up for it?"

The hawkwoman nods at that. "Ragnar would love to give his advice on larger-scale battles. I don't know if he was ever involved in any himself, but he at least has a lot of historical knowledge of dwarven battles. If nothing else, I'm sure he'll have advice for defending the beachhead."

"Cool. Is tomorrow fine for working on that?"

I tell him that's fine, and Yvonne says that should be enough time for her to let the group know. They'll ask if Aranya wants to come once she gets back from chatting with Larx and Vernew.

Hmm . . . I wonder if Folarn might want to take a look, also.

I let Teemo know to check with her sometime, too. No rush, though.

He smiles and relaxes back into Yvonne's lap, enjoying her company. From her smile as she resumes idly petting him as she reads, she's enjoying his company, too.

Chapter 31

Around sunrise, Yvonne, Teemo, and Aranya go to meet up with Aelara and Ragnar to take a look at the forest and the planned shortcut, so I take a chance to talk with the dwarf through Teemo and see what he thinks about making a move soon.

It takes Teemo most of the walk out to the tree line to explain the basics of the situation, and the dwarf looks contemplative as he takes it all in.

"I dinnae envy ya for this one, but I'd try t' get more info b'fore attackin'. Some sieges can be avoided by a quick attack, but more just fail and lead t' a longer fight."

Teemo chuckles at my reply. "The Boss says that's the feeling he's getting from Leo, too. He's just getting antsy about waiting, I think."

Ragnar nods. "Aye, he's still young an' new t' this. Patience is th' key to most wars, lad."

I grumble to myself for a few seconds before taking a metaphorical deep breath. Crafting an attack plan is just like crafting anything else: it takes a lot longer than most people think. And it will take even longer if the inexperienced keep second-guessing the ones who know more about it. It feels kinda weird that Leo would know more about this kind of thing, but Ragnar taking his side helps reinforce that I just don't know that much about waging war . . . which this kinda is. It's not the grandest war, but it's definitely more than just a big fight.

Teemo smiles as he hears me coming to terms with the advice. "I think he knew that, but it's good to hear it out loud from someone else. Makes it harder to make excuses, heh."

Gee, thanks, Teemo.

"Always got your back, Boss," he replies with a grin, deliberately ignoring my sarcasm. I chuckle and try to focus on the delvers, letting Teemo and the party work without me hovering. A watched pot never boils, and me staring through

Leo's eyes won't make the reports come in any faster. I'll just have to trust him to let me know if anything new develops, or if he gets any ideas about potential gaps in the defenses.

Actually, checking in on Violet wouldn't be a bad way to pass the time. I'd need Teemo to actually *talk* with her, but some bare basics can still be done with just the protégée bond. I've only done the basics of checking in on her since the scythemaws showed up, mostly just making sure she's doing alright and isn't in any trouble with them.

She's got a nice stash of mana now, even with the upgrades I can see to her two scions. I'm not sure if she's named them or not, but they've both made good progress. Her centipede is a bit bigger than when he first spawned, but I don't get the feeling he'll be rivaling Tiny for size. Something about it strikes me more as a mage of some kind, rather than a big brute. Still, it's a Guardian now, so maybe I'm wrong? Or maybe Guardians have a lot of room for their own growth.

The Mushroom Scion is the kind of weird I think the Office of Dungeon Affairs would expect me to get up to. I wouldn't have expected something without legs to be so knowledgeable about what's going on outside Violet's borders. I probably should have, though. Fungus can cover *huge* areas. Something like square miles, if I'm remembering some random thing I read on the internet right. Because everything on the internet is true, and my memory is ironclad.

Either way, I can feel how far he's spread, and where. It looks like he's growing more toward the aquifer lakes than into the hunting tunnels, which suggests to me which way Violet might want to expand next. I poke the bond to see if she wants to start expanding, and I get a feeling of her being in no hurry. She very clearly doesn't like the scythemaws, and I can't really blame her. I don't think they're much of a threat anymore, but better safe than sorry. It feels like she'll be expanding out into the cavern past her door, then start working toward the water. She seems to like the idea of getting some mining nodes of her own, and eventually, some aquatic animal nodes.

She seems to think she'll get either water mushrooms or water bunnies, if I'm reading the impressions from the bond right. I just smile and leave her to it, glad she's doing just fine.

First Mate

The Great White Shark Scion of Hullbreak Harbor is restless, because her Captain is restless. Neverrest is slowing in its attack, but not stopping. The gained mana is slowing, too. Has it realized it's been strengthening the Captain?

Probably not. If so, it'd just retreat and let the Captain starve himself again. Which only leaves one option: it's building up its forces. The Captain's no fool;

he knows a concerted attack from the undead could overrun him and the dwellers. So he's been sending expeditions.

It's not too difficult to track the undead from the tree line to the beach with the gulls, but the woods have been impenetrable so far. Even more, the expeditions sent to town have not been able to get far without getting destroyed by the accursed ravens the cemetery dungeon has picked up.

Still, they know the beach the undead are using, and so some fish expeditions can shed some light on the situation. The initial reports have started coming in, and it doesn't look good. It could look worse, but it would at least be a change of pace for them to look better.

The undead are fortifying a rocky beach, dotted with spires and a reef. It'd be a terrible place to try to launch a boat from or to try to swim, but as far as defensible positions go, it's a dream come true. Or a nightmare, for her and the Captain. She and most of the shark denizens could probably clear them out, but it'd take a lot of the Captain's resources, and it would be a lot closer than they'd prefer.

It'd also leave the dwellers and the Captain undefended. He has an idea to make it worthwhile, but the risk to the dwellers if it fails is one of the big reasons he hasn't tried it yet. Of course, the risk to the dwellers is also why he's considering it in the first place. They need *something* to be able to bring the fight to Neverrest and keep the dwellers safe.

"When can I return to the enclave?"

Speaking of dwellers. The First Mate sighs and changes her route, heading towards the shipwreck, rather than just swimming around it. The merman has been confined there for quite some time now, stuck in the brig with only her and the occasional merfolk to come give him food.

"When you tell me what you were doing, swimming away from the group like that," she repeats for what must be the hundredth time.

"I thought I saw a big fish, and I wanted to get it," he repeats, sticking to his story. She still doesn't believe him. She sighs and swims lazy laps in front of the window to his cell in the brig.

"Which you only happened to spot when I was on the other side of the school that you were *supposed* to be hunting with the others. What were you really doing, Yendo?"

The merman gives her a long look, and she wonders if he'll finally give her the truth. She decides to try to bait the hook a bit. "We know you did something, Yendo. You slip away on a hunt, and not long after, we start getting raided by Neverrest? I know you wouldn't harm the Captain on purpose, but you must have done something to attract its ire."

Yendo deflates a bit, looking less like the dissenting voice he's always been and more like the tired widower that he is. "I . . . was after a big fish."

The First Mate sighs and moves to resume her path around the wreck. He'll tell her eventually, she knows. Maybe after the Captain finally deals with Neverrest. She doesn't like the Captain's new plan, but she has to admit they wouldn't have much other way to strike back at the cemetery. She nods to herself as she continues her patrol, unaware that the rocks had ears for the conversation.

Chapter 32

Tarl

The inspector of the Fourdock branch of the Dungeoneer's Guild grins as he finishes his foe with one final slash. It was a long and arduous battle, but it joins its brethren in the pile of the defeated. He cleans his weapon, not letting it drip, before putting it away.

He takes a moment to relish in his victory, glad to have the horde beaten back, even if only for another year. He glances over to his companion, glad to see her enjoying victory in her own way. Truth be told, she is the far more experienced combatant in this field, with nary a splatter anywhere on her.

He glances at his own hands and can only shake his head at how easily they tell the tale of the conflict. Still, they're victorious. "How do you manage to fill out so many forms without getting any ink on you at all?" he asks as he leans back in his chair, the paperwork and taxes for the end of the year finally complete.

His desk bears many dried blots of ink, but his stack of papers only has the minimum of blemishes. The ones with too many have been destroyed in the fireplace, never to betray Tarl with the truth of his penmanship. His quill and inkpot lie in their spot on the desk, the feathered instrument of bureaucracy and its companion finally finished with their duties . . . for now.

"Experience," Telar replies with a smile over her hot cup of tea. Tarl can't help but give her an exaggerated roll of his eyes.

"Fine, keep your secrets. A master of her craft is entitled to some, I suppose," he says with a laugh as he stands and stretches. "Is there any tea left?"

"Of course. I'm not a barbarian to make you do all this and not let you have at least some kind of reward. We're running low on honey, though. You might want to go on a more ordinary delve if you want to get us some more."

He laughs as he pours himself a cup and adds a bit of milk and honey, too. "It'd probably be a good idea to see how Thedeim's coming along with Hullbreak, too. He hasn't sent Teemo here in a panic, so it can't be going *too* poorly." He chuckles before giving the teapot a shake and listening.

"Should be plenty for at least one more cup," he says as he nods, taking his seat at his desk once more. They'll need to clean up some and magically send the forms, but that won't take too much longer at all.

Tarl enjoys the warm tea as he turns over in his head his plans for how to delve Thedeim. He's seen the gauntlet, but never actually tried it . . .

His thoughts are interrupted as two figures enter the guild. He's a little surprised to see it's Torlon and Staiven. They seem to be in the middle of discussing something, too.

"—impossible!" insists Staiven, while Torlon just smiles.

"Clearly not." The gnome raises his hands to stall Staiven before he can try to argue more. "Magical theory was never my forte. But now we're here, you can ask Tarl yourself."

The aged ratkin sighs but accepts that he should talk to the one with more expertise. Tarl, for his part, waves the two to have a seat as he enjoys a sip of his tea. After a few moments to collect his thoughts, Staiven speaks.

"How old is Thedeim?"

"He was discovered roughly eight months ago."

"But how *old* is he?"

Tarl smiles as his attempt fails. "How old do you think he is?"

Staiven throws his hands up. "I don't know! But I'll tie my tail in a bow if he's only eight months old!"

Tarl raises an eyebrow at the exclamation, and Torlon takes over to let Staiven try to calm down some. "Rhonda and Freddie got their classes from Thedeim, and they're . . . unusual."

"Are they alright?" asks Tarl, worried something could have happened.

"Huh? Oh!" Torlon smiles and shakes his head at himself. "I meant the *classes* are unusual. As far as I can tell, the children are perfectly fine."

Tarl relaxes back into his seat, relieved. "What's unusual about the classes? Did Rhonda become a paladin and Freddie is now a mage?" he asks with a chuckle, recalling how *both* kids ended up with a spider.

Torlon shakes his head. "Rhonda is an Ice Sage, and Freddie is a Legionnaire Paladin of the Crystal Shield."

Tarl looks interested but not shocked. "I haven't heard of those before."

Staiven speaks up. "That's because Rhonda and Freddie are the first. *Sage* and *legionnaire* are *Thedeim's* words!"

Tarl's eyes bulge for a moment as his body wars with itself. Instinct demands he clear his airway of the sip of tea, but his battle reflexes refuse to let something like a spit take ruin the results of the trials of the last several days. He manages to swallow the drink properly before coughing, only vaguely aware of Staiven looking relieved to have his concerns taken seriously.

Torlon looks over to Staiven. "I guess you weren't wrong about that being significant, after all."

"No, he's not . . . !" manages Tarl as he gets his coughing under control. He takes a deep breath before continuing. "You're both sure those are their classes?"

"Rhonda let me scry her," states Staiven.

"I can't scry, but Freddie demonstrated for me. I've never even heard of a paladin of the Shield being able to do what he did."

Tarl sighs and sets his tea aside. "Well, I'm not an expert in classes, but I do know dungeons. And you're right, Staiven: a dungeon only eight months old should not have the kind of strength of concepts to be able to help someone manifest a new class around them."

Torlon suddenly looks serious. "Should we be worried?"

Tarl shakes his head. "Not for the kids, at least. Whatever a sage and a legionnaire are, they were, in at least some way, always part of them. Thedeim being Fate affinity helps explain it somewhat . . . but not fully." He pauses to feel out the geas of secrecy he took for Thedeim and measures his words carefully. "The guild will probably want to classify him as *Cloistered*, once they get the report."

The gnome and ratkin both look confused at that, and Tarl smiles, glad to get away from secrets and into the familiarity of dungeon classifications. "It's a subclassification, like Deep or Submerged. Cloistered means it was stuck for a while in a small area before expanding. Generally, it means a dungeon will be more mentally mature than its size would indicate, as the dungeon spent some amount of time without outside influence and could work through actually forming ideas. And cloistered dungeons often have strange concepts, since they didn't develop with outside ideas to guide them. It's rare, and even more rare for a cloistered dungeon to be cooperative. Thankfully, thanks to his Fate affinity, it's probably not going to raise too many eyebrows. Fate dungeons . . . are always a bit strange."

Torlon simply nods at the explanation. Staiven looks a little more relieved at it, but not fully. "What about Rhonda and Freddie's classes?"

Tarl shrugs. "Teach them? You're their mentors, not me. Thedeim can't exactly take the classes back. Just play them off as obscure instead of something unique from Thedeim if anyone asks. I don't have any advice for *how* to teach them, though." He cuts off Staiven before he can interrupt. "If it's some weird magic, go ask Thedeim. You're probably the magic expert around here, so I can't think of anyone else for you to ask. If he doesn't tell you . . . Well, do you tell just anyone how to enchant something?"

Staiven doesn't look happy but doesn't argue. He doesn't stay silent, either. "Do you have a book on the subclassifications I could borrow?"

Tarl nods. "We'll need a couple days to get these papers settled, but that shouldn't be a problem. You could probably talk to the adventurers' guild if you want to research classes a bit more, too."

The idea of research has Staiven looking much more in his element and much less worried for his apprentice. Torlon stands from his chair and smiles at them both before focusing on Staiven.

"Shall we go now? I wouldn't mind researching a bit of the various paladin variants, too. If Freddie is a paladin of many, I might need to be prepared to teach him a wide variety of things."

Staiven nods and stands, offering Tarl his hand to shake. "Thank you for your time, Inspector, and for taking me seriously. It's been a while since I felt out of my depth about something."

Tarl smiles and shakes his hand. "No problem at all, Staiven. I'm sure the kids will be fine, just as I'm sure you two have your work cut out for you helping them reach their potential."

The two mentors laugh at that and soon leave, and Tarl sits back down to finish his cup of tea.

"What would *you* classify Thedeim as?" asks Telar from her desk.

"Hmm?" he responds, in the middle of a sip.

"You said the guild would classify him as cloistered, but not what *you* would."

He just stays quiet enjoying his tea, though he does turn and give her a smile over his cup.

After a few moments, she smiles back. "Fine, keep your secrets. I suppose a master of his craft deserves some."

Chapter 33

Elsewhere

Smoke drifts from the chimney of the Seaside Forge in Fourdock. While the building is within sight of the ocean, most residents wouldn't count it as being beside the sea. But most residents aren't dwarves. By dwarven standards, Hrunter Redbeard may as well be swimming while he's forging.

Most dwarves are more than happy to stay in the Holds, only seeing the sky on rare occasions. Some, like Hrunter, simply get the itch to wander, to see what there is beyond the Holds. The stout dwarf is hairy, even by dwarven metrics, enough so that some of his beastkin neighbors joke that he's a redheaded molekin rather than a dwarf.

He, of course, corrects them. He's hairier than any mole he saw before leaving the Holds, though he does admit to his eyes being properly beady. He likes Fourdock. The people are simple and friendly, and the adventurers' guild is good for business.

That new dungeon is even better for business. He has no intention of delving, preferring to use his hammer on the inanimate things of steel designed for battle rather than whatever the dungeon makes for fighting.

Sometimes, he wonders if he's the only one in town who hasn't at least gone to take a look. He has to admit, the temptation grows every day. He hasn't had a chance to use a pick since he dug out his proper dwarven forge, way back when he first moved here. Those who *do* challenge it bring him quality ore. He doesn't think it holds a candle to what the Holds can produce . . . but it's not an insult to work with.

The dungeon challenges all who enter it with combat, which is great for a smith like himself. That means a lot more demand for various weapons. Daggers are the most popular by far; a solid tool and a decent weapon all in one. Other weapons are still in demand, especially since people just don't seem to die in Thedeim. They'll see a challenge a dagger just won't be up for and start to wonder if they could manage it with a more specialized weapon.

Oh, he's seen battered and bruised adventurers perusing his wares, weighing the cost of their bruised pride versus the gold they'd have to spend to salvage it. Those ones always try to haggle the prices down, but quickly learn that Hrunter is as good at haggling as he is at forging. They usually realize they're on a whole new losing battlefield quickly, and either leave in a huff or sigh and get something that's within their price range.

He chuckles at the pleasant thoughts before returning his focus to his forge. That catkin finally stopped simply gazing longingly at the sign that lists commission prices and put up some coin for a custom order. It was such an interesting commission that Hrunter even let him haggle a couple coins down. It's not every day someone wants blades with no handles.

They're a challenge to make, especially since they're to be a matching set of four. Double-bladed, slightly curved, shaped like he snapped two daggers at the hilt and welded the broken ends together. They're an interesting challenge. There's no proper end to hold while forging, nor while sharpening. The nicks and burns he's suffered in their creation make him feel like an apprentice again, in all the best ways. Rarely do smiths get to make something new, and it's an even rarer experience for a dwarven smith.

With the blades forged and sharpened, now he just needs to do the runework. He flexes his Meta affinity as he inscribes the blades with durability and sharpness runes. He could add other affinities if the cat wanted, but he said he prefers a simple baseline that he can modify on his own later.

Hrunter isn't insulted. On the contrary, it means his weapons will see steady use instead of sitting in a sheath most of their existence, slowly rusting until their affinity is needed.

Eventually, he leans back, letting himself enjoy a satisfied smile wide enough for his teeth to actually show through his beard and mustache. They're no family heirloom axe or crag plate armor, but he'd put them among his better works.

Chapter 34

With night come the latest reports from the spies in Hullbreak, and Leo dutifully works through them. There's definitely an increase in sharks inside, and it looks like their expeditions have finally discovered the beachhead. They've even tried a flyover with some gulls, but Poe's patrols quickly convinced them it was a bad idea. While I'd prefer they hadn't discovered the beachhead, I'll settle for them not having much information about it.

There doesn't seem to be much activity with the gull spawner, but I also haven't been able to get any of the spies into a position to get a good look. No news is good news, as far as I'm concerned. There's not a whole lot of defending Hullbreak can do with the gulls.

The biggest piece of information is about the merman in the shipwreck. He's been imprisoned, and if the report is accurate, he might have been the one to send the note to the Office of Dungeon Affairs. He's not being mistreated, but he's also certainly in trouble with Hullbreak.

Which gives me an idea, but it'll be a huge risk. If I go through with it, it'll be go time, one way or the other. I need to make sure I have everything ready before then.

The shortcut through the woods is done, and Teemo is taking some time to expand it a bit. Jello and Slash should be able to get through it without any problem at all, but Teemo is working to see about letting an army of skeletons get through it quickly, too. I just leave him to it for now. I'll need him for my risky idea, but I don't need to distract him until I make sure I have all the pieces I'll need.

Like Slash and his axe. If I'm going to potentially call down the wrath of Hullbreak, I want to have as much support as possible to fight underwater. I'm uncertain how well swinging an axe underwater will work, but sound should work great. Water will conduct sound way better than air. The only problem is that it will conduct electricity a lot better than air, too.

It's not the superconductor that a lot of movies make it out to be, however. In theory, the metal of the circuit should still be the path of least resistance, though I'll have Thing make sure to reinforce a bit of lighting essence to help encourage it to behave properly. Heh, maybe he'll manage a magical superconductor. That'd be cool.

I'm a bit more concerned about making the arc work properly. A Tesla coil is so loud *because* it takes a lot of energy to get the electricity to jump through the air, so a lot of energy gets converted into sound. With saltwater being more conductive, it'll need less energy to jump, so less energy to convert into sound. If I'm lucky, the quieter sound and the ease of sound moving in water will cancel each other out, and everything will work fine. If I'm not . . . I dunno. Thing might have to lean more on magic than simple physics.

Either way, the axe is coming along great, and I think I'll be able to give it to Slash in a couple days.

Queen is still working on the water-movement potion, and still isn't having much luck with it. While Staiven and her have compared notes, and he has several formulae for it, we still don't have the stuff to make it. I haven't been able to come up with any kind of good physics workaround for it, either.

Water is a massive pain to deal with. It will drink in ridiculous amounts of energy and hardy heat up at all, it's shockingly dense, and it absolutely *despises* being compressed. Air is easy to move in, thanks to it not having much mass to be in the way, and it's also more than happy to squeeze down. The only thing I can think of to move quickly in water is to more or less turn into a fish and take advantage of hydrodynamic design . . . but that kind of magic is way beyond what we can do now.

At least the Electrolysis potion seems to work like a dream. Oh, hey, I should have her team up with Thing and see if they can use that principle to create a bubble of air around the hat and possibly guitar. Probably just hydrogen, letting the oxygen escape. I'm pretty sure it won't be able to explode if there's no oxygen. Maybe they can kludge together something so it'll just bring a bit of air with it when it first goes under the water. I'd really rather avoid Slash exploding during his debut.

While that prep will still take me a couple days, I don't see anything to theoretically stop my idea. I just want to run it by Leo and see what problems he sees, and if he thinks we can handle Hullbreak's reaction.

Teemo? Can you head to Leo? I want to hear what he thinks about us rescuing/kidnapping that merman.

Teemo pauses in his work for a moment before chuckling and shaking his head as he gets his current work into a spot where he can leave it.

"That's a pretty bold idea, Boss. How do you plan on doing that?"

Well . . . I'll explain once you go meet Leo so I only have to explain once.

My Voice nods and soon hurries down the shortcut. Before long, he's before my Wolf Scion. Leo gives him a nod of respect and a short yip.

"Thanks, Leo. The Boss has a crazy plan about that one merman in the ship, and he wanted to run it by you."

Leo opens his mouth and lets his tongue loll out in a grin while Teemo laughs. "Crazy even for him, yeah. So, what's the plan, Boss?"

So . . . that merman. I'm pretty sure he's the one who sent the letter to Tarl. We might be able to convince him to . . . not exactly turn on Hullbreak, but to at least convince him we want to help and that we need someone Hullbreak might actually listen to. So I'd like Teemo to sneak in, try to talk him into helping, and if he agrees, get him back to the beachhead.

"Uh . . . Boss? I can't breathe water."

We have the Electrolysis potion. And with your shortcuts and natural sneakiness, you could get in, talk with him, and quickly get him out, too.

Teemo doesn't look too convinced, but with the obvious objections out of the way, he goes ahead and relays the idea to Leo, who immediately grumbles in that not-quite-a-whine way dogs sometimes do.

"He says Hullbreak will probably immediately attack if we do that."

Yeah, I kinda figured. Does he think we can hold Hullbreak at bay if he does?

Teemo asks, and Leo paces for a minute or so as he considers. Through the bond, I can feel him going over the troops and the various tactical options at our disposal. He eventually sits and gives Teemo his opinion.

"He says he feels confident, but that we'll be tipping our hand about being Neverrest. He says he'll probably need Slash and Jello, as well as Rocky, to be able to keep the merman safe long enough for the initial panic to lessen. *If* it lessens."

Yeah, that's the biggest risk. Hullbreak doesn't want his dwellers to get hurt. They're his number one priority. If we threaten them, he might go nuts. But if we don't, he won't take us as seriously. If we manage to get the guy out, Hullbreak will probably immediately attack with everything he has. We'll have to keep that assault at bay and make sure he can see the guy's unhurt, and hopefully, have him try to negotiate with Hullbreak.

"What if Hullbreak thinks the guy has betrayed him?"

Then we'll really *need to make sure he's safe, and hope he can give us some kind of idea to get Hullbreak to listen.*

"That sounds really risky, Boss," Teemo points out, and I can only sigh and agree with him.

Yeah . . . but is it riskier than letting the status quo go on? If you two can think of a better plan, I'm all ears. You can even ask the other scions, Folarn, or any other dwellers. Or Aranya and Yvonne. I'd love a better plan, but I don't know that we're going to get one.

The best time to do it will probably be the new moon low tide after Slash's axe is finished. That looks to be about a week away. So we have until then to try to come up with something better than forcing Hullbreak's hand while hoping he'll hold back because of his dweller.

Chapter 35

This is feeling like the longest week of my life, and it's only just started. Sure, I haven't had all *that* many weeks since becoming a dungeon, but the point still stands. Everyone has been brought up to speed on the plan, too, but nobody has been able to come up with anything better.

Larx and the ratkin are taking a philosophical approach to what to do; I'm just glad they're not being yes-men about it. They love a good debate, and while I usually like to hear philosophy being discussed . . . I just can't get into it right now. It also doesn't help that they've been diving pretty hard into hypotheticals and have wandered pretty far from the original topic. It's good to know they mostly agree with the plan and couldn't come up with anything else.

The spiderkin are taking a more pragmatic approach with their own discussions. Norloke hates the idea of letting anyone starve, and Vernew seems offended at the very concept that dwellers wouldn't be able to go out and explore and hunt on their own. Folarn was actually able to look at a diagram of the beachhead and point out a few potential weaknesses. I think she's just more used to thinking of assaulting in three dimensions than Leo is.

Leo, meanwhile, is shoring up the defenses as best he can without revealing himself. The skeletons are doing their best to keep any fish from getting inside the protected area, trying to keep Hullbreak from getting any other information. They're also trying to figure out how to make something to help protect the merman, Yendo, just in case. I haven't been able to think of anything that wouldn't just look like a cell. I think our best bet is to let him wander around—if we can actually get him to come along, that is.

Elf Guy, aka Tarl, stops by for a more casual delve, and I can't resist asking Teemo to get his advice. My Voice pops out of a shortcut near the gauntlet, where Tarl is waiting in line, and squeaks to get his attention.

"Oh, hey, Teemo. How're you doing?" he asks. Teemo sighs. "That good, huh?"

"Heh, yeah. Just trying to get some last-minute stuff together for Hullbreak, and wondering if you had any advice."

Tarl grimaces at that, taking a few seconds to formulate his reply. "Dungeon fights are delicate at the best of times. The guild mostly sits back and tries to minimize collateral to delvers, so there's not a lot of help I can give. Your stunt with Neverrest was, if not *totally* unprecedented, very rare. If it makes you feel any better, even if you subsume Hullbreak, the dwellers should be unharmed."

Yeah . . . it doesn't really make me feel any better, but Teemo thanks him and lets him do his thing.

Watching Thing and Queen finish the axe keeps me distracted for the next couple days, at least. They even manage to get a basic air bubble enchantment on it and the hat. They do a few tests, and everything seems fine, so I call Slash to come collect his new stuff.

Slash

The Composer is close to finishing the axe. Ever since his creation, Slash has had at least a vague idea of what the axe would look like, would sound like. He has longed to be able to actually bring some of that music to reality.

He quietly watches as Thing and Queen put the finishing touches on the axe and hat, wondering for a moment if that's the last thing he'll ever do quietly. He chuckles at himself and discards that idea. While a lot of the music is loud and energetic, there are also more quiet and subdued pieces, no less beautiful for their lack of volume.

No, he'll still do a lot of things without actively playing music, he decides. While the Composer has an odd idea of background music, songs to be played to simply fill a silence, it's also close to an even stranger concept of music: one to be played in an enclosed space, with everything interesting removed. The music of boredom.

The Earth elemental suppresses a shudder at the very concept, but even that helps emphasize the power of music. It enhances emotions, even boredom, no matter how ironic the concept of being actively bored is to Slash.

It takes him a few moments to realize the mood in the room has shifted, and a few moments more to see Thing and Queen step back from the axe and hat. He can feel the guidance of the Composer as he simply takes in the sight of the completed instrument.

Take. Yours, whispers the will of the Composer, and Slash wouldn't refuse even if he could. He first takes the hat, a strange style and strange make. And yet, it feels right in his hands, and *perfect* on his head. He supposes it's heavier than most delvers would want to wear, thanks to the odd metallic disks around it to help channel the thunder. For an Earth elemental like him, however, it's no problem at all. A strange idea of a wig drifts through the bond with the Composer, and after a few moments' consideration, Slash refuses. It might look interesting, but hair like that would get in the way if he's in a fight.

He eyes the axe, wanting to simply snatch it up and hold it close, but he resists. It's no simple treasure, and he's no delver to just grab what he can. The axe deserves his reverence, so reverence he shows as he gingerly picks it up from the table. From the first touch, he wonders if the lightning isn't properly channeled, but soon realizes it's not a malfunction. He feels . . . *whole.* A piece he never knew he needed, but now that he has it, he wonders how he lived without it.

He holds it just as he should and plucks a few simple notes, his new hat crackling with energy as wonderful new music is brought into reality. It's harsh and jagged, yet somehow perfectly tuned as well. No . . . not quite perfectly. He carefully adjusts the knobs to adjust the pitch, and smiles to himself as he gets it just right.

Now, he needs to practice. The Composer intends to do battle soon, and needs Slash's help. This will be his debut, so he needs to be certain he's ready. There are so many songs that he could play to help inspire the Composer's denizens and scions, and he needs to be certain he can play them all. There's no telling what kinds of emotions will need to be stirred to ensure victory.

Thedeim

Thing and Queen seem a little disappointed that the pair of items don't count as an artifact or something. We can all tell it's more than a normal crafted thing, but don't really have the time to try to figure out too much more. My Earth elemental reverently dons the silk top hat and takes the guitar in hand. He gives it a strum, and I can feel him just basking in the sound, the juxtaposition of sweet harmony with the harsher sounds of an electric guitar.

I can actually hear music drifting back from him in the bond, as he lets himself relish in finally having the instrument meant for him from the start. *You've got a lot to live up to for your namesake, Slash, but I believe in you.* Eventually, he gathers himself and heads to the tunnels to have some privacy to practice. I keep an ear on him, the little snippets of songs helping keep me from worrying myself in circles, at least for a bit.

It's only a day away from the plan, now, and the scythemaws are almost all back where they're supposed to be. I wonder if Slash's practicing helped encourage them to go, or if they're all just done with what they needed to do. Either way . . . I don't even have scythemaws to try to distract my thoughts.

My decisions replay as night falls, time seeming somehow to stand still and yet also sprint ahead. Should I have tried just talking? Could it have worked?

Maybe . . . but I didn't have any way to actually talk when this started. I had Teemo, sure, but no water-breathing potion. And no guarantee they'd listen to the Voice of a dungeon they don't know much about. A new dungeon that subsumed Neverrest, even. While I doubt there was any love lost between the two, the cemetery wasn't exactly a pushover. A new and powerful neighbor, a total unknown, wouldn't exactly fill an apparent paranoid with trust.

Should I have pretended to be the devil Hullbreak knew, hoping it'd be taken better? It's probably not the best way to build trust, but I couldn't think of any other way to get Hullbreak some mana so it wouldn't starve. An actual gift would probably be even more suspicious than a raid, weird as that seems. Someone paranoid expects an attack, and it's almost a relief for them when it happens. A gift throws them off-balance, disturbs the delicate house of cards that is their thought process.

At least, I think it does. I'm hardly a psychologist or psychiatrist or whatever. Maybe I'm doing the whole thing wrong, and I should have just let Hullbreak starve and pick up the pieces after, somehow.

"You get a lot of crazy ideas, Boss, but that's definitely one you wouldn't follow through with," speaks up my Voice, shaking me from my thoughts as he looks at my core.

What?

"Leaving Hullbreak to starve. You wouldn't go through with that."

But what if—

"What if what? If you did nothing, it'd slowly starve, and the dwellers would have to watch the whole time." Teemo smirks. "You're too much of a busybody to just watch something like that, Boss. You're always poking your nose in and trying to help."

I start to protest, but Teemo just talks over me.

"Like with the kids. If you were any other dungeon, they wouldn't have been able to escape the basement. Not with a Guardian there. Or like with Aranya and that scythemaw. Or with Neverrest and Yvonne. Or Leo. Or Violet. Or the scythemaws in general! Some have been messier than others, but I think you've done a good job."

Maybe . . . but this one is shaping up to be even messier. Most of those were pretty simple.

Teemo snorts at that. "If you call those simple, I don't want to know what you call complicated. Wait . . . I *do* know what you call complicated. It's the kind of stuff that literally hurts my brain," he says with a smirk, and I have to give him a chuckle. "There you go, Boss. The situation is serious, sure, but if you let your nerves get the better of you, it could *actually* get messy and complicated."

. . . Do you think the plan will work?

Teemo shrugs. "I dunno. I haven't thought many of your plans would work, Boss, but I've been wrong plenty of times. As far as the fighting goes, I'm pretty confident in you, at least. Ragnar, Leo, and Folarn haven't been able to find anything glaringly wrong with it."

You think you can convince the merman to listen, to come with you?

My voice nods. "Yeah. From those reports, it sounded like he's kinda desperate for anything to help Hullbreak. It'll still be a risk. Maybe he'll scream and call that shark immediately, who knows? Maybe he'll be able to talk Hullbreak down, or maybe it'll finally fully snap. There's a lot of stuff that could go wrong, but we've planned for that as much as we can. Now, all we can do is hope it goes right."

And if it doesn't? Can we stop Hullbreak from hurting itself and its dwellers?

Teemo's face softens as he smiles at me. "Do you think anyone *else* could?"

I stop in my mental tracks at the question, my worries derailing from the simple directness. After mulling it over, I'm still not *happy* with the situation, but that's just life sometimes. Sometimes, you're the only one who can do it. You either do your best or do nothing and have to live with that. Sometimes you choose correctly, sometimes not, but you just have to try your best.

I focus my attention back on Teemo and chuckle. *I think you're hanging out with Larx too much.*

Teemo smirks at that. "Who else is going to help me get some mystique? Tiny? He's got tons to spare, but I can't go stealing his style!"

Chapter 36

Thanks to Teemo, I'm feeling a lot better about the whole thing. It also helps that everyone is doing the last bit of prep, which helps solidify what we're going to be doing. Something about knowing this is it helps me focus. Having time to second-guess makes it too easy to get lost in my own head.

Queen's ants deliver a bottle of the Electrolysis potion to the enchanting lab, where Thing is putting the finishing touches on Rocky's disguise. I think he was able to put a bit of an enchantment like the oil idea to help Rocky move easier in the water. I still don't understand why it's easier to enchant something than make a potion, but it is what it is.

It might actually be that it's easier to just make a quick and dirty enchantment that will be easily removed once something better is developed. Whatever the reason, Rocky is looking the part very nicely. He holds himself differently than Neverrest's lich did, but not so differently that it should raise suspicion.

Slash has his axe on his back and is looking equally nervous and excited, and the other scions seem to be doing what they can to help his confidence. Still, he doesn't seem *worried*, so that's all I can really hope for.

Jello is just bubbly and happy and looking forward to seeing what the ocean is like. It's easy to worry she might not be cut out for this, but through the bond, I can feel my soft cube's steely determination. She understands the stakes as well as any of the scions . . . maybe even more. There's a lot of parallels to be drawn between helping Hullbreak and in rehabilitating a mole or gremlin.

We don't have forever to prepare, though. Low tide is early in the morning and in the middle of the afternoon, and I want the morning one. I'm pretty sure Hullbreak doesn't sleep, nor would his scion or denizens . . . but it just feels wrong to start this kind of fight in the afternoon.

Rocky and Slash gather up a few more potions from Queen, and my four scions head for the shortcut. Hopefully, we'll be able to talk Hullbreak down without a fight. Hope for the best, prepare for the worst.

Yendo

The merman lays on the "bed" in the brig, staring at the ceiling. The glorified plank that juts from the wall isn't the most comfortable way to sleep, and he can only imagine it'd be even worse for the land folk to sleep on. They don't have water to help buoy them and lessen the discomfort.

Staring at the ceiling has become a significant part of his morning routine since being thrown in here. He doesn't blame the Captain for it. He really *did* swim off when he thought the First Mate couldn't do anything about it, and sent that message that started the . . . siege? It's been a long, defensive battle, so he supposes it's close enough to a siege for him.

Not for the first time, he wonders if he did the right thing. Was he mistaken? His gull, Whitecap, seemed convinced Neverrest had been subsumed, but Yendo was the only one who believed him. After the endless stream of undead, he can't help but wonder if his companion was wrong, somehow.

"Psst, hey."

The merman frowns and sits up, looking at the barred window, expecting to need to shoo away another young merfolk who is trying to talk with him, but the window is empty. He stares through it in confusion, wondering where the voice could be coming from.

"Down here. Be casual. I don't want attention from anyone but you, Yendo."

The merman's confusion mounts as he lowers his gaze, and eventually spots a very strange sight: a rat peeking out from under his uncomfortable bed. Rats can't breathe underwater. And he's pretty sure they don't talk, either.

"You sent that letter, yeah?"

Yendo's confusion shifts gears to a different type of confusion. "Yes . . . but not to a rat. Whitecap was supposed to deliver it to the Dungeoneer's Guild."

The rat smiles and nods. "Yeah, Tarl got it, and he asked my Boss to help."

The merman doesn't look very enthusiastic about the rat's help. "Unless your boss can help stop Neverrest's attack, I don't know what else you can do, little one."

The rat just grins. "That's not Neverrest. Let me introduce myself: I am Teemo, Voice of Thedeim, the dungeon that subsumed Neverrest. He's been sending those undead so Hullbreak doesn't starve."

Yendo's eyes widen at that, and suddenly, the methodology of the attacks makes much more sense . . . though the reasoning eludes him. "But . . . why? I thought most dungeons don't get along with other dungeons."

Teemo chuckles. "Yeah, the Boss is kinda weird, but he really does want to help. And part of that is making sure he has the situation understood right. Hullbreak was traumatized by losing some dwellers a while ago, yeah? He cut himself off and has slowly been starving. He'd rather die than lose another, and he doesn't trust outsiders."

Yendo can only sigh and nod. "Yes . . . the Captain went mad with grief that day, and he hasn't truly recovered."

Teemo nods at that. "That's about what the Boss figured. He has a plan to try to confront, uh . . . Captain Hullbreak with reality, but he needs your help to do it."

The merman looks incredulous. "How much help can I be? I'm in the brig. And how do you know my name? How do you know so much about the Captain?"

Teemo sits back a bit, getting comfortable as he explains. "You aren't the only one who talks to Tarl. That letter dug up some stuff from *his* past, too, you know. He told us what he and the guild know. The Boss knows a lot more than they do, now. I'm not the first one in here."

Yendo looks a bit shocked at that, but he manages to keep his voice low. "But how? Unless your dungeon has some kind of aquatic spawners, anything they send inside would be obvious!"

Teemo grins at that and shakes his head. "Nah, you just gotta think outside the box. And speaking of outside the box . . . I can get you out of here."

"But how? Even if you're a Voice, I don't think you're going to be able to break the door down and fight past the First Mate once she hears a commotion."

"Who said anything about a commotion? I can get you out of here with barely even a ripple in the water." Teemo pauses for a moment after that, his confidence flowing into caution. "It'll get messy once they realize you're gone, though. The Boss doesn't want to harm any dwellers, including you, but you'll probably be in the middle of a battlefield pretty quickly. He can't guarantee your safety."

Yendo's resolve solidifies at hearing that, remembering how often the First Mate would say that something is forbidden because she and the Captain can't guarantee their safety. Hearing the danger but still being given the choice . . . This is what the Captain needs to understand, what his people *need*.

"I'll do it."

Teemo looks relieved. "Great! Now, this will feel a bit weird. I had some practice with shortcuts underwater on the way in, but the transition still isn't as smooth as I'd like it. Are you ready?"

Yendo doubts he is, but he nods. Whether he's ready or not, it doesn't matter. This may be the last chance he has to help everyone he cares about.

"Good! Just follow me, and try not to think too hard about how everything looks, okay? I'm going to be a little messy about it so they notice pretty quickly. Thedeim wants the fighting, if there is any, to take place at low tide."

Yendo doesn't have much chance to question that as the rat does . . . *something*, and then slips *through* the something. He's already starting to regret this decision, but he's not going to balk at the challenge. He swims forward and does his best to keep his gaze resolutely on the tail of the rat before him. Reality seems to twist and bend, reminding him of when he'd poke his head only barely above the surface of the water and see things all strangely distorted.

He's dimly aware of exiting and entering several distortions as he follows Teemo, and he can feel when they leave the safety of the Captain's territory, but he doesn't get much time to dwell on it. Teemo is still moving. The thought of slipping away crosses his mind, but he rejects it.

No, this is the current he's in now, and he'll see where it goes.

Teemo stops, finally letting Yendo get his bearings, and he fears he may have made a mistake. Skeletons are everywhere! He's in some kind of submerged fortress or something!

"Easy, Yendo. They're not going to hurt you," encourages the rat, though it takes Yendo a few more seconds to understand the truth of that statement. The undead aren't rushing him to tear him apart. In fact . . . they're ignoring him. None are moving to try to even restrain him! As he looks around, his eyes settle on two strange figures.

One is exactly what he would have expected: a lich. It's not acting much like he would have expected a lich to, however, as it seems to just be communicating with the other figure.

At first, he thinks it must be a skeleton weighed down with more rocks than usual, but he doesn't see any bones anywhere! It has a strange style of hat, and an equally strange style of axe on its back, too.

Unsure of what else to do, he decides to swim over, hoping they might give him some kind of explanation, but he bumps into . . . He's not sure.

Teemo chuckles. "That's Jello. The Boss has slimes who are basically invisible in the water. The guy in the hat is Slash, an Earth elemental. The Boss also has smaller elementals to act as spies, too. That's why the skeletons were weighed down with rocks, so they could easily get inside without raising suspicion about sudden piles of rock around."

"And . . . the lich?"

"That's Rocky. If Hullbreak and the First Mate want a fight, Rocky is here to give it to them."

Chapter 37

I watch through Teemo's eyes as he talks with Yendo. I'd be holding my breath if I could, then releasing it with a sigh of relief once he accepted helping us. After just a little more explanation, my Voice makes a messy shortcut out of there, and the two book it.

Those are the shoddiest shortcuts I've ever seen him make, but they're definitely good for getting Hullbreak's attention. Teemo keeps as aware of his surroundings as he can while the two flee. It looks like Yendo is just focused on my Voice's fuzzy butt, as he doesn't seem to flinch at the various denizens who try to stop them. Or he trusts Hullbreak. Could be a bit of both, really.

Once they get out of Hullbreak, Teemo makes the shortcuts a bit better, though he still collapses them behind them as they go. I'm pretty sure he's doing that more for a smoother run than anything else. It's not like Hullbreak can't easily guess where they're going.

Once safely inside the beachhead, Teemo lets Yendo catch his breath, then introduces him to my scions. While he does that, I poke Leo to make sure he knows it's go time. Looks like he expects not much more than five minutes for Hullbreak to get his act together and assault the beachhead.

That gives my attacking scions time to get to their positions. Rocky stands at one of the openings in the walls and strikes his most imposing pose . . . which mostly involves just standing there and letting the tide idly move his robe.

Slash stays back more in the core of the beachhead. He's supposed to be support more than full offense, if all goes well. Well, if *all* goes well, he won't have to be either, but, you know.

Jello is sticking near Yendo, glad the merman is still moving slowly, uncertain of his surroundings. He soon wanders to one of the smaller openings to look out into the sea, waiting for the response from his dungeon.

It ends up taking Hullbreak closer to ten minutes to show up, though what he presents is pretty intimidating, not gonna lie. Out of the murky depths comes a veritable wall of sharks, looking much more organized than I would have expected. Looking through the eyes of my scions, I can even see more shapes further back.

Whoof . . . this is going to be quite a thing if it gets ugly.

At the head of the shark army is what can only be the First Mate, a massive great white who only reinforces the fact that I would not have been able to get a big enough boat. She's not scaled up like Tiny is, but I'm still pretty sure normal great whites aren't quite that great in size.

She stops advancing and starts swimming back and forth a decent distance away; far enough back she should be able to avoid any ranged stuff I might try to pull, but still close enough for my scions to hear as she starts talking.

"I am the First Mate, Voice of Captain Hullbreak! Return Yendo, Neverrest! You won't like what happens if you don't!"

Alright, Teemo. Time to drop the other shoe and hope it doesn't mean we have to throw down the gloves, too.

Teemo nods and climbs onto Slash. "Think you can amplify me?"

My elemental nods. Clearing his throat, my Voice starts speaking, and Slash's hat flashes with electricity to bring his words across the distance to the First Mate.

"I am Teemo, Voice of Thedeim. We freed Yendo because you were keeping him prisoner. You are keeping *all* of them prisoner, Hullbreak."

The shark thrashes as she responds. "The Captain is protecting them! No matter which side of the foam they're from, outsiders are dangerous! With the Captain, they are safe!"

"They're stifled! And you were starving! If it wasn't for the Boss, how would you and the dwellers be faring right now?"

The First Mate scoffs. "You're saying those invaders were charity? At least make your lies believable, Neverrest! You want to subsume the Captain and kill the merfolk! You just miscalculated what it would take to finish off the Captain!"

"I already told you: I'm the Voice of Thedeim, not Neverrest! The Boss *subsumed* Neverrest months ago!"

"Enough with your lies! Give back Yendo!"

The merman's voice carries over the waves in response. "I refuse to go back, First Mate! The Captain is sick with grief, not in his right mind! You know it!"

The shark darts forward a few yards before stopping herself, not wanting to get too close to the beachhead on her own. "Yendo?! Is that really you? Are you alright? Did they hurt you?!"

The merman looks back to the various skeletons around him as he slowly starts to make his way out from the barricade. None of them try to stop him, though Jello quietly follows. "I'm fine! They even told me I could leave if I wanted, but suggested I come here. I want to help the Captain, First Mate! And I believe this Thedeim does, too!"

The First Mate takes more than a minute to respond, slumping a bit in her swimming before she does. "It doesn't matter now, Yendo. The Captain doesn't believe that dungeon can be trusted, no matter what its name is. You either come back with me, or it and the Captain will both slowly starve."

Yendo looks confused, as do my scions. I'm pretty confused, too, and Teemo soon voices that confusion.

"What? How do you intend to starve the Boss? I'm sure you can feel how strong even just Rocky is, and he's not the only scion here right now."

The shark doesn't respond immediately, but Poe suddenly wants my attention. The expeditions are reporting something coming from the ocean. A *lot* of somethings.

"The Captain has a new scion: tThe Quartermaster. That great albatross and the gulls will wipe out the town. No delvers, no mana. No mana . . . we both starve."

"How'd you get the mana for something like that?! All those sharks out there should have taken up everything the Boss gave you!"

The First Mate shakes her head and gives a whistle, and the indistinct shadows start moving forward as she explains. "No point in hiding it now. This whole thing was just to buy time for the Quartermaster to get into position. Only the front line are sharks."

The truth of that statement is quickly apparent. As my scions watch, more ordinary fish come out from the obscuring distance. They're still pretty big fish . . . but there's a big difference between just a big fish and an actual shark.

"Those are the terms, Neverrest . . . *Thedeim*. Yendo comes back with us, or we all die. Even if you beat me and subsume him, your scions are too far away to stop the Quartermaster from razing that town before you do."

We'll see about that. Coda, ring the bell! I know the bats are settling in to sleep now, but we need to get people's attention! Fluffles, get at least Folarn from the spiderkin and get her to the public war room! Thing will do the same with Larx! Leo, take the shortcut back as quickly as you can! It looks like I'll need you to help organize and lead a bit more directly over here, instead of organizing the forces beneath the waves! Poe, try to get Tarl's attention, then head out! Try to delay this Quartermaster until Fluffles can catch up, unless you're sure *you can take him. I don't know how much mana Hullbreak's been pumping into him, nor for how long, so be careful.*

Hopefully, once the dwellers and Tarl see the map, they'll understand at least the gist of the situation and can help keep the town safe. I eye the option to expand outward, too, but leave it alone for now. People will probably be grumpy enough being woken up by the bell and the sound of corvids and gulls fighting. I don't need to make it worse by having a spawner show up in people's basements or something.

I refocus on my scions in the beachhead, where Rocky and Slash look ready to make a go of subsuming Hullbreak before the attack can hit, but I do my best to calm them. Looking back to the First Mate, it looks like she's just waiting for our response to that. She also doesn't look too happy about having to inform us her Captain has a gun to both of our heads . . . or at least thinks he does.

Teemo's voice echoes over the waves. "The scions here *might* be too far away, but these are not all of Thedeim's scions. Call the Quartermaster back, and we can still talk."

It takes the First Mate only a few seconds to reply. "The Captain says you're bluffing. He'll do anything to ensure the safety of his dwellers. If it takes him getting destroyed to end a threat to them . . . so be it."

"We're not a threat to him; we're trying to help him! If he attacks Fourdock, it'll just be another mistake he'll live to regret!"

I can see the shark slump some more, and probably sigh, though it's too far away for it to travel to any of my scions.

"No. The Captain says: if it's not a mistake, he'll be happy, and his merfolk will be safe. If it *is* a mistake . . . he doesn't think you'll let him live to regret it."

Chapter 38

I don't know what I was expecting from the fight with Hullbreak, but this awkward standoff wasn't it. I was expecting to have a big battle under the waves, but my assault force is staring at only a fraction of the sharks I was expecting, and those sharks don't exactly look enthusiastic about a fight right now, anyway.

So while everyone underwater is trying to figure out what they should actually be doing, I'm staring at a blob on the map that's only getting closer and closer to Fourdock. I'm not exactly worried they'll actually be able to do what Hullbreak was threatening, but I'm not so certain that I can keep him from hurting any of the townsfolk.

Sure, there are a ton of adventurers and such, but there's also a bunch of just normal people in town, too. I'm pretty sure even a couple gulls wouldn't be a problem for the average townie, but there's *way* more than a couple gulls coming in, not to mention that scion.

I can't say for certain what affinity it has just yet, but there's a lot of storm clouds rolling in with the huge flock of gulls. If he can drop a lightning storm or something on the town . . . that'd be bad.

The ringing bell seems to be getting people's attention, at least. Aranya and Yvonne are already out to try to organize the town for . . . I don't even know what. Should they evacuate? Where? To me? It'd probably be easier to keep them safe like that, but I don't know how many people would be willing to do that.

My regular delvers probably would, but a lot of them are the ones I'd need to be the least worried about. Even the ones who only run the maze or gather from my nodes still have to do a *little* bit of fighting. Not enough to fight off a gigantic flock of gulls, but at least enough to fend off a couple, I'd hope.

Ugh, I wish I had more time to organize this whole mess. Leo is still trying to get back, but I don't know how long it'll take him, even with the shortcut.

Okay, focus. Less wishing, more doing. Larx and the spiderkin triumvirate are on their way to the public war room, guided by Thing and Fluffles, respectively. I'll just have to hope they can provide the manpower to get the town to do whatever they're going to do.

Aranya and Yvonne seem like they're going to go get Ragnar and Aelara, and then either organize the adventurers' guild or get the ODA's help . . . or both. That means I need to buy time. And by me, I mean Poe. I don't want to put this on his shoulders, but he really is the only one I have right now to try to keep that storm at bay.

Perhaps more precisely: *in* the bay. As long as they're over the water, they can't do much damage to the town. Poe's a smart birb, though, and doesn't need me to tell him that. He caws as he flies over the town, recalling the various expeditions and preparing an army of black to face the invaders of white.

Poe

The Marshal flies quickly, though not as quickly as he can. Rushing like that is a good way to arrive there without any backup. Even though he's a strong scion, he doesn't want to try to fight off a literal army on his own. While his Wind affinity is certainly a boon in the air, he's starting to suspect this Quartermaster has Storm affinity. It's not exactly a counter to Wind, but it would guarantee any fighting will be chaotic and intense.

He caws, loud and clear, to summon any expeditions that are out. While most of the crows and ravens were roosting when this threat was discovered, there are still some out on their various tasks. Poe doubts a fresh scion could stand up to him, but he's not so arrogant that he'll bring anything but his best against this foe. The delvers of Fourdock might not be tied to Lord Thedeim like Aranya and Yvonne, but he still doesn't wish to see them harmed.

The feel of the air changes as he soars over the ocean: a certain saltiness to the breeze now, and weaker thermals. It only takes a small flex of his affinity to maintain his and his army's speed and altitude, but it is still a bit of effort. It will give the gulls a small advantage, but hopefully, nothing significant. He estimates the numbers to be about equal, but he knows he and his birds have a significant edge in experience. They've been active in defending Lord Thedeim for almost his entire existence, as well as challenging delvers. These gulls, on the other hand, only have experience in raids, and have not been having a good time of it recently, either.

Poe calls his forces to a halt as they near the army of gulls. He can see his counterpart among them. The albatross looks to be even slightly larger than Poe, probably following a similar path as Tiny. If so, it will be a tenacious foe, though hopefully, not too far along that particular path.

The Marshal resists the urge to embrace his titles just yet, instead ensuring the winds carry his caw, demanding the other scion leave. His crows and ravens echo the challenge with a cacophony of "Run!", "Flee!", and "Hide!" The chatter is silenced by the albatross's reply, carried by thunder. The other scion has no intention of leaving peacefully.

Poe embraces the power of his titles, the Marshal of Murders and Lord of Unkindnesses having no time for niceties in this situation.

If this Quartermaster will not leave in peace, he can leave in pieces.

He caws his orders and guides his forces, the otherworldly sound and coordination surprising the opposing scion. To his credit, he doesn't back down. The gulls shriek their cries and charge the lines. The Quartermaster starts to gather ominous thunderheads, and that will be Poe's focus for his personal attacks.

The inexperience of the gulls is apparent in the charge, as they don't keep a coherent line. The leaders are easily picked off by diving ravens, and with them uncoordinated, they can't press any advantage of mass to push Poe's forces back. His front lines even let some of the gulls through, to be torn apart by the ravens behind. He loses some corvids, of course, but he's clearly getting the better of the engagement.

The albatross isn't being idle, however, and tries to use the thunderheads as siege equipment, trying to blast holes in the shifting tides of the engagement. While some lightning does get through, Poe isn't exactly sitting idle, either. Blades and spears of wind disrupt the cloud formations, severely weakening the lightning when it's not outright stopped.

Instead of conceding the fight, though, the Quartermaster tries a new tactic. While smaller thunderheads are easy enough to disrupt, there is still a lot of cloud cover. The albatross shrieks and brings forth rain. Starting with a few drops, it steadily grows, quickly putting Poe and his forces on the back wing.

The gulls are more used to flying in poor weather, and it's showing. The chaotic dance of the melee starts to descend into just ordinary chaos. Poe tries to disrupt the clouds, but there's just too many to disperse with his attacks. He needs to wade in and battle the opposing scion more directly.

He caws his challenge, and the albatross screeches in mocking reply before darting into the clouds. Poe knows he'll be at a severe disadvantage in there, but he has to do *something* to try to stop the storm! He pulls several dozen of his crows into the ceiling of clouds with him, using them as extra eyes and ears to track down the Quartermaster.

A bolt of lightning takes one of them, but several others spot the enemy's outline. Poe sends a slash of wind, and is rewarded with a pained squawk from the enemy scion.

Poe can't tell how long he chases the Quartermaster, but he can feel his crows and ravens regrouping under the clouds, fending off the weakening attacks of the gulls. He also manages to lash out many times at his foe, seeming to hit more often than not.

It's with surprise that he suddenly bursts from the wall of clouds into a clear area much colder than the surroundings. In the center is the Quartermaster, looking battered but also somehow victorious. Poe is confused until he feels dread from his Lord Thedeim, and a strange sort of storm flashes through the bond. Usually found in much warmer climates, it's a storm that can scour whole islands to bare sand and rock. He doesn't know exactly how strong this hurricane is, nor how the Quartermaster managed to afford it, but he *is* pretty sure the storm will hit Fourdock even if Poe kills the albatross.

Poe grits his beak as he prepares to test that theory before realizing he and the Quartermaster are no longer the only scions in the eye of this storm. Prismatic colors fill the air as Fluffles makes his entrance, the power of Lord Thedeim *radiating* from the winged serpent.

Fluffles

As soon as he gets the three spiderkin leaders to the war room, Fluffles leaves. The Den Master wants him to help Poe as soon as he can. He's a bit nervous about trying to help the more experienced fighter, but he understands Thedeim's reasoning. Fluffles isn't exactly a subtle scion in his efforts, but when fighting an army, there's not a lot of need for subtlety.

Once he gets to the surface, he can see what the Den Master meant. Even from here, he can hear the sounds of Poe and the enemy scion fighting, their armies cawing and yelling. The huge flocks can even be seen diving and fighting through the thick sheets of rain. He feels a whisper through the bond to go over the low clouds, and to use whatever mana is needed to do so quickly.

If it weren't for the impending disaster to the town, Fluffles would find the speed invigorating, the mana intoxicating. But the seriousness of the situation makes it difficult to truly revel in the experience. He doesn't suppress the bit of pride he feels, however, at his effective use of the mana. Proper application and proper form let him fly faster than he would have thought possible, even forming a subtle cone in front of the flying serpent.

He's pretty sure it only takes him minutes to get over the battlefield, but it feels like hours. Since he was sent high, he must be after the enemy scion, rather than the birds obscured by the thick cloud cover. He frowns as he spots a hole in it, and soon sees Poe burst into the clearing. At the center, he sees the albatross, looking battered but not beaten.

Then the Den Master whispers why. A hurricane. But Fluffles can't stop something like that; he doesn't even have *Wind* affinity, let alone *Storm*!

Momentum.

It is confusing to get that word in a situation like this. With Kinetic as his first affinity, Fluffles understands what it is, but he doesn't understand how it applies to this situation. There's nothing moving out here! Just him, Poe, and the enemy scion!

Fluffles flaps his wings a few more times to help stabilize himself from a stray gust, his attention flicking to the slowly swirling clouds below him. He watches them for a few seconds, the whisper from the Den Master echoing in his mind being soon joined by an odd thing Rocky has said many times: stuff is made of *stuff*.

He has always found it to be nonsensical, but Thing and Queen always agree with a conspiratorial smile. They could be playing some prank . . . but what if they're not. Kinetic affinity is about movement. If the clouds are moving . . . if the *air* is moving . . .

Almost without thinking, Fluffles descends toward the two bird scions. The albatross thinks he's won, even if Poe kills him. Fluffles doesn't know if it has enough power to wipe out Fourdock, but it won't exactly just tickle it. But his epiphany has given him an idea to kill two birds with one stone . . . or one bird with its own stone.

He fully embraces his Conduit title, practically feeling the kinetic energy of the storm singing to him. Poe looks in awe, while the Quartermaster simply tries to flee. It takes but a drop of the Den Master's mana to rob the enemy bird of the kinetic energy he would use to flee, locking him in place as he unworks the storm.

He pulls the energy from the air and focuses it in front of himself, slowly forming a swirling orb of air. A boom emanates from the orb as he adds more and more energy to it, the air inside passing the speed of sound. As he keeps slowing the storm, he muffles further booms, remembering the words of the Den Master that escaping sounds are inefficiencies. He draws deeply of the Den Master's mana as he works. While moving energy takes much less mana than making it directly, there is still a *lot* of energy involved. He finally feels the storm reach a tipping point, no longer having the momentum to keep going.

He turns his focus to the enemy scion, the massive albatross somehow having gone even whiter. Fluffles simply hisses at him, no real malice in it, before unleashing the orb's kinetic energy on the unfortunate scion. The hurricane's eye blinks, the storm dissipates, and only a puff of feathers remains of the Quartermaster.

Chapter 39

The First Mate

The Great White Scion of Hullbreak Harbor looks across the seabed to the forces of the other dungeon. Thedeim or Neverrest or whoever it is, she has given them the Captain's decision: the invaders leave, or everyone dies. She can feel the Captain's confidence through the bond. He's certain the other dungeon will back down.

She's pretty sure he's just killed them all. At least there's a decent chance of the dwellers being able to get out safely.

"The Boss calls that 'mutually assured destruction,'" comes the odd sound of Thedeim's Voice. She's never heard anything like the odd crackles it makes. "The Boss also says it only works if it's actually mutual. You're making this a lot messier than it needs to be, Hullbreak."

The First Mate can hear the Captain's confidence as the Quartermaster approaches the coastal town. She can also feel that confidence move to mild surprise as a black cloud rises and moves to intercept.

"That's Poe, the Marshal of Murders and Lord of Unkindnesses, Thedeim's Raven Scion," comes the sound of the Voice. It's odd, though . . . It doesn't sound proud or boastful, more like resigned.

Her Captain asks her a question, and she relays it. "Are you worried he won't win? You don't sound very confident in your so-called scion."

Her Captain's confidence evaporates as the Raven Scion embraces the power in those titles, seemingly in response to being called out. She can't feel the power directly, but the Captain is scrambling to try to come up with something to counter this unexpected threat.

She can hear the directions given, and it's all but confirmed the Captain has killed them all.

"The Boss isn't worried about Poe losing. He's worried about collateral damage to the town."

"Then back off. The Captain will leave them be if you leave him be."

"And he'll go right back to starving, especially after having spent all his mana on making and upgrading a new scion like that albatross. Then we either do this whole dance again, or the Boss just lets Hullbreak starve."

The Captain snaps a retort at that, and First Mate relays it. She wants to know, too.

"Why do you care?"

"Because he just does," comes the simple reply.

The Captain rages as the First Mate waits and thinks. If this other dungeon really is as strong as it's claiming to be, why doesn't it just subsume the Captain? Why would it try to help?

Will it even still want to help after the two winged scions clash? All she can do is try to feel how the battle is going through her bond with the Captain. She can't see through the Quartermaster's eyes, but she can still sense what the Captain is feeling. Mostly, it's rage, but she can catch glimpses of more, like the ever-present sorrow and pain from the loss of the dwellers; she wonders if the Captain even registers that anymore, or if he just accepts it as his baseline. Smug satisfaction—the Quartermaster has figured out something to use against this Poe.

Movement at the enemy dungeon's beachhead pulls her from what she's doing. A skeleton, weighed by rocks? That doesn't seem quite right. It has a strange hat and an odd . . . axe? She's never used one before, but she doesn't think that's how that's supposed to be held.

The Captain suddenly is in abject terror as the figure comes to a stop, but the great white shark can't figure out why. And then sound. It has the same odd edge that the Voice had, but no words. It starts with a few notes, pure and simple, somehow beautiful even with the harsh edge. Rumbles accentuate the notes as they flow in a simple melody of sorrow, of a battle that didn't need to be. Subtler notes join, adding tension to what should be something of simple beauty. It didn't have to be this way . . . It still doesn't.

A momentary pause before what she can feel should be the final note. The quieter melody and rumblings stop. Even the tides seem to pause for just a heartbeat before the final note falls.

The First Mate gasps when it does. She can feel the Quartermaster vanish, the gull spawner now slowly working to respawn him. What kind of attack could obliterate him in a single hit like that?! She was vaguely aware of him taking a few other attacks, but nothing like whatever it was that ended him.

The opposing dungeon's forces stand still and solemn, and the weight of the song crashes down on her and the Captain. That is *another* scion. A Bard. That song was no battle hymn, no glorious march to war. It was a dirge.

The First Mate shudders, knowing that if it's played again today, she won't be able to hear it.

Thedeim

I watch through my scions' eyes as Slash plays, and I'm glad Fluffles treated that attack with the solemnity it deserved. It took a decent chunk of my mana to do, but it looks to be well worth it. The storm is petering out now, so I let Coda give the bell a break. It's probably still a good idea to let my dwellers continue with their plans to check the city, though. There's probably going to be a lot of people wanting answers.

But I also probably shouldn't count my chickens before they hatch. There's still the First Mate and the sharks ahead of us. I think the song took just about all of the fight out of them, though. I nudge Teemo to try to talk again.

"Will you let us pass?" echoes his voice from Slash's hat, my Voice riding his shoulder.

"I . . . Yes . . ." comes the tired answer from the First Mate.

I leave the skeletons at the beachhead for now, not seeing much point in having them march in. Even if Hullbreak somehow tries to trap my scions, I still have all the rockslides and slimes inside. Marching the skeletons in would just be kicking him while he's down.

Rocky, Slash, and Teemo walk out from the beachhead while Yendo nervously follows. Once they all meet up with the First Mate, she escorts them back toward Hullbreak.

"What . . . *was* that?" asks the merman. It's plain on his face that he knows something big happened, but he doesn't look like he thinks a song was all.

"It was a dirge, for the Quartermaster," answers the First Mate. Teemo nods.

"Thedeim really didn't want to fight, but he's not going to hold back if it's the only option."

Yendo and the great white both look like they're still trying to process that as everyone reaches the edge of Hullbreak's territory. The merman gasps as he sees it.

It looks a lot different than I was expecting it to, from the reports. As my scions move through it, however, I get an inkling as to why.

"He consumed everything, didn't he?" asks my Voice, even though the answer is clear.

The First Mate nods grimly. "The nodes, the other spawners . . . everything except me, the Quartermaster, and the shark and gull spawners. And the enclave, of course. He wouldn't, even if he could."

Slash nudges various rockslides as they go, and the odd elementals distribute the information through the grapevine: no more need to hide. The shark chuckles as she sees the movement.

"Heh . . . elementals? The Captain had no idea."

"Slimes, too," adds Teemo. He doesn't want to pile it on, but at this point, might as well be honest with everything, even if I'm sure it hurts Hullbreak's pride.

As we enter the Merfolk Enclave, I'm surprised to see several merfolk with tridents standing . . . "standing" in the way of the procession. Rocky can see what looks like a big coral sculpture past them, in the center of town, which is where we're almost certain the core is. I can't think of any other reason for the First Mate to lead us here, nor for the merfolk to try to threaten us.

"Go away! We won't let you harm the Captain!" speaks up a merman in what looks like some kind of shell or coral armor. He doesn't sound very old, and Rocky can see the shaking of his hands on the haft of the weapon, but the merman isn't backing down.

"Klyrnev, let them pass. There's nothing we can do," starts the First Mate, but the merman shouts over her.

"No! They'll kill the Captain!"

"We won't," states Teemo.

"Liar!" shouts the merman, then notices Yendo among the scions. "You! This is all because of you, traitor!" With that, he lunges toward the shocked merman.

Rocky's hand moves through the water like it's not there and grabs the haft of the weapon. Judging from the loud crash an instant later, I'm pretty sure he moved it with his Kinetic affinity. The speed and sound make the merman release the trident, and both he and Yendo stumble backward. Terror is clear on Klyrnev's face, as a lich just disarmed him midstrike, whereas Yendo is in a new variety of shock from being saved by an undead scion.

I get a notification while Rocky simply looks at the merman.

Accept Geas? Yes/No?
Hullbreak offers fealty in exchange for no harm ever befalling the merfolk.

I sigh at the pop-up and select no.

"Thedeim will not make an impossible promise, Hullbreak," speaks my Voice as Rocky raises the trident then plunges it into the silt of the sea floor.

"Pain and hardship are just part of life. He has no intention of harming them, and will protect them as he does his own enclaves. And he's going to help *you*, too. He has no intention of subsuming you, either. Things are going to be weird. He'll do a lot of stuff that doesn't make sense; stuff you won't like, maybe even hate . . . but the merfolk and you will all be better for it."

Lordship Accepted. Hullbreak Harbor Vassalized.

". . . The Captain accepts . . . Admiral Thedeim."

Chapter 40

The first thing I feel through the new bond with Hullbreak is abject misery. The First Mate seems to be taking it a bit more stoically, but none of them seem too happy with the new situation. I can't really blame them. I'm looking around, and I'm not really looking forward to this right now, either.

Hullbreak really did consume everything to try to beat me. I can at least respect the commitment, even if it means I have to do a lot more than I was hoping to fix this. I can see a bunch of various depreciated nodes and spawners as I look around.

Right, well, just staring isn't going to make the problem fix itself. I try to push a bit of encouragement through the bond as I start planning how to get Hullbreak back into shipshape. Nodes and spawners are going to need to come back online. Looks like he had a crab and sea slug spawners, too. It also looks like the fish and shark spawners are different things. It seems kinda weird to me, but then again, Violet has a mushroom spawner, where I have mushroom nodes.

I look through the crab options before I spend any mana, wanting to try to plan out a little more than just kinda flying by the seat of my nonexistent pants like I usually do. There are a few options for magic crabs, and a couple resource ones that look interesting, but I think I'm going to try to aim them toward being tough melee fighters. If delvers are going to delve properly, they need something they can fight. Sharks and gulls are not the easiest things to deal with, being in the sea and air, but a crab battle can take place on a beach or something. I'll probably have to expand Hullbreak toward land for that, but I might as well have a plan for it now.

Speaking of the sharks and gulls: they're both more specialized for dealing with invaders than as something a delver can actually fight. The problem is that, while there are still the ordinary invaders, I don't think there are any more dungeon invaders around, so there's a lot fewer to actually deal with.

I have a few ideas that might work for them, however. I'll still keep most of them to help keep invaders at bay, but I think I can do something interesting with the gulls and their little island thing. It seems like a great place for a lighthouse to me. It'll take a lot of work, but if we can give Hullbreak an above-water section for more classic delving, that should go a long way toward making him mana solvent.

The extra sharks, I'll probably send on expeditions out into deeper water. Maybe there's an actual deep-water dungeon out there? I dunno.

The fish have a few interesting options, but one immediately catches my eye: goldfish. Sure, it's a pun, but it also seems to be a specialization for more resources. More resources means more delvers means more mana. That one is definitely on my list of upgrades for Hullbreak.

I'm more uncertain what to do with the sea slugs, though. They seem to be mostly magical, though there are a lot of interesting affinities they seem to be able to be specialized toward. I have no idea how Fire affinity would even work, but it's real tempting to go down that path just to see. I think I'll put a pin in upgrading them beyond just enabling the spawner again, at least for now.

The nodes are an easy decision, at least: bring them all back and upgrade them. Lots of various sea herbs, corals, even a couple beds of pearl oysters—all are on offer, and I want them all and more.

I take a few minutes to look deeper at the coral nodes. Back on Earth, I'm pretty sure trying to harvest coral tends to go very poorly for the coral. Here, however . . . it looks like it behaves similar to an underwater mining node.

Oh, that gives me an idea for the sea slugs!

I dig through the options there, and eventually find what I'm looking for: an upgrade similar to what I got for my slimes back home. Where my slimes seem to help crystalize more ore in my nodes, it looks like sea cucumbers will help feed the coral, and so it will grow better.

Bleh, just don't think about how a sea cucumber feeds something else.

Ah, I almost forgot: Hullbreak's core. As suspected, it's in that big coral structure in the center of the Merfolk Enclave. That needs to move. I can understand him wanting to be close to his dwellers, but they're both going to need room to grow, and in more ways than one. My first instinct is to get it under the gull spawner, but I'm not sure that'll work too well for Hullbreak. The guy definitely doesn't like delvers, and he'd probably be constantly on the verge of a panic attack if they're running around in a lighthouse right above where his core is.

I look around a bit more, and eventually find a spot that could be good. There's a nice area that doesn't have much going on but could be a great spot for a thick kelp forest. It'd be pretty easy to hide the entrance in there. I'm not sure how I'll be able to move him, though.

Hey, Teemo, can you ask the First Mate if she has any ideas for moving Hullbreak's core? I don't think it's a good thing for anyone, long term, for him to stay in the middle of their enclave.

My Voice perks up when I talk to him. It looks like more and more merfolk have been coming out to see what's been going on, and everyone looks a bit lost, even with the First Mate trying to reassure them. Teemo simply swims over to her and perches on her dorsal fin before speaking up.

"Hey, First Mate. Is there any way to move Hullbreak's core without tearing apart that coral?"

The shark looks confused for a moment before looking toward where her Captain's core is, considering. "Ordinarily, no . . . but the Captain is rather drained after . . . today. I should be able to get him out without doing too much damage."

The gathered merfolk look dismayed but don't make any moves to stop them. My Voice tries to explain. "See, the Boss wants to make sure your Captain and you all have room to grow. If Hullbreak wants to tell you how to get to his new Sanctum, that's his decision, and the Boss won't stand in the way of it."

That doesn't seem to make them feel any better, but at least there's nobody else trying to use a trident to stab anyone. Which reminds me: Where's Yendo?

Thankfully, it looks like nobody else is blaming him for what happened. He seems to be talking to a merman who looks on the verge of becoming an adult. They're being quiet, however, so I don't try to interrupt them. I just wanted to make sure nothing happened to him while I was distracted.

In the short time I was looking at Yendo, First Mate's already reached the coral. A quick chomp puts a hole in the big mound, and a little bit of Water mana is all that's needed to wash the core into her waiting mouth. The blue tetrahedron is only about the size of a basketball, which is a bit concerning. From the hole, it looks like he used to take up a lot more space than that, poor guy.

Well, let's get him into some new digs. Slash, I'll need your help. Rocky and Jello, you guys can head back now, or take a look around if you'd like.

Teemo guides the First Mate out of the enclave, and the merfolk watch them go. The mood is tense, like they think they won't ever see the Captain or his scions ever again. Which is fair. All they've seen is me come in like I own the place and walk out with Hullbreak's core, with only a few words to try to placate them.

Time to bring some action into backing up the words, to try to ease their fears. It's expensive, but I should be able to afford the upkeep on all this, as well as the actual cost.

With the dwellers watching, the sea seems to come alive around the scions as they leave. Coral rapidly regrows, kelp and other sea flora growing thick and lush. Beyond what they can directly see, the spawners come back to life and start rapidly producing their new upgraded denizens. Copperfins and silverscales start to form schools and meander, while the sea cucumbers start the slow journey toward the corals.

I don't add any new scions yet, leaving that decision to Hullbreak.

It doesn't take long for Slash to create a small sea cave for the First Mate to deposit Hullbreak's core in, nor does it take long for the new kelp to grow in nice and thick, obscuring the entrance as well as a decent bit of the seabed.

I can't help but feel a little proud of how Hullbreak Harbor looks right now, and I'm encouraged by the small ember of hope I feel from the bond with the paranoid dungeon. There's still a lot of work to do, but I'm already feeling pretty accomplished.

Chapter 41

Tarl

The elven inspector lies in bed, awake far earlier than he'd prefer to be. Thedeim told him today is the day he moves on Hullbreak. Even now, he's trying to sort out how he truly feels about the water dungeon. He definitely doesn't like it, that much is simple. It killed his mentor. And yet . . . he feels sorry for it.

He could have just left the whole mess at that, until that letter. And then he told Thedeim about it, and that crazy dungeon actually said he'd do something about it! He's been doing a lot about it, too, and has been keeping Tarl at least vaguely informed of what's going on: infiltration, espionage, battle plans, and more.

He should feel relieved that the whole situation will be resolved soon, but he's just nervous. Dungeon battles are always messy, and even with Thedeim doing what he can to keep it contained, the elf's teeth are still on edge.

He sighs and gets out of bed, finally accepting that he's not going to get any further sleep this morning. He decides to put on his full inspecting gear today. If things go well, he might want to go delve Thedeim's new area. If it doesn't go well . . .

He shakes his head to banish the thought and focuses on putting his armor and gear on. It's a comforting ritual, requiring his attention to keep everything placed just right, but not so active as to work him up into more worrying. Once properly dressed, he grabs a fruit and a crusty roll before heading out the door. He'd like to stop by Cobble Bread for breakfast instead, but it probably won't actually open for close to an hour still.

Maybe he can surprise Telar by having a hot pot of tea waiting for her when she arrives. His mood lightens as he imagines surprising her in her domain, though his mood drops slightly as he's reminded of her question about Thedeim.

"What would you *classify him as?"*

He stayed quiet at the time, not wanting to worm his way around the geas, but even without it, he's not sure he would have replied, just for the implications of what he would classify Thedeim as.

Honestly, cloistered isn't too far off, if you think about it. It's just a period of isolation at the start of a dungeon's life before being exposed to the outside. He thinks Thedeim *did* have a period of isolation—just that it was more in the *middle* of the dungeon's existence.

The guild calls them lost dungeons—ones that have somehow been sealed from the world, often as a result of either a disaster or a fight between dungeons. Tarl can't think of anything else to explain that strange vision he got when he first saw Thedeim's core. Some kind of society with incredible magic; some kind of people living mundane lives full of wonder. The people . . . or the *holes* where people should have been, seemed to have access to incredible arcane devices and incredible architecture. Probably wonderful music, though he couldn't hear anything in his vision.

His mentor used to talk about kobolds sometimes; about how they've probably forgotten more about dungeons than the guild will ever know. He's tried to get Aranya to talk with him about kobold legends, but she generally changes the subject or talks in the kind of vague riddles that historians sometimes do. It's the kind of talk that Tarl always takes to mean the historian doesn't know the answer but doesn't want to admit it.

Stuff like that is why Tarl never fancied himself an academic. Maybe if he was, though, he'd have more evidence to support his suspicion that Thedeim is somehow one of the kobolds' ancient dungeons. He has no idea how he could have ended up in Fourdock if that's the case, but he can't think of anything else that could explain his development.

His musings carry him to the Dungeoneer's Guild, and as he unlocks it, he hears a bell ringing. He, at first, ignores it, taking it as maybe a call to prayer from the Crystal Shield church, or maybe someone signaling dawn. He's not usually up this early to hear such things. It's not until he's in the kitchen, filling the teapot, when he realizes something is strange. The bell is still ringing?

He sets the pot over the fireplace but doesn't light it yet. Instead, he returns outside, trying to figure out what's going on. He hears Poe's cawing, which sets his instincts on edge. It's not the kind of menacing cawing he used when he faced down that one group of delvers, but it's still strange to hear him. It's even more strange to see the large Raven Scion winging over the rooftops. Tracing his path back, Tarl finally notices the source of the bell: Thedeim's belfry.

He curses and quickly ducks back inside, scribbling a quick note to Telar, which he places on her desk.

At Thedeim
Tarl

He'd like to give more information than that, but he simply doesn't have it. He quickly locks the door on his way out and rushes to the dungeon. It feels . . . *wrong* to not be greeted by a chorus of caws, but he does his best to ignore it. He's also not greeted by Teemo, which also feels weird. Thankfully, he spots Tiny exiting the maze, and so hurries over.

"Tiny! Is something wrong?"

The large spider considers him for a moment, then extends a leg for the elf to climb aboard. He hesitates but a moment before doing just that. It's not like Tiny is the Voice. Hopefully, he can take Tarl to someone who can explain what's going on? Teemo would be the best, but if Thedeim is hoping to negotiate with Hullbreak, the Rat Scion will be indispensable there.

Entering a shortcut is always a strange experience, and it's even stranger when riding Tiny. It really drives home how he shouldn't be able to fit through one. He just closes his eyes and tries not to focus on the surreality of it, and soon finds himself in the public war room. He also finds he's not alone. It looks like Thing is here with Larx, and as he hops off Tiny, he spots the spiderkin triumvirate exit a shortcut with Fluffles.

He's not even sure the Conduit noticed him, as he quickly goes through a different shortcut. He stands for a few moments, awkwardly looking at the spiderkin, before the smallest one speaks up.

"So . . . what's going on?"

"I wish I knew," replies Tarl, his confusion growing.

They're rescued by the voice of Larx, the elder ratkin, speaking up so they can all hear him. "If you all come take a look at this, I think you'll understand." He steps a bit back from the map, letting the others move forward and see what he is seeing.

It takes Tarl a few moments to comprehend what he's seeing, then he quietly curses once he realizes what it is. "Hullbreak is pulling something," he grumbles, his eyes fixed to the encroaching mass of invaders depicted.

Vernew and Folarn look grim, but Norloke still looks like she's in the dark. "What am I looking at?"

"An army," replies the large tarantula woman, and the huntsmistress nods.

"But what is it doing?" asks the orb weaver. "It looks more like it's trying to attack the town, rather than the Weaver."

"That's because he is," speaks up Tarl, gaining the attention of the leaders. "I've read about some dungeons trying similar when they get into a war with a dungeon closer to a town, or situated in the middle of one like Thedeim is. If they can kill the delvers, they can cripple the rival's mana at the source."

Norloke looks horrified at the idea, and hesitates before speaking up again. "Do . . . Do you think Hullbreak could manage to do that?"

Tarl frowns as he considers the question before slowly shaking his head. "I don't *think* so . . . but I don't know if Thedeim can stop him from making a mess of the town and killing at least *some* people." They all look grim at that, but Tarl continues. "What's more: if Hullbreak actually manages to severely injure or kill any of the townsfolk, it'll be reclassified as Murderous. The only thing that's been keeping it from that classification is that it isn't sending hostile expeditions."

The dwellers all exchange looks. Larx is the first to speak up. "What can we do to help? Evacuate the people closest to the sea?"

". . . Maybe?" replies the inspector, looking frazzled. "I've never dealt with something like this before. The standard procedure *is* to evacuate if dungeons are fighting, but there isn't really anywhere to evacuate *to*! Fourdock never really saw a point in planning for something that seemed like an impossibility!"

Norloke speaks up. "We bring them to the Weaver; at least the ones willing to come."

"What about the army of birds?" asks Tarl, and Larx replies this time.

"Leave that to Aranya and Yvonne. They've already gone ahead to rally the delvers to provide a defense, should anything slip past Poe."

Tarl still looks out of his depth, but at least he feels like he has a raft in this storm now. "Okay . . . okay. You get your people prepared to help and meet at the Dungeoneer's Guild. Telar should be there by now. Between the two of us, we should be able to give groups quick paperwork to show that you're all sanctioned to help them evacuate."

Tarl sighs and sags slightly in relief at having a plan now, then steels himself, standing straight. "And after this is all over, I'm going to have a long talk with the mayor and the other guild heads. This is exactly the kind of plan that *should* have been in place, not something we have to throw together at the last moment."

All gathered nod and quickly go where they need to go. It's a lot to try to do on the fly like this, but the consequences for failure could be dire.

Chapter 42

Aranya

The two residents of Thedeim hurry through the streets, both trying not to worry too much about the clouds rolling in off the ocean. They both saw the map; they both know Thedeim is making his move on Hullbreak today.

What they're uncertain of is if he can keep Hullbreak's counter from destroying the town. Thankfully, he won't have to try and do it on his own.

"How long do you think it will take for them to get ready?" asks the kobold of her more experienced feathered friend.

"Some will already be awake, and so should take no time at all. Some . . . may sleep through this in its entirety," Yvonne admits. Aranya can't imagine someone sleeping through this . . . Well, maybe. She's seen Ragnar win drinking contests with people who take days to wake up, and whose hangovers make them wish they never woke up at all. The dwarf always seems to weather such escapades just fine. He doesn't seem to be much of a morning person, but he has that professional demeanor of a soldier who can get up and get right to marching, even if it takes a few miles to truly wake up.

She's not sure she's ever seen Aelara even yawn, much less sleep, so she's not too worried about her being groggy for something like this. She's just worried how many other adventurers they'll be able to gather in what little time they seem to have.

Her fears are partially assuaged as they near the guildhall; she can hear morning activities from within. While the sounds at night are often of raucous party and merriment, the morning sounds are more industrious; the sounds of people eating and chatting as they prepare for the day. Adventurers always have a day of danger ahead of them, so they celebrate a day of adventure behind, she supposes.

The two residents burst into the guild, only drawing a few eyes. Once Yvonne makes a line for the thin orc behind the bar, she draws a few more.

Karn the Slight greets the two as they approach, but doesn't offer them something to eat or drink just yet. It couldn't be more clear they have something important to discuss if they had the aranea carve it on a sign over their heads. "Heya. What's up?"

Yvonne cuts to the heart of the matter with her words, as she often does with her arrows. "Hullbreak is attacking the town with an army of seagulls."

Aranya can see him start to smile, thinking it's a good joke, but he can read the seriousness on their faces. "How bad?" he asks, all business.

"Bad enough that Thedeim is mobilizing his dwellers, too," answers the red kobold. Karn's widening eyes signify he understands the seriousness of the situation. He inhales and speaks loudly.

"Raid quest!"

The general murmurs of the guild go silent for a few moments as they all get the notification and option to join the raid party. Aranya and Yvonne join without hesitation, and they can feel the other adventurers quickly joining as well. In a matter of a heartbeat, the atmosphere inside the guild changes from people enjoying breakfast to people preparing for war. Breakfast is still eaten, but much quicker now.

"Any more details than that?" asks Karn of the two, and Aranya speaks up after a few moments.

"Lord Thedeim is making a move on Hullbreak Harbor. This must be the Harbor's attempt to strike back at him. We had all thought he was limited to only having significant forces under the waves, and so disregarded the seagull spawner."

She closes her eyes for a moment, the orange sphere of her pendant gently glowing for a few moments as she tries to divine details from her home Sanctuary.

". . . There is a scion with the gulls. Lord Thedeim has sent Poe, and will be sending Fluffles soon, too. The dwellers are focusing on plans to get the townsfolk to safety with the help of the Dungeoneer's Guild."

Karn considers that for a few moments, then nods. "Sounds like he's got a better civilian response than the mayor. They can keep the townsfolk out of the fight, so we'll get ourselves *into* it. Any better directions than *the sea*?"

Aranya slowly shakes her head. "None yet, I'm afraid."

The thin orc shrugs. "The docks should be as good a place to gather as any." He raises his voice before speaking again. "Raid leaves in five minutes. If you can't make that, either catch up at the docks or go to the Dungeoneer's Guild to offer them assistance." With that, he makes his exit to start spreading the information about what, specifically, is happening.

Aranya and Yvonne take the chance to head up to Aelara's and Ragnar's room. Inside, Ragnar is putting his armor on . . . Maybe even literally in his sleep. The kobold watches for a few interested seconds before Aelara gets her attention.

"What's happening? There's a raid party," she says with mild concern.

"Hullbreak is sending an army of gulls to attack the town. Lord Thedeim is sending forces to deal with it . . . but it will probably get messy," answers Aranya.

Ragnar grumbles an unintelligible insult to seagulls as he continues putting his armor on. Aelara just smirks at that. "So mostly mages and archers and other ranged attackers will be the most useful?"

Yvonne nods, before giving Ragnar a sideways glance and a small smirk. "He might be able to insult them enough to draw the attention of any that slip past Thedeim, though."

The dwarf mumbles something vaguely insulting to *everything* with feathers, earning a laugh from the gathered women. "That's the spirit," says Aelara with a smile, though it slips some as she looks out the window.

"Do you think the townsfolk will be alright?"

Aranya and Yvonne both nod, with the hawkwoman speaking up first. "Protecting them is our job. Even more than that, Thedeim's dwellers are working with the dungeoneers to help keep people from the worst of it."

Further questions are waylaid by the voice of Karn. "One minute!"

Aelara meets her friends' eyes as Ragnar gets his shield onto his back and his axe at his hip. "Let us go do our jobs, then."

Back down the stairs, most of the adventurers are gathered, and Aranya even spots the trio who tried to attack Yvonne. She still doesn't like them . . . but she has to admit that her Lord Thedeim seems to have knocked some manners into them, at the least.

"Alright, let's get going. I'll be giving more specific assignments on the way," announces Karn, leading the way out of the guild. Unsurprisingly, most of the adventurers with ranged attacks, of whatever variety, are to be stationed at the docks to help attack any gulls they can reach. Most of the more melee-focused people are to be runners and help coordinate, especially with the dwellers and Dungeoneer's Guild.

The rude trio are assigned to be wanderers, to move wherever is needed to get anything that can slip past the main group of defenders. Aranya doesn't like it, but she has to admit it's a good use of them. Their party isn't exactly melee, but they're also not capable of operating at the kind of ranges that true archers and mages can.

The orders given, the adventurers split off to go do their duties. Ragnar is much more lucid as they approach the dock, and at Karn's nod, he steps forward to be the vanguard. Yvonne may have said it jokingly back in the room, but Ragnar's unique ability to get and keep an enemy's attention can help give the ranged defenders more time to deal with their targets.

A gnome walks through the loose formation of mages and archers, passing out potions as she goes, and Aranya moves to help in her own way. Minute orange threads spread from the small orb around her neck as she weaves her faith around all gathered. "Weaver's Gentle Touch," she intones, calling upon the subtle actions of her Sanctuary to help guide them all to victory, and to keep them all safe.

Her contribution made, she and the others can only stare out at the ocean and the battle being waged between the forces of Thedeim and Hullbreak. No gulls seem to be getting past Poe and his multitude, but she can feel a growing tension from the others.

"Something's wrong," says an orc with the look of a shaman about him.

Aranya looks at him, confused. "What do you mean? None of the gulls are getting past Poe."

He shakes his head and points up, to the clouds over the chaotic battle. "The gulls aren't the actual threat. Look at the clouds."

Aranya does, but she doesn't know what she's looking at. She's used to there being rocks over her head, not clouds. A few others, however, look at the slow motion of the cover and frown as well.

"The enemy scion is doing something."

That causes everyone to frown, but what else can they do?

"No . . ." whispers an elf who looks like he'd be more fit standing on a deck than a dock. "I've seen a storm like that, once. Way to the south. The ocean swells and rages as the skies tear at anything in the way. Our ship was out past its wrath, but the port we were trying to get to . . . just wasn't *there* afterward."

A loud boom causes everyone to flinch, and Yvonne squints as she gazes at the hole in the clouds. "I see Poe . . . and Fluffles. And I think the enemy scion. It looks like an albatross."

Before she can explain further, the orc shaman's eyes widen in shock. "What is *happening* out there?" he demands with fear and awe.

"Fluffles is . . . building something. Some kind of orb," answers Yvonne, uncertain of what she's actually seeing.

"He's devouring the storm," speaks the orc as he makes a gesture—calling a natural spirit in the form of a turtle—and starts working his magic to ensure the safety of those around him.

The nautical elf and a few others warily watch the skies, and Aranya suspects they have Storm affinity. While the others can only watch in confusion as weaker booms reach their ears, the ones presumably with Storm affinity seem to be getting more and more concerned.

They and Yvonne all gasp at the same time, while the others can only look on and behold the result of whatever happened. The hole in the clouds closes in an instant before the storm simply starts to dissipate.

Everyone stands around in different states of confusion or shock as the looming threat just fades. Nervous cheers are heard, though the ones with Storm affinity don't join in. Eventually, the orc shaman seems to remember something and looks at Aranya.

"What did your dungeon just do?" he asks, less as an accusation and more as someone who just witnessed something profound.

"I . . . don't know. What do you think he did?"

The orc looks back to the clouds, his eyes tracing the large raven and the winged serpent making their way back toward town.

"It ate a storm and spat it back at the one who made it."

Chapter 43

After the morning's excitement, delver activity is . . . *different.* Most of the gatherer delvers are basically delving like everything is the same. I dunno if they managed to sleep through the whole thing or if they think it's something that doesn't really concern them. Either way, they're all happily delving and gathering, and it's situation normal on that front.

The Crystal Shield guys are also more or less normal, though they seem to be enjoying the return of the more ordinary undead. I think their lower-level members were having difficulties with the vined skeletons and fungal zombies, and their resistance to a lot of anti-undead stuff. With the normal skellies not needing to go harass Hullbreak, they can train a lot smoother now.

I probably shouldn't be surprised that the more adventury delvers are taking a break to evaluate. Fluffles put on quite a show with that storm. He's picked up Wind and Storm affinity both, as well as a new title: Stormeater.

I'm pretty sure he could easily expand to get Lightning, Water, and probably Thunder/Sonic, too, but he's been training with Rocky enough to see my Boxer working on his "fundamentals." I think he agrees that he should focus a bit more on truly mastering his new affinities before trying to expand to new ones. A strong house needs a strong foundation, right?

And speaking of strong foundations, I'm working on managing that with Hullbreak. I think what he has now should be a good stepping stone for getting back into the black, as far as mana is concerned. His dwellers are still looking pretty uncertain about things, but Yendo is trying to raise their spirits about the whole affair. It looks like most of them are just going to explore Hullbreak and the changes, but Yendo actually has convinced a few to go explore a bit outside! I consider sending one of my scions out with them, but decide not to. They need to take some steps on their own, even if they don't have feet.

Hullbreak is building up a good head of worry over it, but he hasn't tried to stop them nor send the First Mate out with them. She has her jaws full already trying to keep the dwellers calm. My new vassal is trying to distract himself by looking at the various new nodes and refreshed spawners. I can still feel a good knot of worry through the bond, but there's also a bit of . . . I think *peace* is a bit strong of a word, but something along those lines.

I'm probably going to try to keep new changes on hold for the moment there, let them try to get a feel for their new normal. Hullbreak will have to deal with new delvers eventually, but for now, I want him to get a bit more comfortable with the idea of a new way, first.

I think his first delvers might be my own dwellers, though I'll need to wait for the leaders to get back before I can even float the idea . . . And I'll need Teemo to get back, too. I nudge him about that, and he just nods from atop the First Mate's dorsal fin before speaking up.

"The Boss wants me to start heading back so he can give people more details and plan stuff with his own dwellers. You have everything in fin?" he asks with a smirk.

The First Mate smirks and nods.

"Yes, Teemo. The Captain should be fine with his new Sanctum, and the dwellers just need time to adjust." She pauses for a moment, uncertain, before continuing. ". . . The Admiral is really fine with the Captain revealing his Sanctum to his dwellers?"

Teemo nods. "Yeah. He keeps his own pretty secret, but he's not going to force Hullbreak to do the same. Besides, him and the merfolk are too close for the Boss to expect them to be able to just cut ties."

"What are the Admiral's further plans for the Captain?" she presses, looking like she's worried she's pushing too hard. She deflates a bit as Teemo chuckles.

"Heh, I dunno if I'd call any of it a 'plan,' but he has some vague ideas. Long term: he wants to normalize delving again. He knows that's going to take a bit of time, probably for you and Fourdock both, but the sooner he starts, the sooner it'll be done. For the next couple days, he's gonna just let you guys try to adjust . . . Though you might see a visit from his own dwellers, heh."

"I admit to wanting to meet them and hear their development," the shark states.

"Cool. Welp, I'm outta here. You guys go ahead and explore and adjust. It's different, I know, but the Boss is pretty good at different." With that, he releases her fin and starts shortcutting his way toward the beachhead. Oh man, I should probably clean that up some . . . Or maybe leave it as is and eventually get Hullbreak to expand to it. Could be a good spot for small encounters or something.

As Teemo makes his way back, my prodigals return as a group. Aranya, Yvonne, Aelara, and Ragnar, along with the skinny orc Guildmaster Karn, as well as Larx, Vernew, Folarn, Norloke, and Tarl. My dwellers all inhale and sigh at being back home; Aranya and Yvonne both look happy to be back, too. Ragnar and Aelara smile as they see the activity of the gatherer delvers, while Karn looks like he's scheming . . . or just looking. He's kinda hard to get a read on. Tarl has his business face on as he approaches the porch.

"Dungeon Thedeim, the Dungeoneer's Guild would ask you bring forth your Voice so we may talk about what happened today," he says solemnly. I don't think I'm in trouble, but there's definitely a lot to talk about, he's not wrong there. I poke Fluffles to lead them to the public war room. Hopefully, they'll see Teemo's location and understand that they're on hold until he can get back.

My wingnoodle uncoils from atop the belfry and glides down. The orc tenses for a moment when he sees my scion. "That's not the Voice. The Voice was the rat, right?"

Larx chuckles and nods. "Indeed, Teemo is the Voice. Lord Thedeim tends to use his Conduit when Teemo isn't immediately available." Tarl nods at that, and Karn relaxes slightly . . . and stumbles a bit as Ragnar elbows him.

"Calm down, Guildmaster. Th' Conduit's perfectly safe!"

Karn looks like he strongly disagrees, but he doesn't voice it with Fluffles settling on the ground before them. My noodle gives the gathered group a hiss and motions with his tail for them to follow him, which they do. The walk is quiet, but thankfully not very long, and soon, they all can take seats around the map table. Fluffles points at Teemo's location, and though they can see him moving much more quickly than he should be able to thanks to the shortcut, it's still going to be a bit until he arrives.

Tarl sees that and sighs, deflating a bit in his chair, but doesn't speak up yet. Karn follows suit, but I can tell he's feigning being relaxed. There's still a bit of tension to him, and his eyes keep wandering to Fluffles.

Yeah, he probably saw what Fluffles did, or has had a bunch of reports on it.

The silence grows more than a little awkward, and soon, Larx does what he does best. "Tarl, you said there was a Merfolk Enclave in Hullbreak?"

It takes the elf a moment to realize he's being addressed before he nods. "Yes, Hullbreak Harbor had a Merfolk Enclave."

"*Has*," corrects the aged ratkin, pointing at the area still clearly labeled. Tarl squints as he scrutinizes the map, then is forced to nod.

"Right, has." After a moment, he groans and rubs his face with his hands. "Vassalized, not subsumed, then."

Folarn quirks an eyeridge at that. "You'd prefer the Weaver subsume Hullbreak?"

Tarl sighs. "I don't know. I mean . . . it'll probably be better for everyone with him vassalized instead, but it's going to be a mess for a while . . . Not to mention all the paperwork . . ." he finishes with a grumble.

Aranya laughs at that. "You have a whole year to prepare for it, right?"

"Oh boy, a stay of execution," replies Tarl flatly, earning a laugh from everyone, and the tension mostly evaporates. Karn still keeps an eye on Fluffles, but I don't see his fingers twitching anymore.

"Well, we can at least tell him what's been going on in town," says the guildmaster, deciding he'd rather talk than just wait. "He might not be able to talk, but he can still listen, yeah?"

Aranya nods, so Karn continues.

"Well, on the adventurer side of things at least, people are uncertain. Feelings are mixed. On the one hand, Thedeim dealt with a threat to the town. On the other, it's arguably a threat he caused, and there's a potential *new* threat."

"Fluffles," says Yvonne as a statement, not a question. She's probably noticed Karn's unease. He nods at her.

"Yeah. Everyone knows he's a Conduit, but knowing it and *understanding* it are two different things. Most of the guild can only guess at the actual power needed to do what he did, but there are a couple people with Storm affinity who could feel what he was doing."

If I had blood, it'd run cold at that. Did I accidentally let out the secret of affinities and science linking them?

"They could feel Fluffles there taking apart the storm and focusing it. I've heard of mages being able to steal the strength of an enemy's spell to power their own, but it's the kind of talk you hear rumors about, not something you get to watch unfold out in the bay."

I relax a bit at that, and feel Fluffles relax some, too. They're not putting it together just yet, seems like, so that's good.

"Are they scared of the Weaver?" asks Norloke. Karn shrugs.

"I wouldn't call it *scared*, but they're definitely reevaluating how they feel about him. The various Storm affinities seem to be in awe, especially Basger. That's the shaman," he clarifies as he glances at Aranya, who nods in recognition. "He's probably going to try to come visit Fluffles for wisdom or something. I doubt he'll be the last."

Fluffles looks surprised at that, and I laugh to myself as I imagine a Fluffles fan club. I feel a bit of indignance through the bond at that, which only makes me laugh more.

"So yeah," finishes Karn, "things with the guild are going to be a bit messy for a couple days as people adjust."

There are various nods around the table, and it takes a few seconds for someone to speak up and put in their two cents. Said person is Tarl.

"The Dungeoneer's Guild, officially, doesn't have much opinion now that it's plain that Hullbreak has been vassalized. It'll be more paperwork for me and Telar—mostly Telar—but that comes with the job. Unofficially, I think the townsfolk are going to have a reaction to this, as well as the mayor."

Folarn sighs and speaks up. "The people we helped evacuate, while appreciative of the help, seemed to want to know what the town government was doing about all this. We didn't have any answers to give them. While some were upset with us, most were understanding and seemed to be saving their ire for a different target."

Tarl nods at that. "Most towns with an active dungeon, like Thedeim, will create and prepare various contingency plans for things just like this. Even without a potential dungeon clash, there are always potential monster attacks or brigand sieges—other things that could pose an existential crisis for the town. As far as I'm aware . . . Fourdock doesn't have any."

Karn speaks up to add, "I don't know of any, either. I called a raid party once Aranya and Yvonne explained the situation because I couldn't think of anything else to get a response going any quicker."

Aelara groans after hearing that, drawing the eyes of everyone gathered. "I understand what you two are hinting at. It really *is* going to be a mess for a while, isn't it." Tarl and Karn both nod, though everyone else looks confused. After a few moments, Aelara continues.

"Thedeim has accidentally stepped on the toes of the mayor, and he may or may not see it as an accident. The dungeon identified a threat, organized a response to protect the entire town, and dealt with the threat, all before the mayor could even get out a statement. He snubbed the established political power, making it look both weak and incompetent, and he did so publicly."

Glances are exchanged around the table as that sinks in. It's not a very charitable interpretation of what happened, but it's also not inaccurate. I've been deliberately trying to stay out of anything with the local government or politics, but that might have just led to me accidentally jumping into it with both feet.

Chapter 44

"Alright, what are you guys all talking about that has the Boss feeling so out of his depth about?" demands Teemo as he is finally able to join everyone in the war room.

I'm not that *intimidated.*

Teemo just smirks. "Sure you aren't, Boss."

I make a note to figure out a way to properly huff later. *Short version: I've stepped in politics.*

Teemo shudders at that. "I'd rather you stepped into a sewer, Boss."

Tell me about it.

Further snark is derailed as the gathered people start failing to stifle their humor at the half-conversation they're hearing.

"Here I thought our gracious Lord Thedeim was letting us govern ourselves so we could grow. Now I find out it's because he hates politics," says Larx with a grin as he feigns being offended. The spiderkin triumvirate grin and nod, each pretending to be scandalized in her own way.

"It can be both," retorts Teemo, and everyone laughs. He lets them get it out of their system, waiting for them all to calm down before continuing. "So, how bad is it?"

Tarl and Karn both consider the question, though Karn speaks up first. "It depends on how the mayor decides to take it, and how much spin and lies we're willing to make."

Tarl sighs and nods at that. "I've only seen the mayor a few times, so I don't know how he'll react to something like this."

"I've only seen him once," admits Karn. "Though I try to keep up on noble intrigue."

Tarl blanches at that. "Better you than me."

Karn smirks. "Helps keep the rust off, heh. Anyway, our Lord Mayor Rezlar Herjan Kalsorthoth Niyeroul if'Gofnar the Eighth is probably not going to react poorly to what's been done, but he's going to need to do *something* if he doesn't want the various guilds complaining to his father. Rumor is, his family sent him here to try to get him some backbone. Live a more rugged life, deal with the humble people who aren't going to just kiss your boots because they cost more than their house, stuff like that."

Aelara sighs. "Instead, he's holed himself in his manor and left the actual running of the town to the guilds," she says, clearly used to the games nobles play.

Karn nods at her. "It wasn't a bad situation, to be honest. Even with Neverrest, things were pretty stable. A noble who doesn't interfere is way better than one who sticks his nose in and ruins everything. Things like trade deals and such are implied to have his consent. The dungeon dealing with a threat like that is clearly not something the mayor planned, and clearly only happened *because* the mayor didn't have a plan for a situation like that."

"So what should the Boss do? Send me to negotiate something? Pretend there actually *was* a plan?" asks my Voice. Karn shakes his head.

"Negotiating would probably be a good idea, but there's no pretending there was a plan. The guild members will be talking about how I had to call a raid party to try to deal with this."

Tarl speaks up. "And the citizens we evacuated will have noticed how fresh the ink was on the letters of affiliation we gave the dwellers. I imagine there's a crowd of unhappy people around the town hall already, and probably some outside the Mayoral Manor, too."

"Are we looking at a revolt?" asks Teemo, echoing my concern. Even if the absentee mayor is absolute scum, things can get really messy if the people decide to oust him.

Karn shakes his head. "Nah. Politics actually acts in our favor on this one. He's the only noble in town, so the only means to remove him are . . . not pretty. People will be upset about all this, but nobody is going to want to go *that* far. It should mostly be a lot of yelling and complaining, and probably letters getting written."

Hmm . . . a letter. I give Teemo a quick explanation of my idea. He doesn't look so sure about it, but he floats it for the others.

"What about a formal apology?"

"From the mayor?" Karn grimaces. "I wouldn't bet on it. Showing that kind of weakness could get his father to recall him and send someone else."

Teemo shakes his head. "Not from him. From the Boss."

While most of the table looks confused at that, and my dwellers look plain unhappy, Karn and Aelara both look thoughtful. Teemo decides to continue with the idea.

"Something that says the Boss knows he overstepped, he made a mistake in underestimating Hullbreak, blah, blah. The kind of thing that says he still understands who the town belongs to."

Karn chuckles. "I think everyone will see through it, but it's still a good idea. The mayor can even pretend to be magnanimous and accept your apology."

"Will the townsfolk buy that?" asks Aranya, not looking very convinced.

Karn shrugs while Aelara speaks up. "He'll have to present a plan for dealing with dangers going forward, but it could work. People will see through the pretense, but as long as it's clear something is being done, most will be willing to let it slide. Nobles hardly ever apologize to each other, let alone to ordinary citizens, so that's the closest they can reasonably expect."

"But he *doesn't* have a plan," points out Norloke.

Karn grins. "Which means we can hand him one and let him pretend it was his the whole time."

Norloke gives him a flat look. "*We* don't have one, either."

Karn deflates a bit at that but presses onward. "We don't *not* have a plan. Evacuate civilians, marshal the fighters"—he winks over at Teemo—"petition the dungeon for help, heh."

"Evacuate where? F'r how long? How will ye feed 'em, keep 'em safe?" asks Ragnar, getting into the kinds of details that will be needed.

"Here, for now?" suggests Karn. "Thedeim should be able to feed and keep people safe for at least a couple days, and we can work on some kind of mini hold or something?"

Ragnar strokes his beard as he considers that, and Larx speaks up. "My people will help. We're working on expanding our warrens, and should be able to house at least some people, should the need arise. We'll also be working on our own evacuation plans, too, should something decide to attack from the depths instead of from the sea."

Folarn nods at that. "As will we. We need to make sure we're ready for the next time something like this happens. We've been working on plans slowly, since we expect the scythemaws will be a semiregular occurrence, but after this, I think we need to get plans solidified sooner rather than later."

I let them get to working out the details as I'm reminded of something I asked for a while ago but never actually got around to looking at. I asked Tarl for records of as much as he could give me. While he delivered, I've been too distracted to actually sit down and pay attention to them. No time like the present.

It doesn't take me long to find the books and notes; of course, Honey has organized them into the library. I focus on them and the information therein. It's weird, bringing the information to the fore. It's less like I'm learning a new thing and more like I'm remembering something I already know.

Some bits were already obvious to me, like that we're pretty northerly located.

Snow by the ocean isn't something you see in the tropics, after all. The ocean out west is also plain. To the north there are mostly mountains, and to the east it looks like rivers and farmland. Far to the east is a lake, and beyond the rivers that feed it are the Orcish Wanderlands and the Beastkin Principalities. Further east past them lie more mountains, claimed by the dwarves, seems like.

To the south of Fourdock is more of the kingdom of Horlon, apparently the country I'm in. It looks like it's mostly farms, rolling hills, and loose forests, though there's only so much detail Tarl could reasonably give me without giving me an entire library. It would have made Honey happy, though, heh. It does show we're a long way from the capital, at least. No wonder there's not much worry about defense—we're in the back end of nowhere. The orcs are apparently nomadic but have agreed to "not cross the Gofnar," which I suppose explains why there's a Lake Gofnar, Gofnar River, and *Also*-Gofnar River.

Wait . . . Gofnar? Isn't the mayor something-something Gofnar? Maybe his family is from around the lake. That looks like it'd be a pretty big trade hub. Waterways are always great for trading. There's not much info about it in the packet, which is disappointing, even if it's not surprising. I might need to start asking the aranea to give some quests for various books. While just seeing Honey's happy dance is a pretty good motivation, I also need to get more info.

Now that I have a vassal *and* a protégée, I'm probably going to be a major economic hub all on my own. Depending on how the stuff with the Southwood goes, I could be even more of a mover and shaker. I'm not really looking forward to having to butt heads with nobles and other political entities, but that's the price to pay for prosperity, I suppose. You get more, people want some. The hard part is making sure to share with the right people, and to make sure the ones who *don't* want to share can't just take what they want.

Chapter 45

I look over the maps and try to figure out what my next goal is, while the others continue to plan what to do with the mayor and such. I'm pretty sure I could just fully ignore him and the larger government if I really wanted. Tarl said I'm my own thing, and nations tend to try to stay out of dungeon business, after all. Still, I don't want to be a jerk of a neighbor. I'm confident they can hammer and smooth things out, especially if I give the mayor the lip service of an apology.

So . . . what else do I need to do?

I need to sort out Hullbreak; that's definitely a major thing I need to do. He's all set for delvers now, but how do I actually get delvers to go delve? After the day's events, even *I'm* seeing a bit less activity, and I don't have the reputation of being dangerous.

There's also the simple fact that, even if Hullbreak had no problem with delvers, everything except the seagull spawner is underwater. But I'm pretty sure it used to be friendlier, before the accident. So how did people delve?

I take a moment to look through what Tarl gave me on it, but nothing really mentions how Hullbreak was actually being delved. Were people just able to make water potions and go like that?

I take a moment to get Teemo's attention, and he hops over to Tarl while the others are discussing a few details.

"Hey, Tarl . . . how did people delve Hullbreak?"

The elf blinks for a moment. "What? Oh, right, your new vassal. Ah . . . I believe most of the delving was fishing."

"That counts?"

He nods. "A lot of aquatic dungeons are prime fishing locations. It's a different sort of contest, but it's still a battle between delver and denizen."

Teemo's thoughtful look mirrors my reaction to that. If fishing works . . . that could be a lot easier.

"Thanks," says Teemo with a smile, and lets Tarl slip back into paying attention to the discussion at the table.

Fishing shouldn't be too difficult to get going, at least. Hullbreak doesn't seem close enough to any of the shores for it to work without a boat, but that's at least an option.

Okay . . . other goals.

Violet, definitely. I think she's procrastinating expanding past her door, but now that the maws are done, I'll probably try to encourage her to do that. From what I can tell, she'll get the immediate cavern that's past her borders with this expansion, and I think it'll take another to get next to the aquifer lake. I can't tell if she'll be able to get the entire lake in one go or if she'll have to take bites, but I can definitely feel her curiosity about the water through our bond.

I also need to check the progress of the trail to the Southwood. The last reports from the expeditions were that everything was progressing slowly yet smoothly. With Hullbreak no longer needing his butt kicked, I should be able to send Leo out to help direct and keep track of the progress. I should also see if Teemo can help; maybe making shortcuts between the little outposts or something. I'll just need to be mindful of when, or even *if* I send him. Helping the Southwood is probably a good idea, but if Teemo's out making shortcuts, he's not going to be here, able to talk to people.

Come to think of it, though . . . I'll need to send him to talk to the Southwood at some point. Talking is his main job, after all.

On the home front . . . should I work on my next enclave? It feels a bit early for that, though. My spiderkin are getting a lot more settled now, but I think I want to wait a bit longer for that.

I could expand again. I consider that for a few seconds before setting the idea aside, too. No, I should consolidate my territory and get working more on the deep-cavern areas first. My Earth elemental spawner is still really low level, and I should put the finishing touches on the place before getting more.

That was always my biggest problem in games like *Civilization* and *Stellaris*: expanding too quickly instead of developing what I had. Of course, in those, you have to war if you want to expand after the early game, as everything gets colonized. I haven't seen another dungeon down here except for Violet. There might be more, but my gut says I won't find another for a while.

And if there's no pressing need to go grab everything first, I might as well make sure I develop what I have properly. So . . . what *do* I have?

I have the main manor house and the yard, as well as the hedge maze, for the surface. Tiny's in the maze, Poe's on the roof, and I keep most of my low-level stuff in the area: rats, snakes, birds, the occasional slime.

Hmm . . . I never realized it, but my snake and bird spawners are pretty low level. I could get some tougher birds for . . . maybe the rooftop? The back of the cemetery, with the wolves?

The birds will probably have to wait until I expand past the cemetery. I just don't have a good place for them.

Stronger snakes could be a good addition to the deep caverns, though. Right now, they're mostly elementals and a few spiders. I'll put a pin in that for the moment and think harder about it once I get down to brushing up in there.

Below the manor are the tunnels. Snakes in there *would* rule. Maybe I should test there, first. Right now, they're mostly bats, slimes, and spiders. With the bats specialized as fruitbats, and the slimes specialized for purifying ore . . . it's mostly spiders and a few of the tougher vipers and rats. I'll see about encouraging the stalactsprites to come in, especially since they seem to do such a good job on the gremlins.

Right, I also need to get a mole and a gremlin to join . . . and maybe one of those cave stoats that like to eat Violet's cave bunnies.

Pin in that. Back to taking stock.

Below the tunnels are the deep caverns, which really only have the rock-slides and stalactsprites. Definitely need something more normal for down here. I think the snakes will be a good addition, along with the new things, if we can get them. The access shaft also runs from the caverns up to near the entry cave in the yard. There's also the Spiderkin Enclave down here, of course, with the underswamps past them. The cave lobster hatcheries seem to be working just fine, and they help round out and stabilize their diet with what they hunt in the swamps. Oh, and the dire mosquito invaders.

Yeah . . . not really in the market to add them to my spawners, thanks.

Back on the surface, there's the cemetery. It's mostly for ordinary cemetery things, though there is the wolf spawner in the back, as well as the zombie (technically fleshy undead, but they're close enough to zombies for me), skeleton, and crawling hand spawners. Oh, and the second rat spawner, as well as the bee one.

That's a thing I should have my ratlings do: make some apiaries. Most of the honey stuff is down in the library. Even with Honey running a tight ship in there, messes can happen. I could set up the apiaries in the back of the cemetery and let the wolves guard them. I'll keep it basic until I expand past the wall up there. Don't want fights to range too far or get too loud in there.

Under the cemetery is the crypt complex, where it's wall-to-wall undead, with the occasional wolf or widow thrown in for variety. I like my green skeletons and fungal zombies. They're encouraging some new herbalism nodes in there that the Crystal Shield guys seem to love.

The Ratkin Enclave is deeper in, and they're nice and established by now. They have some good mushroom beds stacked in rooms in there, and they're cultivating all kinds of different varieties. Their staple is something that looks a lot like a portobello to me: big fat caps with short stems. There's even a weird one that grows tall and thin which they dry out, grind, and use similarly to flour. The mushroom bread is still a work in progress, but it fills bellies and supplements their hunting.

There's also Rocky's arena down here. I should give that the polish it deserves before I go do anything else with spawners and expanding and such. It's been dug out, and the arena itself is made, but the boxing area is still sadly missing its boxing *ring*. How do they even make a boxing ring? Boards with a tough silk tarp will work for now, but I'm pretty sure there's a lot more give to the floor of a proper boxing ring.

I chew on options as my mind wanders, and my attention drifts to the underswamps past the spiderkin, reminding me of something I've been idly wanting to do for a while but seemed too far out of my reach. It's still a ways off . . . but close enough for me to actually consider, now.

I'm pretty sure Aranya must have come from somewhere past the underswamps. The aquifer lake isn't something you just cross on foot. The swamps aren't a picnic for that, either, but it's at least feasible. Somewhere past the scythemaws, there must be more kobolds.

I look over my goals as I consider that.

Hullbreak needs proper delving—get fishing boats. Violet needs to expand—just give her a little push, maybe a quest for it. Spiderkin need to get settled properly—just need time. The caverns need more encounters—add in snakes and maybe moles/gremlins/both. Assimilate moles/gremlins—just need to let Jello do her work. Rocky's arena needs finishing—shouldn't be too difficult to get a basic ring built. The Southwood needs help—Leo can focus more on that now that Hullbreak is my vassal.

Aranya's people are out there. Find some way to contact them.

Chapter 46

Alright, so: what first? I really want to get delving going with Hullbreak, but I really should give him a bit more time before I start trying to give quests to fish in there. It'd probably be a good idea to let Tarl inspect before I try that, anyhow.

Violet is probably a good place to start. All I need to do to encourage her to expand is to give her a quest to do it. While my income isn't as far out ahead of my expenses as I'd prefer, I still have plenty saved up to pass a quest through the bond. I can feel her taking her time to examine and consider what she should do with it, and I leave her to it. I'm not trying to shove her out of the nest; I just want to give her the little nudge she needs to do a bit more.

I also tell the aranea to start occasionally giving quests to do something in Violet: hunt a rabbit, pluck a mushroom, something like that. With the maws done, delvers should be able to delve her properly without needing to worry about getting eaten.

Next up . . . get Rocky's ring made. I had been putting it off to try to get the flooring just right, but the whole thing seems like it's more complex than I expected. Or maybe I'm overthinking it. What if boxing rings really *are* just a wooden floor with a thick cloth over it?

At least the turnbuckles and ropes shouldn't be too difficult to make. I spend a little time drawing up some basic plans before giving them to Coda. It's not *quite* in his wheelhouse, but he seems to like building stuff, and his ratlings are only getting more and more sure in their craft. Most of it was digging and carving, but there are still the smithing ones he can get help from, so I'm not too worried.

Now, the snake spawner. I haven't been paying it the attention it deserves, even with my Conduit calling it home. I have normal little bitey snakes, venomous little bitey snakes, bigger venomous bitey snakes, and spitting cobras who are not technically cobras . . . I think. I specialized them for venom a while ago, and looking at it closer, it seems to be a variety of magic specialization. So whatever else I get will probably be things you don't want to bite you, and maybe things that will be able to cast actual stuff at you, too.

Welp, might as well spend the mana and see what we get!

I pour the required amount into the spawner and watch with excitement as I wait for what it'll make! And it makes . . . two snakes at once? That's it? More spawn speed? Not the *worst* upgrade but—Oh, I'm wrong. That's a single snake, two heads. They(?) look around a little before taking a shortcut down toward the cavern layer, and I take a moment to get a better look at what they are.

A twinsnake. Fair enough, I suppose. That's an interesting little critter. I think *they* is the right term, since each head apparently has a different job. It's like someone stapled a classic fighter to a classic wizard. And made them both snakes. One head has Kinetic affinity and the other has Poison affinity.

I wonder if they differentiate between Venom and Poison affinities here? I hope not. If you're venomous, it's bad when you bite someone. If you're poisonous, it's bad if someone bites *you*, and it seems like the kinetic head is all about avoiding that.

I watch as they stalk a small swarm of dire mosquitoes, and am glad to see the poison head is definitely able to be offensive with its affinity. The kinetic head can be a bit offensive, too, as it starts telekinetically grabbing and smashing the invaders. The poison head launches little poison projectiles . . . venom projectiles? I feel like the distinction falls apart a bit when the nasty stuff is being thrown around. Whatever the technical term, the doublenoodle has no trouble dealing with the small swarm, so I'm calling it a win.

I watch my new denizens as they start to spread out in my domain, enjoying the new little bit of weirdness they bring.

Karn

The thin orc can't help but smile as he slips into the mayor's manor after sunset. Used to be, if he was doing this, he was going to be taking as many valuables as he could unreasonably hold. This time, however, he hopes to drop something off, and maybe even leave with something valuable that he can't actually hold.

A good deal can be worth . . . well, a *good deal*, after all, and is a lot harder to stuff in a bag and sell to a fence. Those candlesticks are tempting, though. He resists his rusty urges as he slips through the estate. The guards are trying, bless them, but a rogue who has survived to be able to retire is way above their pay grade.

He finds the young lord in his chambers, looking like a student who has gotten behind. Except, instead of books surrounding him, it's letters, scrolls, and whatever else the people could send to show their ire. Long auburn hair is looking frazzled and frayed, either from the stress itself or from the young elf trying to tear it out. Mysterious blue eyes are looking shallow and unfocused, the angry words hardly able to make the journey from the page to his mind with those as their portal. Expensive silks are rumpled, pale skin is even paler, and ink stains manicured hands. The lad is an adult, if only just, and clearly has no idea how to handle the mess that Thedeim has accidentally given him.

Karn nods to himself as he sees the lad. Someone that deep will take any rope to get out of it, even if they have to wrap it around their own throat. Luckily for the young Lord if'Gofnar, Karn is there to offer an actual lifeline.

Considering how to best approach him, he attempts some unsubtle subtlety. He quietly paces around the room, looking for a loose board, and finds one without too much effort.

The noble elf slumps as he hears the sound and speaks as he stands. "What should I *do*, Mill—" He stops as he sees Karn standing there, the orc's hands behind his back. ". . . You're not Miller."

Karn chuckles and shakes his head. "No, I'm not. I also know it's not something that actually inspires confidence, but I'm not here to hurt you. I'm actually here to help."

The elf just falls back into his chair and gestures listlessly at the pile of angry correspondence. "I don't think I need an assassin for any of them, thank you."

Karn laughs and shakes his head. "I'm not an assassin. I never was. I always preferred burglary to assassination. Always sat easier on my conscience to make off with a few trinkets than a life."

". . . Is that what you're here for, then? Come to pick over the corpse before the other vultures can swoop in?" asks the young noble elf bitterly. Karn shakes his head and pulls the fat rolled scroll case from behind his back, the result of the long meeting in Thedeim's war room.

"Actually, I'm here to help salvage the mess and save you a lot of face among the townspeople," he replies as he holds it out for the beleaguered elf to take. The mayor stares for a few seconds before reaching out to accept the scroll.

"That'd be a trick. What's the price for me to only have my name dragged through the mud instead of being disowned?" he asks with a sigh.

"I'm not here to offer to pull you out of the mess with a noose, lad . . . Lord Rezlar," Karn corrects himself. The elf before him might be battered and beaten in the political sense, but there's no point in adding insult to injury.

He just rolls his eyes at Karn's informality and opens the case to look over the papers therein. His defeated attitude chips and frays as he quickly skims the papers, and he looks at Karn with respect and a spark of hope.

"Is . . . Is the dungeon actually on board with this?"

Karn nods. "Thedeim is. He is fully willing to apologize and pretend that plans had been in the works, and you just needed funding from the kingdom at large to implement. His rapid development has put you in an awkward spot, but it also gives you an opportunity."

The elf starts looking more uncertain, now that his future is not certainly ruined, and looks back at the papers. "Yes . . . that's in the draft of a speech for me to give, too. But . . . why? Why not try to oust me and prepare Fourdock to be taken as an enclave?"

Karn shrugs. "Because he doesn't want to. Politics, at large, seems to repulse him."

Lord Rezlar sighs at that. "At least he gets a choice in it," he states quietly before speaking up a bit. "But what do *you* get out of it?"

Karn grins like a teacher whose student has aced a test. "I get a stable town for my adventurers to recuperate in, and a stable dungeon for them to delve . . . *Three* stable dungeons for them to delve, in fact."

The lord mayor considers that for a few seconds before his face lights up. "Ah, Miller! *There* you are!"

Karn's blood runs cold as he hears a polite voice from behind him. "I was making tea for the young master and his guest." A silver tray with two steaming cups of tea makes itself known in his periphery, supported by a spotless white glove. It's attached to an immaculate black sleeve, which is in turn supported by an older elf with gray skin and short slicked white hair. If there was a Butler-affinity dungeon, this elf would be its scion and Voice.

"Sir's is the cup nearest him," offers Miller, and Karn slowly accepts it. He doesn't drink as the elf moves to offer Lord Rezlar his own cup.

"Ah, thank you, Miller. My friend here, uh . . ."

"Karn," fills in the orc, still trying to process what's going on. There was nobody else in the room. As the young lord starts to explain to Miller what Karn's proposal is, Karn absently takes a sip of the tea, then locks up again. He knows this blend. He knows the spicy honey in it. It's his own blend that he dabbles with; something more for energy than taste. The spicy honey is the only thing he's found that makes it palatable.

Miller meets Karns eyes, and his mouth tilts upward just a hair as Karn swallows his sip heavily. Those guards aren't the only ones in here trying to deal with something outside their pay grade.

Chapter 47

Rezlar

Today has not been a good day.

Miller wakes him up just after dawn, warning him the town is under attack! How could it be under attack?! The orcs have shown no intentions of crossing the Gofnar, there are no bandit groups large enough for something like that, and there's nothing else around that could have the numbers to lay siege to the city!

Yet Miller opens the curtains and the window behind them, and Rezlar can hear the tolling of a bell and see an unnatural storm blowing in from the ocean.

Before the young noble can even ask for details, Miller's attention snaps to the cloud. Rezlar isn't sure he's ever seen his butler look more focused.

"Interesting . . . Young Master, the situation has been resolved, but now we have a different problem to deal with," he says with an apologetic bow.

"Wh . . . What do you mean, Miller?" asks the still sleepy young noble, getting the feeling he'd rather deal with a surprise siege than whatever this new problem is.

"You will need to address the people and guildmasters, and make a show of truly taking the reins of Fourdock, Young Master."

Rezlar's eyes widen at that. He'd *definitely* rather deal with a siege! At least attackers already hate him! The idea of saying or doing something to get the people upset, or even worse, trying to *inspire* them . . .

He shudders at the very thought of so many eyes on him, weighing and judging his every word and action. Just the guildmasters are bad enough, and he's only had to meet with them in person a handful of times!

"Young Master," comes Miller's voice, slicing through the growing panic and getting Rezlar to focus on him. "I would humbly suggest breakfast. Change is often easier on a full stomach."

He sighs at that and gets out of bed, glad Miller is there to help. The simple wisdom definitely helps him get through the day, too, as he finds himself too busy to have time for lunch, and only has dinner at Miller's insistence. There are so many letters of complaint to try to get through, and so many hurried reports of what happened.

While he had been vaguely aware of a new dungeon, and even of it somehow subsuming Neverrest, he simply never gave it much thought. It's not even a year old—how much trouble can it cause?

From the reports, it seems like it's actually trying to find out! So now he's scrambling to try to read the various updates from the guilds about it while also dealing with the growing number of unhappy letters and messages. He'd love to simply toss them in the fire and hide in his room, but Miller insists that's both rude and wasteful.

Many noble houses have found themselves in ruin, financial or otherwise, from ignoring the will of the citizenry. He might feel less helpless about it if he actually had any idea of what to *do*.

And then Guildmaster Karn appeared. He hadn't even known he was one of the guildmasters until Miller addressed him with his title. Thankfully, the thin orc made his exit fairly quickly after finishing his tea. His entire proposal was on the papers in the scroll case, anyway.

"What do you think, Miller? Will it work?" He pauses for a moment as his butler simply looks at him like he hasn't finished his sentence. *What else . . . Oh!* ". . . Can I trust him?"

Miller gives a slight smile. "He's of no threat to you, Young Master. I believe his stated goal is true; that he wants a stable city and stable dungeons for a stable guild. He may want more at some later point, but for now, I believe he is trustworthy in at least this."

"And the plan?"

"It is remarkably detailed and thought-out, Young Master. They had to guess on the specific budget, but I believe it is a workable plan, at the very least. The dungeon has significantly increased our tax revenue, and so too our defense stipend. A few of the other guilds will need to be pressured to discount or donate time and supplies, but public sentiment is that something needs to be done, so I don't see much problem."

He gives another small smile.

"And the dungeon apologizing will help your legitimacy in the eyes of the people and the nobility. The townsfolk will recognize that the dungeon is helping you, Young Master, but they generally like the dungeon, so will be more willing to let you fix this and guide the defensive response. A hold, or similar, in the mountains to the north could work, especially if you can negotiate with the dungeon to help."

"And the speech?" asks Rezlar, knowing the answer but still wishing to be wrong. Miller's smile dashes those hopes.

"An excellent idea, Young Master. The people have not had the pleasure of making your acquaintance yet. Might I also suggest something to help you in your further negotiations with the dungeon?"

Rezlar sighs and slumps but motions for Miller to continue. He might not *like* all of his butler's advice, but he's not going to pretend he's ever lead him wrong.

"Delve the dungeon. Your fencing form is getting quite good, to the point where you will need practical experience rather than just my small tutelage."

Rezlar snorts at that. "Sure, Miller. At least I'll be safe with you at my side."

Miller's smile drips ice into the young elf noble's veins. "Not with me, Young Master. But there is an entire guild that specializes in helping a young adventurer find a party."

"But . . . But they'll know who I am, especially after I give the speech!" he tries in desperation.

"Identities are simple to fabricate, Young Master, especially if a favor is offered to the master of the adventurers' guild."

". . . Do I have to?" mutters Rezlar in defeat.

"Of course not, Young Master. It's simply a suggestion from your humble butler," Miller says without missing a beat and bowing, not even giving Rezlar the dignity of taking the decision out of his hands.

He'd dearly love to ignore this particular bit of advice, but he is forced to admit he can't afford to. Getting some real levels can only help him, and from the reports on the dungeon, he's probably safer there than in his own manor . . . Miller aside. What galls him and almost makes him decide against it in spite is that he knows what else Miller is trying to do.

He's never been welcome among his peers, seen as too quiet and reserved, too shy, too worried about what they might think. He wouldn't even be surprised if that's the *real* reason Miller wants him to delve. He could use more friends than just his butler.

He sighs, knowing he's going to accept the advice, then yawns as the late hour catches up with him. "When should I give the speech, Miller?"

"Tomorrow after breakfast, Young Master. The people must believe swift action is being taken on their behalf."

Rezlar groans but doesn't argue. "I'm going to bathe and get to bed, then. Good night, Miller, and thank you."

Miller gives a small, genuine smile. "Young Master is too kind. Sleep well, Young Master Rezlar."

Surprisingly enough, he does, though he awakens with a sense of dread. He briefly wars with himself to decide what he fears more for the coming day, but the answer is clear: the speech. He eats breakfast without tasting it, too distracted by the impending presentation to the town to appreciate the skill that went into preparing his morning meal, but as Miller said: change is better on a full stomach. He just hopes he doesn't manage to puke it back up from his nerves.

By the time he arrives at the town hall, he's more worried about fainting than vomiting, taking some small comfort in how well breakfast is actually sitting. Miller directs him into his mayoral office, where a strange sight is awaiting him. Strange enough to derail his nervousness.

On his desk is a rat wearing a small hat and a bow tie. Even stranger, as it sees him, it stands and takes the hat off in a theatrical bow. "Ah, you're the mayor, yeah?"

Rezlar just nods dumbly, and the rat puts his hat back on and takes a seat on the desk. He gives Miller a look before continuing. "I'm Teemo, Voice of Thedeim, the dungeon who's been making waves. The Boss wanted to get a look at you before we do this whole speech thing."

Rezlar moves up and takes a seat in one of the chairs usually meant for people wanting to talk to him, still trying to understand what he's seeing. "But . . . the dungeon's scions are big and threatening. A giant spider in a treacherous maze, a huge raven that commands enough birds to blacken the skies, a beautiful and terrifying winged serpent, a simple yet imposing skeleton in a robe, an intimidating zombie elementalist . . ." he starts listing the scions that stuck in his mind, only for the rat's laughter to interrupt him.

"And me, the Voice of Thedeim. Tiny, Poe, and the others are for when negotiations break down. If someone can't deal with talking to just a rat, that's their problem. They can talk with me, or they can try to deal with them."

Miller hums at that, and Rezlar does his best to push down his confusion. The reports said the dungeon was strange, and he'd certainly classify having a simple rat as his Voice as strange. He falls back on what he can remember of etiquette and holds forward his hand for a few awkward moments before instead offering his pointer finger.

"Um . . . pleased to meet you, Voice Teemo. I'm Re—er, Lord Mayor Rezlar Herjan Kalsorthoth Niyeroul if'Gofnar the Eighth," he manages without stumbling. The rat gives him a humoring smile and shakes the offered digit.

"I hope you don't mind me just calling you Rezlar. That's a mouthful."

Something about the tone makes the young noble fight not to laugh. "It . . . is, yes. May I simply call you Teemo?"

The rat nods. "Fair's fair. You read the whole thing and are on board, then?" he asks, getting straight to business.

Rezlar nods. "Yes, it's a good proposal." He pauses for a moment before continuing. "I . . . thank you for this. I never thought something would show up to threaten the town, so never tried to have something planned."

Teemo shrugs and waves it off. "The Boss didn't think it'd happen, either, so he can't blame you. Heh, he says he screwed up by underestimating Hullbreak, so he acted quick to screw it back down. While it's your job to get the people prepared for something like that happening again, it doesn't mean he can't give you a hand."

Rezlar doesn't know what to say to that. He can't remember the last time someone talked so candidly to him. A rat, talking to a noble like . . . like two commoners! Even his family doesn't speak to him so informally!

"Young Master, the hall is gathered and ready for you," speaks up Miller, once again slicing through Rezlar's thoughts and bringing him back to reality.

"Let's go knock 'em dead, heh. Mind if I ride your shoulder, Rezlar?" asks Teemo. The elf nods, uncertain how to respond to something like that. Permission granted, Teemo hops onto his shoulder.

Rezlar follows Miller out to the packed main hall, trying not to think too hard about how much has changed in just over a day's time. He actually finds his nerves more under control than he expected as he starts to read the speech. Maybe because his mind is more focused on his planned delve, later. Maybe his new party won't be the only potential friends he could make today.

Chapter 48

I watch and listen through Teemo as Rezlar starts his speech.

"Citizens of Fourdock, I am Lord Mayor Rezlar Herjan Kalsorthoth Niyeroul if'Gofnar the Eighth. Many of you have never even heard my voice, let alone seen me. It's not because of a lack of interest but because of the simple fact that the day-to-day life here is so stable. There's no need for me to interfere when life and business are working so well already."

He glances at Teemo before continuing. "Then we got a new dungeon, last spring. Fourdock has not had great luck with dungeons, so plans started to be drawn up for what to do about it. For those somehow unaware: Thedeim's growth has been *much* quicker than usual, which makes planning difficult. An ordinary dungeon may take a year or more before its first expansion, and typically a decade before its first enclave.

"Plans are hardly made before they're woefully out of date, thanks to his rapid progress." He pauses, which is Teemo's cue.

"I'm Teemo, Thedeim's Voice, if anyone didn't know." He looks around the crowded hall, seeing a few faces light up as they realize why Rezlar had a rat with him. "He won't apologize for his quick growth, nor for taking decisive action against Neverrest and Hullbreak, though he *does* recognize he's put the local government in an awkward position. He understands that he could ignore all this and just do his thing, but he says he wants to be a good neighbor.

"And while a good neighbor will do his best to fix any mess that spills onto someone else's property, a good neighbor also lets the neighbor know if a mess might be incoming in the first place. The Boss didn't do that, so he apologizes not only to the lord mayor but to the people of Fourdock, too."

Rezlar smiles at that, and at the surprised murmuring of the crowd. He lets them do so for a few moments before clearing his throat and continuing. "And a good neighbor accepts an honest and earnest apology, so: thank you, Thedeim. Moving forward, he's agreed to work closer with me and my people to ensure further plans can keep up, as he seems to have no intention of slowing down his growth."

Teemo grins, earning a few chuckles from the crowd, before Rezlar continues once more. "Which is something that will be good for Fourdock. Revenues are up across the board, and delvers and crafters alike are seeing a spike in their growth, thanks to his unique style of challenge. Much like I had no intention of interfering in the lives of Fourdock, I have no intention to interfere in Thedeim's."

He holds up the scroll case. "I have here some preliminary plans, primarily focused on security for the town and trade routes. With the increased wealth all around comes increased tax income, which will be put to good use to ensure that, should another evacuation become necessary, a proper shelter will be available. The guards will also see increased funding, both to be able to facilitate such emergency measures but also to patrol and secure our road to the rest of the country.

"I'll be in communications with the various guild heads to work out the specific details and to hear their input, as well as keeping in touch with our local dungeon. For us both to grow strong, we must work together. Thank you," he finishes and nods at the gathered people before heading back out the door he entered from. Teemo follows him, so I get to see the young noble deflate once out of the view of everyone else.

His butler is there to help guide the shaking elf to a chair. He offers him a warm cup of tea without prompting, which Rezlar sips gratefully.

"That was a good speech, Rezlar," says my Voice, hopping up on the arm of the chair.

"Do you really think so?" he asks, sounding more battered and tired than a lot of my delvers after a boss fight.

"Yeah. The Boss isn't a great speaker, but you avoided humming and stuttering, had good posture, and made eye contact with people. He says those are important," encourages Teemo, earning a small, relieved smile from Rezlar.

"Well . . . he is not wrong." Rezlar sets his cup aside for a moment and shakes out his limbs, working the stress away before he takes his cup back. "Will you be able to help with the construction of a hold in the mountains?"

Teemo nods. "Yeah, the Boss says he might even get Coda to help with the design. I don't know if the ratlings will be able to provide much help, but they do pretty good work for the Boss, so who knows? I can even make a shortcut to it, once you guys find a good spot. Probably can't go looking until spring?"

The young elf nods. "The town itself has manageable snow, but not even the dwarven citizens are going to want to wander the mountains until after the thaw."

Teemo nods at that. "The Boss says he could spare a few tundra wolves to survey, but they're not exactly experts in what's actually needed to build a hold."

"Nor am I," admits Rezlar. "They'll probably look over what maps of the region we already have and look for a place near a river source. Access to water means access to food. As for how to actually carve . . . that's up to the miners, masons, and carvers." He sighs in relief as he finishes his tea, sagging in his chair. At least until Miller clears his throat.

"If the young master is recovered, perhaps we could see to the rest of the business of the day?" asks the prim butler of his charge. Rezlar sighs deeply but nods before standing. He pauses midstep and gives Teemo a weighing look.

"Teemo . . . would Thedeim be upset if I delved in disguise? Or at all?" he asks. Miller raises an eyebrow at that.

"Young Master?"

Rezlar grimaces but pushes forward. "I know it's supposed to be a secret, but . . . it just feels wrong not to at least let him in on it."

Teemo smiles. "And the Boss will be less likely to let it slip if he knows you want it to be kept quiet. He's not against it, but he says you'll get the same treatment as the other delvers."

Rezlar smiles in relief at that. Miller bows at him in acquiescence, though I get the feeling he would have preferred I not know. I'd probably be able to tell pretty quickly anyway . . . right?

"Thank you, Teemo and Thedeim." With that, the lad and his butler make their exit, and Teemo soon does the same. I turn my attention to the ratlings and Coda working on Rocky's ring, watching them go through the process of prototyping the strange arena.

Karn

The skinny orcish guild leader looks over his desk at his latest applicant, then glances at the gentleman at his side. Miller has done an impressive job disguising the two. Rezlar's hair is darkened to almost black, and his skin is far darker, making him look like a wood elf rather than the city elf he actually is.

The light leather armor and other adventuring gear also helps hide the identity of the young noble, as well as the rapier at his hip. Rather than some fancy filigreed thing, it's much more simple and practical. At least the lord mayor is smart enough to know the difference between something for some aristocratic duel and something that's going to see actual sustained use.

Miller is done up to look like the lad's father: similar skin tone and hair, as well as well-used equipment. He wouldn't look out of place as part of the guard in any caravan.

Honestly, Karn wouldn't have even realized who they are if not for the fact the forms are incapable of recording falsehoods. He double-checks the seals to confirm, and they're still fully functional. Rezlar's full name is clearly there, though his adventurer alias simply has him as Larrez.

"I take it you'd like the public records to be redacted?" Miller gives a nod. "Alright, that's fine. Lots of people get into adventuring to get away from something, so that's not going to raise too many brows. You're not joining?" he asks, already knowing the answer from the lack of a second form for the "butler," but it'd be rude to ask directly.

Miller shakes his head. "The young master needs to grow on his own. Despite my desire to safeguard him from every potential danger, he must still learn to handle some things on his own."

Karn nods at that and taps his foot as he considers the situation. "It'll be a bit awkward for him starting without a party, though. I have a few solo delvers, but they're natural networkers, so they don't have trouble proving their worth to get quests."

Rezlar looks nervous about that. "There are no open parties?"

Karn shakes his head. "Nope. We've had more adventurers showing up lately, but we're still out of the way enough that only solidified teams or dedicated soloists have actually joined." The orc's foot stops as he gets an idea, and he grins at the newest member of his guild.

"Though there *are* two strong people in town who haven't joined up yet. They only recently got their classes, so that's fair, but still. I want them in my guild." He grins as "Larrez" shrinks a bit in his seat. "I think your first quest for the guild will be to recruit them. They're a bit younger than you, but don't let that fool you. Inspector Tarl is probably the only person in town who has more experience with Thedeim than they do . . . and possibly not even him."

Miller frowns slightly at that, while Larrez looks confused. "How can they have only just gotten their classes, then?"

Karn shrugs and smirks. "You'll have to talk to them . . . and probably their mentors, too. I'd like your first quest to be to recruit Rhonda and Freddie to the guild. And make a good impression with them, alright? They're probably your best bet to form a party with."

Chapter 49

Rezlar Larrez

The young elven noble does his best to suppress his anxiety as he walks down the street. This is the first time in a *long* time that he's not been accompanied by Miller. There is, at least, the small comfort that nobody seems to be paying him any attention, thanks to the disguise.

He suppresses the urge to look around for his butler, knowing it won't do him any good. He's appeared between blinks before. If he doesn't want to be seen, he's not going to be seen. Still, he'd like to have the reassurance of his presence . . . which is probably why, if he even *is* around, he's not going to make himself known. Rezlar is supposed to be learning to stand on his own. If he can't even walk down the street without help, how is he supposed to run even a small backwater like Fourdock?

Especially with the town making strides toward becoming a frontwater, at the minimum. He sighs and takes a moment to collect himself. Nobody recognizes him. Nobody has any cause to bother him. Everyone is just trying to do their thing, which does not include scrutinizing his every move. His eyes wander as he repeats that to himself, showing the truth of the little mantra. The only people around paying him any attention at all are the merchants hawking their wares, and even that is simply because he's there, not that they have a specific interest in *him*.

Nerves calmed, he continues down the road, following the directions toward Staiven's Emporium. He's vaguely aware of the establishment being one of the premier alchemy and enchanting stores in town, with Old Staiven being a well-respected member of the community. Even if he didn't need to pick up Rhonda from there, it'd be a good idea to stop in and get some potions. He's confident in the status of his equipment, but he doesn't have much in the way of consumables.

He steps through the door, and a little bell rings to alert the goblin sitting behind the counter, a spider the size of a hand sitting on her wide hat. She smiles at him as he enters.

"Welcome to Staiven's Emporium! Is there anything I can help you with, or would you like to browse some first? If you're looking for true Aqua Affinity potions, we're out of stock, but Master Staiven has plenty of water-breathing potions inspired by the dungeon Thedeim!" she says, going through the spiel. Rezlar probably shouldn't be surprised that people are apparently asking about Water-affinity potions. He has no intention of going into Hullbreak, but proper adventurers are always pushing boundaries. Even with what happened just a couple days ago, it's no surprise that some are looking to delve the watery dungeon.

His thoughts are interrupted once he realizes he's staring and hasn't said anything yet. He coughs and looks away. "Uh . . . I'll browse a little, I think."

The goblin smiles and gestures at the shelves. "If you have any questions, just ask!" With that, she turns her attention back to her book on the counter, resuming scribbling in it.

Rezlar peruses the shelves as he considers how to try to approach her. If they're going to be a party, the direct approach is probably the best, but he doesn't know what to say! He picks a red potion from the shelf, seeing it's labeled as a healing potion. He thinks about how many he should get as he considers his options with Rhonda.

Just blurting out he wants to join her party would be too weird, so how to approach the subject? He sets the bottle down, resolving to get five, and looks at the Lightning Resist potions, wondering why there are so many of them. Is Thedeim a Lightning-affinity dungeon?

He examines the bottle as he comes to a realization. Karn seemed to be at least passingly familiar with Rhonda and Freddie, so perhaps he should bring up the guild. It'd be a better preamble than nothing. He nods to himself as he takes a resist potion to the counter, then brings several healing potions as well.

Rhonda looks up as the first bottle meets the countertop and smiles as she watches him gather the rest. "Will this be your first time into Thedeim, then?" she asks, and he almost drops the healing potions on the floor at her question.

"Is it . . . that obvious?" he asks, uncertain how else to respond.

"Eh . . . a bit. I know the regulars, but I haven't seen you before. Are you a caravan guard or something?" she asks, making conversation as easy as she breathes.

His cover story is easy to remember and relate, thankfully. "Was. I was a guard for a caravan coming up here. I heard the local dungeon is pretty good for learning the basics. I just joined the adventurers' guild, actually." He shows his wooden emblem, and she nods at that.

"Guildmaster Karn seems like a smart guy. He usually sends all the newcomers here to make sure they're prepared. Thedeim hasn't killed anyone, but that doesn't mean there's no danger."

Rezlar jumps on the opening. "Guildmaster Karn actually *did* send me here, and for more than simply potions."

That gets her to tilt her head in curiosity. "Oh?"

Rezlar nods. "He says you and your friend just got your classes? He'd like to offer you two membership, and . . . I don't have a party yet . . ." he weakly finishes.

Rhonda seems to chew that over for a few seconds before letting her eyes wander over Rezlar. She's clearly taking his measure as an adventurer, her eyes lingering on his leather armor and the rapier at his hip.

"Hmm . . . Freddie and I do pretty good, but we *could* use a dedicated damage dealer. Is that what you specialize in?" she asks, and Rezlar nods.

"Yes, I'm a fencer with Kinetic and Water affinities."

Rhonda's eyes widen at that. "Water? Ooohh, that could be really good. I'm an Ice—er, I have Ice affinity, so we should be able to work together great!" She beams for a moment before deflating slightly. "I'll need to ask Master Staiven if he's okay with it, though. He's been teaching me so much ever since I got my class, I wouldn't want to mess anything up." She looks up and shakes her head slightly. "Lucas? Could you go get him?"

The spider on her hat, apparently Lucas, chitters and jumps off, quickly making his way through a hatch behind the counter.

Rezlar realizes he hasn't introduced himself yet. He starts a formal bow before remembering what Miller said about how to blend in properly. Bows might be tradition in higher society, but handshakes are more commonplace in the rest of the citizenry. He holds his hand out a little awkwardly and tries to put on a brave face.

"I'm Larrez, by the way."

Rhonda smiles much more naturally and shakes his hand. "And I'm Rhonda. Pleased to meet you! Though you probably know my name already," she finishes with a giggle. It fades after a few moments as she seems to realize something.

"Does Karn know what my class is? Or Freddie's?"

Rezlar quirks an eyebrow at that. "Not specifically, no. He said you're some kind of ice caster, and Freddie is a paladin?" he offers, uncertain what she seems to be fishing for. Whatever she was hoping to hear, he apparently said, because she smiles.

"Ah, good! Our classes are . . ." she trails off, uncertain how to explain it. A new voice from the hatch, however, saves her the trouble.

"Nothing to be embarrassed about with your class, Rhonda. An Ice Sage might be a rare class, but it still takes diligence and work to use, like any other."

An aged ratkin climbs out of the hatch in the floor, spider on his head. Once up, he plucks the arachnid off and lobs it at Rhonda's hat. "Back home with you, you hairy leg-beast," he says with a smirk, turning his attention to the new elf in his shop.

"So, you're here to get Rhonda to join the adventurers' guild," he says, clearly not as a question. Rezlar gulps and nods.

"Er, yes, sir." He tries not to sweat as Old Staiven peers at him, weighing and sorting everything about him. After a few uncomfortable seconds, the ratkin speaks, looking and sounding much less intimidating.

"I had expected Karn himself to come trying to beat my door in, or trying to sneak a letter or something to her. Rhonda, do you want to join?"

The young goblin nods. "Yes! Freddie and I delve so often anyway! It'd be a great resource for us!"

Staiven nods at that. "Yes, it would. Just be sure to read whatever quests before you accept them. You're still my apprentice, and I'll not have you running halfway across the continent because you accepted a quest you shouldn't have!"

Rhonda giggles at that. "No, Master Staiven. I'll be careful."

He harrumphs, though the ghost of a smile ruins his crotchety master look. "Good. You three run along and talk with Freddie. The latest batch of potions are cooling, and I'll have you bottle them and clean the cauldron once you return. I'll mind the store until then."

Rezlar is confused about the number of people Staiven seems to think will be leaving the shop, at least until Rhonda whoops in excitement and hops off her stool.

"Come on, Lucas! We need to get our stuff!" Rezlar watches her go, surprised at how apparently intelligent the arachnid is. His thoughts are interrupted by the voice of Old Staiven.

"You make sure she's safe, Larrez. Freddie does a good job of it, but I'll be holding *you* responsible if anything happens to her." The aged craftsman is staring at him again, making Rezlar feel like he's a specimen in a jar. He gets the feeling that, if he somehow manages to get Rhonda hurt, that might be a preferable fate compared to whatever else the ratkin might do to him.

Chapter 50

Larrez

The elf stands in awkward, tortured silence as he waits for Rhonda and her spider to return. Old Staiven seems to be relishing in the silence, seeming to dare Rezlar to break it. The ratkin is lord of his domain, and Rezlar isn't certain he's seen higher nobles use silence more deftly than this shopkeeper.

Mercifully, Rhonda and Lucas don't take too long to return, likely because she only needed a change of robe and hat, and to bring an odd staff with her. Where her shop robe is a bit looser, this one is a closer cut so as to not get easily caught on various dungeon things, yet still loose enough for her to easily move in. Her hat has several little crystals, fangs, claws, and other odd bits tucked into the band around the center cone, and her spider is walking around, checking on them all.

Her staff has two small gems near the end, but the entire thing looks deliberately unfinished, though the red and blue of the gemstones contrast nicely. At her hip, she has a small book and charcoal stick, as well as pouches with potions and other knickknacks.

She smiles as she hits the floor, already making for the door. "Come on, Larrez! Freddie is over at the church!" She all but drags him out, and the smirk on Staiven's face tells Rezlar this is exactly what he expected would happen.

The silence with Rhonda is more companionable, at least, and much less awkward for Rezlar to break.

"So . . . an Ice Sage?" he asks, curious about a class he hasn't heard about. He can make some guesses, like the fact that she's obviously a caster and seems to specialize in Ice-affinity spells, but he would still like to know more about his potential party member.

She smiles, happy to share the information. "Yes! It's, uh . . . pretty rare, as Master Staiven said. I guess the biggest difference between me and a lot of other casters is that I didn't get Arcane affinity."

Rezlar frowns slightly at that. "So you're an ice specialist? But your staff . . . ?" he asks, not finishing his sentence, as he realizes he doesn't know very much about how caster classes actually function.

The goblin smiles at him and holds the staff in question up for him to see. "Looks kinda unfinished, right? That's because it *is*! And I'm not quite an ice specialist, either. I have Fire affinity, too!" she says with pride as she conjures twin spheres of ice and fire around the tip of her staff. She has them orbit each other for a few moments before letting them dissipate, leaving Rezlar looking rather impressed.

"Opposing affinities? No wonder it's a rare class," he says, surprised she'd be able to get a class like that from any dungeon around here. Fourdock is supposed to be unlucky with dungeons, and generally weak besides. Rhonda continues, keeping him from retreating into his thoughts too much.

"There's more to it, too, but it gets pretty deep into magic theory." She blushes a little in embarrassment. "I've tried to explain to a few people, but only Master Staiven has been able to make any sense of it at all. But!" She brightens, and Lucas chitters. "That just means I need to learn more! Learning is definitely part of my class, too, which is great!"

Rezlar smiles at her enthusiasm. He was never one to delve into books and scrolls, but his teachers often were. He could always appreciate that gleam in their eye when they'd get access to some new scrap of knowledge, even if he doesn't feel the same drive they do.

Before too long, the group reaches the Church of the Crystal Shield, and an aged wolfkin smiles as he recognizes Rhonda. "Ah, are you here for Freddie?" he asks, leaning on his broom. Rhonda nods.

"Yep! Larrez here is an adventurer, and he wants me and Freddie to join and be a party!"

"Oh, a party?" he asks, turning a measuring eye to Rezlar. "He seems a stout enough lad for it. Well, don't let me stop you. Freddie should be in the training yard, I expect," he says with a smile, opening the door for the two.

Rhonda enters the church like it's a friend's house, rather than a place of worship, and Rezlar awkwardly follows. While he will pay the gods their dues, he prefers to try to stay beneath their notice. Getting the attention of mortals is nerve-wracking enough; he wouldn't want something like a *god* to pay attention to him!

The various acolytes and scattered worshipers mostly ignore them, though some smile and nod at Rhonda as she leads the way, all of them clearly used to her presence here. She leads Rezlar through a few doors and halls before they come out into a large room for training the more martial adherents of the sect.

Inside is a sight that Rezlar was not prepared for. Four elves surround a young orc and a spider. The elves look practically identical, except for the weapons they are using. One has a spear, one a sword, one an axe, and one has a pair of daggers, though all are training, wooden weapons.

The young orc has a shield with a spiderweb on it, as well as a wooden training axe. His shirt is off, helping him stay cool in the intense training, and Rezlar can see Rhonda enjoying the view of her friend. At the orc's side is a larger spider than Lucas, its body narrower and longer, its legs lithe and thin. Three are held up in front of itself with a web between them, like its own version of a shield.

Off to the side, a gnome watches. He glances over at the newcomers for a moment but doesn't acknowledge them just yet. Instead, his focus is on Freddie.

"Begin," he says simply, and all the forms leap into motion. The sword and axe elves immediately engage Freddie and the spider, while the spear elf stays back slightly, poking his spear forward to try to catch openings his companions create. Such openings are rare, though, as a spectral shield manifests at Freddie's side. The orc's shield, the spider, and the ghostly version all work in tandem to deny any clean hits from the attacking elves.

The fourth elf, however, is hanging back and slowly circling, trying to stay below notice as he tries to maneuver into a flanking position on Freddie and the spider. With the three harrying them, they can't turn properly to keep him in easy view. Soon enough, the elf senses an opening and lunges forward.

The spider chitters, and Freddie responds. "Phalanx Press!" Two more shields manifest as he rushes forward, bodily forcing the three elves back and giving Fiona the room she needs to engage the elf with the knives. He wasn't expecting something like that, and he is soon tangled in webbing before the three others can recover and try to save him.

With the tide turned in the orc's favor, soon the others are incapacitated, then suddenly vanish. The extra shields fade as Freddie slumps, and his spider goes to fetch him some water as the gnome and Rhonda both applaud. While Rezlar is impressed as well, he's still confused about what actually happened here.

The gnome speaks up as the applause ends. "Good work, Freddie! I thought I had you with the sneak attack, but Fiona was on top of it."

The spider chitters as she hands Freddie the water, and he eagerly drains the cup. "She says thank you, Head Priest."

The gnome rolls his eyes at that. "You both know you don't need to be so formal with me, Freddie."

The orc grins as he accepts a towel from the spider and wipes the sweat from himself. "But we have guests, Head Priest Torlon."

"Your friends and a guest of theirs. I don't think formality is going to be a major concern for someone Rhonda and Lucas bring along," says the gnome with a chuckle, turning his attention to Rhonda, Lucas, and Rezlar.

"You don't usually bring someone else, though, Rhonda. What's the occasion?"

Rhonda smiles and gestures at Rezlar. "He's from the adventurers' guild, and he wants to recruit me and Freddie! He needs a party!"

Torlon strokes his chin as he considers that. "You two *did* get your classes, didn't you. Hmm . . . Freddie? What do you think?"

Freddie gets a shirt on and joins the others, his own spider seeming to like to cling to the shield on his back and peer her face over his shoulder. "I'd like to join . . . but are we ready?"

Torlon nods. "Yes. Honestly, you're more than ready. Not ready to *leave* just yet, but joining the guild would be a good thing to do. Karn is smart enough to not go sending you off abroad. I'm not even sure he has the abilities to accept quests that aren't local, come to think of it . . ." he trails off as he thinks, but soon shakes his head and continues. "Yes, I think you joining the guild would be a good way to grow, Freddie."

"Besides," speaks up Rhonda with a wide smile. "We go delving enough we're practically members already! This will just make it official."

Torlon chuckles and nods. "That too, heh. So, this is to be your third member?" he asks, looking at Rezlar. The elf noble tries his best not to shrink under the gaze, and the lack of judgement helps him manage it.

"This is Larrez! He says he's a fencer! We could use some dedicated damage, right, Freddie?" says Rhonda, and her friend nods.

"We could. We do pretty well, but from what the experienced adventurers say, we take a bit longer to deal with encounters than most." The spider on his back chitters, and Freddie smiles. "And Fiona says it'd be nice to have someone else in melee. She's right; it's a lot easier for me to manifest a phalanx with friends closer to the action."

"Is that was that was?" asks Rezlar before he can stop himself, and Freddie glances at Torlon before answering.

"Yes. I'm a rare variant of paladin who focuses on combined shield teamwork instead of a single shield."

Rezlar's eyes widen for a moment at that. *Two* rare classes? No wonder Karn wanted them both in the guild! "I'm, uh . . . I'm going to have to work hard to keep up, then. I'm just a fencer. Uh, Water and Kinetic . . ."

Freddie steps forward and claps a hand on his shoulder, smiling at the elf. "I'm sure you'll do great with us, Larrez. If we're going to be a party together, we'll have to work together to succeed!"

Rezlar feels like he'll be slowing them down, but it's still . . . nice . . . to be relied on, to be trusted. His fears of failing to live up to that trust flare for a moment, but a squeeze of his shoulder trips them before they can get a grip on him. Can he live up to their expectations? He's not sure . . . but he also gets the feeling they'll help pull him back up if he falls, instead of pushing him further into the dirt.

Chapter 51

I spend much of my morning watching Coda and my ratlings working on Rocky's ring, though I do check in on Violet, too. I'm trying not to get impatient and rush her, especially after Rezlar said I've been growing way faster than other dungeons.

She's actually sending centipede expeditions to scout the area before she expands, being cautious. To be fair, I don't know what will happen with the scythemaw eggs in the area when she expands. The scythemaws proper are delvers, so would they become residents? Dwellers? Delvers? I think Tarl said the townsfolk would become residents if I expanded . . . or did he say dwellers? I'd think dwellers, since residents seem a bit more connected.

Violet doesn't seem too concerned about them, however, seeming more like someone looking to buy a house and wanting to make sure they don't discover the pipes are garbage or something. Whatever the eggs do, I just have to be patient and not push her too hard. She'll get there.

Around noon, I feel familiar feet, with an unfamiliar set joining them. I smile to myself as I see Freddie and Rhonda, along with Fiona and Lucas, as well as an elf who feels familiar but I can't quite place. I don't need to send Teemo to go say hi, as he's already on his way.

The kids are looking eager to do some delving, while the new elf is looking a bit nervous, but he's doing his best to hide it as Rhonda points at the porch.

"And there's the notice board and the quests from the aranea!"

"We should get a quest. It'll be a good way to help him get used to how Thedeim works," points out Freddie. Teemo walks out from under the porch and grins as he sees the new elf.

"You guys snagged a newbie, eh?"

The kids look a little confused at the term while the elf blushes a bit in embarrassment, so Teemo continues. "Nothing wrong with it. Everyone has to start somewhere. And with these two, you'll be just fine."

"He'll be a great help to us, too," points out Freddie. "He's a fencer. We've been missing a good damage dealer."

"Could have fooled me and the Boss. You kids can pull out some serious hurt when you need to."

Rhonda waves that off. "We have to do a team-up attack to do most of that kind of stuff. I only beat Rocky that one time because I tripped him up and basically made him hit himself."

The elf's eyes widen at that, as does Teemo's grin. "You think the new guy could go toe to toe with Rocky?"

Freddie and Rhonda exchange a look before Freddie shrugs. "We haven't really seen him in action yet. I think the three of us together could at least give him a proper challenge."

Teemo is definitely enjoying the poor elf's misery at the idea. "What's your name, anyway? Sorry about talking about you like you're not here. Freddie, Rhonda, Lucas, and Fiona are friends of Thedeim, and any friend of theirs is a friend of his."

He looks even more terrified at that thought, but Rhonda and Freddie smile and motion for him to introduce himself, so he tries to steel his courage. "I'm Re—er . . . Larrez. Uh . . . just Larrez," he manages, tripping over his words a bit.

Teemo eases up on him a bit at that and nods. "I'm Teemo, Thedeim's Voice. Just Teemo's fine, heh. Anyway, you kids were looking for a quest?" he asks of the whole group, and everyone, even Larrez, nods. "There should be one to do something down in Violet. You kids could take that one and take the long way. You know, show him the ropes and what all the Boss has to offer, maybe introduce him to a few of the other scions."

"Is Rocky available for a sparring match?" asks Freddie, clearly wanting to actually test if he's right about how they'd fare.

"Eh . . . kinda. The Boss is working on a new arena for him. The big lug won't say no, of course, but he might be a bit distracted by the call of his new ring."

Freddie looks interested at that, and Rhonda speaks up. "Maybe we'll just stop by to say hello, then. I'd love to learn more magic from him, too, but I wouldn't want to interrupt."

Teemo shrugs. "I don't think he'll mind if you drop in. Anyway, I'll let you get to it. It was nice to meet you for the first time, Larrez. Just take it slow and learn to work together, and you'll all be fine." Larrez pales at Teemo's exit, which makes me certain I've seen him before, but I still can't place him. Teemo chuckles as he heads down a shortcut, and I decide to keep watching the young party while they look over the quests.

As they peruse the hanging pieces of wood, Rhonda speaks up. "Oh, this reminds me!" She levels a finger at both Freddie and Larrez. "You two should get a gathering skill!" Larrez looks confused, while Freddie looks thoughtful.

"We probably should, yeah. I don't think I'm interested in any crafting skills of my own, but gathering could be useful. What do you think, Larrez?"

The elf, still looking a bit uncomfortable after having talked with Teemo, slowly nods. "It . . . would probably be smart, yes. I do not know if I would be any good at a crafting skill, but gathering is a good way to supplement adventuring income." He gets a little more confident as he speaks, and I can practically see him reading it out of some book or another on adventuring.

"Anything stick out to you two?" asks Rhonda, excited her suggestion is getting followed. Freddie shrugs.

"I think the classic for a paladin would be mining or maybe lumberjacking. I even have an axe. But . . . neither really sounds that interesting to me. Larrez?"

"Um . . . I have always been intrigued by mining," he admits, to the curious looks of his party. After a few moments, he continues. "It just seems . . . relaxing? Slow and methodical, nobody around to bother you while you work?"

Freddie nods at that. "You could even take up smelting to turn your ore into ingots. It's not the most glamorous crafting job, but there's no shortage of demand for metals."

Larrez looks relieved for the support, even being bold enough to ask his own question. "And you, Freddie? If not mining or lumberjacking, what gathering skill would you like to pursue?"

Freddie considers as his eyes wander the quests before he picks one. "Field dressing is interesting. There's a lot of magic in the herbs Rhonda gathers, but there's also a lot of stuff in the things we fight, too. If nothing else, most skins and hides are worth something to a tanner. And . . . maybe cooking as a crafting skill." He chuckles as he nods to himself, smirking at Rhonda. "If we're going to be a party, *someone* should learn to cook. Alchemy doesn't count."

She sticks her tongue out at him. "Alchemy soup totally counts," she says with mock seriousness before giggling and not arguing the point. She grabs a quest plaque to gather mushrooms in Violet, and Freddie shows his to skin three cave bunnies.

"How about you? Violet doesn't have any mining nodes . . . I think, but Thedeim has ones all over in the tunnels and caverns," says the goblin.

"I . . . do not have a pick," admits the elf, but Rhonda doesn't accept that excuse.

"We can get one from a ratling. Or if they don't want to let us have one, you can use your Water affinity to erode the rock and get some ore, right?"

". . . In theory?"

"Great! Then grab a mining quest, and we'll give you the grand tour of Thedeim!"

He reaches out and takes a quest to mine some tin, then looks confused as he looks over at what the other two accepted. "Why do your quests say *Violet*?"

"Ah," starts Freddie, realizing they haven't been explaining things very well, then motions for Larrez to follow him off the porch. "Violet is another dungeon; one pretty deep down. Thedeim found her and has taken her as his protégée."

His eyes widen in concern. "*Another* fast-developing dungeon?!"

Rhonda giggles and shakes her head. "Nah, she's a lot milder than Thedeim is, at least as far as Freddie and I can tell. Though she *was* kinda stuck behind the scythemaws for a while, so there wasn't much expanding she could really do anyway."

"But now the tunnel horrors are gone," points out Larrez, still looking worried. Freddie smiles.

"Sure, but she's still young, and Mr. Tarl says she's still acting like it. Thedeim is helping guide her and giving her advice, but if she was like him, she would have expanded as soon as the maws were gone. I'm pretty sure she still hasn't."

"She's also looking like she'll be a toybox," points out Rhonda as they round the house and head for the simple herbalism nodes. Her quest might be for mushrooms in Violet, but the simple herbs seem to be a base for a lot of things, so might as well get some on the way.

"A *deep* toybox," emphasizes Freddie. "Apparently, most deep dungeons are belligerent at best. If she keeps this up, the dungeoneers will probably expand their guild here to ensure she's safe and happy. The kind of resources she could provide could end up putting Fourdock on the map, even if Thedeim wasn't here. *With* him here . . ."

Larrez sighs, and I finally recognize him as he speaks. "With them both, the mayor is going to have his hands full."

Chapter 52

I might know Larrez is actually Rezlar, but it seems the kids haven't realized it. It's not like they've shown any indication of paying attention to politics. With Teemo off helping Jello, it's not like I could tell them even if I wanted to. No, I told him I'd be willing to keep that secret, and I don't see why I should change that.

At least I know why Teemo was grinning and acting like he was. He probably recognized him as soon as he saw him.

Well, what's done is done. I look through what I have available to greet the group and decide on a significantly harder probing encounter than usual. A viper and a few rats wouldn't even slow down Rhonda or Freddie on their own, so I need to step up my game a bit.

Oh, I should try painting some of the snake scales with the metal transmutation stuff some time. If we can get it to only infuse the scales, that should be a good way to toughen a snake up.

I file that idea away for later as I nudge an electric dire rat and a spitting viper to go test the kids. The gatherer groups give the two denizens a wide berth, and it's not long before Fiona taps the back of Freddie's head, pointing.

The young orc looks and nods as he readies his shield and axe. "Looks like Thedeim is ready to get started. Electric dire rat and a spitting viper."

Rhonda nods at that as Lucas pulls a little shard of metal from the brim of the goblin's hat, the goblin herself opening her book to a specific rune. "There should be an opening to attack after they start. They like to fire from range before closing," she explains as magic starts to awaken the rune in the book.

Rezlar looks pretty nervous, but seeing the confidence in the other two helps steady him. He takes a deep breath before shifting his feet. "Tide Stance . . ." he murmurs as he settles into the classic fencing stance: feet wide, sword forward and raised slightly, back hand held behind and high for balance. I'm a bit surprised to see a watery duplicate of his rapier appear over his head. I can still see a bit of unease in his eyes, but his form looks pretty solid to me.

"I can counter the spit," he says as he steps up beside Freddie. The orc smiles.

"Rhonda and I can handle the lightning, then. Funneling Bulwark!" he shouts as the dire rat starts to spark with the beginning of its attack. Back with Rhonda, Lucas's metal shard glows slightly as the rune on Rhonda's book flashes.

"Lightning Rod!" Freddie's ethereal shields help channel the bolt of lightning as the dire rat unleashes it, focusing it into the earth at Freddie's feet thanks to the magical influence of Rhonda and her familiar.

The spitting viper hisses and launches a glob of poison. This time, it's Rezlar who reacts.

"Riptide Riposte!" he shouts as he lunges toward the dire rat, the watery rapier intercepting the attack from the viper. It turns an unpleasant purple as it absorbs the attack, but that's not all Rezlar is up to. His lunge meets the dire rat and scores a good gash down its side, and the water doppelgänger of his weapon flashes forward to deposit the unpleasant purple into the wound.

Rezlar steps back as Freddie steps forward, raising his shield to deflect the enraged bite from the wounded, unusually sized rodent. Freddie sidesteps to take the attack from the viper as Rezlar steps in once more, and I start to get an idea for why he called it Tide Stance. Each time he hits, the water rapier hits again a moment later. It's like watching waves on a beach erode a sandcastle. I kinda want to see him fight the rockslides; he'd probably do pretty well against them.

Fiona, still on Freddie's back, weaves a quick net and manages to entangle the viper, giving Rhonda an easy target for an Icicle Spear. The group holds their combat stances for a few moments until they get the experience, and then they relax. Rezlar brings his water rapier to overlap his regular one before flicking it away to splash on the ground, carrying with it the blood from the electric dire rat.

Freddie smiles at the newest member of their party and claps him on the shoulder. "Good work! That would usually take me and Rhonda a lot longer to clear!" Rezlar looks a bit embarrassed at that, but he doesn't argue as Rhonda pipes up.

"Yeah! That's some fancy swordwork, Larrez! With you, I think we can take some of Thedeim's more defensive monsters, like the slimes and rockslides!"

"Is . . . that a good idea?"

Rhonda shrugs. "It's not a *bad* one. We've been avoiding them because they take too long for just me and Freddie to handle, but your Tide Stance looks like it's great for getting through defenses!"

Rezlar slowly nods at that. "It is, yes. Water is very good at getting around defenses, finding the smallest weaknesses, and expanding them. It works very well with my fencing," he says, looking more comfortable talking about theoretical application rather than actually applying it. Luckily for him—or unluckily, depending on how one looks at it—Rhonda is all about applying theoreticals.

"Great! We'll show you the maze, and then head down to the caverns to see if we can handle what's in there!" Plan made, the group sets off. They don't end up going into the maze, as the line is looking a bit long, but that doesn't stop them from getting on top to get a good view of what's going on.

I can feel Rezlar tense once Tiny looks at the group, but the big spider simply waves a foreleg at them and continues on his way.

"Is that . . . normal?" asks the poor noble. The others nod.

"Yeah," says Freddie. "If you're up here just to look, he'll ignore you. I don't know what he'll do if you try to get through the webbing to cheat the maze, but I wouldn't try it."

"I half expected to see Vernew up here," Rhonda idly states, scanning the flat expanse that is the top of the maze, interrupted only by the trees of Tiny's lair.

Freddie shrugs. "She must be busy."

"Yeah . . . maybe we can visit her in the enclave? With Larrez, we should be able to get through the encounters there without having to spend so much time."

"Vernew?"

Freddie smiles and starts walking back the way they came. "Yeah, she's one of the leaders of the Spiderkin Enclave. She's the huntsmistress. Kinda bold and brash, but she's cool."

"I wonder if her spear and javelin techniques would translate into fencing," asks Rhonda, looking to Rezlar for the answer.

"Maybe? I've sparred against various spears before, and they've never been especially insightful for my own techniques, but I've never sparred with a spiderkin," he admits.

"She's hard to pin down. I feel like you two would be chasing each other all over the battlefield, trying to land a solid hit," says Freddie as he thinks on how the two might face each other.

Rezlar quirks an eyebrow at that. "You've seen her fight?"

Rhonda nods. "Yeah, beating her was one of our challenges to get our classes. We were lucky and she underestimated us, so we managed to get her caught in a big web tangle."

Fiona and Lucas both chitter, and Freddie chuckles. "Heh, and ourselves, too. It took Tiny several minutes to untangle everyone. I think she'd be up for a friendly spar if she has time. She might be out on a hunt, though," he points out. A *huntsmistress* isn't likely to just laze around the enclave all day, waiting for plucky youngsters to come challenge her to a spar.

"We could follow our first plan and go check in on Rocky, then?" suggests Rhonda as they start to get off from the top of the maze.

"Might be the better idea, yeah. I don't want to be out *too* late. I'm supposed to do a vigil around sunset."

"Yeah, and I need to bottle some potions, too."

Rezlar doesn't seem to have anything pressing, or at least nothing he'll admit to. "Where are the mining nodes? We could let me mine some tin, make our way to Violet for your quests, and go visit, uh . . . Rocky . . . before calling it a day?"

Freddie frowns as he goes over the timeframe. "I think we'll have to come back later to play with Rocky. We can get some mining done on the way to Violet, but we'll probably see enough encounters on the way that we should just head to the Ratkin Enclave and through the cemetery to get back home on time."

The group nods and sets off, having a plan to be done before their other responsibilities have to be attended to. I watch them go about their fun as I nudge Queen with the steel scales idea, and she seems all for it. She even wants to try giving Electric affinity, which I like the sound of. The kids might not get to spar one of my scions or one of the leaders of an enclave, but I still want to give them a boss battle.

You know, something to remember their first delve as a party by.

Chapter 53

The kids make pretty good time as they head deeper toward Violet, and I make sure one of my ratlings drops a beat-up pick along their path before it continues on its way. They don't miss it, and soon enough, Rezlar is whacking away at any nodes they come across in the tunnels.

Even I can tell he has a lot to learn about mining, but he's pretty good at pacing himself, so he's not wearing himself out. Freddie is also slowly learning how to field dress things, though he's still making a pretty big mess. He doesn't have too much difficulty getting a hide off of a dire rat, and skinning a viper is pretty simple, too, but any magical bits of my denizens are still out of his reach.

Rhonda isn't having much difficulty with her gathering as they journey underground, easily plucking various lichens and fungi as they pass the nodes. To be fair, though, she's had actual experience with her gathering. She gives Freddie a few pointers with some of the dressings, but she has clearly learned more about herbalism, despite how easily I saw Staiven process that widow a while ago.

While they travel and have fun, I check on how the scale painting is going for the twinsnake, and it seems to be going great! It might *look* like the snake is being devoured by a swarm of ants, but they're actually carefully applying the metal transmutation to the scales, and the snake doesn't seem to be suffering any for it. Queen is waiting to give it the lightning essence until after the scales are done, not wanting either process to potentially interfere with the other.

That's fine by me. While the twinsnake would respawn if anything went too poorly, I wouldn't want to waste the time on failing. I would worry about traumatizing them with a brutal death, but my denizens don't really seem to mind dying all that much, as far as I can tell. Death is probably a bit less traumatizing when you know you'll just respawn.

I take my time to watch the ants work on the twinsnake as the kids get close to Violet. They'll be safe with her, and Queen would probably like me to relay anything particularly interesting later, via Teemo.

Violet

The young dungeon takes her time deciding when to expand. While her mentor has given her a quest to do so, there's no true urgency to it. She has the mana for it, but she's still a little nervous about expanding beyond the solid door her mentor gave her.

Her Mushroom Scion is confident there will be no danger in the small cavern outside her current borders, even with the scythemaw eggs. He doesn't know what they'll do when she expands, and that's honestly part of why she's been delaying her mentor's quest. What if she gets a scythemaw spawner? What if she gets a Scythemaw *Enclave*?! What if the poor eggs just *die?!* She doesn't really like any of those possibilities, and her scions can't think of anything else that might happen when she expands.

Her mentor doesn't seem to know what might happen either, but he's not worried, which makes her at least pretty sure the eggs won't just die on her. There's still the possibility of her gaining scythemaws, however, which she doesn't like. They're big and scary and mean. Her Centipede Scion thinks they could be nicer if she raised them, but she doesn't know how to do that. She doesn't have the kind of water a scythemaw would need to live in, anyway.

She could upgrade some of her own things a bit more to further delay, but her mentor is right about her needing some more room. Her little cavern is pretty overrun right now. She likes the movement of her denizens and her bunnies, with the latter being great bait to lure things for the former to kill. She doesn't like hurting delvers, but she has no qualms at all about destroying invaders. They only give mana when defeated, not when they beat her denizens or kill a bunny, and her mentor has no problem with wiping them out, either, so she's happy to follow his lead on this.

Her door slowly creaks open, and she sees some familiar faces, though their clothing is different. Oh, and they've brought one more, too. She still sometimes thinks of the two as walking mushrooms, remembering her first experience with Rhonda, Freddie, and their spiders. She still thinks Rhonda looks a lot like a mushroom, even after Teemo explained her wide cap is a hat. She's been hoping her mushrooms will develop caps like hers. It just looks interesting.

Freddie is at least easier to identify as not a mushroom, though his shield on his back makes her think one is growing from him, sometimes.

Their new friend is not a mushroom at all, but he seems friendly enough. He has a new weapon she hasn't seen before, which reminds her of one of her centipede's legs, except it doesn't bend and move like they do. She simply watches as they enter, their weapons ready. She knows they know she won't actually attack them, but outside is still dangerous, and something could have slipped in.

They quickly see everything is as it should be and so relax, putting away their weapons, and Violet enjoys them simply wandering around. Rhonda starts picking mushrooms, and Violet enjoys the mana gained from it. She's a bit surprised when she gets a surge, but a question through the bond to mentor Thedeim gives her a simple answer: quest.

Teemo had told her about her mentor giving quests, about how it gives more mana all around, and she would very much like to be able to give her own quests if that's how they work.

Rhonda continues to walk around, gathering some mushrooms and being a good delver while Freddie and the new one start to hunt her bunnies. Her bunnies are quick, but so are the delvers, and the newcomer's sharp leg easily dispatches whatever bunnies he gets close to. Freddie takes his time to skin them, and another surge of mana lets her know he had a quest, too.

She watches the newcomer, wondering if he has a quest, but it soon becomes clear he probably doesn't. He says something to the others, who simply shrug and shake their heads. Maybe he was asking about a quest? She should ask Mentor Thedeim about it later . . . or Teemo. She thinks it's a complicated enough answer that she'll want the Voice to help.

As the delvers prepare to leave, she gets a feeling from her mentor. He . . . wants to have a boss fight in her territory? She's reluctant, remembering how scary the scythemaw was, but he assures her it shouldn't be as dangerous as that. He even indicates he'll have some healing ants and slimes nearby, just in case, which eases her concern a lot.

She decides to let her mentor challenge her delvers, knowing they're some of his favorite ones, too. He wouldn't hurt them just to give her some mana.

Just a few seconds after she gives permission, she feels the doors open, and she sees what the boss fight will be.

The delvers do, too, and immediately draw their weapons, watching as the odd monster enters. She's seen some of her mentor's snakes before, but this one is larger than most and has two heads! Even more, it's shiny, looking like it's made of the same stuff Freddie is wearing.

The ten-foot-long snake rears up as it coils itself some, an arc of electricity traveling up the connection of the necks to the body with a crackle. The lightning dissipates as the two heads hiss, one revealing wicked fangs, and the delvers prepare to deal with her mentor's challenge.

Freddie draws his shield, then draws it another few times. Violet doesn't know how he does that, but she can't think of any other way for him to have so many shields around him. He shouts as he slams them into the ground, forming a wall.

"Palisade!" While their conversation may elude her, skills are a lot easier to understand. The newcomer conjures a water version of his stabber as Rhonda and Lucas start working together on some kind of spell.

In response, the twinsnake starts its offensive. The two heads hiss once more, each with an attack to test the delvers. One sends a strong kinetic punch at the shields, while the other delivers a bolt of lightning that arcs along the barrier. Something in the protection fails, letting some of the lightning through, giving all of the delvers a nasty shock.

Fiona jumps forward to start patching the barrier, but Freddie lets it come apart as the attacks come to an end. He, Rhonda, and the newcomer all charge the snake, which seems to catch it off guard. It recovers just enough by the time Freddie barrels into it, catching his charge and only being pushed back a few inches. The heads try to strike around his shields, but Freddie's friends don't give it much chance to do so.

Fiona is working on trying to tie the two heads together with her silk, while the newcomer lashes and lances with his weapon, the water double striking a heartbeat behind each time and driving the fanged head back. Freddie gets a good swing of his axe, but it only skids along the shiny scales of the boss, rather than biting in.

He shouts, and the newcomer stabs at the main body of the snake, having better luck. The shiny protection has small gaps, Violet realizes, which the stabber is perfectly made to take advantage of. Not that the snake is going to just let him.

It tries to focus on the stabby one, but Freddie and Fiona are experts at getting in the way. Rhonda shouts from the back, and the stabber nods uncertainly as his water stabber intercepts a stream of green fluid from the fanged head. After a few more moments of attack and defense, the stabber takes a step back and shouts.

"Undertow!" Water seems to bubble from the ground and move with speed, breaking the stability of the snake. Rhonda takes the opportunity to unleash her own attacks, and the stabber shouts with her.

"Rime Tide!" The water crystalizes, holding the snake in an awkward position for a few moments, though it quickly starts to regain its posture.

But not quickly enough. As the ice formed on the snake, fire started to lick around Freddie's axe, and this time it's him and Rhonda who shout.

"Blazing Strike!" The heat of the attack, combined with the snake being off-balance, lets Freddie find or perhaps create a large enough gap in the scales for his axe to bite deep. The fanged head gurgles a hiss before going limp while the other head shatters the ice with a kinetic burst.

It brings its tail around and bashes Freddie back a couple steps, then turns its focus on the stabber. He looks nervous, but a shout from Freddie helps stabilize him and his nerve. Freddie shouts again, and the stabber shouts as well.

"Urchin Stance!"

Freddie's shields move to surround the stabber as he draws several more of his water weapons. He goes on the offensive, his attacks poking through small holes in the shield coverage to score hits on the wounded snake. It tries to attack back, but each strike is not only blocked by the shields but countered with the sickly green water of the stabber.

The snake fights valiantly, but each strike weakens it, slows it, and before long, the stabber gets a clean shot through one of the snake's eyes, and the beast falls. Rhonda whoops with excitement as they get their experience, and Freddie smiles wide. The stabber, however, practically collapses to the ground, rolling to his back to stare upward as he tries to catch his breath.

Violet is surprised at how well the delvers fought. It wasn't the singular overwhelming attack she saw defeat the scythemaw, but it was still very impressive! And it wasn't as scary as the fight with the scythemaw, either. She lets them relax as she digests the fight. Should she try to make a boss? She doesn't want to have a fight like that all the time . . . but maybe a scion would work?

Her mentor has a scion intended for fighting—maybe she should copy that?

She looks at her own scions, and slowly decides neither of them would be really fit for something like that. Her centipede protects her core, and her mushroom keeps her informed of the outside.

If neither of them will work . . . maybe a new one?

She considers the expansion available past her door with a new perspective. Not only would she get new territory, but she should get a new spawner or two, and her mentor will certainly encourage her to get a new scion for each one. Perhaps she'll try to make one of them into a boss.

She's still not going to do much fighting . . . but she *did* get a lot of mana from that scuffle. Maybe an occasional battle wouldn't be so bad.

Chapter 54

I smile as I watch Rezlar collapse after the fight. He's not hurt, just exhausted. I can't really blame him, either. He did a lot of heavy lifting in that fight, which Freddie and Rhonda clearly appreciate. The goblin pulls a little blue potion from her belt and hands it to the supine elf, who eagerly downs it. He sighs as energy fills him, or at least his mana. I dunno if it's technically a different thing from something like stamina.

He gives Rhonda a tired thumbs-up, to the laughter of all gathered, and I let them enjoy their victory. The twinsnake was a great challenge for them, and I'm glad to see it seems to be keeping the new properties as it waits to respawn. I think it might need the occasional touch up, but they'll be great as a wandering boss in the caverns.

I can feel Violet looking more seriously at the expansion, too. She seems to be a bit inspired by the show, which I didn't even intend. Still, if it gets her to expand quicker, I'll take it. Expanding gets a dungeon so much good stuff to play with.

I don't quite cross off getting Violet to expand from my to-do list yet. Don't go making checks before they're cashed . . . or something. I also can't quite check off Rocky's new boxing arena, even if it's progressing nicely. It does make me look at two of the other items that I should really get going officially on, however.

One is getting Leo to go check on the Southwood and the progress of the trail there. I could just poke him to get going, but I instead poke Teemo to go check on him. He's been gathering a few supplies and ensuring the tundra wolves will be ready to join him. As I focus in on him, I even see Honey buzzing around, which seems strange. Probably a good idea to get Teemo in there to see what they're up to.

Only a minute or two pass before Teemo exits a shortcut in the library, where Honey is buzzing around, her bees covering Leo's saddlebag things. The Wolf Scion stands stoically as Honey works, though he nods at Teemo as he enters.

"Heya, Leo, Honey. She helping you get ready?" asks Teemo, unable to keep from smiling at the scene.

Leo considers for a moment before shaking his head and growling a response.

"*Us*?"

Honey does a little buzzing dance before returning to her work. Teemo looks confused.

"Uh . . . Boss? Honey says she's going with him."

Huh. Why?

Teemo relays my question, and Honey starts doing an elaborate dance routine, which Teemo quickly interrupts. "The Boss doesn't need an itemized list, Honey. He just wants to know why you'd want to leave the library, especially for something potentially dangerous like this."

Her reply dance feels a bit curt, and I don't doubt for a moment that she's upset about not getting to actually dance out a detailed essay on why she should go. Still, she gives Teemo the TL;DR, which he relays.

"She says she wants to make sure Leo has all the information he'll need. She can create maps and explore easier than he can . . . at least for a while. She has calculations to prove Leo and the wolves can keep her and the colony she'll be taking warm, too, but I don't think she'll need to show them, yeah?"

Uh, yeah, I believe her. I'm not against her going, just a bit surprised, is all.

Leo yips with a grin, getting a laugh from Teemo.

"Leo says she just wants to get closer to the new information. There's not much on the Green Sea, so of course she wants to be one of the first to actually provide details."

Honey manages to huff and buzz at the same time before returning to her packing.

"She's probably loading up a few other wolves with stuff, too?" Teemo asks. Leo nods. "That's fine then. Bats and birds will still be sent out, too, so you should be easily in contact with the Boss. When will you two be ready to head out?"

Leo tilts his head as he thinks before giving a soft woof, which Teemo nods at. "He says not long after sunset. It'll be easier to rally the tundras and make a quieter exit that way."

Works for me. Do they need anything special?

Teemo asks, and Leo shakes his head. "Nah, looks like they have everything they think they'll need. Honey actually has some go-juice and a bit of the metal elixir, too. I have no idea what she'll use it for."

How about healing?

"She says she'll be bringing along a lot of healing ants. She'd like a healing slime, but they just don't fit in a saddlebag."

Ah, right. Did you and Thing ever figure out how to make bags of holding?

"Not quite, but I think we can manage. Probably not until after they go, though."

That's fine. We can send a wolf with a healing slime in one later. Heh, probably along with you, Teemo. I'd like to have shortcuts between the outposts, if you can manage that?

My Voice whistles at that. "That's gonna be a thing. I should be able to manage, but it won't be quick."

Can you manage before the end of winter?

"Hmm . . . probably. Having a tundra wolf to ride would make it a lot easier, too. Winter's supposed to be pretty rough, but at least it can't snow inside one of my shortcuts."

Cool. Well, if Leo and Honey don't need any help preparing, I do have one other thing I'd like to at least get started on today.

"Sounds like you have another something big in mind, Boss."

Yeah . . . I want to ask Aranya more about how she came here. She's implied there are more kobolds, and that they're not doing great. If I can, I'd like to be able to do something to help.

"Where is she?"

Looks like . . . she's hanging out with Norloke, having a nice bit of tea and chatting.

"Then I'll be there in a couple minutes, Boss."

No rush.

I focus in on their conversation, and I see Aranya smile as she sets her tea down.

"Ah, Lord Thedeim is here."

"He always is," replies Norloke with a motherly smile, before realizing Aranya doesn't mean it metaphorically. "Oh! The Weaver is paying us attention?" She looks around while Aranya nods.

"He is, though I don't think it's anything too serious."

"I should hope not! He considers things like the scythemaws and the attack by Hullbreak to be serious! I've had enough seriousness to last me a while, thank you."

"Well, you know the Weaver, Norloke. He's not happy if he's not whittling away at something that most would just leave alone," Aranya replies with a grin. She might be able to hide it from Norloke with her cup, but I can still see it. Are all High Priestesses so cheeky, or am I just rubbing off on her?

"The Boss says you're being cheeky," says Teemo as he enters the cozy room. Aranya simply smirks.

"And yet I haven't been *smited*." Teemo laughs with her, though Norloke rolls her eyes like a mother whose child refuses to be as reverent as they should be. "Does Lord Thedeim need me?" she asks with more seriousness.

"Yeah, but nothing dangerous. Well, nothing that he expects will be dangerous, at least. He wants to know more about how you got here, and how the kobolds are faring deeper down. He's going to be expanding more eventually, and he wants to help more than just the people on the surface, you know?"

Aranya grimaces as several emotions flicker across her features. Not really a surprise that her past is complicated. She takes a deep breath and tries to focus herself, nodding.

"I . . . had been hoping He would be interested, but I didn't want to ask. He's already given so much." She sighs again and firms her resolve. "This is probably a good time to talk about it, too. May I ask the rest of the triumvirate to listen, as well as Elder Larx? The enclaves may have to deal with more than just tunnel horrors if You expand much deeper."

That's fair. Teemo, you want to go get Larx?

"You want me to bring Larx here, or do you all want to go visit him at the Ratkin Enclave?"

"We can go visit him," speaks up Norloke. "No need to make him walk all the way here, even if he uses a shortcut. I'll gather the others, and we can meet him at his enclave."

Aranya nods at that. "Would you please tell him to expect us, Teemo?"

"Yeah, I can do that. See you there!" With that, Teemo slips into a shortcut, leaving Aranya and Norloke to prepare to get going.

I leave them to it as I try to not let my mind wander with the possibilities of what Aranya will say. I've been trying to ignore this partially because I didn't think I could do much about it. With her state when she first got here, it's easy to guess kobolds aren't doing so hot. If I can't change it, I'd rather not know the details. But after dealing with Hullbreak, or at least getting past the first hurdle, there's a very real chance I could actually help them.

Chapter 55

As Teemo exits the shortcut into Larx's kinda open-air temple thing, I see the ratkin easily chatting with Freddie, Rhonda, and Rezlar. He's smiling as they recount the fight with the electric twinsnake, enjoying their youthful energy as well as Rezlar's fidgeting as the other two talk him up.

Larx spots my Voice and waits for a lull before saying something.

"Is this an official visit, Teemo, or did you want to hear how they handled Lord Thedeim's latest challenge?"

The kids and spiders all look to Teemo, happy to see him, and he takes a moment to bask in the attention before speaking.

"Official . . . kind of. Aranya and the triumvirate are going to be visiting. She has something important to discuss."

"What is it?" asks Freddie with a tinge of concern, but Teemo waves him off.

"Just some underground stuff," he deflects. Rhonda and Freddie seem to accept that, but Rezlar appears to have more experience being deflected. He doesn't say anything right now, but I wouldn't be surprised if he asks about it later when he's here in a more official capacity.

"We should probably get going anyway," notes Rhonda, and Freddie nods as he stands.

"Me and Rhonda have stuff we need to do, too. Tell them we said hi, Elder?"

Larx nods. "Of course. They'll be sad to have missed you, but we wouldn't want to keep you from your responsibilities. May Lord Thedeim bless you," he says with a wave of his hand, and a subtle breeze of orange drifts across them all.

Rezlar's eyes widen at that, but Freddie and Rhonda get him moving before he can work himself up into the panic it seems he wants to. Once they're well out of the enclave, Larx breaks the silence.

"So that's the young mayor."

Teemo bursts into laughter, and I still need to figure out a good way to give a flat look to my Voice. After a few moments to calm down, Teemo finds his ability to speak. "So, what'd you think?"

"He's not what I expected. The lad needs to learn some confidence to go with whatever schooling he's had and will have. I think Freddie and Rhonda will help him with that. Nothing builds confidence like successfully doing a challenging delve." He pauses to muse, then continues. "So, what does Lady Aranya and the triumvirate actually need?"

"To talk about underground stuff. Specifically: her past, and how the kobolds fare."

Larx leans back into his chair. "Ah, that makes sense. Lord Thedeim acts above and below. He feels He's ready to tackle the darkness of deeper down, which even the glowmoss can't dispel?"

Teemo nods. "Yeah, though I don't think he's going to actually tackle it. More like sneak in and take it apart, piece by piece."

Larx nods at that, taking his staff in hand to stand. "Then I'm going to need more tea, and some of the mushroomsnap cookies. We haven't managed anything like actual bread just yet, but some of Honey's honey and some ginger makes a decent cookie to dip into some warm tea."

Teemo follows as he heads into his chambers. While Larx prefers to keep the little temple fully open to the public, he recognizes something like this might be the kind of thing Aranya would like to keep private. A subtle orange glow envelopes things as Larx works, his faith helping him prepare for guests. His timing is incredible, too. As he's pulling a second kettle from the fire, a knock sounds from his door.

"Come in!" he calls as he places the last jar of tea leaves on the table, next to a large plate of cookies. My Head Priestess and the triumvirate enter his humble abode. It's a little cramped, thanks to Folarn's size, but it feels more cozy than anything as they all settle around the table.

"Would you like some tea and cookies before we begin?" he asks.

"Just some tea for me, please," replies Aranya, Folarn echoing her.

"Those cookies smell *good*," speaks the eager Vernew as she grabs a couple, mostly ignoring the tea. Norloke is more patient, however.

"Both for me, please, and thank you."

Larx smiles at them all, and soon, everyone is enjoying his hospitality. Norloke even gets Vernew to have a cup of tea and shows her to dip the cookies, much to her delight at the new flavor and texture.

Aranya lets everyone get settled before she begins. "If you all don't mind, I'd like to start." Nobody seems to mind, so she continues. "Lord Thedeim has asked me to tell more of how I came here, about where I came *from*, and I wanted you all to hear this. You are His dwellers and live below the surface. If He expands much further, I think the Deeps will start to truly notice us, and we all need to be prepared."

She pauses to let everyone take that in. Half-eaten cookies are quickly finished, and soon, the red kobold has everyone's undivided attention.

She takes a few more seconds to compose herself, then she begins. "While Lord Thedeim is a Sanctuary in the truest sense, the ones deeper earn being called dungeons. There may be other Sanctuaries there, but I've never heard of them. At least not in anything besides legends.

"The dungeons of the Deeps are . . . I'm not even sure where to start," she admits, taking a few more moments. "My enclave was in one of the dungeons. It had no spawners we could have developed from, which isn't a surprise. My people are treated as slaves there, and were probably taken instead of developed. They're forced to do the dungeon's wishes, which mostly involve labor. There is a settlement not far from my home, mostly pale elves and pale dwarves. They worship it and delve to make it stronger. They tithe much of their materials gained, and we kobolds must collect and process it.

"Ores are smelted, metals forged, weapons, armor, and more are made, and the dungeon uses it as loot for the delvers. The town and dungeon grow together, almost a mockery of how Lord Thedeim nurtures us and Fourdock."

She closes her eyes, trying to resist tears as she continues. "My people are *sacrificed* to the dungeon, murdered by the pale followers so the dungeon can grow. They sacrifice anything else they can get their hands on, too, but my people seem to be what the dungeon likes the most.

"*I* was to be sacrificed, but I wasn't the only one that day. They were also going to offer some monster they had found; some terrifying mass of tentacles and mouths. I don't know how they captured it, or even what it was, but it got loose and started wreaking havoc. It picked up my cage and threw it, and I fled in the confusion.

"I ran until I collapsed, then crawled into a crevice in a wall. Only when I woke up did I realize I had no idea where I was. I continued that way for days, running when I could find the energy before finding some small place to hide and get some mockery of sleep. Eventually, I came to what Lord Thedeim calls the underswamps, and I slowly made my way across. I was almost out when one of the tunnel horrors decided I looked delicious."

She stops there and slowly smiles at the memory. "And I found Lord Thedeim, and he killed the monster and took me in. He gave me clothes. He gave me a weapon. He gave me a true home . . . He gave me *purpose*. I never brought up my people because I didn't think there was anything to be done for them. I don't even know where they *are*; how can I help them? And He already gave me so much, I couldn't try to ask for more."

She stops there, unable to think of anything else to say. Everyone is clearly digesting her story. Larx looks sad to hear that a dungeon could do something like that. Norloke looks like she feels similarly but is leaning more toward horror than sorrow. Folarn has all her arms crossed and is frowning. I can practically see battle plans forming in her head. Vernew looks like she wants to skewer something, but she has to settle for snatching up and devouring a cookie. Teemo is looking almost shocked at how bad it is.

And I'm trying to resist getting Poe to send as many bats on expedition past the underswamps as possible. It's certainly going to be the priority for underground expeditions going forward, but rushing will only make a mess. Being angry is one thing, but letting it explode into a fiery rage doesn't help anyone. No, I'm an engineer, and making heat do work is practically the profession in a nutshell.

So . . . let's get down to business.

Chapter 56

Unfortunately, it's easier to *want* to get down to business than to actually *get* down to business. The biggest hurdle is that I know even less than I did about Hullbreak when I started. At least I knew where Hullbreak was! So . . . time to do what I can. The most I can do directly is ask Poe to focus the underground expeditions out past the underswamps. If I want to kick that dungeon's butt, I need to find it first.

The other thing I can do is to make sure the home front is well and secure, which means making sure Violet and Hullbreak can support themselves. Violet is fine on that, technically. She doesn't have many delvers, but she also doesn't have much in the way of expenses. With me sending quests for delvers for her, she should be getting a lot more mana now, too. I can also feel her shuffling closer to expanding, so I poke Teemo to go visit and see if she has any questions or wants any guidance for her first expansion.

Thankfully, it looks like the mood has lightened significantly in the meeting, my dwellers doing their best to reassure my High Priestess, who reassures them in kind as she can feel me moving. They've moved on to the more idle chatter between friends, which lets Teemo slip out without making much of a fuss.

"What's up, Boss?"

Heya, Teemo. Can you go check on Violet? I think she's about to expand, and I'd like to be able to answer any questions or worries she has.

"Like with the scythemaw eggs?" he asks with a cheeky grin, slipping through a shortcut.

Har har. Like help with whatever new spawners she gets, and with whatever the eggs do.

"You still think they won't cause any problems?" asks my Voice, letting his sarcasm fall by the wayside.

Yeah. I get the feeling they won't do much at all. I think, worst case, they'll count as delvers who aren't doing very much.

"Any idea for how to help them hatch?"

Mostly to just leave them alone. I'd probably suggest she keeps an eye on the temperature and humidity, and probably mana, too, but try not to interfere with anything. The maws have been doing this long enough to know how to make it work, right?

Teemo shrugs. "I guess?"

It's not like either of us has any better ideas. It's not too much longer before Teemo exits the shortcut, and then it's just a little further until he can slip into Violet's area.

"Heya, Violet! How'd you like that boss fight?" He listens for a few seconds before relaying her opinion. "Sounds like it wasn't as scary as she thought it would be, and she kinda wants to have a scion she could use for fights like that."

Oh yeah? Which one is she thinking to use for that?

"Hmm . . . she says she wants a new scion for it. She likes Legs as her Guardian, and Cappy for information."

Nice, she's named them? I can feel my happiness at the thought filtering through the bond, and Teemo smiles.

"She says she's glad you like the names. So yeah, she plans to expand and get a new scion or two. Do you have any advice for her before she does?"

Nothing specific, no. Just to take a moment to take it all in before she spends more mana on upgrades. She has enough to cover expanding as well as some upgrades to things, yeah?

Teemo nods. "Yep. Sounds like she's as ready as she's going to be. Go ahead, Violet."

A couple beats later, I feel her territory expand, rapidly claiming the entire small cavern outside her door. A few more seconds pass before I get a notification as her mentor, giving me a basic list of what she's gained. What I see has me interested, too.

"She says she can make mining nodes now, and she picked up a pair of spawners. Wait, really?" He listens to her reply while I nod to myself.

She got moles and shadow spirits, and I can see the spirits can upgrade to gremlins for practically a song.

"Yeah. That's . . . probably not a coincidence." I can feel some concern through the bond, so I pat it to reassure her. "Nah, you didn't do anything wrong, Violet. It just seems like one of the Boss's experiments wasn't going as badly as he thought," he finishes with a grin. I don't dignify him with a response, instead taking a closer look at my protégée's new spawners.

Looks like the gremlins are a resource specialization, which could be good for her mining nodes. The moles also have a mining specialization, but I can't get too much detail. It's probably more efficient to just go with the gremlins for the resources and decide on what to do with the moles later on.

Teemo relays that, and Violet quickly takes the discounted upgrade. We all watch as a gremlin almost flows out of a crack in a wall like smoke before moving to one of the nodes—looks like tin or something? Either way, the gremlin picks with its claws at the rock, leaving the metal ore behind, and I can even see it somehow adding to the metal there.

I take a closer look at the gremlin and see why. Huh, looks like they picked up Metal and Earth affinities. That's cool.

Teemo speaks up, drawing me from my examinations. "Hey, Boss, Violet wants to know if she should make scions, and if she should make any of them fighters."

I take a quick glance at her mana flow and give Teemo the go-ahead. *It's a good idea to get scions, but what kind of fighters does she want?*

Teemo snorts when Violet gives him her reply. "She says she wants something like what you have, heh."

Well . . . I think she'll need to do some more prep before she can manage someone like Rocky or the Jacob's Ladder snake. She should probably make a few basic rooms before trying to specialize her new scions. Her Mushroom Scion will probably make a good Marshal, so she should make a war room for a map.

I take a few moments to see what rooms she has available before continuing. *I don't see alchemy or enchanting labs . . . but she has access to a metalworks, which could be interesting. If she wants to pull some kind of surprise, that's probably her best bet.*

Oh! Speaking of surprises . . .

I trail off as I focus on one of the scythemaw nests, seeing something surprising but not shocking. The nests each count as a very small enclave, with the eggs counting as dwellers. Violet notices, too, and I can feel worry dripping through the bond until Teemo speaks up.

"Hey, easy there, Violet. You'll be fine; they're still just eggs. Just keep an eye on them, don't bother them, and they should hatch and head out for the water. The Boss says the maws know the best way to let them grow, so just try not to disturb them, okay?"

I can tell she's still nervous about the eggs, but the little pep talk from Teemo seems to keep her from doing anything rash.

"Any advice for how to organize her new denizens?"

Well . . . I'd leave the moles mostly alone for now; maybe a couple upgrades to make them stronger, but don't specialize them just yet. Moles and centipedes are probably good to send on expeditions, but make sure she keeps enough at home to deal with whatever new invader she has. She might actually see wild gremlins, so she might want to upgrade her centipedes to be able to deal with them, come to think of it.

For her new scions . . . I'd suggest giving them both turns in running the metalworks, see which one likes it better. Whoever doesn't like it, she can try to see if it likes to fight. If it still doesn't feel quite right, let it focus on dealing with invaders and helping out wherever it can. Some of my scions I had a good idea of what to do with them, and some of them took a while, like Coda. Poor bat was kinda just flapping in the wind for a while.

Teemo relays that, and I'm happy to see Violet not just implementing everything I said. She's her own dungeon; I'm just giving her advice to avoid pitfalls. For the moment, it looks like she's getting those rooms I suggested, and getting Cappy to organize a few expeditions.

I lean back and idly watch her work as I think. It's *definitely* not a coincidence she got spawners for the two things I've been trying to gain. Were the ones we released just hunkering down in here, waiting for her to expand and join her? Is that even how it works? I could try to experiment with other invaders . . . but the only other one that comes from down here are those dire mosquitoes. I feel like having those as a spawner would traumatize Violet even more than a scythemaw spawner!

I'll let Jello know she's kind of succeeded with the mole/gremlin stuff, though I doubt that'll get her to stop. I don't think I'd want her to, either. If she can pacify them, and they go to Violet, that's perfectly fine by me. I'll probably ask Violet if I can have one of each once I do my own next expansion. For now, though, I'll just let her get used to the new stuff she has to deal with.

Violet is making strides . . . Now it's Hullbreak's turn. I'm going to need to ask Tarl to do an inspection. That's probably going to be difficult for everyone . . . but it still needs to be done.

Chapter 57

It doesn't take me too long to decide if I should check on Hullbreak or Tarl first for an inspection. While it's not likely to be easy for either of them, I think the consequences will be worse if Hullbreak isn't ready. With that in mind, it just takes a bit of the Electrolysis potion for Teemo to head to Hullbreak to check in.

I've spotted a few delvers in the days since the battle, but they've all just barely looked around, maybe snagged a little coral or something, then scooted on out. I don't think the Delver's Guild has any quests in there, so it should just be delvers being adventurous and taking risks.

I can tell Hullbreak isn't happy about them, just as I can tell he's uncertain what to do about it. His instinct is clearly to attack, but after seeing what I did to repair his territory, he's been fighting that. It probably doesn't help that the delvers are skittish when they're there. Makes me think of how most dogs only chase cats because they run.

Yeah . . . I think I'll ask Teemo to kind of be a dry run of an inspection. It'll be a good chance to try to get to know the dwellers a bit better, too. From what I can tell, the Merfolk Enclave has organized itself similarly to my ratkin in that they have an elder who tries to give the will of the dungeon, and the others mostly follow it.

After the whole thing and Yendo's part in changing things, they all seem a bit aimless right now. I think they're just getting used to having actual freedom to do things, and the elder is trying to understand Hullbreak's new perspective. Heck, *Hullbreak* is still trying to understand his new perspective, so yeah, not a surprise things seem a bit off in there.

With Teemo popping through a shortcut into Hullbreak's territory, it's time to actually chat instead of just trying to look and infer things. The First Mate doesn't take long to come say hello, either.

The Great White Shark Scion bobs in the water in an approximation of a bow. "Greetings, Voice of the Admiral."

Teemo blows a raspberry at that. "Just call me Teemo, you know that. How're you guys doing?"

"We are . . . rudderless," she admits, and I can feel a flash of shame through the bond with Hullbreak. I send a bit of understanding through the bond as Teemo speaks up.

"That sounds about right, to be honest. The Boss has really upended stuff for you guys. He's given you some space to try to come to terms with it, and now he's ready to give some advice for how to move forward."

The First Mate sags in relief, and I can feel it echoed through the bond. Teemo smiles as she speaks. "The Captain has been reluctant to do much. He says he feels like all his maps have suddenly been replaced, and the stars changed. These waters are new . . . and he doesn't want to run aground."

"Is he alright with people delving properly again?"

The shark hesitates at that. "I . . . I don't know. He's willing to try, but he's so used to repelling boarders."

Teemo smiles in encouragement. "The plan is to start slow and easy. Tarl said that fishing boats count as delvers, and you have those copperfins and silverscales now. The Boss isn't very sure how to make a true underwater encounter, anyway."

I can still feel a bit of nervousness through the bond, but it's also backed by a subtle feeling of steel, of wanting to try.

"The Captain likes that idea. The early days of boats and lines . . . those were good times," she reminisces. Teemo lets her enjoy some happy memories for a few seconds before speaking up once more.

"The Boss also wants to get to know your dwellers a bit more. Them and Hullbreak are close, so they also seem like they're floundering a bit. And if Tarl is going to do an inspection to clear you for delving, he'll probably want to try to normalize relations between them and Fourdock, too."

I can feel a spike of fear through the bond, which Hullbreak tries to quickly smother, and Teemo can see the First Mate tense for a moment.

"Easy there," calms Teemo. "The Boss isn't going to let another accident befall them. Trade and such will be slow to start. And if the dwellers want better trade, the Boss and Coda can get a *proper* dock built. A proper place to moor ships, strong enough that even a deliberate ramming attack wouldn't hurt it, let alone a freak wave catching a boat."

"And . . . if they don't want to trade? If the dwellers wish to be left alone?"

"Then they can do that, too. The Boss isn't going to force them, but they will need to decide how to handle growing. Their enclave is bigger than the ones the Boss has, so logistics and stuff are more pressing concerns."

The First Mate slowly nods at that. "Their growth . . . was a strain on the Captain's resources, but he couldn't bring himself to try to stop them, especially since they were trying to not drain his resources."

Teemo nods once more and swims up to hold her dorsal fin. "So let's go talk and see about hashing some things out, yeah? Once you get some regular delvers, Hullbreak should be able to afford to support the dwellers a bit more, but I expect they'll need to learn how to swim in the waters outside if they want to really thrive."

The First Mate silently leads the way to the enclave, and on the way, they pass several merfolk doing some small gathering: a few mining coral, a few spearfishing, even a pearler. It seems like most are staying in the enclave.

The First Mate isn't too difficult to spot at a distance, so much of the enclave is gathered by the time she and Teemo arrive. There's a lot of curious murmurings once they notice Teemo hitching a ride. I'm sure they all remember the sea around them blooming back to life the last time he was here.

Some of the faces look curious, some hopeful, some are even angry, though a few look conflicted, too. Looks like they're still not quite sure what to make of me.

"The Admiral's Voice is here," declares the First Mate, and the crowd murmurs until Teemo speaks up.

"Just Teemo is fine. The Boss has been trying to let you all adjust before making more changes . . . and it's about time for more. Probably not quite as drastic as the last time I was here . . . at least not at first. I know you guys are conflicted about delvers, but the fact remains Hullbreak will starve without them. Now, the Boss isn't going to just open the floodgates. He wants to take things slowly, and that will start with small fishing boats."

Some of the older merfolk's eyes widen at the memory as Teemo continues. "Hullbreak has some good fish for this now, so that should be enough to easily get him back into a positive mana flow. The Boss also has a few other plans to help with mana, but those can come later. For now . . . has anyone gone outside, yet?"

The merfolk all shift awkwardly, looking like they're not sure if they'll get in trouble for having done so—or for *not* having done so.

The First Mate speaks. "You won't be in trouble either way. The Admiral simply needs to know. And the Captain knows some of you definitely *have* left."

After a few more seconds of silence, a few hands tentatively raise. I recognize Yendo and his apparent son among the group.

"You have a house or something, Yendo, where we can all chat?" asks Teemo. The merman nods. The other merfolk take that as their cue that they don't need to stick around, and Yendo leads the group to a modest coral house near the edge of the enclave.

"I just want to thank you again, Thedeim, for helping the Captain," he says as everyone gets close and he starts ushering them inside. "Things have been much better since you, uh . . . intervened?"

Teemo chuckles at that, though the other merfolk still look a bit nervous. "The Boss is happy to help. So, what all have you guys been up to outside of Hullbreak?"

The merfolk exchange glances until everyone is looking at Yendo for direction. He doesn't look too happy about it, but he *is* the one with the most experience talking to my Voice.

"We've mostly been exploring. The others prefer to look more toward the open ocean, while I've been taking a closer look at the shoreline. There's actually quite a lot of lobsters and crabs not too far from your beachhead, Thedeim."

"Anything interesting out deeper?" asks my Voice. Yendo nods.

"They've been finding some great spots for various fish as they've been mapping out the currents. Lots of stuff gets carried out to attract them."

"Have you considered trying to plant anything outside, either to eat yourselves or to bring in more wild fish?"

Yendo and the others all stare for a few moments, having clearly *not* thought of something like that. Teemo smiles at them.

"You should probably look into it, then. A lot of the Boss's dwellers like to hunt outside, but also farm. Right now, they can fit their farms in the enclave, but you guys are big enough you'll probably have to plant out past Hullbreak's territory. If you can be self-sufficient on food, that's a *huge* pressure relieved," informs Teemo.

The merfolk look thoughtful at that, seeming to be planning how to make that work in their heads. They soon start to voice their ideas, and Teemo and the First Mate mostly stay quiet, letting the merfolk figure things out. They'll need to talk to the others, since it's going to take a lot more farming than just this handful, but it's a start. Sometimes, all someone needs to walk on their own feet is a little help to find a path. Drop someone at a crossroads, and they won't know where to go. But just a little information about where the paths lead can get them walking on their own, get them thinking about what they actually want to do, where they want to go.

Even if it's a long road to travel, having at least some idea where it leads can bring a lot of confidence and peace of mind.

Chapter 58

Watching through Teemo's eyes as the First Mate takes him around Hullbreak really helps put things in perspective, which makes sense, now that I think about it. Most of Hullbreak is still a work in progress, but we do identify something that he should probably work on himself: the location of his core.

Riding the First Mate, it's not difficult for Teemo to spot the various merfolk around the kelp thicket that hides the small cave with Hullbreak's core inside. "He told the dwellers, then?"

The shark nods in her odd way, undulating her entire self up and down a few times. "Yes. You said that'd be fine?" she asks with a little hesitation.

"Yeah, that's fine. The Boss likes his secret, but you do you. What are you going to do about delvers being around, though?"

The First Mate freezes for a moment, and I can feel Hullbreak is blindsided by the question, too. "Uh . . ."

Teemo chuckles as I get an idea and pass it on to him. "The Boss says it shouldn't be too big of a problem. Back in one of his first inspections, Tarl said his basement was off-limits thanks to the presence of the Boss's strongest stuff at the time. If you put strong denizens in and around, he could do the same . . . especially if the merfolk act as guards, too. Strong denizens can sometimes *draw* delvers rather than discourage them, but dwellers are a different story."

"Would the merfolk be safe?" asks the First Mate immediately.

"Not perfectly, but if they look official and have the backing of not only your strongest denizens but also official ODA info that the area is to be avoided, they'll be as safe as we can make them."

Hullbreak isn't exactly thrilled with that answer, but his scion doesn't argue the point, and soon, they continue on. The only other real place to take a look at is the gull island. The First Mate can't join Teemo on land, but he doesn't stray too far from shore as he looks around.

"So, what does Hullbreak think of building something here?" he asks as he pokes around. The gulls eye him but stay out of his way.

"He hasn't really thought about it. He doesn't have much that *could* build," points out the shark.

"The Boss does, though. He thinks a lighthouse here could be a good way to give some traditional delving, and it would fit the feel of the place." Teemo hops up on a large rock to look over the rest of the island. That's when the Quartermaster finally notices him. The albatross's eyes widen, and he scrambles from his nest of seaweed to stand at attention.

"Nah, none of that. The fight wasn't personal; you were just getting ready to do something the Boss couldn't allow."

The Quartermaster squawks a reply that gets Teemo to sigh, even as the First Mate grins. "Then . . . at ease? As you were? Whatever I have to say to get you to sit and settle down."

The sit part is simple enough, but the Quartermaster looks anything but settled in his nest. Teemo gives him a flat look before speaking up again.

"How about you? What do you think of a lighthouse here?"

Teemo frowns at the squawk he gets. "No, I don't want what you think I want to hear. What's your honest opinion?"

The Quartermaster nervously glances at the First Mate, who somehow manages to convey a shrug. "Just tell him what you think."

Uncertainly, he gives a few squawks, and Teemo smiles. "See, that wasn't so hard. It *would* give you guys plenty of space to perch *and* give you a good chance to actually challenge some delvers, yes. It'll probably be mostly crabs inside, though."

The Quartermaster looks thoughtful at that, and he seems to be actually relaxing some as he chews it over. Teemo takes the chance to focus back on the First Mate. "The Boss also thinks you should try expanding toward the shore once you get the mana for it. Tide pools or a sea cliff cave could also be great places for delvers to do their thing."

"The Captain was thinking something along those lines, but didn't bring it up since it'll probably be some time before he has the mana for something like that."

"With luck, it might not be so far away, after all." Teemo looks out over the waves as we both think about what other plans I have, but that's really all of them for Hullbreak.

Oh, actually . . .

Teemo looks a bit surprised as I tell him, but he's more than happy to pass it along. "The Boss would also like for your Quartermaster to visit his territory eventually so the Captain can have a better idea of what Thedeim's goals are, and how he accomplishes them."

The Quartermaster stops looking relaxed and instead looks positively panicked at the idea. Hullbreak, however, seems to like it the more he chews on it.

"The Captain says that could be arranged. When should he come see?"

Teemo shrugs. "Probably in a few days or something? Poe can come escort him after the inspection. The town would probably be nervous if he just flew in on his own, after all."

The scions look a little uncomfortable at the understatement but don't say anything. After a few moments, Teemo fills the silence. "That's about everything, though. I'll head to town and see when Tarl can do his thing."

"Let me give you a ride, then. Unless you have some shortcuts from here to there, I'll probably be a lot faster," offers the First Mate, and Teemo smiles as he accepts. True to her word, she makes great time back to Fourdock. The shark earns more than a few stares from the people at the docks, but no shouts of alarm. A few quick shortcuts later, and my Voice is at the ODA, atop his favorite shelf.

From there, he can see Telar working away at some paperwork or another, while Tarl is reading some ledger, looking lost in thought.

"Heya, Tarl."

The elf jerks in surprise before looking to the shelf and my Voice sitting on it.

"Ah . . . Teemo. I was wondering when Thedeim would want an inspection for Hullbreak," he says, sounding a bit hollow.

"Maybe he just wants his own inspection? Or one for Violet? She just expanded, you know," tries Teemo, attempting to lighten Tarl's mood, but the elf gives a rueful chuckle and shakes his head.

"Heh . . . I can schedule those, too, but I know he needs Hullbreak cleared for general delving. He makes a lot of mana, but supporting Hullbreak means he can't do whatever other crazy things he wants to do. It might make for easier paperwork, but Thedeim isn't the type to let a problem like that sit, especially when the solution is so simple . . ." he trails off as he looks back to the ledger and sighs. "Even if simple doesn't mean easy."

"You alright?"

Tarl sighs again. "I don't know? Your support at his grave helped a lot, but this . . . going back?" He closes the ledger and sets it down. "I've been back close to fifty times since then for inspections. Each time, I take the small boat out; each time, I think about that day on the long trip out there; each time, I anchor just outside . . . and each time, the First Mate tells me no delvers will be allowed in, that those few who do manage it will not be allowed *out*."

He shakes his head and stands, starting to pace. "I almost want to be turned away again. It'd be easier not to have to confront the past like this. But he wouldn't want me to shy away from this. Not only is it my duty as an inspector, but this is the kind of thing Listor *believed* in. He was a ranger before becoming an inspector, and he always said dungeons were a part of life."

He stops and rubs his face.

"He was always better at explaining it than I am. My point is . . . I don't even know what my point is," he finishes with another sigh, then looks to Teemo.

"I guess my *actual* point is: no, I'm not ready to do the inspection, but yes, I'm willing to do it anyway. Thedeim needs it, Hullbreak needs it, and I need it, too." His posture straightens, though his face looks tired and worn. "Is Hullbreak ready for an inspection?"

Teemo takes a few moments then nods. "Yeah. Me and the Boss just did a check of our own. Your fishing idea should be a great start. There are various nodes underwater, but no real intended encounters. There's a no-go zone, but I'll let the First Mate fill you in on that once you're there. It's not something people should be able to just blunder into."

Tarl nods and heads into a room in the back while Teemo follows. It looks to be where Tarl keeps his delving/inspecting gear, because he's putting various things into a new bag of holding as he talks. "Then I'll head down to the docks once I'm prepared." He has his inspector face on, looking all business, but Teemo and I both can see he's still apprehensive about this.

"Mind if I tag along?" asks my Voice, stopping Tarl in his tracks. The elf gives him a blank look for a moment before giving a small smile.

"That would be most appreciated, yes."

Chapter 59

Tarl

As he takes the small dinghy out toward Hullbreak, his thoughts return, as they always do, to the day his mentor died. The day Hullbreak went mad.

However, much as his mind would like to wander down those dark paths, it's difficult to get a proper brooding going. For starters, Teemo is with him this time, and the Voice is enjoying the speed of the small boat across the waves thanks to the enchantment.

His presence also reminds Tarl that a lot has happened since the last time he made the trip out here. Thedeim has grown incredibly quickly and been an impossible boon to the town . . . and to himself, if he's honest. He might affect an air of detached optimism when inspecting, but that's more thanks to his training and experience than how he actually feels . . . or felt, rather.

The day at Listor's grave was like alcohol on a wound: not exactly pleasant, but a good start toward actual healing. This inspection will be another step toward that, too. He doesn't doubt Teemo when he says Hullbreak is making a genuine effort toward being delvable again. It's just . . . there's a lot of dust on how he and the watery dungeon interact. It'll be difficult to get used to doing things in a new way.

Even now, he finds himself slowing the boat and preparing to heave the anchor over the side, though this time he does so under the curious gaze of a rat who's far too smart to still be an ordinary rat. The splash of the anchor is echoed by the splash of the First Mate bringing her head above the gentle waves.

Tarl clears his throat before speaking, falling back on the way he's greeted the Shark Scion dozens of times. "The Dungeoneer's Guild would ask the Voice if delvers will be able to delve in peace."

Instead of a hard look and firm refusal, the First Mate actually looks . . . *uncertain* as she speaks. "The Captain doesn't know if he can promise it, but he dearly wishes it. Come, Inspector. Much has changed."

Tarl just stares at her for a few moments, uncertain what to do now that the well-trodden path must be abandoned. The First Mate doesn't look like she quite knows what to do either, until Teemo speaks up.

"Well, weigh anchor! Or draw anchor? Pull the stupid thing up and let's do this."

Tarl shakes himself and gets to pulling the anchor back up while Teemo takes the chance to help the elf back into his inspection.

"You're gonna try some fishing first, yeah?"

At his nod, the First Mate speaks again. "The eastern part of the Captain should be the best for that. The fish spawners are away from the enclave and reefs, so anchors shouldn't be a hazard to those below."

With the anchor soon back in the boat, Tarl pulls out his note-taking stone and speaks to it. "Entrance granted; inspection will proceed. Hullbreak's Voice is guiding, along with Thedeim's Voice as an observer. Will attempt fishing before attempting a more in-depth inspection."

The two Voices exchange a glance at the formality, but he doesn't explain further. The rigidity helps him concentrate, helps him keep his mind focused on the now rather than on years ago. He follows the shark to the designated fishing area before securing the boat and getting out his tackle. He was never very good at fishing, but a few enchantments on some lures help cover that weakness.

Teemo looks out over the expanse of blue, his ear twitching for a few seconds, before he looks at the First Mate and speaks up. "The Boss says we should make some buoys to help designate the fishing area. He might need to send some ratlings out on an expedition to try to build them on the shore somewhere. Wood will probably be easier than metal, Boss."

Tarl returns his focus to his fishing rod as he lands a fish, mostly ignoring the talk of how a proper buoy is made and secured. His first catch is a decent-sized silverscale, close to two feet long. He tosses it into his holding bag and resumes fishing, soon adding two large copperfins before pulling out his stone once more.

"Fishing area is in the east; appears to have silverscales and copperfins." He pauses and looks to the two Voices, who nod. the First Mate speaks up before he continues.

"The Captain should also get goldfish eventually."

Tarl nods at that and speaks into the stone again. "Voice confirms fish population and indicates Hullbreak intends to invest more into fishing as well." He tucks the stone in his pocket and puts his fishing gear away before looking around.

"May I anchor near the gull spawner?"

The shark nods and motions for him to follow. It doesn't take long before they arrive at the small island covered in gulls. He watches them as they take off, though they don't seem interested in trying to fight him at the moment. He pulls out the stone once he has his boat secured.

"Inspecting gull spawner. Gulls don't seem interested in combat, but not confirmed yet." He trades the stone for his daggers as he explores the small island. The large Albatross Scion stands at attention as he spots the elf, much to Tarl's confusion. After a few seconds, he switches back to the stone and speaks as he walks back toward the boat.

"Little of interest on the gull island. Recommend leaving it alone, as it is the roost of the Albatross Scion."

"The Admiral wishes to build a lighthouse here, eventually, and have crab and gull encounters," informs the First Mate, which Tarl nods at.

"It's a good plan. Most delvers who would want some combat won't be able to get much. Potions of the Sea are difficult to come by." Of course, he has several. He can't expect to give a proper inspection without them, can he. He pulls one from a belt pouch and downs it before pulling out the stone once more.

"Potion of the Sea consumed; proceeding with inspection." Stone secured, he dives into the salty water. Only the First Mate follows, which earns her a curious look.

"Ah . . . the Admiral's Voice forgot to bring his water-breathing potion. He intends to return with it, but doesn't want to slow your duty, Inspector." She looks as uncomfortable being without the rat as Tarl is, but the elf doesn't let that stop him.

He simply nods and continues to dive deeper, recording his observations as he does. "Crab denizens confirmed; appear to be melee focused. Will be difficult for most delvers. Engaging."

He swims down toward a stout-looking crab and draws his daggers. The crustacean clacks his claws in challenge, scuttling closer, and Tarl dodges a few swipes. He can feel how sluggish he is in the water, but thankfully, crabs aren't exactly known for their grace. Tarl wishes he had more attacks that would be appropriate for under the waves, and resolves to brush up on that part of his training. He does at least have *some* answer for this.

Shadows lick along his blades for a moment before he stabs them both forward.

"Murky Strike!" Twin lances of darkness skewer the crab, who manages a few weak clacks of its claws before going down. Tarl quickly removes the two large claws to put into his bag before speaking once more into his stone.

"Crabs are resilient, and the water makes it difficult to bring to bear most attacks. Piercing techniques still work well." He glances at the First Mate to see if she has anything else to add, but she looks lost in thought. With no guidance, he decides to wander, though he stays away from the west. The Merfolk Enclave should lay in that direction, and he intends to speak with them after the rest of the inspection is finished, to see what relationship they wish to have with the land dwellers.

The central portion of the dungeon is full of various nodes and life, and he can't help but feel a pang of sadness at seeing what was lost with the tragedy of so long ago. He tries to distract himself with gathering, pulling out tools as needed from his bag of holding. Once he's sampled enough, he pulls out the stone. "Central areas appear to be focused on gathering. Various kelps and other herbalism nodes abound, as do coral and mining nodes. Have spotted at least two clam beds for potential pearling, too."

As he puts the stone away, he notices the First Mate wandered off at some point, which leaves him with mixed feelings. Her presence and absence both stir warring emotions, but he does his best to put them aside for now as he heads west, toward the Merfolk Enclave. Along the way, he spots a dense field of kelp with armed merfolk swimming around it. At first, he wonders if that's the enclave, but swimming upward shows there to be no bare area in the center for an actual enclave to live. He makes a mental note of it as he continues west, and soon finds the enclave, as well as the wayward Voice of Hullbreak.

Most of the merfolk are staying well back, though one who looks to be a High Priest seems to be waiting by the scion, watching Tarl approach. He stops outside the enclave, not stepping into their territory yet, and speaks.

"Enclave of Hullbreak. The Dungeoneer's Guild would ask what relationship you wish to have with those above the waves."

The merman glances at the First Mate, then speaks. "Our Beloved Captain wishes peace between us, and we are more than happy to echo His desire." He looks at Tarl, then back at the First Mate before continuing. "However . . . there is an old matter that still clouds these waters. Come, inspector. Be welcome in our enclave and swim with me, that the path can be made clear once more."

Tarl is glad the lump in his stomach only *feels* like lead so that it can't weigh him down as he swims forward to join the priest and the scion. The merman leads the way, and soon speaks once more.

"The Tragedy. Many lives were lost. Our *way* of life was lost. We even feared our Captain was lost. In the aftermath, he was inconsolable in his grief, and yet we tried. We tore down the old reef that held the trading post and built a memorial. The Captain even placed his core there, that he would not be far from their memories. We carved their names, so none could forget."

He leads the two to the center of the enclave, where a large coral structure stands, and Tarl can see the names and icons of the lost: an underwater memorial.

The First Mate takes over as they continue to move toward it. "But . . . we *have* forgotten. More were lost than the Captain's precious dwellers. In grief and rage, he lashed out. Only now does he understand it helped nothing. No, it only added to the Tragedy. So we need to add to the remembrance."

Merfolk swim forward and add pieces of coral and smoothed stone, and the High Priest turns to give Tarl his full attention. "I know you won't have all the names right now, inspector, but are there any that you would add now?"

After a few stunned seconds, Tarl slowly nods. It takes him more than one attempt, but he soon croaks out, "Listor. Inspector Listor Greybrows."

Chapter 60

At least there's not much more inspection to do after that. The merfolk show Tarl to the kelp thicket, and he simply notes that the thicket is to be avoided, happy to leave it at that. Teemo doesn't manage to get back by the time Tarl is ready to leave, so the First Mate sees him off instead. He gives Hullbreak a tentative reclassification as a cooperative dungeon and assures the First Mate the info packet will be full of warnings and directions. I think most delvers will be swimming on eggshells for a while, but I'm happy with the effort of my vassal.

Hullbreak might still be a bit of a work in progress, but who isn't, right? And speaking of works in progress, it's probably a good thing Teemo didn't get back to help with the last of the inspection. With the sun starting to dip below the horizon, I should probably give Rezlar an update. If I'm going to go picking a fight with one or more dungeons in the depths, I should probably give him a heads-up.

"Probably a good idea, Boss. I don't think you'll be able to cause much actual trouble any time soon, but best to give him as much warning as possible. He might even have some advice for this. Should I ask Aranya if she wants to come, too?"

If she's up for it, sure. She might have to act as a bit of an official liaison for my enclaves to him, Fourdock, and the kingdom, though. Larx and the triumvirate probably wouldn't mind doing that themselves, but I don't want to overwhelm Rezlar.

My Voice nods at that as he slips down a shortcut to the Sanctum, where Aranya looks to be simply relaxing and reading a book. She's not as quick as Yvonne, but ever since my birb resident helped her learn, reading has been one of her favorite pastimes.

She looks up as Teemo enters, marking her place with a finger for the moment. "Ah, hello, Teemo. You just missed Yvonne. I believe she's off to the guild to see if they have any maps of the local depths."

The rat shakes his head as he hops onto the small table. "Actually, I'm here to talk with you, if you don't mind?"

She smiles and marks her place with a scrap of cloth, then sets the book aside. "Of course not. What do you need?"

"Well, the Boss is going to let Rezlar know about his plans with the depths and stuff, and wanted to know if you wanted to come, too."

The kobold taps her fingers on the book as she thinks. Reluctantly, she answers. "Not . . . *really*, but it would probably be a good idea."

Teemo chuckles at that. "Yeah. You could also bug him about an actual trade agreement between the dwellers and Fourdock, too. Larx and the triumvirate could probably do that on their own, but the Boss doesn't want to overwhelm Rezlar."

Aranya sighs and nods as she stands to put on her scythemaw sword. "From what I hear, he's . . . high-strung?" she settles on, uncertain of a more diplomatic way to put it.

"Yeah, kinda. He's a good kid, though, just needs the chance to actually do something so he can prove to himself that he actually *can* do something."

"And what is Lord Thedeim actually planning to do about the depths? I could feel Him moving, but I don't know His plan."

Teemo smirks as he hops onto her shoulder, the two now ready to go. "I'll save the details for once we're at Rezlar's, just so I don't have to repeat myself. For now, though: nothing *too* outlandish, even for the Boss. Just more expeditions and looking for a good way to expand deeper."

My High Priestess looks relieved at that, taking the indicated shortcut as she talks. "Ah, alright. I admit . . . I thought he might send Rocky or Fluffles past the underswamps to tear a swath through the depths until they found something."

"Oh, the Boss considered it, but he's smarter than that. Besides, if he let Rocky and Fluffles off the chain, they might collapse the depths and make a huge sinkhole!"

Aranya giggles at that, not taking it too seriously. Not that they probably couldn't but that they *wouldn't*. They both know how dangerous they could be if they're not careful.

Teemo and Aranya chat until they arrive at my gate, and I ride along Teemo's senses as they head for Rezlar's manor. Huh . . . I wonder who owned my manor before me? Maybe some early noble, or even a founder? Maybe a rich merchant whose fortune waned? I let my mind wander, with Teemo occasionally snorting at my increasingly wild imagination.

By the time they reach the manor, I'm theorizing about a family of creepy but friendly kooks, and Teemo knocks me out of my thoughts.

"Hey, Boss, we're here."

Aranya smiles as she greets the guard at the gate, who is eyeing her and Teemo with curiosity. "Excuse us, but could you let Lord Mayor Rezlar know he has guests? Teemo and Aranya, of Thedeim."

The guard wordlessly nods and turns to someone behind the wall. Teemo can't quite make out what they're saying, but he *does* notice when the guard stiffens and quickly nods before turning his attention back to my rat and kobold.

"Uh . . . yes. Mister Miller will lead you in. The young lord will soon be having dinner, if you'd like to join him?"

Teemo looks suspicious, but if Aranya noticed, she's better at hiding it as she answers for them. "If it wouldn't impose on him."

The guard glances to the side before shaking his head. "Uh . . . no imposition, ma'am."

"Then we'd be delighted and honored."

"Ah, excellent," comes the voice of Miller from behind the wall. The guard does his best not to flinch when a hand rests on his shoulder for a moment. "I've informed the young master he'll be receiving guests for dinner. If you would please follow me?"

He offers Aranya his arm as a gentleman, and she accepts it with dignity and grace. Teemo continues to look suspicious, but he also continues to remain silent for now. Miller leads the way, making conversation as he does so.

"What brings the High Priestess and the Voice of Thedeim to call on my young master?" he asks. Aranya answers without missing a beat.

"The promise of closer communication and cooperation. A matter has come to my Lord Thedeim's attention which may come to concern the lord mayor."

Miller tilts his head slightly, possibly in surprise? I have such a hard time getting a read on him. "Oh? Is it something pressing?"

Aranya waves it off and smiles. "No, but that's why we're here: to inform him before it can become pressing, and possibly even keep it from ever becoming so."

He smiles at that and changes the topic to the various bits of art along the walls as he leads them toward the dining hall. Soon, he enters the room before them, speaking clearly. "Lord Mayor Rezlar, I present Aranya, the High Priestess of Thedeim, and Teemo, the Voice of the same." With a flourish, he steps aside, letting Aranya enter and give a curtsy to the elf noble.

Said noble looks about as nervous as I've seen him, but he manages to keep it out of his voice as he speaks. "Welcome to my table, High Priestess and Voice. Please accept my hospitality and enjoy yourselves."

Teemo finally decides enough is enough and speaks up. "Cut the formal crap—it's just me and Aranya. I don't even have my hat and tie . . ." he grumbles as Aranya giggles. While Miller dons a sly smile, Rezlar still looks uncomfortable.

"Apologies, Teemo, but my young master could use the practice," admits Miller. "But please, take a seat. Tradition would dictate you sit at the opposite end, but I get the feeling there will be business discussed over the meal, so sitting closer will be fine, too."

Aranya takes the seat at Rezlar's left, with Teemo hopping onto the table to sit at her own left. Miller, of course, pulls out her chair for her and helps push it in as she thanks him for the assistance. My Voice takes a moment to get settled before looking to Rezlar and speaking.

"Why do you look so nervous? You look like you're about to go give another speech in front of the town or something."

The young elf looks to Miller for help, but his butler is the very image of stoicism as he simply stands with his arms at rest behind him, ready to help his master with anything *except* whatever has him so unsettled.

After a few moments, Rezlar deflates slightly, looking less like he's relaxed and more like he's accepted his doom. "Why didn't you tell me Thedeim was a god?"

Ah. That's . . . complicated. So much for trying not to overwhelm him.

Chapter 61

When someone asks if you're a god, you say yes, right? Not to argue with Winston's wisdom, but there's some valuable context to keep in mind. If you're staring down a seven-foot-tall freak show flanked by monster dogs and a weird extradimensional pyramid/staircase behind them, probably a good time to build yourself up. Maybe avoid having to fight a giant mascot.

But when you're sitting at someone's table—someone who is a bit prone to overreacting—maybe go with some more humility. It's kinda hard to just say no, though, with my High Priestess sitting at his left. It'd ring a bit hollow, even if I don't think I actually have anything to do with her magic. At least no drain that I've noticed. I may or may not have been trying to not think too hard about it.

Teemo also seems to be uncertain how to respond. Thankfully for the both of us—or all three of us if you count Rezlar—Aranya speaks up smoothly.

"It wasn't important at the time."

"How is something like that not important?!" exclaims Rezlar, avoiding a screech only by not being particularly loud about it.

Aranya sighs and looks Rezlar in the eyes. "Because Lord Thedeim doesn't like to throw His divinity around. He could have chosen Tiny or Fluffles to be His Voice, to present an imposing or majestic front to those He interacts with. Instead, He chose Teemo." She gestures at my Voice, who gives her a flat look.

"Thanks, Aranya," he says, dripping with sarcasm, though the twitch of a smile at his lips shows it for the act it is.

The kobold smiles. "Any time, Teemo. I fully agree with Lord Thedeim's choice, too. Fools look and see a rat, even a rat that talks, and assume Lord Thedeim is simple or weak. But just like you, He has hidden strength."

She shakes her head and turns her focus back to Rezlar, who is looking pretty lost. "Sorry, sidetracked. The point is that you engaged with Teemo like a person instead of as some jumped-up noble talking to a rodent. How you treat the least is a show of how a person is."

Rezlar fidgets in his seat for a few moments before Teemo steers the conversation toward the actual reason we're here.

"You two can talk theology later if you want, but the Boss wanted to keep Rezlar informed on what he's doing."

The elf continues to look uncomfortable, but at least he looks like he's in familiar uncomfortability. "What *is* he doing? I understand Hullbreak just had an inspection. Did something go wrong . . . ?"

Teemo shakes his head as a salad is brought out for each person, including a smaller version for him. "That seems to be going as well as can be hoped. Delvers can delve there again, but should take it slow and not push things. Mostly, they'll be fishing."

Rezlar looks relieved at that, though only momentarily. "Then . . . what else? Has he learned something of what's bothering the Southwood?"

"Nah, but he has sent Leo and Honey to investigate and secure the supply line for actual support. I'll probably be going that way fairly soon, too, to make shortcuts. What the Boss needs to talk about is . . . well, about the Deeps. The deeper tunnels and caves, where Aranya came from.

"See, there are other dungeons down there. Not a shocker, right? Well, they don't seem to treat kobolds right—or *anyone*, for that matter. Her old dungeon would sacrifice kobolds and whatever else the local town there could get their hands on."

Rezlar looks horrified at the idea, and even Miller looks displeased, but neither interrupts as Teemo continues.

"As you can imagine, the Boss doesn't like that. We don't know exactly where this dungeon is, but the Boss figures he should let you know he's probably going to be picking a fight with a dungeon that actually has its act together."

"Does he know when?" asks the mayor, his concern shoving aside his unease for the moment.

"Not yet," admits my Voice, shaking his head. "Like I said, we don't know where it is. Aranya crossed the underswamps to get to the Boss, but before that, she basically wandered for days without knowing where she was going. We'll keep you informed, however. There's a settlement of pale elves and pale dwarves, too, so just trying to sneak in and go for a decapitating strike is probably off the table."

Rezlar thinks for a few moments before looking to his "butler." "What do you think, Miller?"

He bows before answering. "I think it will be a most delicate situation, Young Master, but not one that can just be left to continue. My humble advice would be to try to expedite the construction of the hold in the mountain as much as possible, and perhaps offer quests to gather materials in Thedeim. Having a stockpile for the spring will make the excavation and construction go quicker, and if I understand dungeons correctly, it will help Thedeim have the resources to prosecute his war in the depths."

Rezlar perks up, his eyes bright. He seems to feel much more comfortable with logistics and planning than with dealing with people. "Ah, excellent idea, Miller! Teemo, does Thedeim have the kinds of nodes we'd need for something like this?"

I take a moment to consider my nodes and what would be useful for a vault or a hold or whatever you want to call what amounts to a panic room big enough for an entire town. I have plenty of metal, and Violet can even get in on the fun once she upgrades her own. She'll probably need to expand again to be able to provide the kind of volume they'll want, but every little bit helps.

Timber is probably going to be a big deal. I'll see about removing some of the hedge walls around a few of the wood nodes and let them atrophy a bit. Right now, they're fancy wood that seems to be used for crafts and maybe furniture. The difficulty of getting to them helps make them easy to rank up and maintain at that level. If they need beams and stuff, however, I don't want Tiny chasing them through the maze the entire time. I can probably aim for some volume upgrades instead of value, once they're free of the maze.

My various stone nodes are similarly more focused toward value than volume, but the caverns should have easily enough room for me to expand one into a true quarry. I'll just need to ask what stone they need. I'd think granite for strength . . . or we could do like the Romans do and try some cement . . . concrete? I always forget the technical difference, but we should be able to grind limestone, add gravel and water, and make something good. I think volcanic ash is also a part of it, but normal ash might work? Sounds like something for my ratlings and maybe even Queen to experiment with. Honey is going to be sad she missed this.

For food . . . I don't think I have much. My herbalism nodes are more for alchemy and enchanting than cooking, I think. People can cook some of my denizens, but I don't think most of them are very good for eating. We *did* just get Hullbreak set up for fishing, though. I have no idea how edible the fish are, but they sure look like mostly normal fish to me.

I nod to myself, and Teemo speaks up. "Between him, Violet, and Hullbreak, the Boss thinks he can provide a lot of supplies for this. He and Violet have metal nodes, he can adjust the maze to make some of the lumber nodes more accessible, Hullbreak has fish, and Violet has bunnies for food . . . and the Boss has a weird liquid-rock idea."

The others gathered all look curious about that, but I'm mentally patting Teemo on the back for remembering Violet's bunnies as another source of food.

Aranya eventually breaks the silence, since Teemo is refusing to elaborate without someone asking. "Liquid rock?"

"Yeah. The Boss says you crush limestone, mix with gravel and maybe ash, then add water until you make a thick mud. Once it dries, it's supposed to be incredibly strong, and since it starts out liquid, you can shape and apply it easily."

"Is it really that simple?" asks Rezlar, to which Teemo shrugs.

"The Boss says there's probably more to it, but ground limestone and gravel are the two big parts. He'll test on his own to see if there's anything else, and if you can give him a few samples of the stone that would normally be used, it'd help him have a goal to beat. If he can get it to work, it has uses beyond just making holds."

Aranya and Miller both look politely interested, but Rezlar looks almost enthralled by the idea. I'd bet he's learned more than just a little about infrastructure and how much of a pain it is to actually make big projects. If nobody has been able to make actual concrete here, it'll be a quantum leap forward for cities. Stone and mortar can only do so much, can only last so long. Literal magic has to help a lot, but I seriously doubt it comes cheap. But a proper concrete is why Roman stuff is still around on Earth, and it is arguably one of the big reasons they were so successful. A good army will *get* you land, but things like concrete improve the lives of people, and so lets you *keep* it.

And it looks like Rezlar understands that. While the topics drift to more ordinary things as they all start to eat, I get the feeling Rezlar is chewing on that idea more than he is the food. I wonder what he's imagining making, and just how much he's underestimating what it can do.

Chapter 62

The next couple days see a sharp increase in delvers. I think it's a bit of a combination of them wanting to get in some more quality delving before winter really sets in, and of Rezlar's quests being put out. It also helps that people are checking out Hullbreak now, too. For the moment, people seem content to mostly fish. There's been a few people diving in to get at the nodes, but it's getting pretty dang cold to want to get soaked and then have a long boat ride back to town. Still, he's mana solvent now, so that's a weight off me.

Violet is also raking in the mana, at least for her size. She's picked up Gremlin and Mole Scions named Onyx and Nose, respectively. Onyx is fairly self-explanatory, but Nose I can only think is because it's got that star-shaped nose that some moles do. Oddly, neither seems very interested in the metalworks, but Legs, her centipede, is.

With both of them being pretty self-sufficient, I have my mana basically all to myself, so I should probably do something with it. With the boxing ring finally complete, Rocky is probably going to be bringing in a lot of mana soon, too. So . . . what should I do?

Expanding is always an option, and while I have the cavern layer about where I want it now, I don't want to go expanding until I have a better idea of what's out there. And I don't really want to expand into the underswamps. I'm pretty sure I could leave plenty of it for the scythemaws to live and for my spiderkin to easily hunt, but that's not the most defensible of territories. Sure, it'd be a pain for invaders from an enemy dungeon to slog through, but it's also not something I want to build a castle on. I'd need to let two sink, then another burn down, fall over, *then* sink, just to give me a foundation for a fourth. That's a lot of work.

Poe's been sending expeditions through the other passages; I'm just glad he's the one trying to keep track of all that instead of me. There are countless tunnels and cracks to chase down and try to map. Most don't have much of anything interesting in them, though deep to the north there seem to be signs of volcanic activity. That could be a good direction to expand in, but that will have to wait for later, until we get more information. So let's turn our attention inward.

There are a couple spawners that could use some love. I upgraded my birds to ravens pretty quickly, and I have basically ignored them since. My bats have been even more ignored, just having the fruitbat specialization and left at that. But the most neglected, by a mile, is my poor crawling hand spawner. I switched it to crawling hands instead of the skeletal ones Neverrest had, and then never did anything with them except make Thing.

Thing is doing great, but his spawner is . . . kinda shameful, really, and it's my fault. So let's see if we can fix that. What niche do I have that could use some filling? Well, a lot of my stuff is more physically than magically focused. If things aren't specialized toward resources, they're usually geared toward mundane fighting. The Jacob's Ladder snakes are a good step toward fixing that, but they're for the cavern layer, which is more directed toward stronger groups.

While I have electrical stuff in the house and around, people basically have that problem solved with Lightning Resist potions. So I need to diversify. But the crawling hands are more me removing a specialization than setting one, so I take a good look and settle on a magic specialization that should give me just what I want: arcane hands.

Listening to delvers talk shop as they delve, Arcane seems to be an affinity that's a bit of a magical catchall. It's not individually strong with any of its spells, but it can do weaker versions of practically everything. My gamer sense tingles at that bit of balance, even as my engineer sense grouches about that only being feasible if magic is an extra fundamental force, and so Arcane should be incredibly powerful. Maybe it's specifically limited to only magic instead of massaging other forces, like a sledgehammer to open a door instead of using a key.

I should leave that kind of speculation to Honey, and not just so I don't explode Teemo's brain or something. Chasing theoreticals is an easy way to distract you from doing actual practical things. And the practical thing is to get practically-Things all around the manor and crypt complex to spice up encounters and get people thinking how to counter more magic than just lightning.

Other practical things I should do include actually doing the node stuff I told Rezlar I'd do.

It doesn't take Tiny long to web off a few of the wood nodes in the maze, and then my ratlings can get to work tearing the hedge down in those spots. The fruitbats will be able to grow new hedge . . . probably in the spring, actually. For now, Tiny's webs are more than enough to keep people from sneaking in that way.

It costs a pretty penny in mana for me to change the nodes, but the delvers seem ravenous for the wood. I wonder if any of them are intending to use it as firewood? Not that I mind. While the mana per gather is a lot lower, there are a *lot* of gathers going on now. It might actually be making more than before.

I also set a limestone node not too far from the access shaft in the caverns, but don't upgrade it to a quarry just yet. I have the room to, but I want to make sure our concrete mix is up to snuff before I get into industrial-scale production. And that's a job for Queen.

It doesn't take long for Teemo to explain everything I know about concrete, because I don't know all that much about it. I know limestone dust, sand, and gravel, but there's probably more to it than that. Will any sand work, or does it need to be silicate? Is all rock silicate, technically? What actually makes granite and marble and limestone so different? Is ash needed? Does it specifically need to be volcanic?

Sheesh, maybe I shouldn't be so surprised concrete doesn't exist here yet.

I hedge my bets and make sure I have at least basic nodes for as many types of rock as I can, then let Queen loose on the problem. She immediately calls on Thing, Slash, and Coda to help her out. I can feel her intense hunger to figure this out, and I'm just glad her nature is turned more toward learning than combat. She'd probably be a nightmare to fight if she ever actually needed to.

The selected scions are also eager to help her figure this out. While Thing is also a scion who enjoys new information, it seems like Queen wants him to be more than just someone to bounce ideas off of. He's probably one of my scions who knows the most about magic, and getting a bit of magical knowledge could let them make a magical solution to the mundane goal, or to refine and improve it once they figure out how to make it work.

Slash isn't too interested in the academic aspect, but he likes working with the stones and doing some of the heavy lifting. He's easily the largest of the scions involved with the experimenting, so he's basically playing Igor to the mad civil engineering going on.

And speaking of mad engineering: Coda has a fire in him about the entire affair. I can feel his drive even without the bond, and I'd put money on him listening to his Fate affinity, along with his Architect title, to guide the creation of concrete. It's all in the gathering phase right now, but once they get down to mixing . . . it might end up being his show even more than Queen's.

As it is right now, I'm enjoying watching them work together as I consider further plans. I should probably see about maxing out another spawner and getting another enclave going, but I'm hesitant. Any enclave is going to need more room, and that means expanding. If I expand deeper, the risk of Aranya's old dungeon noticing us increases, or we could even trip over some other undiscovered one.

I have the option to expand up, but I'm also nervous about that. It could be something as simple as a beanstalk sprouting and blooming a huge cloud at the top, or I could accidentally bring a hurricane that will stick around. It might even float chunks of the town around me, or something else destructive. Maybe it'll just tear a hole in the sky which may or may not be full of unpleasant things. There are just too many unknowns about it, no matter how curious I am.

No . . . until I get more info about what it entails, I'll leave that big shiny button unpressed. Hopefully, thinking about it like that will help keep the temptation at bay. Sure, big shiny buttons are tempting, but how often do they actually do something besides blow things up? I think I'll try to keep everything from exploding for a while longer, at least until I know exactly what will detonate, and what the minimum safe distance is.

Chapter 63

Honey

The Bee Scion sighs and takes flight, unable to fight the twitchy feeling she has. It's nothing she can do anything about, which is probably the worst thing about it. If it were something within her reach, some detail she needed to fill Leo in on, she could do it and be done with it. But no, this is something beyond her reach right now.

The Emperor is sharing knowledge with the others, and she's not there to witness it! If she were less rational, she'd suspect he's doing it on purpose, too! But no, she *is* a rational bee, and she knows she can't expect the Emperor to stall his plans just so she can raid the flowers of his knowledge. No matter how much she might *like* him to.

"Are you alright, Honey?" asks Leo in his gruff, direct way, almost knocking her out of the air in her surprise. Has she really been *that* obvious about her . . . Well, to be honest, *jealousy* at not being able to hear what the Emperor has to share? Apparently, if Leo feels the need to speak up.

She buzzes a sigh and lands on his nose to do an apologetic dance. He watches as he walks, nose twitching to pick up the nuances of the pheromones that help guide the meaning of her movements.

"Ah, Alpha Thedeim is revealing one of his secrets? No wonder you're perturbed," he says with a chuckle. "I could send you back with one of the wolves, if you'd like?"

That earns him a stubborn dance of refusal, which in turn earns her a laugh. "Fine, fine. I know, Honey. You're not going to get distracted from this, no matter how sweet the tempting nectar is. Besides, I'm sure he'll be willing to share it with you once we get back."

She gives a curt nod before letting her demeanor soften. She doesn't mean to be so defensive about coming along. It's just that nobody seems to think she can handle this! Sure, it's a challenge, but just think of the rewards! And even more than learning something new, she can help Leo protect the Southwood, and so advance the Emperor's plans, too!

"We're close to the next outpost. Are you ready with the inspection plan and reports?" Leo asks, once more pulling her from her thoughts. She buzzes and gives her best dance of salute before returning to the hive to gather her drones. The travel hive isn't much, but it's at least enough to house enough of her swarm to let her take notes and organize reports.

She swarms back out and into the bags of the wolf behind Leo, as even the Wolf Scion can only carry so much. This wolf carries the papers and completed reports. While it's cold outside, it's warm enough in the bags to at least check everything. She even takes a moment to go over the reports for the preceding outposts.

The first outpost is located in a bramble thicket about a day's travel by wolf outside the Emperor's territory. While neither she nor Leo are particularly happy about the state of it, there isn't much other option discovered yet. At least it's moderately defensible, and the fruitbats have been tending it to ensure it can dissuade all but the most determined of curious intruders. If the location is discovered by an actual hostile force, it won't hold long, but with how close to the Emperor it is, that's a minimal concern.

The next outpost is another day from the first, located in a small cave. It's much more defensible, but also a bit more obvious. Leo ordered them to encourage the growth of various plants around the entrance to conceal and discourage others from taking a closer look.

The third is in an abandoned shack in the woods, slowly being reclaimed by nature. It's honestly Honey's favorite one so far, and she agrees with the bats stationed there that the fireplace is nice, thanks to the clogged chimney. There's still a bit of soot, but it's secure and dry. The wolves have a bit of trouble staying out of the rain and snow, but it's still better than just being outside.

This upcoming one will be the fourth, and it's supposed to be situated under the branches of a cluster of pines. She pokes her head out of the bag, seeing what must be their destination. From the outside, it looks like a solid clump of trunks and green needles.

Before heading inside, she and her swarm return to Leo, and they make a lap around the outside, the Wolf Scion nodding as Honey takes notes. She doesn't see any way inside, nor does she see any sign of activity. Only knowing it's supposed to be there gives anything away.

After her scribbling ends, Leo steps forward and is granted entrance once the wolf inside pushes aside a bow of green needles and white snow to reveal the interior. It's hardly grand, but there's still room for several wolves to fit, along with plenty of perching space for the bats.

It's also much warmer inside the enclosed space, the wolves proving themselves to be excellent heaters. It's hardly like a nice fire to relax near, but it's much more comfortable than outside.

She lets her swarm out to relax on the low branches, where they can be out of the way while still taking notes. Leo gives her a few moments to get settled before turning his focus to the wolf that let them inside.

"How has the outpost been faring?"

The wolf tucks his tail and lowers his head in a bow before speaking. "The outpost itself is secure and safe. The scout bats have been keeping an eye on the surroundings, and none have come to disturb us. If the longer scouts are right, we're at about the halfway point between the Southwood and our home, yes?"

Leo nods. "Yes, roughly. Honey?" He glances to the bee, who dances an affirmative. "Are there any problems with the outpost?"

"Only that it's a bit small, Warden. The bats have enough room, but the pack has to pack in fairly tightly at night."

Honey takes a note on that, dancing that she'll make a note for Coda to attempt to expand the space in a more mundane way if Teemo can't.

"Duly noted. You have enough supplies?"

"Yes. Even in the winter, food seems abundant. It might change once winter truly sets in, but the bats say there is a fruiting vine that enjoys climbing the pines. They call it a frost plum, and it is the favorite of the squirrels, so we and the bats both are well-stocked."

Leo nods as Honey takes notes. "Send a few of the plum pits back when you rotate out. The Alpha seems to always be on the lookout for new seeds."

"Yes, Warden," the wolf replies, hesitating before continuing. "And . . . word of home?"

Leo gives an understanding smile before answering. "The Alpha is healthy and strong, and has made a vassal of Hullbreak. My and Honey's presence here is because he wishes to make good on the promise to aid the Southwood. I can also feel him making plans for the depths below even the caverns and beyond the underswamps, but I don't know the details."

The wolf looks relieved, and Honey buzzes in sympathy. For the scions, they can always feel the bond with the Emperor, no matter how far away. Or at least as far as they've been able to test. For the denizens, though . . . they're more or less on their own once they step outside of the Emperor's borders. She can hardly blame the wolf for wanting some details about how the Emperor fares.

"Is there any word on the Southwood?" asks Leo, shattering Honey's thoughts for the third time today. She's been so easily distracted of late!

The wolf shakes his head. "None yet. I've heard the sixth outpost has had some communication, but I don't know what. It's probably not especially dire, at least. How soon do you think we'll be able to start to actually support them?"

Leo sits for a moment to consider. "Once Honey and I get to the Southwood, I expect operations will be picking up a lot. Voice Teemo will likely be through to help secure the supply lines and route before we can truly provide much assistance, however. The Alpha wants to get ears and nose on the problem before he commits any sort of solution. Once the Voice comes through to truly talk with the Southwood, then I think we'll see an actual mobilization."

The wolf nods at that. "You'll be staying until the morning and heading to the next outpost then?"

"Yes. Myself and the entourage will take the guard shifts tonight so we don't try to all cram in here at once."

The wolf bows his head and tucks his tail again in appreciation. "At least the next outpost should be roomier. It's in a crevasse in the hills. The top is overgrown, so there's really only one way in, but much more room than these trees give."

"I look forward to it. Let's compare and update our maps, and then I'll get the watches squared away."

Once the wolf produces the maps, Honey and her swarm descend on them to ensure both are updated properly, much to the relief of Leo and the other wolf. While the bats are . . . *passable* as scribes and cartographers, she and her bees are much better equipped to handle the finer details. She rather thinks she and the Wolf Scion make a good team together. She records and reports the details, giving him what he needs to carry out the Emperor's will properly. Much like with her swarm and flowers, she gathers nectar and pollen, helping the flowers do their duties and getting her dues at the same time.

It makes her warm and fuzzy inside to think of the stores of knowledge she has, to know she can use it to help the Emperor and those he deems worthy. One of the concepts he's gifted her that she holds dearest is that knowledge is power. The fight with Hullbreak truly showed that, with the tricks and countertricks at play. So she is proud to follow Leo to the front lines, even if she never draws a drop of blood. She will do her utmost to reveal the tricks leveraged against them, and so take away their power. That kind of help will be far sweeter than her namesake.

Chapter 64

I don't know how they declare winter officially here, but I'm willing to call it with the first snow in town, which started about an hour before dawn. It's not a very heavy snow, nor is it really sticking, but it's there, so I'm counting it. And with winter officially-by-me here, it's time to make sure I'm all adjusted for it, and to make sure my other plans will be able to handle it.

Underground, it's like winter doesn't even exist. It's not like it snows down there, so I don't think the plans to find that dungeon and kick its butt will be slowed much; at least not directly. Miller wasn't wrong about saying I'll need mana to actually apply boot to butt, and lessened delving aboveground would hinder that.

I'm not seeing too much drop-off just yet, but it can't be helped but for it to lessen at least some . . . right? While on the one hand, there's not a whole lot else for people to do in winter, I wouldn't want to try to have an encounter in a foot or more of snow. My snakes have already transitioned to being mostly inside, with the ravens and crows swapping in for yard duty when they're not out on expedition on the surface.

My herbalism nodes on the surface are slowing down, but I'm actually surprised to see they're even still working at all. On Earth, they'd be dead and drying on the surface, and either wintering in their roots or waiting for volunteer seeds to sprout in the spring. But they're all still doing their thing, if a bit slower. I think it's because the fruitbats have been stepping up their game.

I was all resigned to let Tiny's webbing secure the maze wall near the exposed timber nodes, but my bats are working around the clock to nurture new hedges even with the gentle snowfall. They're also paying extra attention to the herbalism nodes and even the timber, ensuring they keep doing their thing properly. It's kinda weird to see them flying around and being active in the daytime too, but they seem content enough to work harder in the winter.

Further abroad, I've been peeking through Honey's and Leo's eyes, checking up on them as they travel, and it's a *lot* snowier out in the mountains and forests. I can see why the Southwood isn't expecting much to happen in the winter. He doesn't even need strong denizens with the help of good old General Winter guarding his borders. Still, with the progress my two scions are making, I should probably get Teemo ready to head that way and get the shortcuts rolling, too. I don't know exactly how long he can make them, nor how short, but he doesn't seem too worried about it.

I think he's more worried about what Yvonne, Ragnar, and Aelara are planning to do. They'd been mostly wandering around in the woods outside, doing ranger things. What with winter being here now, they didn't want to go out too far, even if they're pretty confident that Yvonne doesn't have to constantly come back to my territory to keep herself perked up.

After hearing Aranya's story, however . . . Well, what do you think a group of adventurers is going to do when they hear a story like that? Especially one about one of their friends and technical party member? Yeah, they want to help track the dungeon down, even if they understand they can't assault it on their own. They've even managed to claim a standing quest from the Office of Dungeon Affairs. Apparently, they are always looking for new dungeons, which is technically what they'll be doing.

Right now, everyone is in the public war room, looking over the maps available. The adventurers' guild somehow has a map of the Deeps, but it's basically a bunch of faint scribbles on faded leather. Even the basic topography is in question, considering the quake I triggered to get access with my downward expansion, way back when.

Ragnar idly toys with his beard as he looks over the maps, and Aelara looks rather frustrated as she tries to match them with my own maps from the expeditions. The elf sighs and stands, stretching her back with a grunt.

"I don't think we're going to get much use out of the old map. It doesn't show anything remotely like the underswamps, nor the aquifer lakes. It might connect through one of the various cracks, but . . ."

Yvonne sighs and finishes. "But that's not the way Aranya got here. She came through the swamps, at least enough to attract a scythemaw. I wouldn't be surprised if one of those cracks eventually can weave its way to this dungeon through other tunnels, caverns, and tubes, but it's not the way she got here."

My kobold inhales like she wants to apologize—at least that's how she looks—but Ragnar cuts her off. "It's nae yer fault yer no cragwalker, lass. They'd have a tough time retracin' their steps after what ye went through, too."

She still looks more than a little ashamed that she can't help more, but at least she doesn't try to continue with her apology for something that's not her fault. Instead, she takes a calming breath before speaking.

"Where should we start, then? Just go through the underswamps and explore from there?"

"That's probably our best option," admits Yvonne, to the nods of the other two.

"It's not the perfect start, but it's at least a start," confirms Aelara. "We'll need to supply ourselves for this, too. It's pretty simple to forage in the woods, but I don't think any of us has much experience finding food in the Deeps?"

"Only some. I might keep m'self fed, but I wouldnae want t' bet on even tha' much," says Ragnar. Nobody looks too surprised at that. If even the dwarf doesn't think he could scrounge up much food, they'll probably want to bring everything they plan to eat, instead of planning to find something in their travels.

"We should be able to at least resupply without too much issue," speaks up Aranya. "The spiderkin are working on setting up a scouting outpost past the underswamps. I'm certain we can get at least basic supplies from them to make our own scouting forays."

Yvonne nods at that idea. "That would also make it a lot easier for us to give our reports and update everyone's maps. Thedeim will probably have the most accurate ones, but we can help with our own contributions."

"Aye, an' we c'n fight through things easier'n th' bats."

"Even if we won't be quite as sneaky as they can be," adds Aelara with a small giggle. "They can find the routes to sneak information; we can focus more on the routes that will let Thedeim attack."

My Voice makes his presence known by speaking up, having been listening and silently trying to not worry about them scouting underground. "Don't forget that, with my shortcuts, the Boss can even use the small cracks to send big attacks," he points out as he hops onto the table. He looks over the maps like he hasn't been eavesdropping the entire time.

"Yes, but you'll be busy with the Southwood for a while, securing the routes that way first. Besides," points out Yvonne, "the other dungeon will have to use more traditional movement to get its troops mobilized against us. While we can probably avoid provoking that kind of reaction, it will surely notice something is amiss well before we're trying to batter its walls down and take its core. We'll need to have those passages scouted anyway."

"Sure, but . . . the Boss can scout those, too."

Yvonne smiles at him and pats his head. The two are close enough that she can recognize when he's trying to keep her safe. "We'll be fine, Teemo. With Aelara's Earth magic and Ragnar's dwarfish senses, the only ones doing any ambushing will be us. And if something goes wrong, we'll have Aranya to patch us up after."

Teemo grumps at being shot down like that. He pouts for a few moments and sits, folding his arms. "I still don't like it . . ."

Ragnar and Aelara try to hide their chuckle and giggle respectively while Yvonne's smile softens. "I know, Teemo, but this is what I do. You're not the only one allowed to take risks to help people." Her soft smile shifts to a cheeky smirk. "And I've been doing this a lot longer than you've been alive, so I know what I'm getting into."

Teemo holds his little sulk for a few more seconds before finally relenting with a sigh. "Fine . . . Yeah, you're right. It's what you do. I just don't want to be missing the next time someone needs to jump in front of a sword."

Ragnar grins at that. "That's *my* job, ye little weasel. But be assured: we'll be turnin' tail and fleein' back home if there's any Lifedrinkin' around." His confidence slips as he glances toward Aranya. "Will there?"

Aranya looks uncomfortable. "I honestly don't know. I don't think so, but that does sound like the kind of enchantment it would want to pursue. Hopefully it won't be an issue, at least for now. If we come across anything actually familiar to me, we should immediately return to Lord Thedeim and have Him investigate."

Everyone easily agrees to that notion. The very best case of making contact is spotting them without being spotted. The cases get a lot worse pretty quickly after that. The pale elves and dwarves are not exactly going to throw a welcome party for the group if they catch them. And if they do . . .

Well, the party will probably be the appetizers for the dungeon.

Chapter 65

Coda

The Architect finds it difficult to focus, despite how excited he is! Probably *because* of how excited he is, honestly. The Foreman's idea, this concrete—the very concept sings to his soul! The kinds of things he could create with it . . .

The bat shakes his head, refusing to get too far ahead of himself. He and the others have only just started, and there is so much to figure out! The Foreman has only vague guidance for them, but Coda knows they're on the right track, as does Queen.

It's always a bit awkward trying to talk with her about most things, but with this, it's like they both speak the same language. Forces, mixtures, ratios, reactions . . . there is so much more going on with the ugly-looking mixtures than meets the eyes!

They have already created their first tests of the concrete, attempting to follow the sparse instructions from the Foreman to get an idea of what they're working with. All of them, even Foreman Thedeim, know it won't be very strong, but even failures teach how to reach success.

The drying process takes enough time for them to get some testing devices created, too. Queen's lab was starting to get a bit cramped until the Foreman had mercy and created a secret workshop for the process. Thankfully, the actual testing equipment is very simple. The first is to test compression: a small divot in the floor with four steel posts around it, and a plate that will slide down the posts. The sample is placed in the divot, the plate placed over the sample, and weights added until the sample fails.

The next is a simple hole in the wall, which a sample can be placed into, with several inches left to hang in the air. Weights can be hung from the end, and get its strength from that kind of force. And lastly: a threaded hole in the ceiling. The samples will have to be carved slightly (with Slash's help) to thread them like giant bolts, and weights can be suspended from that, too, until it breaks.

It was such a strange thing to learn, when he was first being directed on how to build and carve the stone of the underground, that things have different strengths in different directions. The beautiful slopes and arches the Foreman required were not simply artistic but carefully designed. Stone is stronger when pressed, and weak when pulled, like the opposite of a rope. Pull a rope, and it will resist. Push a rope, and it won't resist at all.

If they can get this concrete to work properly, it should be very strong no matter the direction! Yes, it will still be strongest when pressed, but should stand up to pulling and even attempts to bend it, like what will be tested with the hole in the wall!

He shakes his head again, trying to focus on the paper before him and the charcoal stick in his grasp. The concrete samples should be ready by now, and they've received several blocks of different stones to test, too. Slash has already manipulated them to the dimensions needed, so the testing can begin.

Most of the process isn't especially interesting, but getting numbers is important to actually knowing they're making progress. The only real surprise in the first round is that granite is stronger than what they can bring to bear on the test, but more than fifty weights is still a number to keep in mind. The bending tests go quicker, as everything breaks before they run out of weights, and the pulling test is similar.

Then comes the test with the first batch of concrete. Unsurprisingly, it's weaker than the other samples in all tests. While it did at least set and seemed to be like any other stone, it crumbled pretty easily under the various loads.

Not surprising, but Coda can't help but feel a twinge of disappointment. That there is no echo of disappointment from the Foreman helps ease the sting, at least. He and the others created it as well as they could, and the Foreman accepts that it won't be a success on the first try.

So now, to get working on other batches. But where to even begin? His Fate affinity and his title both resonate as he tries to think, and both point at the limestone first. He doesn't need the entire thing, but *something* in it is core to making this work. He can feel other resonances in many of the other potential ingredients, but they won't be able to do their job if they can't refine the limestone somehow.

While Thing and Slash are at a loss for how to actually do that, Queen has a glint in her eyes at the proposition.

"Pieces, components, *elements* . . . Yes, purify, distill, extract . . ."

Coda still misses much of the subtlety by not being able to understand her pheromonal communications fully, but he's hardly alone in that. Besides, she understands what he needs, and she is all too happy to run her own experiments to help him find what he needs for this.

Limestone is ground and powdered, sifted, separated, dissolved in water, dissolved in acids, and yet, nothing feels quite right. On a whim, he suggests taking some to the furnace. Maybe the limestone is actually like an ore for what he needs, and it just has to be smelted out? Neither he nor Queen are particularly confident in that, but it's not like they're short on limestone to try. Slash delivers the samples to be smelted, and even tries different coarseness of grind, from powder to sand, gravel, rocks, and even a single solid piece.

While they smelt, he considers the other ingredients. The sand and gravel feel right, but he also feels there could be something else added; something that doesn't quite integrate like the various powders are supposed to.

He's seen flashes from the bond of concrete being not simply poured into molds but poured over lattices of metal. He knows this is important, and he suspects it comes back to strength working in different directions. Metal is very good in most directions, but seems to be very good at pulling. If one needs a stronger rope, reach for a chain. But . . . metals rust.

While the Foreman has a concept of a strong one that doesn't, none of the ratlings nor ratkin have been able to quite replicate it yet, so perhaps it won't be the best solution. So what else can he use that could be good at being pulled?

The obvious solution is spider silk. Foreman Thedeim has countless spider denizens to provide it, after all. He chews over that solution, scribbling notes as he thinks. While the silk is *very* strong for pulling, it also has a lot of give to it. If just put in the mix like the gravel, the concrete will crumble away before the silk actually starts providing resistance.

They could try to pre-stretch it? He frowns at that idea as he draws a few diagrams, not liking what he's seeing. Stretching it would be putting force on the whole thing before anything else, which will be like adding a few plates of weight before even starting the experiment!

Perhaps the spiders can make silk with less give to it? Or it can be worked out of it somehow? He lets his gaze drift as he thinks, and his eyes fall on the barrel of metal-transmutation elixir. Could that work? Or would it have the same rusting problem of other metals?

Well, either way, he'll need to get some silk, so he may as well see if he can recruit some of the aranea. It will take time for the limestone to smelt, so talking will be a more productive use of his time. With a nod, he flaps off to the spider lair to see about recruiting some help.

"*Not* stretch silk?" comes the reply of the first one he asks, looking at him like he's asked her to walk on only one leg.

"Yes. I need it to not have any give at all, or at least as little as possible."

The aranea looks askance at him but calls over a couple others to discuss this strange new idea.

"But bad socks!"

"Help strange job?"

"What can do?"

They take a few more minutes before they seem to get an idea, and the first one Coda talked to returns to him. "Not us. Them," states the aranea, pointing at one of the widows. "Bad sock silk. Good you silk?"

"Huh . . . maybe?" He'd still prefer to have the aranea make the silk, as they're the experts. Then again, if the experts are pointing at a widow, he should at least give it a shot.

He flaps over to stop one before she can go out to patrol, and she regards him with eight curious eyes.

"Can you make silk that doesn't stretch?"

Her pedipalps twitch as she considers that. Without a word, she weaves a short segment of thread and offers it to him, and he can feel the attention of the Foreman upon them both.

Dragline. Strong.

The two concepts drift through the bond, and Coda is encouraged. He accepts it with a small bow. "Thank you. I'll test this and get back to you."

He swiftly returns to the workshop, eager to see just how stretchy this silk is—or isn't. He has a good feeling about this, just as he's getting a good feeling of the limestone down in the smelters. He doesn't think these two pieces will be the full solution, but they feel like two of the proper steps to take for this.

He's heard Tiny say that every journey starts with one step. If he can start this one off with *two*, he'll be on a very nice pace.

Chapter 66

So, I'm looking at the map for the stuff beyond my borders, above and below the ground, and . . . I think I have my timescales messed up. Below the surface, I was expecting to be tripping over Aranya's old dungeon fairly quickly, or at least finding some trace of it with the long scouts. But so far, they've not seen hide nor hair of the thing.

It's making me wonder if I could expand underground and maybe set up a third enclave after all.

Above the surface, I've underestimated how much the snow will slow things down. While the tundra wolves have been making great time with actually moving around, setting up the outposts is going a lot slower than I was hoping. Travel time isn't a problem for them, but building is. I should probably try to design something to standardize the outposts, too.

Or maybe not. Coda could probably make quick towers or something even with just wood and whatnot, but that's not exactly stealthy. And he's a bit preoccupied with the concrete. He had a really good idea with the dragline silk, and I hope he can get it to work similarly to rebar. It could also be a good use for the metal elixir, depending on how resistant it ends up being to rust.

None of the mixes seem quite right yet, but with the baked limestone, they seem to be making some real progress. I almost wish Fourdock had an actual need for an aqueduct or a dam or something. Probably better to start with roads, though. Water stuff is big and impressive, but roads are the ultimate test for durability and longevity. If I'm *really* being honest, however . . . the lighthouse might be the first large-scale use of the stuff, once Coda gets a mix he likes. Hard to say, really. My personal instinct is to go with the lighthouse, since it will be able to start on bare rock. I've dipped my toes into a lot of waters, but one of the things I've never had to deal with is soil stuff and how it will react to, say, a huge slab of concrete being poured over it. It might make a nice road to start with, but then water can erode the soil away and make potholes, or all sorts of problems.

Ugh, I really hope we don't have to make a sewer system before putting in roads. I think Fourdock has some kind of sewer system already, but not the kind of thing that can handle the change in drainage from concrete roads all over the place.

Anyway: expansion. I really am starting to feel a bit cramped, and I don't know if it's just from me being me, or if it's something about being a dungeon and having a growing cache of mana that I could be using. I've already basically upgraded my spawners as much as I feel like I can right now. Sure, there are a lot of upgrades left, but where will I let the new denizens do their thing?

I could also expand on the surface. I've been so focused on the underground lately that it's easy to forget I could expand out past the cemetery. It'd give me a place to really let the tundra wolves do their thing. I wonder if they could actually keep the area cold, even in the summer? That'd be cool, pun only kinda intended. It could also be a place to let my birds do their things, too. Stretch their wings and all that.

I could probably see about taking the forest toward Hullbreak, even, and do stuff in there. I could even be *really* stupid and expand above and below at the same time. Pretty sure that'd be stupid, but it's still really tempting to take a big bite and test just how much I can chew.

I wouldn't go for two enclaves at once, though, even if I do decide to be reckless. Testing limits is one thing, but I want to give each enclave the attention it deserves. Make sure they're going to be good to be mostly independent before working on the next.

Besides, winter is a terrible time to try to set up a settlement on the surface. It might not be the worst time to set up a wintery section to give my delvers something new and challenging to face, though. I stare at the cost for a few seconds before noting it down. I want to know how much I'd have left over if I do decide to follow this wild hair and expand both ways.

Deep underground, I look toward the volcanic area. It's a bit of a downward north direction to get there, and it might end up being two expansions on its own to actually *get* to the volcanic stuff, instead of warmer and probably more dangerous passages. Looking at the maps and reports, it looks like . . . I don't know if lava tubes is the right term, but it feels like something along those lines. They're not exactly lined with obsidian, but the way they twist and loop makes me think of lava tubes.

Whatever they are, they don't look like they're even remotely active. The reports show all sorts of the glowmoss around, as well as other signs of life. I'd imagine it'd be a lot more barren and hot if lava was still occasionally passing through. The actual volcanic area isn't as well scouted. At least not yet. I hope my bats can handle the heat of an area like that. Can they even breathe there? If this was home, it'd be a suicide mission to send them in, but here . . . it's hard to say. I trust Poe to know what he's doing with the scouts, though, so I don't worry too much about it.

I do look at the cost to potentially expand that far, and whoof, that's spendy. I could get the tubes without too much difficulty, but the volcanic area beyond it would be a lot more than I want to spend right now, even with reckless being on the table. I'll want to wait for the scouts to get a better idea of it first, and let that lower the cost.

That still leaves me feeling kinda cramped, though. The woods could give me a good place to do some stuff, but no enclave yet. The lava tubes could get me an enclave, but I don't know how good of an area it'd be to set one up. Of course, the volcanic area isn't going to be all sunshine and roses, even if magic will let people actually live there.

There's really only one enclave I'd put in the tubes, at least right now: the snakes. It'd just be cruel to put a Birdkin Enclave so far underground.

Oh, wait . . . there's one other enclave that might work perfectly in the tubes.

I have one other spawner that I've been kinda neglecting, partially because it just works so much differently than the others: the ant spawner. Queen technically produces most of my ants, but the hill still spits out other varieties seemingly on its own, and I think two of them could be very useful in the lava tubes, if I do end up expanding that way. Firstly, the fire ants. Fairly obvious why they might be good in there. Fire affinity has to count for something close to magma and such, right?

The other would be the carpenter ants. Bigger ants in the tubes could make the whole system into basically a huge ant farm, which would be neat. But how do I make an Ant Enclave? Is it even an option?

I take a closer look at the hill, seeing a confusing mess of options. Right . . . there's a reason I haven't kicked this particular anthill very hard. Well, you're out of excuses now, my guy. Get in those trenches and figure this thing out.

I mentally roll up my sleeves and dive in.

Well, the first thing I can do is to immediately rule out various things. While the hill will happily spit out practically any ant up to the tier the hill is at, the odds lean it toward the specialization. It also looks like Queen has more than a little influence on what it makes, too, as it seems like leafcutters are the top, followed by carpenter ants, then alchemical, then fire, then arborists (which look to be a subclass of the carpenter ants), and then a huge list that I don't think Queen even bothers to add to her army. That particular list is *gigantic*, and just snipping it off at everything below one percent chance helps clear the confusion a ton.

There's also an option for other entrances to the hill. While I can feel that the hill takes up a space on my lawn, the feel of it gets a bit fuzzy as it goes deeper, reminding me of one of Teemo's shortcuts. Which would make sense, if I'm allowed to put in little entrances practically wherever. They look to have a *lot* of restrictions, though. For starters, only ants can use them, and any ant that wants to go back *in* has to wait for a respawn timer like everything else.

Still, the advantages are pretty nice. While most of them don't really matter to the leafcutters, the other ants will have much easier times getting to where they need to get to. Queen can't just hatch a carpenter or fire ant, so I could put an exit in her lab marked for them, and she'll be able to integrate them easily. One more for arborists in the lumber nodes would help, too.

And that's without upgrading and designating more ants. The leafcutters are basically as good as they're going to get, seems like. Well, without Queen further specializing them. She definitely has more leeway here than what I seem to. Could I make a Leafcutter Enclave, then?

I dig a bit, but don't even see an option for it. I wonder why not? Are they too closely linked to Queen?

Whatever the answer, the hill isn't telling me. How about the others?

I don't even bother looking at the huge list, instead focusing on the fire and carpenter ants. The carpenters seem to have the option well down the line, but I can see it requires access to a forest. While I do have access, or I guess *could* have access with an expansion, I'm not going to make them try to get situated in one in the winter. Looking at the fire ants, they also have the option to make an enclave, and they don't even have any requirements! Well, they can't be placed underwater, but duh.

I eye the costs for the upgrades and the expansion, and how much it would cost to put in hill access that far down. Oddly, it doesn't seem to matter how far from the actual hill I place them, just the maximum allowed rate for that exit. While it looks like the whole thing will cost a lot, I don't need to spend everything all at once. In fact, I'd prefer not to. Not only can I keep a healthy reserve in case I actually need to do something in an emergency, but if I take my time, I can get more used to the new ants and how they behave.

Nodding to myself, I purchase the lava tubes and sprinkle in hill access for the fire ants. What better way to help keep me sane in the winter months than an ant farm?

Chapter 67

In hindsight, in my eagerness to get an enclave and so a project to keep me busy, I may have forgotten that an expansion gets me more than just a bigger sandbox. I blame how long it's been since I expanded. Totally a good excuse, right?

Well, this is why I drill into Violet the need to have plenty of extra mana before expanding. Before I get into the new stuff, I focus a bit on my fire ants first. The basic ones aren't all that impressive, but I have easily enough mana to upgrade them to cinder ants. Interestingly, the resource focus I've taken the main hill into seems to work even with these. I might not actually need to get into the volcanic section if I want volcanic ash for Coda to play with for the concrete. Even better, the ants seem to build little nests out of coal and what I'm pretty sure is coke. If my ratlings can get that, steel production should get *way* easier.

I'll probably want to encourage the bats to help the plants in here along, too, as the ants are working on processing them. Plants become coal, coal becomes coke, coke becomes steel . . . once my ratlings start gathering it, at least.

Interesting as the cinder ants are, they're far from my only denizens down here. Yes, a new expansion means a new spawner! It's even dragons! Technically. They don't look very draconic to me, but they have the little tag or whatever it technically is. What they actually look like are tiny graboids from *Tremors*, but made out of magma. They're wyrms, and are Magma affinity.

As is tradition, I spend the mana to make a new scion, watching with interest as she crawls out of the little wyrm den. Little being relative. The wyrms are around a foot thick and around six feet long, but I get the feeling they could easily get big enough to take up a full lava tube with enough upgrades. But back to my new scion . . . what should I name her?

Cinder or Ember are pretty classic, but they don't feel quite right. Sure, she's fairly small right now, but if she ends up being a big actual dragon, the name just won't fit anymore. I could call her Grendel, but that doesn't feel right, either. I should lean more into the fire and heat, rather than the dragon. Not a lot of lady dragons to name her after, feels like.

Corona? That's certainly leaning hard into the heat aspect. People often like to talk about the surface of the sun as being hot, but it's tame compared to the corona. I think the surface is around ten thousand degrees, while the corona can top 100k? I honestly don't remember, just that the corona is the hottest part.

The name feels closer, but still not quite right for her. What's hotter than a star's corona? Hmm . . . Well, there's one other thing stars can do that's probably hotter. I don't know if it's *technically* hotter, but a nova has some ridiculous energy output.

Yeah . . . Nova sounds perfect.

She seems to slump a bit under the weight of the grandiose name, and I do my best to encourage her. I don't need her to live up to the raw power of her namesake, but I figure we might as well aim high. Even if we miss, we'll land among the stars, right? *For now, Nova, just try to get used to life and living. I'm sure the other scions will come visit you soon.*

In fact, I poke Teemo to visit her and help her get settled before he heads out. We've kinda both been procrastinating on that, but we really should get on it. I think I'll send him out in the morning with a tundra wolf. I don't think there's much else that I'll need him here for, even if I'd like to have him around anyway. While talking with delvers is good and helps build trust, I kinda *need* to start building it with Southwood, especially if I'm going to be helping him with defense.

I watch my wyrms and ants as they start to populate the lava tubes, and wonder what kind of invader I'll be attracting as I wait for Teemo to make his entrance. If it's anything like in the caverns, I might be getting the attention of something from the next biome, or whatever it technically is. If the caverns got those dire mosquitoes from the underswamps, what kind of critter will the volcanic area send at me?

Maybe just some lava variant of what I've already seen? Lava slimes, fire bats, obsidian snakes? Hmm. Those sound pretty cool, but I don't think it's going to be something that simple. Maybe an elemental? Or even something draconic? I don't have much information to base my imagination on, so I just let it wander until Teemo arrives in the tubes. Nova is a bit deeper, so I nudge her to make her way to him instead of making him start making shortcuts just to get to her.

"You know I don't mind looking around and making them, right, Boss? What kind of Scout doesn't enjoy blazing trails?"

Heh, that's fair. I just feel like I'm putting more work on you lately, so I want to try to lessen it when I can.

My Voice smiles. "Yeah, I get that. But it's good to have something to do. Helps keep me from worrying . . ." he trails off as he glances in the direction of the underswamps.

Yeah . . . I know that feeling. Having something to do is why I decided to expand. I'd probably go nuts if I didn't have something to work on while waiting for word from the Southwood or from the Deeps. You can make some shortcuts after chatting with Nova if you want. I'd like to get you on the trail to the Southwood in the morning.

"Sounds good to me, Boss. Try not to be too lonely without me, yeah?" He smirks, and we share a laugh as Nova pokes her head through the wall of the tube Teemo's in.

"Ah, heya, Nova! The Boss wanted me to check in on you. Things can be a bit hectic, especially right at the start. How're you doing?"

She rumbles and does a little bow, earning her a resigned look from Teemo. People and scions both are only going to get more and more nervous talking to him for the first time as I grow, after all.

"Just Teemo is fine, Nova. Yeah, I know what your name means. Don't think of it as an expectation but as a goal. The Boss will take care of you even if you never get a single level. I'm still just a rat, after all," he says with a smirk, though it doesn't seem to have eased her concerns.

"Don't worry, Nova, I'm sure you'll grow into it. And don't worry about the Boss not immediately having a specific job for you to do. For now, just try to get settled, and maybe visit some of the others when you get a chance. Did you have anything else you wanted to ask the Boss besides your name?"

She wriggles uncertainly and gives a quiet rumble, somehow managing to look and sound rather shy. Teemo just gives her a smile. "Yes, you can wander wherever you like, though you might need to be careful in the manor to not burn it down. And you can go talk to the others, too. You'll probably like Jello, in fact. She's very friendly and mostly patrols the caves and tunnels for invaders. Most of us did basically that at the start, and a lot of us still do."

Nova looks like she's trying to chew on that idea for a few seconds before she turns and looks at the wall.

"You spot something? If it's an invader, go kill it," encourages Teemo. Nova looks like she doesn't want to just take off on a hunt where he can see, but a little shooing motion from him gets her into gear.

Wow, *really* into gear. Teemo's going to need to be on his A-game to make his shortcuts work faster than the wyrms can tunnel, or at least Nova. She dives into the wall like it's made of water, leaving behind a plug of molten rock as she goes.

As I watch her, I can see it's more than just a plug. She really is basically just swimming through the rock, melting it and zipping through like an eel in water.

I quickly look ahead to see what she's after, and I get to see the new invader. It's . . . I don't know what it is. It's labeled a fire elemental, but aside from being really hot, it's not like what I would expect a fire elemental to be. It's not a vaguely humanoid flame, nor even a floating fireball. It's more like an amoeba made of napalm.

It doesn't move like my slimes, either. They move more like slugs or snails, mostly gliding forward as a single mass. This thing launches a tendril of itself forward and then flows into it. It's kinda disturbing, actually. It's also surprisingly quick, though that's only compared to my slimes. Jello can manage about a brisk walk when she's at top speed, but this thing is moving at a jerky gallop. It probably averages a decent jogging pace, but trying to fight something like that in melee would probably be a very bad idea.

Or a bad idea if you're flammable. Nova does a remarkable missile impression as she exits the wall, and her triple mandibles snatch the thing up before it can react. I think. The elemental is so alien I have no idea. She simply swallows it and chews a bit of the tunnel that has bits of it left while I make sure to send her some feelings of praise through the bond.

She's certainly not what I expected of a dragon, but she's strong and fierce like one. I can trust her to keep the tubes safe, and depending on how quickly she advances and how long it takes to find the other dungeon, she might even get to go on a proper rampage.

Chapter 68

Nova

Heat and pressure, building . . .

building . . .

Building . . .

BUILDING . . .

Existence. The newborn scion takes a few moments to try to adjust and take stock. While the empty magma tube she's in is fairly simple to understand, things only get more complex from there. Her fealty is to a dungeon that looks to be very established. She's well beneath the surface, but she can feel the reach of her new home spans that impressive distance.

And then the attention of her home is upon her. Its presence is heavy, almost oppressive, yet the feeling filtering through the bond with it is curiosity. Thankfully, it's not the kind of curiosity that would take her apart to see what makes her tick. Instead, it's the kind to watch and figure it out that way.

It . . . No, *he* seems confused by her, though she can't fathom why. She's a magma wyrm with nothing unusual, right? She self-consciously pays more attention to herself, but the lack of finding any particular flaw only increases her anxiety. Is something wrong with her that she can't even sense?!

The budding panic is nipped as concepts drift through the bond, and she realizes she's going to be named. Already? What did she do to deserve such an honor? The first few potential names sound almost cute, and she finds she likes them. Her new home, however, finds them lacking.

Crown of Stars seeps through the bond, and the concept nearly takes her breath away. Could she live up to that kind of majesty? To that kind of power? She greatly doubts it. She sighs in relief as her new home seems to discard the name, before feeling like she's being crushed under the weight of the next one.

Nova. Death of Stars. Something so violent and majestic, playing at scales she can feel even the mind behind her home has difficulty comprehending. How can she even hope to live up to something like that?!

The gentle encouragement from the bond helps her somewhat, but she still feels overwhelmed by the weight of her name alone. She's still trying to come to terms with it when the Voice appears from nowhere and asks if she's alright.

She, of course, gives a humble greeting to the Voice. She's not going to let his simple appearance fool her. She feels barely able to handle her home's attention for a few minutes. No simple rat would be able to handle being the primary conduit of her home's will.

The Voice echoes the encouragement she felt through the bond, but it's not that simple! How is she supposed to even *start* living up to that name?!

He suggests she simply explore and see how things are done, which feels strange to her. Shouldn't she immediately try to strengthen herself? Confusion and inadequacy rage in her mind before she feels something that seems to cut straight through everything. There is something *wrong* moving below her.

The Voice encourages her to eradicate it, and so she does. She doesn't think her handling of it was anything special, but she can feel pride for her through the bond, and she realizes something strange: she wasn't ordered to go kill it. She was just encouraged to deal with the problem in whatever way she saw fit.

In a way, she finds that rather intimidating, perhaps even more than being ordered. She could let him order her . . . but he prefers to guide her, instead. Her name is a goal to be guided toward, rather than an expectation to be met, just like the Voice said.

While it may be easier to be ordered and obey, she can feel her name rejecting that idea. No . . . strength and majesty are more than just physical. She needs the strength of self to actually take the path the Guide shows her. She must be strong and do what she needs to in order to live up to her name!

Her bravado wilts as she feels how much room the Guide has, how many other scions he has. The daunting task looms before her, but she also feels another *wrong* thing in the tubes. Right . . . the Voice said to take her time and adjust. She'll hunt the elementals, at least for now. It's not an excuse—it's a job that needs to be done.

She can't help but feel like the Guide knows the truth, but he doesn't seem to be upset at her choice. She gets the feeling she won't be able to hide in the tubes for long, but that will give her time to build up her courage.

Right?

Chapter 69

I mostly watch Nova wander around as night falls, letting Teemo make some shortcuts to help keep himself distracted from worrying. I'd tell him not to worry if it wouldn't make me a gigantic hypocrite. I know the group can handle themselves, but that doesn't stop my mind from spitting out horrifying what-ifs.

Better to have something to do, especially if it's something that will help them with their mission. It's a bit of a tangential help, but the ratlings have already started using the coke from the cinder ants to make the forges hotter, and so make steel easier.

Oh, which reminds me. Steel might be one of the biggest things back on Earth, but I bet there are fancy metals to play with around here, thanks to magic. Something like mythril, orichalcum, adamantine, and so on would be great. If unobtainium actually exists, I will refuse to process it just on principle.

I can actually put in some gold nodes, but I hold off on that for now. It probably has some good uses in enchanting, but I don't want to deal with that metal. It's too soft and too likely to get attention I might not want. Maybe a secret node down there, but not yet. My other options do actually include orichalcum and mythril, and I take some time to figure out what they actually do. Or at least try to.

The menus aren't exactly forthcoming with information, but concentrating on them gets me at least some basics.

Mythril
Light and durable metal, often sought for enchanting.

Orichalcum
Light and hard metal, highly resistant to magic.

I note that one says durable while the other says hard, and I wonder if an alloy of them could manage anything special. I go ahead and put in a node of each for now, and can feel some of my slimes starting their slow way down to do their little slimy business of helping the nodes along. I also put in a few high-purity iron nodes and a smattering of other more ordinary metals. I even notice I can get a diamond node and put in one of those. It doesn't look like it will be especially good for jewelry, but I'm more looking forward to trying some industrial applications.

I'd love to get some titanium, too, but I'm not exactly going to hold my breath on that. I'm actually a bit relieved to see there's no option for a titanium node, at least not in the lava tubes. Titanium is actually incredibly common, but processing it is a massive pain, as the strong metal will actually burn before it melts. I wouldn't be surprised if Queen could manage some kind of alchemical processing method for it, but she's still pretty focused on the concrete with Coda.

As the night goes on, a few of my scions even go visit Nova. I can feel her curiosity about the rest of my territory, but she's taking the time to get more used to the tubes first, and to hunt down more of the fire elementals. The other wyrms have been hunting them down, too, but Nova takes to it with gusto, and she's really good at it, too. Still, a little nudge is all it takes to get her to greet whatever scions come down to say hello.

Fluffles is the first to visit, and seeing my Conduit seems to both intimidate and motivate her. Fluffles is a good role model, and he is more than happy to help give her some suggestions and encouragements. He's curious about her Magma affinity, and while she's happy to tell what she knows, I don't think she quite has the words to explain it to him. I don't know how many people here could explain the mechanics of breathing despite doing it their entire lives, and it seems similar for her.

Next is Rocky, comfortably back in his boxing gear. He had kept the lich outfit for a little after dealing with Hullbreak, but now that his arena is up and running, he's more than happy to put back on his familiar gear. Unsurprisingly, he seems to chat with Nova about fighting and about affinities. I don't think he's tried to lay on her any of the actual concepts for expanding them yet, but he did watch her demonstrate some of her magma stuff with great interest.

Tiny pays her a visit, too, and I'd wager he gave her some philosophical stuff about what names actually mean. He's the opposite of tiny, after all, so Nova shouldn't feel too intimidated nor defined by her name. At least, that's the impression I get from the bonds.

Grim stops by next, though I don't think the stoic skeleton says much to her. Instead, he seems to have a bit of a housewarming gift for her in the form of a small plaque with a flower carved into it. Nova carefully accepts it, making sure not to melt it, and thanks him for the gift. She doesn't seem to know what to do with it, though, and eventually decides to set it near the wyrm spawner, where the denizens get to appreciate it before going about their duties.

Even Jello pays her a visit. I'm pretty sure Jello was the first to want to come visit, but her speed puts her in last place to chat. And, like Teemo said, the two seem to hit it off. They talk and hang out for basically the rest of the night, and Jello even gets to eat one of the elementals. I don't think it quite agrees with her, but she's tough enough to not care too much about its opinion on her digestion methods.

Sunrise starts to threaten, so I ask Teemo to head up to the wolf spawner. He's gotten a lot of shortcuts done in the tubes, but I can tell he considers the job hardly started. Still, it's better than nothing, and we really do need to get the shortcuts to the outposts done.

You ready to go on an adventure?

Teemo smirks as he exits the shortcut near the wolf den. "Last time I went on anything like an adventure, I got impaled by a sword."

Yeah, but you got better. Besides, you've been outside a bunch since then.

"Yeah, but not for anything like an adventure." He glances at the wall and the little staircase over it. "And never for as long as this is going to take. You gonna be alright with me out there?"

I mentally smile and pat the bond. *Yeah, I should be fine. I managed without a Voice for a while. I'll miss you while you're out there, but we should still be able to easily talk, even while you're outside.*

"And how about with the delvers, or with Hullbreak or Violet? You still need to take the Quartermaster on a tour, remember?"

I know. I'm sure Fluffles can handle that on his own. I might even try to get him to invite one of Violet's scions to come along, too. She'll probably get a kick out of basically anything on the surface.

Teemo chuckles at that, nodding. "Yeah, she probably will. Want me to head down and ask her?"

I'm tempted to say yes, but instead, reluctantly decline. *It's a good idea, but I think we'll both keep finding little excuses and things to do that will keep you here, Teemo.*

He deflates a bit at that and nods after a few moments. "Yeah. You can handle it. It's just . . . It's a bit scary to head out there. Making the shortcuts has me excited, but trying to negotiate with a large dungeon like the Southwood . . ."

Yeah. We haven't had great first impressions with most dungeons. Even Violet was terrified of us at first.

"We've had to work hard to change their opinions to consider us allies. With the Southwood . . . it already wants to be an ally. I just don't want to mess it up."

I don't think you'll mess it up, Teemo. You've been great at making friends with people who didn't even know they wanted one. Now that we have someone who actively wants our help, I'm sure you'll do great.

Besides, who else am I going to send?

That earns a bark of a laugh from him, and my Voice shakes his head as a tundra wolf exits the den. "Send your best instead of trying to wait for perfection, hmm?"

Eh, I think you're at least . . . fifty percent of the way toward perfection.

"Such a vote of confidence."

It is. If I had half-perfect concrete, a lighthouse would be no challenge. I don't need perfect, or even half perfect. It's the flaws that make things interesting; the problems that invite unique solutions. You are my unique solution to talking, and you've been, if not perfect, *at least up to each and every challenge. I know you can do it, Teemo.*

My Voice sits there for a few moments before he clears his throat. "Thanks, Boss."

With that, he hops onto the wolf, and they hop over the wall. I could still talk to him, but I can feel the roiling emotions of his through the bond, and I don't doubt they echo my own. I trust him to do this. I'm not just sending him because he's the best option I have right now. I'm sending him because I can't conceptualize anyone being better suited for this.

If this somehow falls through, I very much doubt it will be because of him.

Chapter 70

Just because there's technically no snow on the ground right this moment, it doesn't mean it's not cold outside. Early delvers are pretty sparse, mostly just the miners with their escorts heading down the access shaft. There are a few on the grounds and in the manor, but not much else. The catacombs are mostly empty right now, too. I think most of the Shield people are turning their focus onto more spiritual than physical pursuits with winter here.

There is one big exception to this, as I notice a certain elf step through the gates and get greeted with the traditional clamor of caws. I smile to myself as I spot Tarl, looking like he's here on official business. Hopefully not *too* official; I don't want to need to recall Teemo already. He seems to be in the middle of making a shortcut, and deep in thought besides.

It doesn't look like I'll need him, however, as the elf simply gives the birds an exaggerated scowl before shaking his head with a smile and taking a look at the noticeboard.

Hey, Fluffles, would you go greet him, please?

My wingnoodle nods and makes his way up from the tunnels with a quick but not rushed pace. I think he likes zipping through them at speed, makes me think of riding a roller coaster. He makes his exit via the cave mouth and lazily glides to Tarl, who watches his descent with vague interest.

"No Teemo?" he asks, curious but not concerned.

Fluffles shakes his head and motions for Tarl to follow, and the elf comfortably falls in behind him. I don't bother sending any encounters, though he does notice the hands. He pulls out his little note stone and talks as he follows.

"Appears crawling hand spawner has been upgraded; can see arcane hands in the manor. No change in hostility. Without the Voice present to confirm, would speculate they are to be a new challenge to broaden the experience of new delvers. Lightning Resist potions unlikely to be the only way to protect from magic anymore."

He glances to Fluffles for any other input, but my noodle simply nods once more. Tarl accepts that and continues taking notes.

"Currently following Conduit. Voice is apparently indisposed at the moment. Likely being taken to something that will shed light."

Fluffles leads him down to the public war room, and Tarl looks surprised at how much bigger it is than the last time he looked at it. "Public map is greatly expanded and detailed since last inspection."

Fluffles gets his attention before he can go into much detail for the stone, pointing at Teemo out on expedition. Tarl's eyes follow the tail tip as Fluffles shows him the route, and he speaks as he watches.

"Voice appears to be on expedition toward the Southwood. Thedeim appears to be making good on his word to contact and potentially provide support." He pauses and squints at the map for a moment. "Appears Warden and Librarian are checking the route while the Voice solidifies it with shortcuts. Odd . . . Thedeim has marked several small locations as territory, but they can't be actually part of him . . . right?" He looks to Fluffles, apparently not willing to bet against me finding some way to claim those little spots. Fluffles shakes his head, and Tarl sighs in relief before continuing.

"Conduit confirms locations not officially claimed. Appear to be designated resting and possibly planning locations once Thedeim starts sending actual support to the Southwood." His eyes follow Fluffles's tail as he points out my new expansion.

"Ah, it appears Thedeim has expanded again. Map dubs the area 'lava tubes.'" He lowers the rock for a moment before addressing Fluffles. "Will I need specialty gear to delve?"

Fluffles shakes his head, but he does point at the volcanic area past the tubes. Tarl considers that for a moment before nodding and bringing the stone back up. "Territory doesn't require specialty gear, but it is in close proximity to more active volcanism. Preliminary estimate that the far reaches of the tubes be avoided, but nearer portions should be fine. Will inspect with caution."

He shakes his head and pockets the stone. "I actually came here to inspect Violet, since Teemo said she recently expanded. Looks like I might as well inspect you some, too. I didn't expect you to expand, though, considering the . . ." he trails off as he tries to find a subtle way to put it, but instead decides to start a new train of thought. "That's why the map is bigger now, right? Looking around to find that other dungeon?"

Fluffles nods, and I have him tap the expansion then Rezlar's home. Tarl frowns as he thinks for a few seconds before he seems to get the gist. "You want me to tell him about the expansion? You haven't already?" Fluffles nods and shakes his head, respectively, in reply.

"Alright. From what I've heard, the dungeon isn't in that direction. So why expand?" Fluffles just stares at him for a moment before Tarl shakes his head at himself. "A question for Teemo once he gets back, then." He takes a moment to trace the route to the Southwood with a finger, then shakes his head again. "Probably will be a while, too." He changes his attention to Violet's location and taps it, looking like he's making a mental note before turning his attention toward the cavern layer.

"I'd like to take a look over here before going down to Violet, if you don't mind? The miners have said there are a bunch of small stone nodes, and I've heard there are rare snake monsters?"

Fluffles nods and motions for Tarl to follow. The elf pulls out his stone once more. "Proceeding to caverns to confirm reports of new nodes and new denizens." He follows my Conduit in comfortable silence; my snek seems to be pretty satisfied, too. It's been a while since he's had to step up for something like this, and I'd say he might have missed it. If he could talk, I might see if I could have him organize tours or something, but I don't know how that could even work.

Maybe if I make a museum. Could be interesting. Or he could be a good escort for caravans to the various enclaves. I have no idea how we're going to try to organize any kind of commerce at that kind of scale. It feels weird to just let caravans through without a few tests, but I also don't want to mess with the trade of my enclaves. Probably something else to talk about soon.

It doesn't take Tarl long to examine the various little stone nodes. "Can confirm variety of stone nodes, though inspector lacks the qualifications to tell precisely what each node is. May require a contractor to provide official appraisal of nodes, but no true reason to suspect error in the initial reports for what the nodes contain. Will now attempt to verify new denizen reports."

He lowers the stone and looks to the Conduit-turned guide. "He has some kind of new snake?" Fluffles nods and leads the way once more, and I make sure the nearest Jacob's Ladder snake is prepared to play nice.

Tarl's eyes widen as he sees it. He draws his daggers immediately, though his tension slowly drains as the snake calmly observes him. After a few more seconds, he sags in relief and sheathes his daggers, pulling out the stone.

"Twinsnakes confirmed. While there are certainly ordinary ones around as well, there is an alchemically enhanced version, too. Appears to have metallic scales and increased size . . ." he trails off as an arc of electricity travels up between the two heads. ". . . As well as Lightning affinity. Designating Arcsnake. Level too high for inspector to safely challenge solo; recommend for seasoned groups only. Others should take care to avoid."

He lowers the stone and gives Fluffles an incredulous look. "The kids really handled one of those on their own?" At the nod, he simply keeps his incredulity apparent. "And how much did it hold back?"

Fluffles manages a shrug. I can see Tarl adding another item to the list of things he wants to ask Teemo. Maybe he'll even try to catch up to him on the trail soon. For now, he pockets the stone and lets Fluffles lead him to Violet.

"Confirm expansion for Violet. Appears to have gained mole and . . . shadow spirit spawners." He watches a few of the gremlins, despite them doing their best to stay out of sight. "Appear to be gremlins already. Odd. Will need to confer with Thedeim's Voice when convenient, but not concerning. Unknown if new scions."

He looks to Fluffles, who gives another snakey shrug, and I gently nudge Violet with a suggestion to show off her new scions if she likes. I kept Queen a secret for a while, so I can't really demand she put all her cards on the table. I can feel her thinking it over as Tarl wanders around, gathering as he goes. He takes a peek into her first room, too, and does a little gathering in there as Violet comes to a decision: she'll show him her scions.

Fluffles taps his shoulder to get his attention, and Tarl smiles as he spots the scions gathering. "Confirm Centipede, Mole, and Gremlin Scions. Also confirm . . . appears to be a true metalworks, rather than Thedeim's simpler forges." He eyes the metallic pieces attached to the legs of the Centipede Scion before continuing. "Centipede is Guardian, and is likely one of the scions will gain a title for the metalworks soon, too."

As he makes his notes, I can feel Violet asking if she could test Tarl. Feels like her gremlin might want to follow in Rocky's footsteps to be a boss. I do my best to gently dissuade her from that, at least for the moment. Her gremlin being a fighter is fine, but Tarl is strong enough that I don't think she'd gain much from fighting him. She could probably test the kids the next time they show up, however.

She seems to accept that, and soon, Tarl heads out with Fluffles to see the tubes. He immediately pulls out the stone once they enter them. "Fresh expansion, likely in the last day or two. Appear to be volcanic tubes of some variety, hence the designation on the map. Little actual volcanic activity apparent, judging by some very basic herbalism nodes," he notes as they walk. He stops as he spots one of the ant nests.

"Interesting. Cinder ants. Speculate Thedeim will lean heavily into them, but too early to tell just yet. Only single small nest observed yet. Will continue inspection." He notes a few more nests before he notices one of my new metal nodes. He brings the stone up slowly, as if sudden movement will somehow scare the node off.

"Mythril node," he says solemnly, as if that's all that needs to be said. I have Fluffles take him to an orichalcum node, too, and he just glares at my Conduit once he spots it. "*And* orichalcum?!" He sighs, pulling out the stone. "Orichalcum node, too. At least that explains the cinder ants. Thedeim appears to be preparing to lean heavily into more advanced metals production, which means the local mining, smelting, and smithing guilds will be able to, too."

He lowers the stone and gives Fluffles a flat look. "What's the new denizen, then? And I can only assume scion, too. He's not going to just give this away for free."

Fluffles manages a smirk and motions for Tarl to follow, leading him to the wyrm den. Tarl furrows his brows as he spots the hole in the wall, but it seems to take him a little longer than usual to figure out what he's looking at. Once he does, he gives a short bark of laughter before bringing up the stone.

"Wyrm den in lava tubes. Magma affinity, looks like. Will need proper protection to challenge for the new nodes." He pauses to think. "Will need to confirm new invader. With rare metal nodes, invaders could be a danger to delvers."

Fluffles nods to that and leads Tarl deeper into the tubes, where he can see the wyrms—or at least the signs of their passage. He also spots a smear of soot on a wall, a sign of a fire elemental, and I see him frown at it as he stops. He seems to glare for a few moments, until Fluffles hisses to get his attention to keep following.

After a few more smears of soot, Tarl sighs and pulls out the stone. "Signs of fire elemental invaders. Attempting to confirm," he says, sounding very unhappy about it.

Fluffles tilts his head in curiosity, conveying a bit of concern, too. Tarl waves him off and motions for him to keep leading. "No, they're nothing actually concerning. I just don't like them. They move all wrong," he says, suppressing a shudder. At least I'm not the only one who doesn't like them.

I help steer Fluffles toward one making its way up an adjacent tube, and I even see Nova stalking it. I gently nudge her not to get it just yet, doing my best to get the idea of a guest through the bond to her. The idea seems to be a bit confusing to her, but she accepts the direction.

In the tube, Fluffles grabs the elemental with his telekinesis, not needing to worry about how hot it is since he's not actually touching it. Tarl eyes the floating blob warily as he speaks into the stone once more. "Fire elemental invaders confirmed. Shallow depths in the tubes may not need proper fire protection, but deeper will."

His note done, I let Nova know she can eat the invader if she likes, which she does with gusto. Tarl shouts in surprise, losing grip of his note stone as Nova bursts from the ceiling and eats the elemental in a single bite before diving through the bottom of the tunnel.

Fluffles hisses in laughter at Tarl's undignified response to my newest scion, levitating the lost stone to the elf. He glares at my noodle, but his voice is the epitome of professionalism as he speaks into the stone.

"Wyrm Scion confirmed."

Chapter 71

With Tarl's latest inspection out of the way and him certainly writing some kind of report about it, I'm back to working on making my new expansion actually be something useful. I still need to get my enclave in there, and there are a fair couple of upgrades to do to get access to it.

I'm already seeing some activity in the tubes, which is encouraging. My ratkin are in the middle of a small mining and gathering expedition. They're all pretty happy, talking about how it gives them vague memories of when they were still my ratlings and would do this sort of thing for me.

The two new metals seem to be pretty tough to mine, too. I think they're only going to manage about a wheelbarrow's worth of each before they head home. They have a much easier time gathering the coal and coke, their eyes alight with the possibilities the fuels will open up.

Especially since they've discovered something that I probably should have mentioned to them when I first made the limestone nodes. The rock has more uses than just making concrete, which is progressing very well now, too. I think my scions have a mix they like, but I can see Coda working to make something else, too: cinder blocks. I have no idea what they're actually made of, but they must be made of something similar to concrete, right? They're clearly molded instead of carved. My bat scion is toying with molds and new mixes now, too, and I think he wants to make the idea of the lighthouse become a reality with cinder blocks and concrete.

But coming back to the limestone, it's also used in smelting as a flux stone. I don't know if it reacts with impurities and grabs them for easier skimming, or if it acts as an oxygen barrier to keep the metals strong. What I do know is that they saw Slash baking some limestone and wanted to see what would happen if they added some to the ore when they smelt, and they were able to get more ingots than usual.

I'm looking forward to seeing what they can produce with not only coke but also flux. Will they be able to make better steel? More steel? Both? I get the feeling they'll need the flux and coke to process the mythril and orichalcum, but I don't really have advice for them for it. My ratkin are smart and experienced in the forges and smelters, so I'm not worried. Maybe a little anxious to get to see what the new metals actually do, but not worried.

I am a little worried about how bare the tubes feel right now, though. Definitely need more stuff in there.

I upgrade the Earth elemental spawner so it will make more, and send the extra stalactsprites and rockslides to help populate them, deciding to stick with the rocks-and-magma theme in there. Miners are probably going to be the main delvers, so I'm not against letting them use their picks as effective weapons in the tubes.

They'll still need some answer to the ants, after all. I wouldn't imagine a heavy pick would be very good for dealing with a bunch of them. While the cinder ants are generally about the same size as Queen, they're still pretty small to try using something like that.

I also need to upgrade them if I want to get this enclave anytime soon. No rush, but I do want to get the enclave placed before I get too settled in how I want the tubes. Wouldn't want to have everything working how I want it, only to realize I need to delete a bunch of stuff to make room for the Ant Enclave. A quick check of my mana shows that I'm in no danger of running low, so I go ahead and upgrade the cinder ants.

The new ants are immediately different from the cinders. For starters, while the cinders act like the spawner access points are their homes and build hills over them, the new ants immediately have a nuptial flight and disperse through the tubes. They're also a fair bit bigger than the cinders. The cinders are about pinkie sized, but the new ones are closer to a hand's length from end to end.

They're also called crucible ants, and it's not difficult to see why. They prefer nesting near my various metal nodes, so I sprinkle in a few more. They don't seem specifically drawn to the new ones, looking to happily settle near the pure iron and copper nodes. I even decide to put in a gold node pretty far into the tubes. From Tarl's reaction, it might not be that interesting compared to the orichalcum or mythril, but I still want to be careful with it.

The crucible ants all settle fairly close to a node or two, then start making their hills. While they mostly seem to dig into the tunnels for it, they also send workers to the nodes to nibble at the material there, and start making the hills out of metal! The ants themselves seem to act like little anty crucibles, which is pretty cool. I wonder if they can alloy things, too, so I drop in a few more nodes to experiment, mostly a tin node near a copper one to see if they'll make bronze.

I spend some time enjoying them just doing ant things before I return my focus to improving the tubes. For the moment, there's only one more thing I want to do with them, and that's upgrade the wyrm spawner a little. I'm not ready for whatever the next tier of wyrm is, but I would like a few more around. Having some more will give Nova the freedom to explore around a bit and see more than just her starting biome.

My newest scion helps organize the wyrms to ensure the elementals hardly get inside before they get eaten, which is fine by me. They're probably drawn to the fancy new metal nodes, and I don't want the weird little blobs to get away with my cool stuff. With that problem mostly solved, she's free to explore a bit, and I watch her as she wanders.

She doesn't go into Violet, though she does give her territory a curious look before continuing. I think she'd rather get a bit more familiar with my territory before she tries to figure out someone new, even if they're my protégée.

Or she really wants to see the surface, because after her curious looks, she makes her way there. She doesn't take any shortcuts, and I wonder if she doesn't like not being surrounded by rock. I'm pretty sure she can move just fine on the surface . . . but yeah, probably a lot faster when she's swimming through it.

She causes a bit of a stir when she pokes her head up through the grass, charring what's nearest her but not starting a fire, thankfully. She curiously watches the grass wilt and blacken, but the ramifications don't seem to sink in until she looks a bit further and sees just how much grass there is on the surface. She may be young, but she can guess that a fire up here would probably be bad for all the people moving around, not to mention the destruction it would wreak on the manor and maze.

While she's just looking around, one of my regulars notices her and decides to investigate. He's a catkin named Berdol, and usually, he escorts various gatherers around. He also usually doesn't pay my scions any mind, happy to do his work and leave them to theirs. I guess curiosity finally got the best of the cat with my new scion.

Nova spots him and sinks down a little into the ground, giving a soft, nervous rumble as she clacks her mandibles in uncertainty. He just gives her a smile as he gets near.

"Well, you're new. I guess Seaside Forge's hunch is right, then," he says casually as he stops a couple feet from her. Nova just sinks a little more before he speaks again.

"I'm not going to try to hurt you, don't worry. I don't think I could, even if I wanted to, which I don't. Could you help me? I have a quest to scout Thedeim's newest expansion, but I don't know where it is." He speaks gently to her, seeming to recognize her shyness.

Nova stares at him for a few seconds before sinking fully beneath the ground. For his part, Berdol doesn't look too upset and just shrugs. He smiles when he sees her peek above the ground near the side of the manor, though not close enough to harm it any. He strides toward her with confidence.

"Thank you! I'll be happy to fight whatever Thedeim wants me to on the way, too. I just have no idea where to start." As he gets near, she dips beneath the surface, and an electric dire rat rounds the corner. He draws two long daggers and levitates two more hiltless blades as he prepares to fight.

I prepare to watch, wondering about his floating weapons. I'm pretty sure he has Metal affinity, but I still don't know what that actually means. Is it magnetism? Is it actually just metals? I've seen him fight before, but never paid it too much attention. While a new affinity can be interesting, I have a lot on my plate already with figuring them out. But if he's going to potentially be a friend to my new scion, well, I'd like to know more about him.

Chapter 72

Berdol and the electric dire rat square off for a few moments, each measuring the other up. I'm pretty confident the catkin will win without too much trouble, but I still pay attention to see if I can learn anything about how he fights and how his affinity works.

The rat isn't going to just give him the victory, however, and releases a strong bolt of lightning! As soon as it starts to move, Berdol swiftly changes the position of his floating blades.

"Chain Link!" The lightning flies and catches the tip of one floating blade, flows down, and arcs to the second before arcing to the ground. The lightning makes a bit of a messy circle, but it's still more than enough to ensure the energy can't reach him. He's already moving before the light show is even finished, giving the rat two slashes with the blades he holds before following up with two slashes from the still-hot floating ones.

"Flashing Steel!"

After a barrage like that, the rat can only slump, defeated. Berdol checks to see if there's anything he'd like before he sheathes his blades, looking around for a few moments before spotting Nova some distance away, watching him and waiting for him to follow her.

As he does, I consider how he handled the electricity. While I didn't exactly have any fancy tools to measure the magnetic fields, my gut says his Metal affinity isn't magnetic . . . or if it is, he can't use it to influence the electricity. If he could, he probably would have only needed one blade to direct the current. Instead, it looked to me like he simply gave the lightning a better path of least resistance to ground out.

I watch him fight a few other of my denizens, and I get the feeling he's just an experienced fighter rather than someone who knows how electricity and magnetism work together. His whole style is about flowing motions and subtle setups.

It's not much of a stretch to assume he's dealt with a few lightning attacks before and knows it likes metal better than just about anything.

Nova also watches him fight, and the bond is practically glowing with inspiration as she sees how he wields his affinity. Even a widow is no match for him, though he does treat the fight with care. He even pulls out two more blades to dance with, and I have trouble keeping track of all of them. So does the widow, who finds her webs sheared through before she can use them, and herself constantly harassed by flickering whispers of sharpness.

She manages to land a solid kick with two legs, sending him back and his held weapons flying. As she lunges forward, I almost tell her to stand down before Berdol smiles.

"Irising End!"

All six blades swoop in on separate arcs, like a brutal mix of a camera lens and a guillotine, and the widow falls with two thuds. Berdol exhales as he stands and wipes his blades clean. "Hard to keep all those eyes looking where I want . . ." he mutters to himself. He considers the corpse for a few moments before continuing on. I don't know if he has any of the . . . whatsit skill. What Freddie's still picking up. Butchery?

Field dressing! Yeah, I don't think he has that. I bet he knows how to mine; it'd probably be a cakewalk for him with his affinity.

I poke Nova to lead him toward Violet before heading to the lava tubes, figuring he could be a good first test for her fighting scions. I don't think Nose is really up for fighting, but Onyx definitely is. It looks like she has a sharp-fingered gauntlet now, and it also looks like Legs has gained the simple title of Smith.

Man, I need to see if I can trade her some rooms or something. My forge and smelters aren't bad, but Violet's metalworks is so much better equipped to make quality stuff.

Berdol is a bit confused when Nova leads him outside my territory, and he looks a bit more confused once he sees Violet's mining nodes.

"Is that Thedeim's expansion? It doesn't look like anything for a dwarf to be particularly interested in . . ." he trails off, glancing around before looking to Nova, who shakes her head. He continues to look at her, confused, before she nods toward where Onyx is slipping from a crack in the wall.

"A gremlin . . . Gremlin Scion? What . . . *Oh*." He chuckles as he seems to put it together. "Right, I heard Thedeim had a protégée. I thought she was more of a toybox, though?" he asks, eyeing Onyx. The gremlin is smiling wide, looking eager to fight, but also not looking too threatening.

Berdol studies her for a few moments before shrugging. "Well, she doesn't seem like she actually wants to hurt me. She looks like a new adventurer, eager to learn. Is that right? You want to fight to learn?"

Onyx's smile widens and she nods, doing her best to take a fighting stance. The catkin looks amused as he draws his more normal daggers. "Alright, I can do that. You don't mind if I finish the lesson properly when we're done?" he asks, and Onyx continues to smile, eager to learn. A bit of time respawning is worth the knowledge. Besides, she'll probably earn a fair bit of mana for Violet from it, too.

He nods at that, taking a few seconds to try to figure out where to start. He shakes his head and sheathes one of his daggers as he steps forward, motioning for her to mimic his stance. "This is why I don't teach much at the guild. My style is pretty unique, but I think I can help you with some of the basics. Gremlins are Shadow affinity, right?"

When she nods, he continues, moving to adjust her stance a little. He keeps her in a pretty low stance, the gauntlet forward and hand loose and slightly open. "You'll probably want a second gauntlet when you can. Close-in work is better with the ability for both hands to do work."

He guides her through a few basic swipes and grabs before standing and speaking again. "So, Shadow affinity. I don't have any of it, but my style would work really well with it. The whole point is to keep your opponent guessing. If they know where an attack is coming from, they can react to it. So, use some misdirection. Here, try this."

He curls and flourishes his fingers like a magician, and Onyx does her best to mimic the complex motion, catching some of the light in a display that just naturally draws the eyes. Berdol smiles at that and nods.

"That's the idea, you've got it. Now, if you do that in a fight, you can try to keep a foe's attention on that hand while the other gets into position for a proper strike."

Onyx is nodding and already practicing the motion, not noticing as the catkin steps back a few paces and draws both his daggers once more.

"Alright, let's spar. Make sure you pay attention to how I move. Daggers are a bit different from gauntlets, but you can probably fill in the gaps on your own. Ready?"

The Gremlin Scion nods and takes her low stance. Berdol smiles at his swift learner as he takes his own. From the start, I can see him holding back, moving much slower than against the widow. He scores several shallow cuts on Onyx's arm as he slips through her guard, teaching her where to tighten it up with the pain of experience.

While the transfer is a lot more muted than with my own scions, I can feel her having fun even with the pain, and Violet is having some conflicting emotions about it, too. She's happy for her scion, though not very happy to see her hurt. As she slows from the wounds, Berdol speaks up once more.

"I think that's enough practice for now. I hope we can practice some more later." One quick stab, and Onyx dissipates like smoke in the wind. Violet is conflicted about that, too, but I think the countdown timer for Onyx's respawn helps ease her concern. Yeah, it was weird for me the first time Tiny ate it. Onyx will be fine. In fact, she'll probably be itching to do it again, heh.

Teaching done, Nova leads the catkin to the lava tubes. He looks around in surprise as they get there. "Huh, you really can tell when an area is a work in progress with him, can't you? It just feels like there's . . . more to be done in here. Niches he hasn't filled yet."

Nova nods at that, then kinda awkwardly sits there, uncertain what to do next. Berdol looks a bit confused for a few seconds as well before smiling in realization. "Ah, right. We're here. Well . . . can you show me around? The Seaside Forge thinks there are new metals to be had here."

Nova is uncertain if she should, or if she's even allowed to, so I pat the bond with some reassurances. Delvers are technically why I made the nodes, so there's no problem with her guiding him to at least a few of them, if she doesn't mind.

It seems she doesn't mind at all, and she eagerly shows him around. The crucible ants get an odd look from him, as do their nests. His interest is definitely piqued when he sees the special nodes. He uses his affinity to get a good chunk each of mythril and orichalcum ores to bring back, and I get a good chunk of mana from him finishing his quest.

"Looks like his hunch was right. You're going to be up to your ears in miners," he says with a chuckle, laughing as Nova tilts her head in confusion. "Or whatever you use to hear with, hah! I'll probably be down here more, too, once Hrunter explains the kind of things he can make with this stuff."

His quest complete, he bids her goodbye and makes his way back to the surface. Nova, rather than follow, decides to practice her own affinity. She makes a nice mess of the tunnel as she lobs bits of magma around, and I'm looking forward to seeing what she can manage. I don't know if what Berdol was doing would be more or less dangerous with magma instead of steel, but I wouldn't want to be the target either way.

Chapter 73

Tarl

Tarl considers his report, brushing the feather of his quill against his cheek and not minding the ink staining his fingers. It's not often he gets to update two dungeon reports at the same time, but he really should understand by now that things simply work differently around Thedeim.

At least the actual contents of the reports aren't too out of the ordinary, if one ignores the dates. Violet is progressing slower than her mentor, thank the gods, but still at a rapid pace compared to other dungeons. Her tentative designation as a toybox is still valid, which is nice. He could see the Gremlin Scion wanting to fight when he was there, but she looked less like a killing machine and more like a child wanting to show what she's learned.

He'll have to keep an eye on Violet, if only to ensure delvers understand the implied rules of delving. His gut says she'll stay as a toybox but have a single chest—or maybe a small section of her territory—where delvers will actually need to fight to get whatever goodies she has. Perhaps she'll lean hard into metals. It'd help explain why Thedeim expanded and looks to be focusing on that himself.

Thedeim's lava tubes will be interesting. Mythril and orichalcum will draw miners from across the kingdom once spring returns, as well as adventurers to guard them. While he expects Karn's guild will have enough who can handle magma wyrms for the demand over winter, he doubts he'll have enough people for the influx in spring. In fact, the appropriate adventurers might be more occupied with the miners in the caverns. They might shift their operations to the tubes once they learn of the bounty of rare metals in there . . .

He shakes his head, banishing his wandering thoughts. Those details are for the adventurers and miners to sort out. His job is to provide the information they need to make the decisions, not try to guess what they'll actually do with it. He'll need to pay attention to the local smiths and see if he can get an upgrade for his daggers, though. His steel ones are the highest of quality, but mythril should help him hone his techniques better.

He sighs and closes his eyes for a moment, setting the quill down. He needs to focus. If he can't stop his mind from wandering, there's probably not much else to add to the reports. He holds that in the forefront of his mind as he opens his eyes once more and checks the reports for mistakes. After a few minutes, he nods to himself, satisfied.

Thedeim's new expansion is marked as hazardous, partially because of the potential threat the elementals and wyrms entail, but also because the specifics of the area are likely to change rapidly. The adventurers and even the townsfolk at large are still careful around Thedeim's new projects, but they also trust him enough to take a closer look than might be strictly safe. With how remote the expansion is, at least the only ones who will likely be able to get down to look will be ones experienced enough to tread carefully.

Violet's expansion is also interesting, as is her apparent secret metalworks. He'll have to wait and see what she actually cooks up. If Thedeim is helping her, Tarl isn't even going to attempt to guess. He might somehow give Thedeim ideas, and that dungeon has enough of those already.

Before his mind can wander to what absurdity Thedeim could get up to, the door to the guild opens, and a catkin enters. Tarl is drawing a blank on his name, but he watches as he introduces himself to Telar.

"You guys want information on the local dungeon, right?"

Telar nods from behind her desk, motioning for the catkin to take a seat. "We do, though our inspector finished an inspection of Thedeim and Violet just the other day. If you have information you believe to be more recent, however, I can still pay coin for it."

He takes a seat as she talks, and Tarl can tell he feels less confident in a payout after hearing that. "Ah. Well, I had a quest for Seaside Forge. Uh, Hrunter will probably be by soon, come to think of it. I just turned it in with him. Anyway, he wanted me to scout out the deepest sections of the dungeon to check on a feeling he had. I didn't know the way down that deep, since most of my clients prefer the manor or the caverns at most.

"I spotted the new scion peeking up through the dirt in the yard, so asked her for directions. She seemed pretty shy, but also seemed to agree to help guide me. I fought a bunch of various things on the way down—nothing out of the ordinary—until she led me out of the dungeon, then into the other one, the small one?"

Telar nods. "Violet, tentative toybox designation. She probably won't receive her proper one until she gains a Voice."

"Oh. Well, she has a little Gremlin Scion with a bladed gauntlet, and she wanted a fight. Not like she wanted to kill me, but she wanted to fight. Does that make sense?"

Telar smirks. "Not especially, but I understand what you mean. So you and the scion battled?"

He shakes his head. "No. Well . . . yes, but first, I showed her a basic stance, attacks, and blocks with her gauntlet. It was maybe thirty minutes of training before we sparred. I killed her at the end, and the dungeon . . . Violet? Violet didn't seem upset about it. Then the Wyrm Scion—Thedeim's new scion is a wyrm, by the way—the new scion lead me to the tubes.

"I spotted a mythril and orichalcum node and gathered a bit, and I also saw a bunch of ants in there. Some were making their hills out of weird gray dust, but others were making them out of metals. Those ants looked a lot bigger than the dust ones, too."

Tarl's eyes widen at that, and he gets up. Telar's eyes follow him as he approaches, and she stays quiet to let him speak up.

"Crucible ants already?"

The catkin turns to look at the other elf. "Is that what they are? I haven't heard of them before."

Tarl nods and stands beside Telar's desk. "They're uncommon in our kingdom, but many dungeons in the dwarven holds have them. Their warrior-smiths will often specialize in fighting them, giving them access to high-purity metals without needing to pay a smelter or smelt it themselves. Are you a smelter?" he asks, curious about the catkin.

He shakes his head. "Technically, I suppose, but I'm a Steeldancer by class. I only have some mining and smelting skills to help pay the bills. Metal affinity makes it a lot easier to gather and purify."

Tarl nods at that, eyeing the catkin up and down. Well-used yet well-maintained gear; implied to be a solo adventurer; strong enough to delve deep in Thedeim; careful and smart enough to engage the dungeon himself and achieve at least a working relationship.

He nods to himself and holds out his hand.

"I'm Tarl, inspector for this branch."

The catkin shakes his hand pleasantly. "I'm Berdol, solo adventurer."

"Have you considered a change in career, Berdol?"

The catkin shrugs. "Not really? I like doing the odd jobs and quests in the adventurers' guild. Gives me the freedom to mostly do what I want. Why?"

"Have you ever considered becoming an inspector?" Tarl can see Berdol almost laugh the suggestion off. The elf's honest look makes him pause and consider for a few seconds.

"What all does it entail? And will I still be able to delve? Can I be in both guilds at once?"

Tarl smiles at that. A proper inspector needs to think things through, yet also be prepared to take advantage of new situations. "You'd apprentice under me, and yes, you can still delve. You can even remain part of the adventurers' guild until your apprenticeship is finished, though you'll have to take a few oaths to not share information for free. Trade secrets and so on. I'd expect Karn to get an oath or two out of you for similar secrecy about his business, too."

"Why me?"

Tarl takes a few seconds to consider that question before answering. "Do you know how many people ever even *attempt* to communicate with a dungeon or its scions?"

Berdol looks slightly taken aback at the question, and a frown slowly develops on his face as he thinks about it. ". . . Not many? I don't think I personally know anyone who has."

"Yet you did. Not only did you try, and not only did you succeed with the rather personable Thedeim without the benefit of addressing his Voice, but you were also able to communicate with Violet's Gremlin Scion, too. There's more to being an inspector than being strong enough to delve solo. You also need to be able to communicate with the dungeons and their scions, to be able to recognize they have needs and wants, even if you don't know what those needs specifically are."

Berdol chews that information over for a few more seconds before smiling. "What's the pay like?"

Tarl grins and prepares to answer, but he is interrupted by the door to the guild slamming open.

In the doorway stands the hairiest dwarf Tarl has ever seen. A thick leather apron and rugged pants attempt to hold the tide of red hair at bay, and thick leather gloves cover hands that only *probably* don't have much hair on them. A bulbous nose sticks out above the braided mustache, and beady eyes perch above that, though they are wide and wild at the moment.

"Orichalcum and mythril! It has orichalcum *and* mythril!"

Perhaps Tarl should have put some thought into how the local smiths would react, after all.

Chapter 74

Another day, another set of delvers. Today's set is starting early . . . and they don't look much like my typical delvers. Most of them come in with some variety of armor or at least a wizard's robes, but not these ones. These ones come with what looks like forge gear: heavy leather aprons, gloves, and such. The half dozen or so at least have picks and hammers they probably know how to swing, but I seriously doubt they can handle my deeper stuff.

That doubt turns to certainty as I probe them with a few encounters on the surface. One of them gets a nasty bite from one of my vipers, and he hobbles back toward the gates to recover, giving me some "defeat delver" mana. The rest of the group decide to turn back when they meet a widow in the tunnels. I'm just glad they understand what they can't handle.

The next group actually tries their luck against the widow, and she leaves them nice and wrapped up for my ratlings to haul to the gates on the surface.

On the one hand, I'm enjoying the mana for victories. On the other, I'm starting to think I should have been more careful about the fantasy metals. While smiths theoretically could be after gold, I seriously doubt it. These guys look like they make adventuring gear, not jewelry.

I'm sure they'll learn. It doesn't look like it will even take them long to do so. The more experienced miners show up around noon, a bit late in the day for them, but it looks like they were spending their time organizing a big group. I wonder if it's even technically a raid party. That'd be kinda cool, even if it'd really show how much I underestimated how desirable those fantasy metals are.

Usually, mining groups going to the caverns are about three-to-one miners to adventurers, but this group is looking almost one-to-one. They all consult with a map and check their route, and I'm much less concerned for this group than the others. I bet the others heard about my friendly disposition and the valuable ores and thought they'd be able to run in and get some quickly. These guys have been in the caverns and know I can bring some heat if I want, so they've prepared accordingly. I'm actually a bit proud of these guys.

I make sure I have some healing slimes down in the lava tubes anyway. They probably have some fire protection, but I don't know exactly how dangerous my wyrms actually are. They've been having an easy buffet of the fire elementals, but that's thanks to the ambushes. I don't want my wyrms to just swallow limbs and dive back into the rock. Hopefully, it'll be good training for my weird little dragons to actually have to fight instead of relying on surprise tactics.

I keep half a metaphorical eye on them as they steadily make their way down, cool and professional. The rest of my attention is on the tubes as I consider what else to do in there. One thing that catches my eye is the herbalism stuff. I had been expecting them to mostly just be fuel to make charcoal and coke for the cinder ants, but it looks like some of the seeds the fruitbats have found on expedition are starting to grow down here with their help.

There's a variation on a lumber node called a deepapple. I think they actually specifically want to get fruitbat attention, as the mushrooms grow pretty thick and tall, putting the caps close to the ceiling. Instead of the typical mushroom gills, they have little round . . . spore pods, I guess? Makes me think of a video I watched before I met truck-kun about stinkhorn mushrooms. I think the little pods are full of gleba, which is not just fun to say but also basically spores in liquid. Thankfully, it doesn't seem to be too stinky. I think. I'd imagine they'd get a ruder name if they were. Deephorseapples, maybe.

Whatever the smell or nutritional value, they should be perfect for the cinder ants to do their thing, and let me grow some of the more exotic stuff my bats have managed to recover. I'm pretty sure they've gotten them from the volcanic area past the tubes, which bodes well for delvers being able to do stuff in there, eventually.

One that catches my eye is Fool's Coal. I sprinkle a few of them around as I look over the description, which is interesting. The plant looks like it mostly grows inside the rock and produces a little black fruit on the surface. It has a lot of alchemical uses, apparently, and is called Fool's Coal because only a fool would try to burn it. It looks like it tends to explode when too hot. I guess that's one way to get your seeds away from a place too hot for them to survive.

Magmoss is an interesting one, too. It grows close to the surface of rocks and such, making them look like they have veins of magma, but they're not hot. In fact, they actively cool, and I'd bet they're a primary ingredient in a lot of fire-protection potions.

I have a few others that I'd like to plant, but I think I'll need to expand again to get them. Lava Lillies actually require lava pools to grow in, making me wonder if the volcano area will be more like the underswamps but with lava instead of water. Magma. Magma is inside, lava is outside. Thank you, *Dwarf Fortress*.

I also check in on my crucible ants to see if they alloy stuff properly, and it sure looks to me like they can. I see a few hills made of bronze over by the copper and tin nodes. It makes me want to place a whole bunch of nodes close to each other and see what the crucible ants can cook up, but I think I'll hold off on making more of the fantasy ore nodes for now.

I might upgrade the ants again, though. I like the crucible ants, but they're still not going to make me an enclave. I think I have at least one more tier of ants before I reach the max ones. My mana is still doing fine, especially after defeating those earlier miners, so it's not a difficult decision to upgrade to the next tier.

Wow, that's a big and *ugly* ant. It's called a tunnelbore, which makes the ugliness make a bit more sense. And the size. They're easily going to be my biggest denizens at around four feet tall and around ten feet long. They're kinda squat and thick ants, with a huge head like a major might have. Instead of the big mandibles a major would have, though, it has a big flat ugly lumpy spiky face. It reminds me of the head of a big tunnel-boring drill, but organic instead of metal.

I'm glad it doesn't look like it can just rotate its face like one, however. That'd be some nightmare fuel. It does like to dig, at least, and I watch as it starts, rubbing its face against the wall in a circular motion, looking like it wants to wax on, or maybe wax off. Probably off, because the wall of the tunnel is easily being dug away. Once it can put its entire face against the newly flattened part of the wall, the ant crawls around in circles, like a breakdancer spinning on his head. But with more limbs. And on the wall.

. . . Maybe not so much like a breakdancer, then. Whatever the correct metaphor, it's making good progress, and I spend a bit of mana to give it some direction. I'd usually have Coda do this, but he's busy with the cinder blocks and cement. I tell the ant to make a bunch of side chambers along the tunnel for now, and am glad to see the next tunnelbore ant start to work on a new one. I'm sure they'll congregate a bit once they can start opening the boreholes into proper chambers.

I'm really happy with my new tunnelbore ants, watching them work as the miners reach the tunnels. It looks like the adventurers have some form of fire protection, which is great for my wyrms. Not letting them ambush is one thing, but how can I expect them to attack if a touch would give third-degree burns? First degree?

Really bad burns!

The wyrms keep them on their toes, opting to start with making very obvious and slow magma holes before leaping out, forcing the delvers to dodge or otherwise deal with the simple momentum of the attack. The delvers' strategy is simple but effective. The adventurers will lock down the mandibles of a wyrm in various ways, and the miners will come in with hammers and picks to get at the more vulnerable sides. It's not especially fast work, but it's effective and pretty safe. Burns and wounds still happen, but they have some healing on hand for that.

I absently nod to myself, glad I won't need to babysit the delvers as I watch the ants dig. That's part of the fun of an ant farm, after all.

Chapter 75

Rhonda

The goblin hums to herself as she carefully measures out doses of potions into bottles, Lucas dutifully following after to properly cork them. He likes to put a thin webbing over them as well, enough to ensure the corks stay put, yet not thick enough to interfere when someone actually needs to quickly drink one. This batch is healing potions, but the two will be working on Aqua Affinity potions next.

She might brew a few of Thedeim's water-breathing potions in the next few days, too. Something about them draws her class to it. She has a hunch Master Staiven is wrong about what they do, but she has no idea what else it could be. The idea of experimenting to find out tempts her to hurry, but she stomps that impulse down. Fast work with potions is sloppy work, and sloppy work with potions is *dangerous* work. Besides, if she's been taking stock properly, she's pretty sure there are a couple of those potions left unsold yet not on the shelves. Her master might be ahead of her in wanting to experiment. She might get to help design one!

That hope leads to a stronger urge to speed up, and a harder one to ignore, but she manages. She's been having to learn patience with her studies after Thedeim vassalized Hullbreak. With the dungeon now open to delvers, the demand for water potions has skyrocketed! Once the first wave started bringing back kelps and other ingredients, Master Staiven was more than happy to blow the dust off the old Aqua Affinity recipe and teach it to her.

It's easily the most complex potion in her repertoire now. It's mostly water and life essences, expressed through a transmutation formulation. The gills and fins it gives are weird, but not uncomfortable. She and Master Staiven had tested the first batch out just past the docks to ensure they had it right. While the water is murkier than she would have preferred, there were no other problems. She's even been toying with the formula to see if she can fix the murkiness issue. She can feel another essence will be needed, but she's not sure what. Her first instinct was light, but that doesn't feel quite right.

Maybe she can try to talk with the First Mate? All accounts of the Voice of Hullbreak say she's intimidating but reasonable. Old sailors say sharks are supposed to have incredible senses, but whenever she tries to ask one in the shop about it, they start on a wild fish tale and never reach the point before they need to pay and leave.

She's starting to suspect that's the point, and that most of the sailors don't actually know if sharks have good senses. It might be better to get it from the shark's own mouth. The more she thinks on it, pouring doses into bottles, the more she likes the idea. Another delve would be great!

"Lucas, do I have any spell spore in my personal stocks?" she asks her spider familiar. He's always been better at keeping track of hard numbers than she is, and she pouts slightly when he shakes a negative.

"We'll need to delve Thedeim again if we're going to try to delve Hullbreak. Master Staiven would probably let me borrow some, but a proper adventuring alchemist keeps herself and her party stocked with potions from her own gathering. Or pays for the ingredients, like Master Staiven does."

Lucas chitters approvingly at that, and Rhonda can tell he's looking forward to some adventuring too. She's pretty sure he's somehow picked up Meta affinity. She doesn't know how else he can use the odd bits and pieces he's gathered to help her spellcraft. She's also not certain where he's gotten them all. She has no idea what creature could have created the small chip of bone that has Earth affinity in it. If it was a whole piece, she might be able to puzzle it out, but a small piece could have come from anything!

She finishes pouring the potions and scrubs the cauldron before heading up to the shop floor to check if her master needs anything. His grumpy look doesn't look like an act like it usually does.

"Is something wrong?" she asks, concerned. His look softens slightly before he sighs.

"No Aqua Affinity potions today. The delvers I sent to gather bubblekelp came back with bubble*weed* instead! Sure, I can use it in something else, but not the affinity potion," he grouses from the stool behind the counter.

His sour mood pauses when he sees the considering look in his apprentice's eyes. That look means mischief, or some other version of plotting. He's always equally proud and concerned when his apprentice gets that look.

"What if we get it? Me, Freddie, and Larrez? We'd need to delve Thedeim for some spell spore, but then I can make his version of the water-breathing potion, and we can go gather stuff in Hullbreak," she suggests.

Staiven weighs that plan for a few seconds, looking for holes to poke in it. He *has* kept her brewing a lot recently. Stretching her legs would be good, especially with winter here. It's easy to forget Thedeim has plenty of space belowground to delve, not just the house and yard.

He nods. "Gather enough for warming potions, too. The trip to and from Hullbreak will be cold." With that, he offers her the quest to gather the bubblekelp. "You can prepare with Thedeim today and get an early start on Hullbreak tomorrow. Go have fun," he says with a smile, shooing her up the stairs to gather her gear, then waving her farewell as she leaves with all her kit.

Getting Freddie is as easy as going to the church and asking. She finds him in prayer and quietly waits. He cracks open an eye and gives her half a smile before continuing, and soon finishes up. It only takes a few minutes to explain, and only a few minutes more for him and Fiona to prepare.

The hard part comes when they both realize they don't actually know how to get in contact with Larrez. They know he was a caravan guard, so he's probably guarding something, but they don't actually know where he works.

Well, besides at the guild. With no other leads, the intrepid youngsters and their spiders head there. Inside, the first floor is fuller than usual, the adventurers taking a bit more time between quests and delves to warm up and unwind. A few groups see them and nod in greeting, but most are too busy with what they're doing to even notice.

One major exception is Karn the Slight. The guild leader smiles at the small group and waves them to the bar. "Well! If it isn't two of my newest members! How're you kids doing?" His eyes shine with mirth as they drift to the spiders. "You two keeping them from getting into too much trouble?"

The spiders chitter in affirmation, and the two youths smile at the friendly orc. "We're doing well," answers Freddie. "We're actually looking to do some delving. Old Staiven gave Rhonda a quest to get some bubblekelp from Hullbreak."

Karn nods at that. "Sounds like a good way to expand your horizons, get a feel for a dungeon besides just Thedeim."

"Yeah, but we don't know how to let Larrez know. If we're a party, we should delve together," points out Rhonda.

Karn leans back and folds his arms, his gaze drifting over the tavern as he considers the problem. His drifting gaze freezes for a moment before he nods to himself and leans forward again. "I don't know his contact info off the top of my head. Let me check his paperwork to see what options we have. I'll be back in a sec."

They let him go to his office without any fuss and take the chance to look around the first floor a bit more as they wait.

Karn

He probably should have expected a wrinkle like this in Rezlar's plan to keep his identity secret. While he doesn't doubt the young lord has plenty of people to handle most of the work of being the mayor, it's not like the kid can just hang out in the guildhall all day. He was trying to think of some way to deflect when he noticed Miller standing outside a window.

Their eyes met, and the definitely-just-a-butler pointed upward, then vanished. Karn might not have planned for something like this, but it's looking like Miller did. The orc suppresses a sigh as he heads to his office, and he isn't surprised to see Miller inside, waiting for him.

"So, what's your solution?" Karn asks, taking a seat behind his desk.

Miller smiles like he'd prefer to play this out a bit more but is decent enough to get to the point. Not everyone enjoys the intricacies of a good cover story. "Young Lárrez has secured himself a job as a guard to the young master's estate. His party should be able to request his company with the gate guards, though he will not always be available."

Karn mulls that over for a few seconds and nods. "That'll do it, yeah. I'll let them know where they can gather up their friend."

Miller's professional smile relaxes just a hair at that. Karn is perceptive enough to notice, and smart enough to pretend he doesn't. There's not a lot he knows for sure about Miller's motivations, but one thing has been pretty consistent. It might be yet another cover, a part of the act, but Karn's gut tells him it's genuine. The "butler" cares deeply for his charge, and about more than just his safety.

It's pretty plain Rezlar sees Miller as a father figure, possibly more than his actual father. Seeing that smile makes Karn think Miller sees the young noble as a son, too.

Chapter 76

~~Rezlar~~ Larrez

The young elf noble does his best to ignore the curious glances of his guards as he selects a bunk at the back of the barracks. While he does have his disguise on, his guards *do* still need to know where he is, at least when on the grounds, so the veterans are read in on the ruse.

When Miller suggested telling them, Rezlar was against it. The fewer people who knew, the fewer people who would blab. Miller smiled at that argument but shut it down with his usual ruthless efficiency. The veteran guards are trusted, otherwise they would not be veterans at his estate. Just as Miller takes his job seriously, so too do they, and they would not be able to do their jobs if kept in the dark.

Even Rezlar's protests that they'd see it as weird were only met with a smile and a twinkle in the older elf's eyes.

"The so-called common folk expect *some* strangeness in their lords, Young Master. I recall hearing of one lord who greatly enjoyed baking pastries. He and the head baker had a very close relationship. The noble enjoyed doing something so uncouth as to leave him filthy and sweaty, and his mother was happy to be able to provide an outlet for that which didn't involve him being in any actual danger. As far as I'm aware, while it was an open secret among the staff, none of the nobles ever knew. While I'm certain they all enjoyed sneaking some of the baked goods, it's also something that endeared the noble to them. It helps break down a bit of the us versus them that so many people think in. If you are them, at least in some small way, they will tend not to question your decisions as hard, and grant the benefit of the doubt so long as they don't suffer because of the choices."

When he was even younger, Rezlar would have gasped at the very idea of the ordinary citizenry questioning the decisions of the nobles, but now, he understands that the citizenry will always talk and have opinions on it. Any noble who pretends otherwise—or worse, tries to stop it—tends to not have the chance to pass their noble title on further.

He shakes his head to clear it, focusing on the task at hand, which is to get his bunk and locker organized and secured. While the veterans know who he is, the other guards do not, so he'll be disciplined if he doesn't keep his "assigned" area properly.

Speaking of the vets, a halfling with a sword on his back bigger than he is comes up to Rezlar. "You're the new one, Larrez, yeah?" he asks, looking amused to be talking to his boss like this, but staying in character. Rezlar does his best to stay in character, too, and stands stiffly at attention.

"Uh, yes, sir!"

The halfling smiles and points a thumb over his shoulder. "Your friends are at the gate, wanting to know if you're free to delve. Adventurer guild rules say we have to give reasonable accommodation for delving." He makes a show of looking over the bed and locker. "Looks like you need to practice tucking your sheets, but I don't see anything that would bring shame on Lord Rezlar. You're free to go."

The elf is surprised at the news of his friends being at the gate, and for a moment can't think of who they could even be. His eyes widen, and he barely manages to not facepalm himself. It must be Freddie and Rhonda! Miller must have learned of their plans to delve, and that's why he's been furthering this alternate identity. They can't exactly come and ask the lord mayor to go delving, can they? But asking their friend who happens to be a guard should garner hardly any attention at all!

He hurries to get ready, and the halfling leaves him to it, shaking his head and smiling. Rezlar is dimly aware of one of the newer guards complaining about him getting to leave, and can't help but feel a spark of pride when the halfling responds.

"Get strong enough to get accepted into the adventurers' guild, and you can take off on delves, too. Until then, thanks for volunteering to cover his watch!" The guards, vets and new, laugh as Rezlar leaves, and he's soon at the gate, seeing his party. Rhonda and Freddie both smile as they see him, and their arachnid companions wave. He doesn't bother to fight his smile as he hurries, and his quick salute to the guard at the gate is returned with practiced ease. So dismissed, he turns to the rest of his party.

"Hello! What is, uh . . . what's up?" he asks, trying to remember to talk more casually with them. Among nobles, misspeaking can be leverage to be used against you. With friends, flubbing words is ignored, or a good way to share a laugh.

Freddie smiles but stays quiet, letting Rhonda give the details. "Master Staiven needs some bubblekelp, so I accepted the quest. But I don't have what I need to make water-breathing potions, so we're going to delve Thedeim today and get the stuff, and then delve Hullbreak tomorrow to get the kelp and whatever else we can get!"

Rezlar is nervous about the idea of delving Hullbreak, but Thedeim *did* vassalize the dungeon. He's even been getting financial reports already about the fishing vessels, and the jewelers have started selling pearl pieces already.

Freddie notices his unease and nods.

"Yeah, Hullbreak will be different than Thedeim, but it'd be a good idea for us to get used to other dungeons. And I'm looking forward to just exploring underwater. I've only really splashed around in ponds before."

They all chat as they head to Thedeim, mostly about how much swimming they've all done. The consensus is that Larrez will probably be relied on heavily for their first delve in Hullbreak, until Freddie and Rhonda get more used to the water.

As they enter their favorite dungeon, the conversation shifts to the details of their delve, and Rhonda explains what they'll need.

"It'll probably be a shorter delve. I need a bunch of herbs in general, but we need ochredill from the yard, spell spore from the basement, and mustard moss from the tunnels. Do you guys mind carrying any extras I gather?"

Freddie and Larrez shake their heads, not minding at all, and look over the hanging quest boards, considering what they should take. They both are looking at the various slaying quests, with Larrez wondering if they could handle a rockslide. A clatter of wood draws his attention, then the front door squeaking as it opens. Freddie picks up a quest offer as Larrez looks at the door. His confusion turns to wary concern once he spots the zombie Boxer exit the manor.

The zombie grins around his mouthguard, showing his sharp teeth for a moment before he pounds his fists together. Larrez's growing concern turns to abject terror as Freddie reads the quest.

"Challenge Rocky?"

What kind of fool would challenge Rocky?! He's Thedeim's only scion specifically trained for battle! Even the mighty Fluffles, who *ate a hurricane*, isn't trained for battle!

Rhonda's gasp at least lets him know she understands the insanity of the quest.

"Your arena is finally finished?" she practically squeals with glee, and Rocky happily nods. Larrez just stares at the two, trying to figure out when the punch line will hit. Freddie dashes his hopes of it being a joke.

"Don't worry, Larrez. Rocky was part of our quests for our classes. I bet he's been itching for a rematch ever since." Freddie smiles at the undead Boxer, who eagerly smiles back.

"Rematch? You *fought*?!"

Freddie shrugs. "Technically. And technically, Rhonda dealt with Rocky. I had to deal with Aranya."

Larrez isn't exactly comforted by that. Rhonda smacks Freddie's elbow before turning her attention to the elf. "It was . . . more like a game of tag, and Rocky was it. Staying away from him gave me insight into his magic, and is why I got the class I did."

As a demonstration, she and Rocky both summon a lick of flame and a thin sheet of snow before letting them dissipate. The goblin eyes Rocky, who grins at her. "It also feels like he's gotten better with his control. I don't think I'll be able to steal it from him again."

Rocky points at the piece of wood with the quest on it, giving a pleading look to the party. Larrez is absolutely against it, but the others all look like they're considering it.

"I'd love to have a match," starts Freddie, but Rhonda continues.

"But we need to get some herbs to be able to delve Hullbreak later. I don't think we can afford to lose what we gather if you beat us."

Rocky waves that off and motions for them to follow him, but Larrez finally digs in his heels.

"You guys can't seriously be considering fighting him! He's *Rocky*! I've heard people talk about full *liches* with less magic than him!"

Rocky smiles at the compliment, but the kids and spiders all shrug.

"He won't *actually* hurt us, Larrez," replies Freddie. "He'll fight us and push us to our limits, but we can always just surrender. Even if we don't, I'm pretty sure the worst we'll face is some bruises . . . and losing some stuff."

Rocky shakes his head at that, motioning for them all to follow him again, earning a confused look from Rhonda. "No?"

Rocky shakes his head and motions for them to follow a third time, which Freddie and Rhonda are ready to do. They wait for Larrez's opinion, which he's immensely grateful for. He wants to argue to stay as far away from the zombie as possible, but he has to grudgingly admit to himself that he's the least experienced when it comes to Thedeim and his scions. The others trust Rocky, and Rocky seems to want to show them all something, too.

He sighs and offers a compromise. "We follow, but don't take the quest yet?"

Rhonda nods at that. "It looks like he wants to show us something about the quest. I guess Teemo is too busy to explain whatever it is? Either way, we can gather stuff on the way, if Rocky doesn't mind a few detours?"

The fighting scion taps his glove to his chin a few times, then nods. While the others are happy at that, Larrez can't help but feel like it's only a stay of execution.

Chapter 77

Rezlar is clearly doing his level best not to panic, and I'd say he's doing a pretty good job of it, all things considered. The confidence of the others probably helps, as do the few small encounters I send as they do their gathering. I only send some minor stuff; just enough to be a warm-up. Rocky would be crushed if I tired them out before he could have a real fight.

At least, a fight as real as the ring will allow. While Rezlar looks like he's hoping his will is in order, the others are looking more and more excited as they get closer and closer to finishing their gathering. After hitting a few nodes in the caverns, Rhonda and Lucas discuss their stores.

"Anything else we're low on, Lucas?"

The jumping spider chitters, and the goblin taps her chin. "Bale morels are mostly for antidotes. What we have should be plenty for now."

Lucas nods and chitters, seeming to agree, and Rhonda smiles wide as she turns to Rocky. "Then I think we're all good! Lead the way, Rocky!"

Rocky raises a gloved fist in victory, and notes start drifting through the air. The kids have no idea what "Eye of the Tiger" is, but Rocky obviously recognizes it. Slash approaches, nodding at the kids and Rocky, then my Boxer leads the way. Rhonda and Freddie are looking even more excited now, but Rezlar is just looking confused as he follows.

Rocky takes the chance to warm up a bit on the walk, looking a lot like his namesake in the iconic montage as he leads the way. My various denizens along the way watch as they go by, many following behind them. Over in the arena, my ratkin and spiderkin are gathering, eager to watch the show.

They cheer as Rocky enters, my zombie reveling in the attention and excitement. Rezlar looks tempted to bolt, but Rhonda and Freddie manage to convince him to smile and wave at the crowd. I'm definitely going to need to get the aranea to make crowd signs for the next big match, and get Teemo to explain how the wave works. That's for next time, though. For now, Rocky shows the kids the sign with the rules.

- *Only those in the ring are in the fight.*
- *Fights will last for three rounds, or until one side is incapacitated or surrenders.*
- *Party members not in the fight may cast buffs and heals on fighters in the ring only between rounds.*
- *Losing does not incur the typical penalties, and Rocky has sole discretion to hand out what rewards are available after a fight. Should Rocky be defeated beyond the capacity to do so, Thedeim will provide the proper rewards.*
- *Once in the ring, challengers may not leave until the fight is finished.*
- *Challengers may not join midfight, nor between rounds.*

Rezlar calms down a bit as he reads, and only Freddie seems to want a clarification.

"All of us can fight at once?"

Rocky eagerly nods, hitting his fists together. The orc nods and looks to the others.

"Are we all in?"

"Yeah!" comes Rhonda's excited reply. Fiona and Lucas chitter their approval as well. Rezlar sighs and holds out the plank with the quest.

"I'm in. Same tactic as with the twinsnake?"

Freddie glances toward Rocky as the zombie climbs into the boxing ring, weighing their options. "If he lets us, sure. We'll probably all need to be ready to move, maybe even scatter, quickly. We won't be able to keep much distance between us and him in there."

The others all nod, and the bell dings to get their attention. Rocky stands atop a turnbuckle, grinning around his mouthguard. He reaches out a gloved hand and beckons them in challenge. The party exchange glances and nod, then move to enter the ring.

My favorite zombie shouts in excitement and takes his corner as Slash stops the music for a moment. Once the kids are in the ring and in formation in their corner, with Freddie, Rezlar, and Fiona providing a front-line defense, and Rhonda and Lucas behind, the bell dings, and the boss music starts. The ground rumbles as Slash has his Earth affinity beat an energetic tempo while Rocky strides forward. The party readies their defenses, and the screech of an electric guitar is all the warning they get as he sends a quick combo at them.

A left hook sends a lash of fire at Rezlar, a right hook sends an arrow of ice at Fiona, and a heavy straight sends kinetic energy barreling down on Freddie.

Rezlar parries the fire with his floating water rapier, though it dissipates into steam from the attack. Fiona catches the arrow of ice with a thick wad of webbing. Freddie, however, seems to have taken the real attack.

A floating shield of light crumples under the assault, winking out of existence, and Freddie grunts as he takes the excess force on his metal one. Rhonda works with Lucas on a response, sending out a pair of spells as Rocky grins and lightly bounces on his feet.

"Ice Armor! Flaming Weapon!" A thick coat of ice covers Freddie and his shield, leaving his joints free so he can still move. At the same time, flames wreath Rezlar's metal rapier.

Rocky smiles as he steps forward, and this time, it's Rhonda's turn to grunt as he tries to take control of the elements from her. It turns into another grin as she fights him off, Rocky loving to have a challenge. In a blink, he summons his own fire and ice and meets the front line with opposing elements.

Rezlar is forced to summon water around the basket hilt of his rapier to try to block the icy punch, knowing it'd be foolish to try to parry or block with his actual blade. "Whirlpool Block!" he desperately shouts, the water moving in a quick circle to try to keep the powerful punch from finding proper purchase. His sword arm and Rocky's fist both recoil from the meeting. Rezlar is pretty sure nothing is broken, so he's willing to call it a draw.

Freddie takes the incoming fire punch on his ice-crusted shield, but there's a lot more follow through than with the ice punch. The ice shatters and melts, and Freddie's shield is starting to get uncomfortably warm already. "Shield Punch!" he grunts as he summons another ethereal shield overtop his mundane one and forces it forward. He's used that against some of my other undead before, and they usually stumble back a bit from it, but Rocky only leans back for a brief moment.

Rhonda shouts as Rocky is momentarily off-balance. "Scatter! Don't give him a single target to focus on!" She darts between everyone's legs as Freddie turns and yields ground to Rocky, this time actually putting the Boxer off his rhythm and giving everyone a chance to scatter to the other three corners.

The party all give Rocky a wary gaze as he turns to face them once more, my zombie looking like he's having the time of his unlife. He points a glove at Rhonda, and everyone flinches before he moves on to point at Freddie. By the time the glove moves to Rezlar, it's clear to the kids he's picking who he's going to focus on. The glove continues to cycle between them as Rocky grunts a little tune, clashing with the boss music, and they all do their best to prepare their defenses.

Freddie plants his feet and summons his full phalanx of five shining shields, each reinforced with Fiona's silk to help absorb blows. "Shield, give me strength!" he shouts, his axe raised high and defiant. Rezlar digs deep into his training, summoning two more water rapiers. The floor of the ring around him splashes slightly as small waves roll, his feet moving nimbly in his new stance. “Dance of the Tides!” Rhonda’s robes and hat billow as she embraces the secrets of fire and ice, Lucas helping her keep it under control. Flaming chunks of ice orbit her, her breath a fog and her eyes wisps of flame. “Inferno Maelstrom!”

The crowd goes wild, seeing the challengers hold nothing back. Rocky’s glove stops on Freddie, and the orc stands proud against my only scion specifically designed for battle. Rocky moves almost faster than Freddie can see, and he reflexively brings all his shields to bear against the overwhelming attack.

Stars almost seem to form around Rocky’s glove, small motes that crackle with the distillation of their elements, fire and ice in forms purer than most can even conceptualize. The first shield vaporizes from a fire mote, while the ice one causes the next to shatter. Raw power obliterates the third, and the cycle repeats in the mere moments it takes for the attack to complete. Raw kinetic energy impacts Freddie’s shield, and the brave orc is driven to the mat from the force, unconscious and hopefully unaware of the broken arm under his broken shield.

Before Rhonda can do more than widen her eyes, Rocky is upon her. His boxing footwork lets him weave through her whirling field of fire and ice, and a gloved hand knocks the wind and the fight out of her with a single measured blow to the stomach.

Rezlar’s fencing reflexes let him attempt to take advantage of Rocky not focusing on him for a moment, and his rapiers flash as he closes the distance. One rapier simply evaporates as another turns to useless ice. He feels a little better that Rocky ducks the third, his attack at least enough of a danger that the Boxer can’t simply ignore it. He doesn’t see the uppercut coming before Rocky’s fist impacts, the tide dashed upon the rocks.

The crowd’s roar is deafening, and Rocky helps the healing slimes get the kids before he raises both fists, victorious! Even sweeter than victory for Rocky is getting to have a proper fight. I know he held back the force, but not his techniques. I’m proud of his skill, even more proud of his control, and proudest of all that he made sure the kids would be fine and get into the slimes.

I have mixed feelings as I watch the party quickly start to heal. I’m *very* glad the slimes work as well as they do, even if I’d prefer the kids didn’t need to learn that firsthand. Should I have asked Rocky to hold back a bit more?

. . . No, I don’t think so. My whole goal as a dungeon is to try to prepare people for other dungeons that won’t be as nice. If they keep being delvers, broken bones are probably among the least of the things they’ll have to face. It’d be a disservice at best not to make sure they’re aware of that fact. I get the feeling none of them will be discouraged from this, though. Some people, if they get beat at their best, crumble into thinking they just aren't good enough. Seeing the defiance in all of them before Rocky's final assault makes me confident they'll see not a failure on their part but a success on Rocky's, and will take up the challenge to match him. Their growth has barely started, and now, they know the kind of heights to strive for and achieve.

Chapter 78

Rhonda is the first out of the slime, probably because she's the least injured of the three. It's hard to tell exactly how hurt Rezlar is, but I'd bet Freddie will be out last, thanks to that broken arm. Rocky helps the goblin out of the slime and back into the ring, where he lifts her hand (and the rest of her, too) to the roar of the crowd! Rhonda looks pretty confused about that.

"But . . . we lost?"

Rocky grunts in laughter while Lucas chitters, confusing the goblin even more, until she takes a few seconds to think.

". . . Winning wasn't the point, was it?"

My boxer grins around his mouthguard at her, nodding, and she takes a bit more time to think about the fight. It's the hardest pressed I've seen them be so far, but it's not like they've had much chance to delve anywhere else. Her eyes widen as she seems to recall the end of the fight, and she looks at Rocky with awe.

"What was that . . . What did you *do* with that attack on Freddie?! It felt like . . ." she trails off, apparently unable to put words to what it actually felt like. Rocky mimes scribbling something, and Rhonda's eyes widen once more before she pulls her notebook from her belt and starts furiously scribbling. Rocky hops out of the ring and digs around underneath it for a few minutes before pulling out a chest, which he places in the center of the ring before helping Rezlar out of his slime.

The elf actually yelps and jumps back when he realizes who's helping him to his feet, earning another laugh out of Rocky before he motions for Rezlar to follow him to the ring. Nervously, Rezlar does as bid, and Rocky raises his arm as well. The cheer is a little quieter this time, for the simple reason that a lot of people have made their way out of the colosseum to head back to the enclaves.

Rezlar looks just as confused as Rhonda did, but she gives him a quick answer, even as she continues scribbling.

"Winning isn't the point. The point is to learn."

Rezlar doesn't look like that's cleared up much. He looks to Rocky, who just nods, and Rezlar can only sigh and accept he doesn't get it. He takes a seat on the chest, the fight replaying in his mind, until he eventually speaks up.

"Did you dodge my one attack because it could have actually done anything?" he asks Rocky, sounding like he already knows the answer.

Apparently, he didn't, as Rocky puts his dukes up, pretends to get hit, and lets an arm hang limp for a few moments.

"Really? You think it could have done that much?" Rocky nods, and then I guess it's his turn for questions. He points at Rezlar's feet before doing a bit of his own footwork. The elf stares for a few seconds before understanding dawns.

"The Dance of the Tides? Footwork is an important part of fencing, so I tend to change stances a lot. The Dance of the Tides is probably my strongest one. It feels like I just let the flow of a fight guide my feet, forward and back with its own rhythm, like waves on a beach."

Rocky grins at that and encourages Rezlar to stand, clearly wanting a better look. The elf sighs and does so, then pauses as he gets an idea. He looks a bit nervous but manages to force himself to talk. "Can you show me some of your footwork, too? You don't move like any zombie I've ever seen, nor any other fighter, for that matter."

Rocky grins, and the two act like they're on an invisible DDR machine for a few minutes before Rocky goes and helps Freddie out of the slime. The orc smiles at him, though it falters as he spots his broken shield on the ground, crumpled beyond repair. He soon spots Rezlar and Rhonda in the ring and raises an eyebrow.

"Did . . . we win?"

Rezlar looks away as Rhonda laughs. "Not even close! I'm pretty sure he could have done that crazy punch a bunch more times, and even *that*, I think, was him holding back!"

Rocky bashfully nods at that, earning him a chuckle from Freddie before my Zombie Scion brings him into the ring and raises his hand like he did the others. He gets a cheer as well from the people who stayed before they start to make their way out as well, the show well and truly over now.

The orc sees his two friends in thought, Rezlar moving his feet and Rhonda tapping her chin as she looks at her book, and he soon follows suit as he mentally goes over the fight. It seems like something sticks out to him, because he speaks up. "Rocky? When I did the Shield Punch to try to get some room, you rocked backward a little instead of just absorbing it."

Rocky nods, holding up a hand and punching it, keeping the punched hand steady. He then shakes his head at that and repeats the motion, but this time more catching the punching hand than simply stopping it in its tracks before nodding.

Freddie thinks on that for a few minutes before he spots the chest and gives Rocky a curious look. My Boxer nods and points at it, taking a step back to let the kids enjoy their loot. Or talk about it, as they seem to prefer to do.

"Is it really okay for us to open it? We lost," points out Rezlar. Freddie just nods.

"It should be fine. The chest wasn't there in the fight, so it must be a reward for us, even if we lost."

Rhonda's eyes gleam as she looks at the chest. "Learning *and* loot! I hope all dungeons are like this," she says as she steps forward, the other two right behind her.

"They aren't," Rezlar informs her, but he doesn't seem too reluctant to help open the lid anymore. All three lift the lid together, and they collectively gasp at what they find. I'm pretty surprised at what's in there, too. That's definitely not ordinary loot.

Rhonda is the first to get her prize, which at first looks like a folded bolt of blue-and-red silk. As she pulls it out of the box, however, it's pretty obviously a robe. And not just any robe.

"Robe of the Sage . . ." she murmurs in awe. It reminds me a lot of a graduation robe, but without the hat. It even has the hanging scarf thing, embroidered with arcane runes. No way my aranea made that. I don't even know if my spiderkin could have made it . . . at least not on their own. I *could* see Thing helping, though. He's had a lot more time for his own projects after the axe.

The next item pulled out is by Freddie, and I know it didn't originally come from me. Well, the raw resources probably did, but that axe is way beyond what my ratlings can make. I'd put money on it being made by Legs, and it's quite the interesting design. At a glance, it looks like a hatchet. Any longer looks show it to be one made of mythril. Paying a closer look shows it's only *mostly* mythril, with the cutting edge made of orichalcum.

How the crap did Legs come up with a composite design like that?! Has Violet been watching the ratkin at their forges? Might Cappy have spread that far? I'm going to need to have Teemo talk with the sneaky little dungeon and let her know how proud I am of her progressing that quickly, and ensure she doesn't go eavesdropping in people's houses. Privacy is important.

Back to Freddie, he's carefully holding the hatchet like it's made of glass. While the weapon's shape is pretty simple when compared to his more traditional single-headed battle axe, it's very high quality and of course made of special metals. Freddie chuckles as he gets the name for it. "Simple Hatchet? Not hardly . . ."

Rezlar is the last to claim his treasure: a new rapier. The leather of the sheath looks different, and so does the blade. "Thresher's Rapier . . ." slips from his lips, and I'm pretty sure he means the shark, not the farmer's activity. The metal of the sword feels weird, and it takes me a bit to realize that's because it's not metal.

I'm pretty sure it's some kind of processed coral. I believe normal coral is way too brittle to be an effective weapon, but seeing Rezlar do a few practice motions with it makes me certain it'll serve him well for a long time.

Rhonda is the first to recover from receiving such an incredible reward, launching herself at Rocky with a hug and a shout of thanks. Freddie soon steps forward and hugs the confused zombie, and even Rezlar is able to put his fear aside for a moment to hug Rocky in thanks.

I just smile as I watch Rocky try to carefully escape the hug, but Lucas and Fiona are working their silk to make it more difficult, and the kids are starting to giggle and laugh at finding one of Rocky's weaknesses. I can feel him try to get help from me through the bond, but I'm staying out of that. You may have outsmarted yourself with those personalized rewards, my guy. I'm sure you can manage a way out of the hug eventually. You're not getting out of that friendship so easily.

Chapter 79

Jarsto frowns to himself as he looks at the dossier on his desk. Unlike many in the guild, he doesn't mind the bureaucratic upkeep required for the guild to run smoothly. He's actually quite good at it, if he does say so himself, and it makes him happy to be able to look over the numbers and ensure they add up.

His frown is from what the numbers are already implying, and he hasn't even opened the report yet. While he doesn't doubt that it will have numbers to explain the oddity, they're going to have to be some interesting numbers indeed.

The elf sighs and opens the folder, knowing that just staring wont force reality to bend to his whims. Even an archmage would have trouble with something like that. He skims the first few pages, the summary of the previous year of Fourdock. Hullbreak is unchanged, unsurprisingly. While the dungeon stretches the definition of simply belligerent, it has never made any moves to send hostile expeditions and tip over into murderous.

Neverrest, however, *is* murderous, and it seems the quarantine is still in effect. It hasn't started starving, it seems, but that should only require time.

The Southwood is still a toybox out in the middle of nowhere, and Jarsto wonders how it came to be so pacifistic. Perhaps the local wildlife is simply strong enough to count as delvers? He's hardly an expert in how dungeons actually work, so all he can do is guess.

With his foundation for the town refreshed, he takes a breath to steel himself for the reports from this year.

Ah, a new dungeon. That alone makes the thickness of the rest of the report make a lot more sense. Dungeon germinated in an abandoned manor; the inspector was able to inspect it very early in its life, too. It hadn't even claimed the entirety of the house by the time he found it. Jarsto nods in approval of the efficiency as he continues reading reports.

His approval quickly turns to confusion, and he double-checks the dates on the report, then skims the dates for the rest. They all seem to line up, at least as a timeline goes, but as he takes the time to truly read the reports, he wonders what has been going on in Fourdock.

Unauthorized delvers—local urchins. Not especially concerning, but their claims of the progress are. The follow-up inspection confirms the growth and multiple scions, as well.

Next report mentions odd behavior of bird denizens. The official inspector is off to inspect Hullbreak at the time, which is unfortunate but reasonable. How could the inspector anticipate what seems to be an explosive growth rate for this dungeon? Adventurers are hired, expenses look appropriate, no definitive reason for the temporary shift in behavior is found, but dungeon seems to be shaping into a cooperative one.

A cooperative dungeon in that area would certainly be a blessing for the locals. With the two nearest dungeons being unsuitable for delving, and the toybox being so far away, a cooperative right on main street could be a gold mine.

The next official report details enough change that it could have easily been an entire year but seems to have been just a couple weeks! Territory expanded, new spawners claimed, scions created and upgraded, and a strange, unique encounter involving a maze made of bramble bushes? Core likely moved, secret war room, secret alchemy lab . . . Is this dungeon older than it appears?

It wouldn't change much with the fees and whatnot, but it would help explain the rapid growth. Dungeons do occasionally spawn cloistered and can take a long time before they actually expand, instead simply getting to know their small territory and developing themselves a bit. He makes a note to inquire about that when he sends the official receipt of the report, and resumes working through the pile of paper.

His suspicions of the age only gain more evidence in his eyes as he finds the dungeon has expanded down and is now a deep dungeon. The quake was fairly minor, all things considered, and didn't seem to require any additional explanation in the report, save that it happened.

The dungeon has gained a resident already? A kobold, according to the report, so likely gained access via the new tunnels from the expansion. The kobold appears to be, not exactly hostile toward delvers but also not exactly welcoming. Seems like she's content to just quietly live in the dungeon.

Oh dear, Neverrest is making moves to attack the new dungeon? He eyes the rest of the report with concern, wondering if all those dates he skimmed earlier were listing violent incursions from Neverrest. Still . . . he's not aware of any requests for assistance with the hostile dungeon, so they must have things in hand.

He blinks at the next report and checks that he didn't skip a page or ten somewhere. No, everything seems to be in order. In a matter of days, the young dungeon formed a plan, recruited local adventurers, and actually *subsumed* Neverrest?! There's no doubt in Jarsto's mind now that the dungeon was cloistered for at least a decade before being discovered. There's no way a fresh dungeon would be able to make a plan, somehow negotiate *without a Voice*, and actually succeed in subsuming a dungeon like Neverrest.

It also gained a new resident, one of the adventurers. The details are sparse, but apparently, the dungeon was only able to save her from death by making her a resident. It's clear something happened, but considering the careful wording of that section, it reeks of legal talk. No, thank you. He'll send a notice to the legal department to take a look, but he's staying well out of anything like that. It has nothing to do with accounting, so he's more than happy to leave that mystery to the people who get paid to look into that sort of thing.

As far as he's concerned, Neverrest is subsumed, and this new dungeon has control of the territory, which is all he needs to know. The rest of the report is almost a comfort. While the details are complex, they're the kind of complex he enjoys, and he's happy to lose himself in the checking of the details of the aftermath of something like that.

Things are accounted for, the new dungeon designates a Voice and also gains a Conduit from the subsuming, both things that are nice and predictable. It even names itself, just lending further credence to the cloistered theory.

There's even a *second* new dungeon? It's located rather deep, and it seems Thedeim has taken it as a protégée, calling it Violet. Thankfully, the growth for the new dungeon seems to be proceeding at a more reasonable pace.

What's less nice and predictable are the ending notes. While the accounting year is over, time continues to advance, and it seems the winter months will not be quiet for this Thedeim. There has been a change in the status of Hullbreak Harbor, and though it happened after the official end of the accounting period, the ending note is very appreciated. It's having mana issues, and Thedeim is intending to help. There's also a note about tunnel horror migration/mating season, but the elven accountant doesn't pay it much mind. Something like that will be more of a local problem than one the guild at large has to worry about. The locals might be able to make some decent coin from the information they can glean from it, but that's for *their* taxes and records, not the guild's. Well, at least until the guild pays them for official access to that information.

About the Author

Khenal is the author of the Dungeon Life series. Born and raised in a small town in Northern California, he studied mechanical engineering but graduated from college in the middle of the Great Recession. Unable to find an engineering job, Khenal turned to content creation, streaming videos on Twitch and posting stories to Reddit and Royal Road.